A TASTE OF SIN

"This is madness," Ashton mumbled as he realized he had begun to undo her gown.

"'Tis a very sweet one." She kissed his throat, savoring the taste of him, and heard him groan softly.

"Penelope, I am close to taking you right here, on the settee in your parlor."

"Aye, it is, perhaps, not the best place for this."

He lifted himself up on his forearms to look at her. Her lips were kiss-swollen, her eyes a hot blue that he now knew was caused by desire. She wanted him. He wanted her.

"You are an innocent," he whispered.

"Innocent, but not ignorant. I live a short walk from a part of London where every sin known to man can be purchased. I may be innocent in body, but I know more than I like to. I know where this will lead and I know I want to follow . . ."

Books by Hannah Howell

Published by Zebra Books

IF HE'S SINFUL

HANNAH HOWELL

ZEBRA BOOKS
KENSINGTON PUBLISHING CORP.
http://www.kensingtonbooks.com

ZEBRA BOOKS are published by

Kensington Publishing Corp.
119 West 40th Street
New York, NY 10018

All Kensington titles, imprints, and distributed lines are available at special quantity discounts for bulk purchases for sales promotion, premiums, fund-raising, educational, or institutional use.

Special book excerpts or customized printings can also be created to fit specific needs. For details, write or phone the office of the Kensington Special Sales Manager: Attn. Special Sales Department. Kensington Publishing Corp., 119 West 40th Street, New York, NY 10018. Phone: 1-800-221-2647.

Zebra and the Z logo Reg. U.S. Pat. & TM Off.

ISBN-13: 978-1-4201-0461-5
ISBN-10: 1-4201-0461-6

First Printing: December 2009
10 9 8 7 6 5 4 3 2 1

Printed in the United States of America

Chapter One

London—Fall 1788

There was something about having a knife held to one's throat that tended to bring a certain clarity to one's opinion of one's life, Penelope decided. She stood very still as the burly, somewhat odiferous, man holding her clumsily adjusted his grip. Suddenly, all of her anger and resentment over being treated as no more than a lowly maid by her stepsister seemed petty, the problem insignificant.

Of course, this could be some form of cosmic retribution for all those times she had wished ill upon her stepsister, she thought as the man hefted her up enough so that her feet were off the ground. One of his two companions bound her ankles in a manner quite similar to the way her wrists had been bound. Her captor began to carry her down a dark alley that smelled about as bad as he did. It had been only a few hours ago that she had watched Clarissa leave for a carriage ride with her soon-to-be fiancé, Lord Radmoor. Peering out of the cracked window in her tiny attic room she had, indisputably, cherished the spiteful wish that Clarissa would stumble and fall into the foul muck near the carriage wheels. Penelope did think that being dragged away by a knife-wielding ruffian and his two hulking companions was a rather harsh penalty for such a childish wish born of jealousy, however. She had, after all, never wished that Clarissa would die, which Penelope very much feared was going to be her fate.

Penelope sighed, ruefully admitting that she was partially at fault for her current predicament. She had stayed too long with her boys. Even little Paul had urged her not to walk home in the dark. It was embarrassing to think that a little boy of five had more common sense than she did.

A soft cry of pain escaped her, muted by the filthy gag in her mouth, when her captor stumbled and the cold, sharp edge of his knife scored her skin. For a brief moment, the fear she had been fighting to control swelled up inside her so strongly she feared she would be ill. The warmth of her own blood seeping into the neckline of her bodice only added to the fear. It took several moments before she could grasp any shred of calm or courage. The realization that her blood was flowing too slowly for her throat to have been cut helped her push aside her burgeoning panic.

"Ye sure we ain't allowed to have us a taste of this, Jud?" asked the largest and most hirsute of her captor's assistants.

"Orders is orders," replied Jud as he steadied his knife against her skin. "A toss with this one will cost ye more'n she be worth."

"None of us'd be telling and the wench ain't going to be able to tell, neither."

"I ain't letting ye risk it. Wench like this'd be fighting ye and that leaves bruises. They'll tell the tale and that bitch Mrs. Cratchitt will tell. She would think it a right fine thing if we lost our pay for this night's work."

"Aye, that old bawd would be thinking she could gain something from it right enough. Still, it be a sad shame I can't be having me a taste afore it be sold off to anyone with a coin or two."

"Get your coin first and then go buy a little if'n ye want it so bad."

"Won't be so clean and new, will it?"

"This one won't be neither if'n that old besom uses her as she uses them others, not by the time ye could afford a toss with her."

She was being taken to a brothel, Penelope realized. Yet again she had to struggle fiercely against becoming blinded by her own fears. She was still alive, she told herself repeatedly, and it looked as if she would stay that way for a while. Penelope fought to find her strength in that knowledge. It did no good to think too much on the horrors she might be forced to endure before she could escape or be found. She needed to concentrate on one thing and one thing only—getting free.

It was not easy but Penelope forced herself to keep a close eye on the route they traveled. Darkness and all the twists and turns her captors took made it nearly impossible to make note of any and every possible sign to mark the way out of this dangerous warren she was being taken into. She had to force herself to hold fast to the hope that she could ever truly escape, and the need to get back to her boys, who had no one else to care for them.

She was carried into the kitchen of a house. Two women and a man were there, but they spared her only the briefest of glances before returning all of their attention to their work. It was not encouraging that they seemed so accustomed to such a sight, so unmoved and uninterested.

As her captor carried her up a dark, narrow stairway, Penelope became aware of the voices and music coming from below, from the front of the building, which appeared to be as great a warren as the alleys leading to it. When they reached the hallway and started to walk down it, she could hear the murmur of voices coming from behind all the closed doors. Other sounds drifted out from behind those doors but she tried very hard not to think about what might be causing them.

"There it be. Room twenty-two," muttered Jud. "Open the door, Tom."

The large, hirsute man opened the door and Jud carried Penelope into the room. She had just enough time to notice how small the room was before Jud tossed her down onto the bed in the middle of the room. It was a surprisingly clean and comfortable bed. Penelope suspected that, despite its seedy location, she had probably been brought to one of the better bordellos, one that catered to gentlemen of refinement and wealth. She knew, however, that that did not mean she could count on any help.

"Get that old bawd in here, Tom," said Jud. "I wants to be done with this night's work." The moment Tom left, Jud scowled down at Penelope. "Don't suspect you'd be aknowing why that high-and-mighty lady be wanting ye outta the way, would ye?"

Penelope slowly shook her head as a cold suspicion settled in her stomach.

"Don't make no sense to me. Can't be jealousy or the like. Can't be that she thinks you be taking her man or the like, can it. Ye ain't got her fine looks, ain't dressed so fine, neither, and ye ain't got her fine curves. Scrawny, brown mite like ye should be no threat at all to such a fulsome wench. So, why does she want ye gone so bad, eh?"

Scrawny brown mite? Penelope thought, deeply insulted even as she shrugged in reply.

"Why you frettin' o'er it, Jud?" asked the tall, extremely muscular man by his side.

Jud shrugged. "Curious, Mac. Just curious, is all. This don't make no sense to me."

"Don't need to. Money be good. All that matters."

"Aye, mayhap. As I said, just curious. Don't like puzzles."

"Didn't know that."

"Well, it be true. Don't want to be part of something I don't understand. Could mean trouble."

If she had not been gagged, Penelope suspected she would have been gaping at her captor. He had kidnapped the daughter of a marquis, brought her bound and gagged to a brothel, and was going to leave her to the untender care of a madam, a woman he plainly did not trust or like. Exactly what did the idiot think *trouble* was? If he were caught, he would be tried, convicted, and hanged in a heartbeat. And that would be merciful compared to what her relatives would do to the fool if they found out. How much more *trouble* could he be in?

A hoarse gasp escaped her when he removed her gag. "Water," she whispered, desperate to wash away the foul taste of the rag.

What the man gave her was a tankard of weak ale, but Penelope decided it was probably for the best. If there was any water in this place, it was undoubtedly dangerous to drink. She tried not to breathe too deeply as he held her upright and helped her to take a drink. Penelope drank the ale as quickly as she could, however, for she wanted the man to move away from her. Anyone as foul-smelling as he was surely had a vast horde of creatures sharing his filth that she would just as soon did not come to visit her.

When the tankard was empty, he let her fall back down onto the bed and said, "Now, don't ye go thinking of making no noise, screaming for help or the like. No one here will be heeding it."

Penelope opened her mouth to give him a tart reply and then frowned. The bed might be clean and comfortable but it was not new. A familiar chill swept over her. Even as she thought it a very poor time for her *gift* to display itself, her mind was briefly filled with violent memories that were not her own.

"Someone died in this bed," she said, her voice a little unsteady from the effect of those chilling glimpses into the past.

"What the bleeding hell are ye babbling about?" snapped Jud.

"Someone died in this bed and she did not do so peacefully." Penelope got some small satisfaction from how uneasy her words made her burley captors.

"You be talking nonsense, woman."

"No. I have a gift, you see."

"You can see spirits?" asked Mac, glancing nervously around the room.

"Sometimes. When they wish to reveal themselves to me. This time it was just the memories of what happened here," she lied.

Both men were staring at her with a mixture of fear, curiosity, and suspicion. They thought she was trying to trick them in some way so that they would set her free. Penelope suspected that a part of them probably wondered if she would conjure up a few spirits to help her. Even if she could, she doubted they would be much help or that these men would even see them. They certainly had not noticed the rather gruesome one standing near the bed. It would have sent them fleeing from the room. Despite all she had seen and experienced over the years, the sight of the lovely young woman, her white gown soaked in blood, sent a chill down her spine. Penelope wondered why the more gruesome apparitions were almost always the clearest.

The door opened, and before Penelope turned to look, she saw an expression upon the ghost's face that nearly made *her* want to flee the room. Fury and utter loathing twisted the spirit's lovely face until it looked almost demonic. Penelope looked at the ones now entering the room. Tom had returned with a middle-aged woman and two young, scantily clad females. Penelope looked right at the ghost and noticed that all that rage and hate was aimed straight at the middle-aged woman.

Beware.

Penelope almost cursed as the word echoed in her mind. Why did the spirits always whisper such ominous words to her without adding any pertinent information, such as what she should *beware* of, or whom? It was also a very poor time for this sort of distraction. She was a prisoner trapped in a house of ill-repute and was facing either death or what many euphemistically called a fate worse than death. She had no time to deal with blood-soaked specters whispering dire but unspecified warnings. If nothing else, she needed all her wits and strength to keep the hysteria writhing deep inside her tightly caged.

"This is going to cause you a great deal of trouble," Penelope told the older woman, not really surprised when everyone ignored her.

"There she be," said Jud. "Now, give us our money."

"The lady has your money," said the older woman.

"It ain't wise to try and cheat me, Cratchitt. The lady told us you would have it. Now, if the lady ain't paid you, that be your problem, not mine. I did as I was ordered and did it quick and right. Get the wench, bring her here, and then collect my pay from you. Done and done. So, hand it over."

Cratchitt did so with an ill grace. Penelope watched Jud carefully count his money. The man had obviously taught himself enough to make sure that he was not cheated. After one long, puzzled look at her, he pocketed his money and then frowned at the woman he called Cratchitt.

"She be all yours now," Jud said, "though I ain't sure what ye be wanting her for. 'Tain't much to her."

Penelope was growing very weary of being disparaged by this lice-ridden ruffian. "So speaks the great beau of the walk," she muttered and met his glare with a faint smile.

"She is clean and fresh," said Cratchitt, ignoring that byplay and fixing her cold stare on Penelope. "I have many a gent willing to pay a goodly fee for that alone. There be one man waiting especially for this one, but he will not arrive until the morrow. I have other plans for her tonight. Some very rich gentlemen have arrived and are looking for something special. Unique, they said. They have a friend about to step into the parson's mousetrap and wish to give him a final bachelor treat. She will do nicely for that."

"But don't that other feller want her untouched?"

"As far as he will ever know, she will be. Now, get out. Me and the girls need to wrap this little gift."

The moment Jud and his men were gone, Penelope said, "Do you have any idea of who I am?" She was very proud of the haughty tone she had achieved but it did not impress Mrs. Cratchitt at all.

"Someone who made a rich lady very angry," replied Cratchitt.

"I am Lady Penelope—"

She never finished for Mrs. Cratchitt grasped her by the jaw in a painfully tight hold, forced her mouth open, and started to pour something from a remarkably fine silver flask down her throat. The two younger women held her head steady so that Penelope could not turn away or thrash her head. She knew she did not want this drink inside her but was unable to do anything but helplessly swallow as it was forced into her.

While she was still coughing and gagging from that abuse, the women untied her. Penelope struggled as best as she could but the women were strong and alarmingly skilled at undressing someone who did not wish to be undressed. As if she did not have trouble enough to deal with, the ghost was drowning her in feelings of fear, despair, and helpless fury. Penelope knew she was swiftly becoming hysterical but could not grasp one single, thin thread of control. That only added to her terror.

Then, slowly, that suffocating panic began to ease. Despite the fact that the women continued their work, stripping her naked, giving her a quick wash with scented water, and dressing her in a lacey, diaphanous gown that should have shocked her right down to her toes, Penelope felt calmer with every breath she took. The potion they had forced her to drink had been some sort of drug. That was the only rational explanation for why she was now lying there actually smiling as these three harpies prepared her for the sacrifice of her virginity.

"There, all sweets and honey now, ain't you, dearie,"

muttered Cratchitt as she began to let down Penelope's hair.

"You are such an evil bitch," Penelope said pleasantly and smiled. One of the younger women giggled and Cratchitt slapped her hard. "Bully. When my family discovers what you have done to me, you will pay more dearly than even your tiny, nasty mind could ever comprehend."

"Hah! It was your own family what sold you to me, you stupid girl."

"Not that family, you cow. My true parents' family. In fact, I would not be at all surprised if they are already suspicious, sensing my troubles upon the wind."

"You are talking utter nonsense."

Why does everyone say that? Penelope wondered. Enough wit and sense of self-preservation remained in her clouded mind to make her realize that it might not be wise to start talking about all the blood there was on the woman's hands. Even if the woman did not believe Penelope could know anything for a fact, she suspected Mrs. Cratchitt would permanently silence her simply to be on the safe side of the matter. With the drug holding her captive as well as any chain could, Penelope knew she was in no condition to even try to save herself.

When Cratchitt and her minions were finished, she stood back and looked Penelope over very carefully. "Well, well, well. I begin to understand."

"Understand what, you bride of Beelzebub?" asked Penelope and could tell by the way the woman clenched and unclenched her hands that Mrs. Cratchitt desperately wanted to beat her.

"Why the fine lady wants you gone. And you will pay dearly for your insults, my girl. Very soon." Mrs. Cratchitt collected four bright silk scarves from the large carpetbag she had brought in with her and handed them to the younger women. "Tie her to the bed," she ordered them.

"Your customer may find that a little suspicious," said Penelope as she fruitlessly tried to stop the women from binding her limbs to the four posts of the bed.

"You *are* an innocent, aren't you." Mrs. Cratchitt shook her head and laughed. "No, my customer will only see this as a very special delight indeed. Come along, girls. You have work to do and we best get that man up here to enjoy his gift before that potion begins to wear off."

Penelope stared at the closed door for several moments after everyone had left. Everyone except the ghost, she mused, and finally turned her attention back to the specter now shimmering at the foot of the bed. The young woman looked so sad, so utterly defeated, that Penelope decided the poor ghost had probably just realized the full limitations of being a spirit. Although the memories locked into the bed had told Penelope how the woman had died, it did not tell her when. However, she began to suspect it had been not all that long ago.

"I would like to help you," she said, "but I cannot, not right now. You must see that. If I can get free, I swear I will work hard to give you some peace. Who are you?" she asked, although she knew it was often impossible to get proper, sensible answers from a spirit. "I know how you died. The bed still holds those dark memories and I saw it."

I am Faith and my life was stolen.

The voice was clear and sweet, but weighted with an intense grief, and Penelope was not completely certain if she was hearing it in her head or if the ghost was actually speaking to her. "What is your full name, Faith?"

My name is Faith and I was taken, as you have been. My life was stolen. My love is lost. I was torn from heaven and plunged into hell. Now I lie below.

"Below? Below what? Where?"

Below. I am covered in sin. But I am not alone.

Penelope cursed when Faith disappeared. She could not help the spirit now, but dealing with Faith's spirit had provided her with a much-needed diversion. It had helped her concentrate and fight the power of the drug she had been given. Now she was alone with her thoughts and they were becoming increasingly strange. Worse, all of her protections were slowly crumbling away. If she did not find something to fix her mind on soon, she would be wide open to every thought, every feeling, and every spirit lurking within the house. Considering what went on in this house, that could easily prove a torture beyond bearing.

She did not know whether to laugh or to cry. She was strapped to a bed awaiting some stranger who would use her helpless body to satisfy his manly needs. The potion Mrs. Cratchitt had forced down her throat was rapidly depleting her strength and all her ability to shut out the cacophony of the world, the world of the living as well as that of the dead. Even now she could feel the growing weight of unwelcome emotions, the increasing whispers so few others could hear. The spirits in the house were stirring, sensing the presence of one who could help them touch the world of the living. It was probably not worth worrying about, she decided. Penelope did not know if anything could be worse than what she was already suffering and what was yet to come.

Suddenly the door opened and one of Mrs. Cratchitt's earlier companions led a man into the room. He was blindfolded and dressed as an ancient Roman. Penelope stared at him in shock as he was led up to her bedside, and then she inwardly groaned. She had no trouble recognizing the man despite the blindfold and the costume. Penelope was not at all pleased to discover that things could quite definitely get worse—a great deal worse.

Chapter Two

"This is ridiculous," muttered Ashton Radmoor as he was stripped of his clothes by two scantily clad women. "A costume, Cornell?" He scowled at the youngest of his four friends, trying to emulate the look his late father, the viscount of Radmoor, had perfected. Cornell was unimpressed, judging by his wide grin. Obviously Ashton had to practice the look a great deal more.

"It is all a part of the game," Cornell replied. "Part of the gift we are giving you."

"I am not sure I ought to accept this gift. I am to speak with Clarissa's brother tomorrow." He had no intention of following in his father's faithless footsteps, the ones that had put his family into the dire straits they were now in.

"Exactly," said Brant Mallam, Lord Fieldgate, "and we all know that, once you do, you will consider yourself bound up tight. You will undoubtedly become quite pious in many ways. Consider this your last hurrah."

Ashton grimaced as one of the women dressed him in a tunic and the other put sandals on his feet. "What sort of game requires me to dress like some ancient Roman?"

"The Pagan Sacrifice game."

"God rot it!" Ashton shook his head. "Whyever should you think I would enjoy something like that?"

"It is harmless and we decided that you needed the memory of something rare and exotic, even a little shocking, before you became a staid, old, married man. If you do not enjoy it, I am quite certain the woman will be able to give you whatever you decide you *do* want. Mrs. Cratchitt trains her girls well. Fly free and wild for one night, Ashton. We have purchased you a full night of delight. Fulfill a few dreams. Even you must have some. After tonight there is only Clarissa and the breeding of heirs."

There was no denying that hard, cold truth. His forthcoming union with Clarissa Hutton-Moore was no love match, not that he particularly believed in love, anyway. It was a union based upon the usual need for an heir and a nearly desperate need for money. Clarissa had the appropriate bloodlines, was beautiful, and had a very impressive dowry. She would be an excellent hostess, which was also important now that he was a viscount. She moved about in society far more comfortably than he ever had. She was a perfect choice for a wife.

So why did he feel as if the weight of the world now rested upon his shoulders? That question kept invading his mind more and more with each step he took closer to marriage with the much praised Lady Clarissa. True, there was no real affection between them, and little passion, but such things were luxuries few men in his position could afford. Yet a little warmth in one's wife would be nice, he mused, and he had not yet detected even the smallest spark in Clarissa.

And that, he suspected, was what made him continue to drag his feet. The thought of a marriage bed where only cold duty existed was a deeply chilling one. He feared it could eventually cause him to act against his own principles and begin to seek out a little warmth elsewhere. Ashton knew his friends thought him too full of ideals or, worse, a hopeless romantic, but he had always wished for a good marriage. He did not want the more common arrangement found in society, one where the wife was simply a hostess who occasionally bred a child for her husband while the husband indulged in a long succession of mistresses. That sort of marriage had destroyed his family, had torn his poor mother's heart to shreds. It began to look as if that was exactly what he would be stuck with, however.

He was abruptly yanked from his dark thoughts when one of the women began to blindfold him. "Is this necessary?"

"Adds to the mystery," replied Cornell.

"I feel bloody foolish."

"It is to be hoped that you will feel a great deal better soon. We shall see you in the morning."

As he was led away from his friends, Ashton was not sure he would want to spend an entire night playing silly games. He was no innocent, but he was not the rake his friends were, despite what rumor and gossip tried to make him. It was an indulgence he had never been able to afford since his father's reckless waste of a fortune on such indulgences and gaming had left the Radmoors nearly destitute. Ruefully he admitted to himself that his father's actions were part of the reason he struggled to remain temperate in all things. That and the disease

that had finally ended the man's life. He was even somewhat staid in his lovemaking. The need was there but
not the inclination to be inventive or daring. He prized
his control in all things.

The problem was that, although he had felt a need
for a woman before, he had rarely truly lusted after the
woman herself. On the few occasions he had felt a stirring of a hearty lust, it had faded quickly when it had
not been returned in kind or he began to think he was
losing control of his passions. He had never experienced that knee-weakening, limb-trembling, fire-in-the-
blood sort of lust others spoke of. That madness had
been fleeting for those who had claimed to suffer from
it, yet Ashton could not help but fear that there was
something wrong with him since he had never felt it at
all. Just once he would like to be gripped by that madness, but since he would be thirty soon and was about to
commit himself to the cool, elegant Clarissa, he doubted
he would ever know it.

"Here we be, m'lord," said the woman leading him
along as he heard her open a door. "I'll just tug ye o'er
to the bed and then take off the blindfold so's ye can
see the fine gift your friends got ye."

When the woman removed the blindfold, Ashton
looked at his *gift* and experienced a sensation that he
compared to the time he had fallen out of a tree and
landed so hard that all the breath had been stolen from
his body. The woman tied spread-eagle to the bed was
small, delicate. Ashton wondered if she were too stretched
out to be comfortable. He was only dimly aware of a
woman setting a tray of wine and cakes on the table by
the bed while another placed his clothing on a chair.
All of his attention was firmly centered upon his *gift*.

The white diaphanous gown she wore hid little from
his gaze. His breath quickened, became something just

short of a pant, as he studied her lithe shape. Her breasts were not particularly large but they were perfectly shaped, round and plump with dark pink nipples. She had a tiny waist and it accentuated the womanly curve of her hips. His palms began to sweat while he looked up and down the length of her beautifully formed, slender legs, and he slowly wiped them dry on the sides of his tunic. Her body was cushioned by thick, rippling waves of brown hair enlivened with glints of gold and red and reached almost to her knees. He wanted to wrap it around his body. His gaze was then caught by the tidy vee of curls between her pale thighs. He trembled and his heart began to pound.

When he heard the women leave the room, he quickly sat down on the edge of the bed. He felt oddly unsteady. Ashton fought the urge to throw himself at her as he studied her heart-shaped face. Her small straight nose was lightly dusted with unfashionable freckles and he wanted to kiss each one. There was the hint of a few more on her breasts and he wanted to count them, too. With his tongue. Fine cheekbones and a faintly pointed chin made for a face that was pleasing, but not elegant. Her eyes, however, were stunningly beautiful. A strange blend of blue and green, they were wide, surrounded by thick, long dark lashes and set beneath neatly arched dark brows. Her mouth would tempt a saint, he mused. It was a little too wide for fashion, was no rosebud or cupid's bow, but it was perfectly shaped with slightly full lips. He wanted to nibble on them.

"Is that uncomfortable?" he asked and decided he deserved the scornful look she gave him. "A stupid question."

"I would never be so rude as to say so."

She spoke very well for a common whore, Ashton thought, and inwardly winced. He hated to think of her as one of that sad breed, which was utterly foolish of him. She was working in a brothel and was tied to a bed, prepared to play the part of a maiden sacrifice in some idiotic sex game with a total stranger. It embarrassed him a little to admit to himself that he was now prepared to play that game; was, in all truth, eager to participate. He would untie her ankles in a few minutes, he decided and reached out to stroke her thigh.

The soft gasp she gave and the sight of his hand upon her thigh made Ashton slightly feverish. This was lust, he realized; that blinding sort of lust he had just decided he would never experience. Suddenly what had seemed foolish now appeared highly erotic. Ashton discovered that he did have an imagination and it was filling his mind with a vast array of truly licentious plans. He removed his sandals and stood up to pull off his tunic. The way her eyes widened flattered him and he tossed the tunic aside. It took an effort not to preen in front of her like some vain fool.

Nick me! Penelope thought; she was looking at a naked man. Even more astonishing, she was looking at a naked Lord Radmoor. She had been infatuated with the man from the moment she had first set eyes on him, but not once in all her silly romantic little dreams had she imagined him naked. And if she had, Penelope decided, unable to stop herself from staring at his groin, she would never have imagined that particular appendage to be so inspiring. The little knowledge she had gathered concerning the male anatomy had come from caring for young boys. She had always suspected that a man's appendage would be larger than a boy's, but would never have guessed it could be that large. Penelope did not know what emotion seized her more firmly, amazement, or terror over the fact that he actually thought he could put that inside her.

It was not only Mrs. Cratchitt's potion that kept her from demanding, loudly and hysterically, to be set free, and Penelope knew it. Her infatuation with the man also held her captive. Until now she had seen him only from a distance or as she indulged in some spying, creeping about her own home like a thief. Everything about the man had drawn her, from his aura of strength and reserve to his elegant handsome appearance. She had been struck stupid by his beauty from the start. Clothed, he had often caused her to sigh with appreciation like some moonstruck girl. Unclothed, he left her unable to find the breath to even sigh.

She was finally able to lift her gaze to his face in the vain hope of easing the odd warmth infecting her blood. The sight of his body had stirred a strange fever inside her and she needed to shake free of it. His thick golden hair was unrestrained, hanging past his shoulders. A shorter strand dangled over his broad forehead. A long, straight nose, elegant bones, a firm jaw, and a mouth that begged for kisses with its slightly full lips equaled perfection in her eyes. It was a face she knew she would never tire of looking at. It was his eyes that held her spellbound, however. They reminded her of the mists upon the moors, a mystifying bluish gray that could lighten to clear silver or darken to the almost black color of threatening storm clouds. Thick, almost feminine lashes of dark brown tipped with the glint of gold encircled those incredible eyes. Sleek, faintly winged brows of that same color added to the exotic look, enhancing the faint hint of an upward slant to his eyes.

Her thoughts about his beauty abruptly scattered when he joined her on the bed, crouching between her spread legs. He stroked her thighs with his elegant, long-fingered hands, and pure, unfettered lust swept over her. Penelope knew the potion was at fault, but suspected its effects were strengthened by all the emotions the man already stirred in her heart and body. The vile potion the madam had given her had also shattered all her shields, opened wide the inner doors she kept shut to protect herself from the turmoil of sensing the emotions of others and from being overwhelmed by the spirits all around her.

Aunt Olympia had always said that those born of Wherlocke blood were passionate. Penelope was not pleased to discover the woman was right, not now, not when she was too helpless to control any of her emotions. Unless some miracle happened, she, who had never even been kissed, was soon to experience the full measure of passion. The fact that that thought more intrigued than frightened her was just another sign that she had no control at all.

"Your legs are so beautiful," Ashton murmured as he stroked them, reveling in the softness of her skin.

"They are too thin," she said, and the small, still sensible part of her drugged mind told her that that was a particularly foolish thing to say. His smile was beautiful, however, and held no ridicule.

"Sleek and strong. And soft. Deliciously soft." He gently nipped the inside of each of her thighs and then soothed the spots with tender kisses and slow strokes of his tongue. "You are too sweet for this sort of life," he whispered and looked at her. The tips of her breasts had hardened and there was a slight flush upon her cheeks. "And very responsive. You are new to this life, I think."

"Oh, aye, quite new."

Ashton would have smiled at her use of the word

"aye," which revealed her country roots, if it had not been so sad. Too many country girls came to the city to find honest work only to end up selling their bodies just to survive. He intended to ask her just how new she was but was distracted by her body and his own lust. She even smelled delicious, he thought as he pressed his body against hers.

Penelope started to explain everything, only to gasp in a strange mix of shock and delight when he settled his long body on top of hers. He held his upper body up by propping himself up on one forearm, but that did little to ease the intoxicating touch of his warmth and his weight. Even more startling was how eagerly her body responded when his hard length pressed against that mindlessly hungry place between her legs.

"Let me take you away from this," he offered, surprising himself.

"Aye, that would be most kind of you," she said, her voice little more than a whisper as she watched him slowly untie the silk ribbons holding the front of her immodest gown together. She should be shocked but she was mostly concerned that he would find her lacking.

"I could set you up comfortably someplace, in a little house all your own." He was not sure how he could afford it but was determined to find a way. Ashton ruthlessly silenced the little voice that whispered in his head, telling him he was acting as recklessly as his father.

"Ah." Penelope was disappointed but not terribly surprised. "So that I might service but one man instead of many and that one man would be yourself?"

"It would be better than this, would it not?"

"Quite possibly, but did you never consider the possibility that I might not wish to service anyone?" Especially not a man who did not even know who she really was and was courting Clarissa, she thought, frustrated by her inability to stop him or to act cold and unmoved by his gentle touch.

"Then why are you here at all?"

"That seems a rather naïve question. Do you truly think a woman wakes up one day and thinks—why, I do believe I will become a whore?"

Lord Radmoor's question had made Penelope think he would probably doubt her tale of kidnapping, drugging potions, and imprisonment. He obviously thought as too many others did, that a woman would willingly choose such a degrading profession. Some might, she mused, for they believed they would find a rich patron, but far too many of the women were dragged into this hell through trickery, force, or dire poverty. Just as she gained enough of her wits to relate her troubles with clarity, he moved his hand over her breasts and her wits were scattered all over again.

Ashton closed his eyes and savored the way her soft breast fit so perfectly in his hand. "Perhaps it was a foolish question. Perhaps you had little choice." He pressed a kiss to the warm skin between her breasts. "I am offering you a choice now." He looked at her again. "What is your name?"

"Penelope," she replied, spellbound by the warmth in his eyes.

"Penelope?" He smiled faintly, not sure he believed her. "An odd name for one of Mrs. Cratchitt's girls."

"I am not one of her girls." Penelope suddenly wondered if the madam was really married, and if so, where was her husband? She hastily buried that thought when the whispers began in her head and she knew someone or something was trying to answer her.

"No? And what are you then?"

She could tell by the tone of his voice that he was just

humoring her. Nevertheless, with what little clarity of mind she could muster, she decided to tell him her tale. She doubted he would believe her, or even falter in his seduction for a moment, but she needed to at least try to plead her case. If nothing else, knowing that she had tried might help ease the sting of shame she was sure to suffer once he was gone and the power of Mrs. Cratchitt's potion faded away. At least she hoped she would feel shamed if she gave her innocence to Lord Radmoor. She had the sinking feeling she might not be.

"What if I told you I was the daughter of a marquis, cruelly kidnapped, and then sold to Mrs. Cratchitt? What if I said I was given a potion, dressed in this scandalous excuse for a gown, and tied to this bed all against my will?"

"Do you really expect me to believe that?" Ashton thought it was just his wretched luck to experience his first taste of blind, hot lust for a woman who was beset by delusions.

"Not really." She sighed. "If you are offering me choices, might I choose to be untied now?"

"In but a moment I will untie your ankles." He began to encircle her long, slender neck with soft kisses and gentle nips. "I thought this a silly game but allowed my friends to push me into playing it."

"This is a game? What is it called?"

"The Pagan Sacrifice game. Did they not tell you?"

"No one told me anything. I did not realize that one played fanciful games in a brothel."

"A lot of games are played in brothels. I was never one to indulge in that. I have never been an imaginative man. Then I saw you. At that moment I realized that I did indeed possess a powerful imagination. My mind became crowded with ideas of how I would enjoy you, pleasure you. I realized I could do anything I wanted to. I intend to make you want it, too."

Penelope knew she was not herself when the heated images his words created in her mind were more exciting than alarming or shocking. She wondered if, somewhere in those many dreams she had had about this man, her thoughts had taken her far beyond kisses and sweet words of love. She did not recall anything particularly lascivious in her dreams but she had enough knowledge to have made them so. That would certainly explain why she woke up so many times all asweat and aching with a need she did not understand. Those dreams worked against her now, almost as much as Mrs. Cratchitt's potion did.

She shivered with pleasure so sharp it was almost painful when he covered her breast with a warm hand and slowly licked the space between her breasts. "Should you not kiss me first?"

When he lifted his gaze from her breasts, Penelope caught her breath too quickly and nearly choked. It was as if she stared into the heart of a thundercloud. The gray of his eyes had darkened nearly to black and there was such heat in his gaze it warmed her skin. There was also the glint of amusement and curiosity. She had obviously just said something else that did not suit the role she was being forced to play.

Such inconsistencies did not prompt him to ask any questions, though, she thought, and anger began to stir inside her. She knew enough about Lord Radmoor to know he was not some thick-witted dandy so it puzzled her that he would so blindly accept what a brothel madam had told him about her. It was not as if a woman who made her living selling other women was one a person should put much trust in. Like far too many people did, he simply accepted what he saw and used that to soothe away any doubts stirred by her words. Penelope wondered sadly how often that happened in such places, how often innocent girls and women were forced into this hellish life because no one asked questions and no one listened to them.

Ashton saw the sadness in her beautiful eyes and gently framed her small, lovely face in his hands. He never kissed courtesans and whores, was even very sparing with his kisses with the rare widow or flirtatious wife who had favored him in the past. It was an idiosyncrasy others shared with him so it did not worry him too much. Despite the temptation of her soft, sensuous mouth, he had thought to hold fast to that rule, but the sadness in her eyes broke his resolve.

He brushed his lips over hers and the warmth of them flowed through his body. "You taste so good." Ashton hoped she could not hear the surprise in his voice, then wondered why he was so concerned about offering some insult. "You are a feast I could linger over for hours."

"My deepest apologies, sir, but I fear you shall have to step away from this banquet before you have had your fill. It would be best for your health."

Chapter Three

Ashton tensed. He was not sure what chilled him more, the subtle threat uttered in that deep, cold masculine voice, or the feel of the hard, cold metal of a pistol muzzle pressed against the side of his head. It astonished him that he had not immediately gone soft, all passion fleeing his body in a rush, but he was still achingly erect. That could prove embarrassing. There was no sign of fear upon Penelope's sweet face. In fact, she looked an enchanting mix of delighted and annoyed.

"Artemis," Penelope said in a gentle but firm tone, "there is no need to hold a pistol on his lordship. It is rather evident that he is not armed."

"He looks cocked and primed to shoot to me."

Penelope lifted her head enough to scowl briefly at the four boys gathered at the foot of the bed who laughed at Artemis's crude jest. She was pleased to be rescued, but appalled by what the boys had risked in coming to her aid. Artemis was only sixteen, Stefan only fourteen, Darius not yet ten, Hector but newly turned nine, and Delmar barely seven. All were far too young to be wandering the dangerous streets of London at night but she could not bring herself to taint her gratitude with a scolding, or to pinch at their boyish pride. She would, however, try to remember to have a little talk with Artemis concerning the fact that Hector and Delmar understood his jest. They were too young for that knowledge. They were also too young to be seeing her tied to a bed with a naked man on top of her but there was nothing she could do about that. She frowned when she realized Lord Radmoor was no longer "cocked and primed."

She also felt a distinct pang of disappointment. It was not just the drug that made her sorry this sordid interlude had been interrupted before she had even gotten a real kiss. Penelope was certain she would never get another chance to fulfill even one of her wishes or have even one of her dreams about Lord Ashton Radmoor come true. The feel of small hands untying her ankles pulled her free of her wandering thoughts and she lifted her head again to smile her gratitude at Delmar.

"Get off her," Artemis ordered Lord Radmoor.

"That could prove awkward," Penelope said, blushing as Ashton began to slowly lift his body off hers.

"I do not think we will be shocked by seeing a naked man."

"I did not think you would be, but *I* am also naked, or as good as." She blushed again when Artemis looked her over and his eyes widened.

"Lads, look away until I can get Pen decently covered," Artemis ordered the boys.

"But what about the man?" asked Delmar as he and the other boys obeyed the command.

"I have a gun on him," replied Artemis even as he

fixed his gaze on Ashton again. "Now, my lord, remove yourself from my sister. Very slowly. Do not think that, because I am young, I will hesitate to shoot you."

Ashton did as he was told. When he finally stood at the side of the bed, he looked across it at the one who held a pistol aimed directly at his heart. His first clear thought was to wonder how such a tall, too thin youth could possess such a deep, manly voice. Then he looked into the youth's icy blue eyes, eyes that remained steadily fixed on him as the youth moved to untie one of his sister's wrists. Ashton had no more doubt that there was enough strong, furious man in the boy to make him a true threat. He could also see a slight family resemblance in the youth's face, an almost pretty face despite how his cold anger hardened his expression.

A fleeting glance at Penelope revealed her having trouble untying her other wrist, and Ashton looked back at the boy. "If you will allow it, I could assist her."

"No tricks," said Artemis.

"My word of honor."

The youth nodded and Ashton quickly untied Penelope's wrist. He moved back to stand by the side of the bed. She struggled to sit up and he frowned at her awkward movements. She acted as if she was a little drunk yet he had not smelled or tasted any spirits on her breath. Ashton studied her very closely as she fumbled with her gown in a vain attempt to achieve some semblance of modesty.

"Were you tied up for a long time?" he asked. Guilt pinched at him over the fact that he had not asked her that before and had hesitated to untie her.

"Oh, nay. I mean, no, I do not think so," Penelope replied, beginning to experience an alarming unsteadiness in her body and her mind. "Where are my clothes? I think I must hurry and dress. That nasty potion

Mrs. Cratchitt forced down my throat does not feel so very pleasant now. I think I may soon be very ill or very unconscious and very soon."

Ashton cursed and heard the youth echo it. "I will get her clothes," he muttered even as he looked around the room. He spotted them piled on the floor near the door and went to get them. "Put the gun away," he told Artemis as he set Penelope's clothes on the bed. "You will need some help getting her dressed." He sighed when the boy hesitated. "It is a little late to worry about her modesty in front of me. I also have no desire to take a woman who has had to be drugged to share a bed with me."

"How late?" demanded Artemis.

There were very few men Ashton knew who could have put such cold, deadly fury into two small words. "Not that late," he replied and was relieved when the boy set his pistol aside and moved to help him dress Penelope.

"But I will be naked," Penelope protested as her brother and Ashton started to remove the thin gown Mrs. Cratchitt had forced her to wear.

"You are as good as naked now," muttered Artemis and then he frowned at her. "You were given some potion?"

"Mrs. Cratchitt forced it on me. It made me very calm for a while, very accepting of my fate. Now it is making me very dizzy and a little nauseous. How did you find me?"

"Paul slipped out and followed you for aways. He saw those men grab you, ran back home to us, and told me about it. I had already sensed that something was very wrong and was preparing to set out after you."

"I was very frightened."

"I know," he said in a soft, gentle tone and he stroked

her hair. "Between that and questioning a few boys here and there, we were able to pick up your trail. Then, well, it was as if a lantern had been lit to lead me straight to this place and this room. I did not have to roam about outside for very long before I knew exactly where you were. The potion, I suppose. It has made things uncomfortable for you?"

"Quite uncomfortable. This is a very sad place, full of ill feelings and angry spirits. Someone died in this bed," she added, sorrow weighting her every word. "Poor Faith."

"What are you saying?" asked Ashton, eyeing the siblings warily as he finished tugging Penelope's dress on her increasingly limp body. He did not completely understand the meaning of their words but what little he guessed at made him very uneasy.

"Oh, you are still naked," murmured Penelope, unable to stop herself from looking him over very thoroughly. He was so handsome, she thought and sighed.

"I can finish this unaided now," said Artemis and he scowled at Ashton. "You can go and get yourself dressed now. Boys, watch him closely."

Ashton moved to where his clothes had been set down. He looked at the boys who had been ordered to watch him, caught the direction of the interested gazes of the younger ones, and hurried to get dressed. He understood a young boy's fascination with that part of a grown man's body but he was in no mood to be the object of their study. He was embarrassed enough by how matters had turned against him.

What little he could hear of the conversation between Penelope and her brother made him inwardly shake his head. They seemed to believe they could feel things and see things others could not, could snatch emotions from the air and speak to the dead. She spoke of this specter named Faith as if the vision were not born of the potion Cratchitt had given her, which it certainly must have been. He then wondered if they were part of that group of charlatans who swindled foolish people out of money by claiming they could contact the dead or tell one what the future would bring.

That would explain their fine speech, that air of gentility, he mused. Unless one went to a gypsy at some fair, most of the charlatans of that ilk dealt with the ladies of society and were as genteel as their customers, or pretended to be. He frowned as he tied his cravat under the intense scrutiny of the boys, wondering uneasily if the game was not over yet. Were they going to try to entrap him in some way? Perhaps even try to claim honor demanded he marry the girl?

A little voice in his head whispered that it would not be such a hardship if they did and he brutally silenced it. It was his lust talking, nothing more. He could not marry just anyone, especially not some lovely woman whose bloodlines and purity were in question. He had a duty to his title and to the future of his line, as well as to his family. He had to marry a woman of the appropriate bloodlines, and one fully accepted by society. He also had to marry a woman with as large a dowry as possible to help rebuild the family fortunes. It did not please him to admit, even if only to himself, how swiftly he would toss aside the need for good bloodlines if this wide-eyed girl were wealthy. In a way, he had already done that by considering marriage to Clarissa for the barony her brother now held was very new. The family had been very minor gentry before then.

For a moment he feared he was like his father, a slave to his passions. He pulled on his boots and shook his head, fighting to dislodge that fear from his mind. One moment of madness with one woman did not make him the satyr his father had been. Ashton knew he could never treat a woman as his father had treated his mother. Nor could he ever leave his wife and children nearly destitute just to sate those unbridled passions. He had to stop fearing that he was going to become his father. That fear could easily choke all the life out of him.

What if I told you that I was the daughter of a marquis?

He tensed as he heard her say those words again in his mind. That would make her bloodlines more than acceptable. Ashton silently cursed. He was grasping at the air, at any reason he could find not to tie himself in marriage to the beautiful but cold Clarissa. Even if Penelope was what she claimed, she was not the heiress he needed. The gown she now wore proved that. It was pretty enough but not of the finest quality. Neither were the clothes the boys all wore. His curiosity was now piqued, however. Just who were these people?

"Pen, may we leave now?" asked Delmar. "There is a bad air here."

Ashton stared at the boy. He looked a little pale and his wide blue eyes shone with fear. It was not an offensive odor the boy referred to. Ashton frowned at Penelope, who now stood by the bed, her brother's arm around her waist to steady her. Did the whole family believe they had strange powers?

"Exactly who are you?" he asked Penelope. "All of you?"

"That is no concern of yours," replied Artemis, tightening his grip on Penelope when she started to speak.

"You can depend upon my discretion." Ashton grimaced and dragged a hand through his hair. "If naught else, I certainly do not wish my name connected to this debacle."

"De—baaa—cle," Penelope murmured. "A fine word." She smiled and closed her eyes.

Artemis staggered when Penelope went limp and started to fall. Ashton lunged forward to grab Penelope before she hit the floor. Four young voices cried out in dismay and Ashton knew he, too, had been frightened by her sudden collapse. The relief that swept over him when she opened her eyes to stare at him was greater than he thought it should be.

"My legs failed me," she said and frowned at the faint slurring of her words.

"The potion was obviously too strong for you," said Ashton.

"I can take her now." Artemis reached for Penelope.

"To where?" Ashton glanced toward the open window. "Out that way? Carrying her?" He could tell the boy wanted to say he could do it but had enough good sense to know it could prove impossible, even dangerous. "I need to find my friends to help us."

"In this place? Do you mean to knock on every door?"

"I mean for you to go out the window, go up to the door, and ask for Sir Cornell Fincham. Tell the man at the door that the Duke of Burfoot has sent you with an urgent message for his son. They will fetch him or lead you to him. Tell Cornell I need him and the others to come to this room as quickly as they can. And as stealthily as possible."

"Which room is this?"

"Twenty-two," Penelope replied and rubbed her cheek against the soft velvet of Radmoor's coat.

"And I may trust in their discretion as well, may I?" Artemis frowned. "Why should I?"

"Because they are my closest, most trusted friends and will protect my name as fiercely as they would their own."

"They will want explanations."

"Tell them they will get answers as soon as they join me here." When Artemis still hesitated, Ashton added in a voice that held both command and counsel, "We shall need their help to get her out of here safely and unseen."

Artemis nodded and, after ordering the other boys to guard Ashton and Penelope, slipped out the window. There was barely a whisper of sound as the youth descended the outside wall and Ashton had to admire the boy's skill. He sat down on the bed to await his friends and settled a limp Penelope on his lap.

She felt right there, fit perfectly in his arms. Ashton heartily wished Clarissa fit so perfectly instead of this unknown girl. Not that he had actually embraced Clarissa yet. Worse, he found himself wondering if the hints of passion he had seen in her were born of his touch or the potion the madam had forced her to drink. It was not something that should concern him but he suspected he would be wondering about it for a long time. He also knew that he would soon question the veracity of the passion his past lovers had shown in his arms, few and far between though they were. Once a man began thinking of such things, he entered into a vicious circle of doubt.

"Is she going to die?"

Ashton looked at the small boy called Delmar. "No. She is just weakened by the potion given to her. It will loosen its grip upon her soon and she will be fine." There remained a glint of doubt in the boy's eyes and Ashton forced as much confidence as he could into his voice as he added, "Truly, your sister will fully recover from this."

"She is not my sister. She is my cousin. Stefan and Artemis are her brothers. The rest of us are her cousins."

"Ah, I had thought you all lived with her."

"We do. She takes care of us."

"All of you?"

"Enough, Delmar," said a boy who looked nearly as old as Artemis. "The man does not need to know our business."

"But, Stefan, I was just talking. I was being polite."

"No need of that, either. The man is not a guest in our home. Recall how we found him and what he was trying to do to Pen."

Delmar glanced at Ashton and then pressed his lips together. Ashton gave the boy a brief smile before looking at Stefan, Penelope's other brother. "She will need to rest. The potion will flee her system but it may take hours to do so and, I believe, she will not feel well afterward. Is there someone who can care for her?"

"We will."

Ashton was about to argue the ability of a pack of boys to care for a sick young woman when Artemis and the others slipped into the room. Brant was the first to reach his side and Ashton waited patiently while his friend studied Penelope and then looked over each of the boys. When Brant finally looked back at him and cocked one dark brow, Ashton sighed. He explained what had happened as quickly and plainly as possible.

"So Mrs. Cratchitt's is not quite the genteel establishment it pretends to be," Brant said and then looked at the boys again. "Do you know how and why she was taken?"

"Nay," said Artemis and moved to braid Penelope's hair. "She was late coming home. The ones who took her must have seen her as easy game."

Ashton exchanged a brief look with his friends. He knew the boy was not telling the truth. The expressions his friends wore told him they shared his suspicions. Penelope had secrets and the boys were holding fast to them. It was hard for Ashton to think they were dark or dangerous secrets, but having tasted the madness of a fierce lust, he was not sure he could trust his own instincts when it came to Penelope.

"The problem now is how to get her out of here without anyone seeing her," said Ashton. "She is incapable of walking out of here and will be for several hours yet. It is not simply to save her reputation, either. I have a strong feeling she was not brought here because Mrs. Cratchitt was on the hunt for new girls."

"Someone is coming for me tomorrow," Penelope said, not surprised at how weak and soft her voice was. She was clutching tightly to a thin, fraying thread of consciousness. "She did not tell me who."

"Yet she sold you to me for the night?"

"Said she could make sure the man did not know. Someone paid for me to be brought here." She ached to say who she suspected had done so, but kept the words back. She had no proof.

One look into her cloudy eyes told Ashton there was no sense in questioning her about that now. She was barely conscious. He looked at his friends, praying one of them had devised a plan. This was not something he really wanted or needed to get mixed up in at this time, but he could not desert the woman and certainly could not leave her at Mrs. Cratchitt's.

"The boys can go back out the window," Brant said. "As soon as they are on the ground, we will draw up the rope. I will tie it about your waist, Ashton, and while you hold the girl, we will lower you out the window. Cornell, you go to the carriage and wait for them. Whitney, Victor, and I will wait here while you take the boys and the lady to their home. There are a few things I wish to do before we leave this place," he muttered and frowned at Penelope.

"We do not need help to get her home," said Artemis.

"Do not be so proud you refuse help when it is truly

needed," Brant told the boy. "She cannot walk far, if at all, and you cannot carry her through the streets without drawing a great deal of unwanted attention to yourselves. Now, out the window with you. We do not want to have someone catch all of us in this room, do we?"

Artemis's lips moved and Ashton suspected the youth was cursing, but he did as he was told. In but moments all the boys were gone and Brant was pulling up the rope. As Ashton prepared to take his turn, he noticed that the rope was similar to what sailors used to catch the side of another ship, the sharp tines of the grappling hook deeply embedded in the wall. He wondered how he had missed the sound of that striking the wood and digging in. Lust had obviously deafened him, he thought as he handed Penelope to Victor with an unsettling reluctance and stood still while Brant secured the rope to his waist. When Brant declared the rope secure, it took all of Ashton's willpower to stop himself from grabbing for Penelope like some greedy child.

Shaking aside his unease over his tortured emotions, Ashton sat on the windowsill. He carefully swung his legs around until they hung outside, and then held his breath as he was slowly lowered to the ground. The way Penelope clung to his neck, her face pressed against his shoulder, told him she was still aware enough to realize what was happening around her.

When his feet touched the ground, he set Penelope on her feet. Artemis and Stefan hurried over to support her as he untied the rope around his waist, but it was clear they were having trouble keeping her upright. Once freed, Ashton waved to his friends who were still in the window and then picked Penelope up again before striding toward the carriage.

"This is a bad business," muttered Cornell as the boys scrambled into the carriage.

All Ashton could do was nod in agreement. He set Penelope on the seat between her brothers and climbed into the carriage to sit down across from her. Cornell climbed in right behind him. It was crowded, and even as he rapped on the roof of the carriage to tell the driver to move, Delmar climbed into his lap. He would have preferred Penelope there, he thought, but put a steadying arm around the boy when the carriage began to move.

"Do you live far from here?" he asked Artemis.

"Nay," the boy replied. "I told your man the way to go as we waited for you and Pen."

When they pulled up in front of the house Artemis said was theirs, the tiny hope Ashton had not even realized he had been cherishing died a swift death. The area was home to mistresses, minor aristocracy with empty pockets, and those in trade who had progressed beyond living above their shops. Even if Penelope had good bloodlines and the training to be a viscount's wife, she would have little or no dowry. He detested being so mercenary in his choice of a wife but the small horde of dependents he was responsible for required him to be so. Penelope might really be the daughter of a marquis but the man had obviously been as reckless with his riches as Ashton's father had. Or she was not the marquis's legitimate child.

Ignoring Artemis's protest, Ashton lifted Penelope out of the carriage and carried her up the steps to the door. He had only just reached the top step when the door was flung open and more young boys appeared, surrounding him. Penelope was taken from him before he could utter one protest. The boys all thanked him for his aid and hurried a staggering Penelope inside, slamming the door in his face.

Ashton considered banging on the door but shrugged aside the urge. He had to put the woman out of his mind.

On the morrow he would be facing Lord Hutton-Moore, taking that first formal step toward marrying the beautiful, cold Clarissa. He noticed a placard by the door that read WHERLOCKE WARREN and frowned. An odd name for a house, even for one bought for a mistress, he mused as he turned away.

Once back in the carriage and on his way to Mrs. Cratchitt's to gather up his friends, Ashton decided he wanted to go home. He needed quiet, needed time to think and strengthen his resolve to do what he had to do for his family. He needed time alone to push all thought and memory of a woman who stirred his blood as none had ever done before right out of his mind.

Chapter Four

"Pearls cast before swine, that is what it was."

Ashton gave Brant an uneasy smile as his friend walked into his breakfast room and helped himself to a large plate of food from the sideboard before sitting down. "What are you talking about?"

"The great wisdom I imparted to you two nights ago."

Was it only two nights ago? Ashton mused. It felt like months. He had not gotten much sleep since then, haunted by dreams of a woman with odd-colored eyes and knotted up with unquenched lust. Worse, he was starting to see Penelope everywhere. He was sure he had seen her pale face in an attic window as he had left Clarissa's home yesterday, but that was impossible. Clarissa would have no reason to hide the daughter of a marquis in her attic.

"Which great wisdom was that?" he asked Brant.

"About waiting before you asked for Clarissa's fair hand, before making it all official."

"But I did heed that advice. I had to keep my meeting with her brother, but I kept the talk very vague, more of an official request to court his sister. The most basic and formal first step. Foolish really because it is time I married and the family coffers definitely need an infusion of funds."

"Well, either you were not vague enough or someone willfully misunderstood you."

Ashton cautiously accepted the paper Brant handed him, wondering why he had not noticed his friend carrying it. He really needed a few nights of good sleep, Ashton decided. He was getting as blind and as absent-minded as his ancient grandfather had been. Ashton had been young when the old man had died, wandering off one night onto the moors to drown in a bog. He felt as if he was drowning in an emotional bog, one that was making him question his every decision.

The paper was folded open to a section listing betrothals, marriages, births, and deaths. It took only a quick glance over the various announcements to find what had brought Brant to his home at such an early hour. Featured quite prominently and filled with a tactless listing of his ancestry and prospects was the announcement of his betrothal to Lady Clarissa Hutton-Moore. Ashton felt his breakfast turn into a seething ball of acid in his belly. He had been trapped.

"I never asked her," he muttered. "No *dear, would you do me the honor.* No ring."

Brant filled a cup with coffee and frowned. "Bad ton, then. Yet what can you do?"

"Nothing, I suppose." Ashton continued to stare at the notice and had the fleeting thought that it would be better placed beneath the obituaries. "My courtship of Clarissa, my marked interest in her, has been very public and an announcement has been anticipated. It was always my plan. I but faltered for a moment."

Faltered was a weak word to describe the turmoil that had beset him since that night at Mrs. Cratchitt's, he thought with a sigh. To say he had fallen on his face would be a better way to describe it. That night he had gone out with his friends fully accepting his future with Clarissa and had come back dreading it to the very depths of his soul. He had not been given time to regain his balance and good sense. Ashton frowned, suddenly wondering if Clarissa's brother, perhaps even Clarissa herself, had sensed the change in him and acted quickly to stop him from walking away. Despite his hesitation of the moment, that would not have happened.

"Scented your change of heart," Brant said, echoing Ashton's thoughts.

"Possibly, but it was only a brief change. I would have wrestled it back onto the path of necessity. My mind was still set on the betrothal. To be honest, my heart was never involved anyway."

"Did not think so. Clarissa is beautiful, a perfect gem of the ton, but I never saw anything there that would bestir you much at all."

"Ah, but there was her dowry and the fact that I would not have to snuff all the candles in order to beget an heir on her."

Brant grimaced. "But you will have to build up the fire in the bedchamber ere you crawl beneath the sheets or you will be chilled to the bone."

"So you think her lacking in passion, too?" Ashton asked.

"The kind that can warm a man who looks for more than scratching an itch? Most assuredly."

"And you think I look for more, do you?"

Brant smiled, but there was a tinge of sadness in the expression. "In the end, most of us do. We just rarely find it. We turn to money and appropriate bloodlines instead, and then spend the rest of our lives trying to find that warmth elsewhere. Thought I had found it once," he added in a soft voice.

"It proved false?" Ashton felt certain he knew exactly when Brant had suffered his disappointment for there had been a distinct hardening in the man a little over a year ago.

"I am not sure. She was a vicar's daughter."

"I suspect your mother was chagrined," Ashton murmured.

"A mild word for dear Mama's reaction to my choice. She was absolutely enraged, especially when the match she thought I should make was lost to her and her chosen candidate was snatched up by another. My chosen one had a very small dowry and was but the child of the youngest son of a minor baron. I was determined to have her, my pretty Faith. But she disappeared. Her father said she had run off with a soldier."

"Do you believe that?"

"Some days, no, but most of the time, yes. Her father is a respected man, a vicar well known for his piety. I find it hard to believe he would lie to me or not search far and wide for his daughter if she had just disappeared. So I decided that, if one cannot trust a pious vicar's daughter named Faith, what hope is there? I will, at some point, find a suitable girl who makes Mama happy and grunt over her until she breeds me a brood of heirs and spares, all the while keeping a mistress to satisfy my less dignified needs."

Ashton felt a chill go down his spine and not because

of Brant's bleak portrayal of his future. In his head he could hear Penelope say, *Someone died in this bed. Poor Faith.* He firmly told himself not to be a superstitious fool. It helped only a little, as did reminding himself that Faith was not such an uncommon name, and even if Penelope could sense such things, it did not mean she had seen Brant's Faith.

He forced his wandering mind back to the subject at hand—his newly announced betrothal to Clarissa. "That is a dark and dismal future," he said, not completely referring to Brant's last statement.

"As titled gentlemen, burdened with history, duty, and far too many dependents, it is a future we all face." Brant spread honey on his toasted bread. "Are you going to even complain about the Hutton-Moores' presumption?"

"Some. A few cutting remarks as I give Clarissa a ring. Mayhap I will purchase one, letting the fact that I did not adorn her delicate white hand with the famed Radmoor emerald speak for itself. I believe I am angry enough to deliver that insult. Although it is little more than a tightly trapped man's last howl of defiance."

"An excellent idea, however. It will be interesting to see how she explains that to all who will rush to gawk at her ring. Myself, I would no longer trust her any further than I could spit."

"Oh, I am not sure I trusted her that much even before this trickery. I trust her brother even less. I cannot really say why, just instinct."

"God's tears, Ashton, if that is so, why are you going to marry the chit?"

"Because she was the only one with a hefty dowry who would look with any favor upon a nearly penniless viscount who has too many people living off his meager and rapidly diminishing funds. And one who carries the taint of a licentious father to whom 'scandal' was just another word."

"Ah, there is that. What about the fair Penelope?"

Ashton slumped in his seat. "I wish I could say I will just forget about her. I remind myself that I am a man of reason. Reason tells me to get my wandering mind back on the path I need to take, the one that will keep my family out of debtor's prison. Reason reminds me, continuously, that I need money, that my estates need money, and that my family needs money. Reason tells me that I need to repair the Radmoor reputation, repair all the damage my father did as he drank, gambled, and rutted his way to an early death. Reason tells me that I will gain none of that if I chase after a girl named Penelope who lives in a house in a just barely genteel part of the city with what appears to be a vast horde of younger brothers and cousins, somehow ends up in a brothel, and thinks she can see spirits and the like."

"Really? Spirits?" Brant grinned. "Fascinating. Do you know what I think?"

"I am afraid to ask." He was relieved, however, that Brant did not pursue the subject of ghosts.

"I will tell you despite that scorn I hear in your voice. I say, bugger reason, bugger Clarissa and her brother, and go see the little Penelope. Either get her out of your head or groin or wherever she has settled or hold on tight, but you do not have much time to do that before you are married."

Ashton frowned. "Weddings take months to prepare."

"And betrothals are usually proceeded by a proposal and a ring. I would never allow myself to be caught alone with the fair Clarissa if you intend to dawdle the usual amount of time before actually standing before the vicar."

"Damn. Never considered that. If the Hutton-Moores feared I would not even propose, they could be very concerned about whether or not I will balk on the way to the altar. The question is—why? With her beauty and her dowry, Clarissa could easily find another husband. *They* do not need *me*. *I* need *them* or, rather, that dowry."

"A very good question. One that definitely needs an answer. Are you very certain Clarissa actually possesses that dowry?"

"I had my man of business check the Hutton-Moores out thoroughly."

"And there is no chance he was lied to or fooled?"

Ashton opened his mouth to say such a thing was impossible, but the words would not come out. Could Hudson have been gulled? And if he had been, how did one find out the truth? Society saw nothing wrong with the Hutton-Moores except for the few who disdained their title. There were no rumors slipping through the various balls and routs that would cause one to question what they claimed about their finances, and they did not live like a family teetering on the edge of ruin. Such a family would not work so hard, so deviously, to marry a lady of their house to a penniless viscount. A search would be on for a man with a full purse, and he said as much to Brant.

Brant nodded. "That would be logical. Yet why this? Why shove you toward the altar? Do you think Clarissa might truly care for you?"

"No," Ashton replied, completely confident in his judgment. "She appreciates a viscount, the title, the family history, and all of that. All the things her family has not acquired yet. In a way, I am being bought. I believe she also has a covetous eye set on those even more impressive titles I am in line for."

"Ah, yes." Brant helped himself to an apple. "Clarissa

hopes to become a duchess. Well, do as you will, but I believe I will begin to take a much closer look at the Hutton-Moores. This trickery disturbs me, especially when there appears to be no reason for it."

"It begins to disturb me more and more as I think on it." Ashton stood up, took the paper to the fireplace, and tossed it in. He did not get the sense of satisfaction he had thought he would as he watched it burn. "Yet I cannot break the betrothal without good reason. If nothing else, I will not subject my family to the scandal that would result from it. They have suffered far too many years of scandal already." Once the paper was ash, Ashton returned to his seat.

"If they have lied, promising you what does not exist, you could easily break the betrothal. Whatever scandal results from it will mark the Hutton-Moores, not you."

"And then I would have to start all over again. That is not something I look forward to."

"Better that than to find out that you have been taken for a fool on the day after the marriage is consummated."

Thus ending up with absolutely nothing, Ashton thought. No money to help his family and a wife he did not care for, trust, or desire. He had soothed his pangs of guilt over wooing a woman for her dowry by promising himself he would be a good husband to her. Yet thinking of marriage to Clarissa sans her promised dowry was chilling. This trickery had been enough to kill what little liking he had for her. He tried telling himself that it could have been her brother who pulled this trick, that she had had no idea of what he was planning, but he could not believe it. Clarissa would have to have been aware of it all if only so she could act accordingly when society came calling to congratulate her as they soon would.

"I had best send a letter to my family to tell them

what has happened," Ashton said and then winced. "I shall have to be at least somewhat truthful or they will be hurt, thinking that I did not care to include them in such a momentous decision. They knew I was courting Clarissa, but they would expect me to have at least warned them that I was about to propose and that I was betrothed before the announcement appeared in the paper. They live close enough to the city that they will hear the news soon."

"And you must find a ring. I may be able to help you there."

"You carry betrothal rings around with you?" Ashton teased.

Brant ignored that remark. "A small token I intended to give my last mistress before I caught her abed with her butler." He smiled faintly when Ashton laughed. "I felt I was gracious by allowing her to remain in the house at my expense for two more months. 'Twas gift enough. It is a pretty little diamond and sapphire ring."

"That is very kind of you, but—"

"Ashton, do not waste what little blunt you have on this sly chit. Swallow your damn pride. I have a ring. Take it. Give it back to me later."

"You do not think I will marry her."

"I do not want you to, especially after this trickery. But if you do, I know you will eventually give her the Radmoor emerald. If you do not, you will get this back from her. If neither occurs, it is still nothing to worry about. Consider it a gift since the last one I tried to give you did not work out and I got my money back."

That surprised Ashton. "All of it?" Mrs. Cratchitt did not seem the type of woman to bow to that demand.

"Down to the last hapenny. You were too angry, perhaps, to ask about all I had been doing while you took the lady home."

"I still think Mrs. Cratchitt ought to be put out of business."

"She will be. For little Penelope's sake, the full truth of what happened cannot be told, but little by little, dark rumors will choke off the flow of clients that bitch needs to survive."

Ashton was a little surprised by the depth of the anger he heard in Brant's voice. He shared it, but it was all tangled up with the fact that it had been Penelope who had been taken and nearly forced into that life. It had begun to drown out the sinful part of him that wished her rescue had not come until he had satisfied that fierce desire she had stirred in him. The anger had grown stronger over the past two days as he continued to recall the things she had said and all the clues he had previously missed or ignored that indicated she was an innocent. Yet surely some of what she had said could not possibly be true, could it?

"Do you think Penelope was a complete innocent?" he asked Brant.

"You mean do I think you were about to break in a virgin for that old crow?" Brant nodded. "There is a part of me, a large part, that does believe that despite the brief time I was with her. Only the cynic doubts, and not too strongly." He smiled faintly at Ashton's look of dismay. "Do not look so appalled. Sad to say, it happens. Not every woman in a brothel came there already taught the hard lesson, shall we say. Nor do they all step into the life willingly."

"That is what she said. She said, *Did you think a woman woke up one day and said I think I shall become a whore.*'"

Brant chuckled but quickly grew serious. "I had thought the places such as Mrs. Cratchitt's were different, that the ones who catered most specifically to the gentry did not indulge in that sort of, er, recruitment. I was wrong. Perhaps even naïve."

"God rot it, now I begin to fear that everything Penelope said was true. I have not been able to shake her words out of my head. After all, she was an innocent, though I had thought her but new at her work. We know she was kidnapped, and she was drugged. Yet how could she be the daughter of a marquis?" he finished in a distracted mutter.

Brant choked on the coffee he was drinking and needed a moment to still his coughing before he asked in a hoarse voice, "She said what?"

"If I recall correctly, at one point she said she was not one of Mrs. Cratchitt's girls and I rather condescendingly asked her what she was then. She said, '*What if I told you I was the daughter of a marquis, cruelly kidnapped off the street, and then sold to Mrs. Cratchitt? That I was given a vile potion, dressed in this scandalous attire, and tied to this bed, all against my will?*'"

"And you did not believe her?"

"Would you have?"

"No. So, the only question left to answer now is—*is* she the daughter of a marquis?"

"What would a marquis's family be doing living in such a house at such an address?"

"Perhaps the man was akin to your father and that is all they can afford. Or they are the man's little family from a mistress he kept for years. Did you ever discover what her full name was?"

"Wherlocke, I believe. It was the name on a placard by the front door. A strange placard, as it said WHER-LOCKE WARREN."

"That is odd. A family joke perhaps. The name is of the gentry, but that is all I am certain of. It most certainly warrants investigation, but we must do it very carefully, and as discreetly as possible. It could be true. You and I do not know enough of each and every family in society to discard that possibility." Brant studied the look that settled on Ashton's face with amusement. "What is that odd expression indicative of?"

"I just realized I may have stood bare-arsed before the virginal daughter of a marquis." He grimaced and then smiled when Brant laughed. "Let us just hope the man is either dead or not the sort to be easily offended."

Brant immediately sobered. "Good point." He sat up straighter when Ashton's butler entered the breakfast room. "S'truth, we can begin our investigation now."

"With my butler?"

"Butlers can be a veritable fount of information on the ton. Marston," Brant said as the tall, slender butler began to remove some of the empty plates from the table, "do you know anything about a family called Wherlocke?"

"I do indeed, m'lord," Marston replied in his deep, well-modulated voice. "A somewhat eccentric, reclusive family, but a very old one. They and the other branch of the family, the Vaughns, have collected up quite a few impressive titles through advantageous marriages and service to the crown." Marston frowned slightly at the shocked looks on the faces of the young lords. "Is there a problem, m'lord?" he asked Ashton. "I would have thought you would know of the family for Lady Clarissa's father married into it. If I recall correctly, the woman was a young, wealthy widow with only one child. I am surprised you have not met that child for she must be living with the Hutton-Moores."

"I have met no one," Ashton managed to spit out, a cold, hard knot of dread beginning to form in his stomach.

"How odd, m'lord. The butler at the Hutton-Moore town house was my cousin, although it had a different name when my cousin worked there. He died shortly after the marquis did. I trust in his word that there was a daughter. I do not know the Hutton-Moore butler well enough to confirm that if that is what you seek."

"But you are certain the marquis's child was a girl?"

"Most certain, m'lord. My cousin had no reason to lie to me about it. In truth, he always spoke quite fondly of the child."

"What did you mean when you said the Wherlockes are eccentric?" asked Brant.

As he scraped the leavings from each dish into a bowl, Marston replied, "'Gifted' might be a better word. It is what has been claimed about them although I have no knowledge as to the veracity of such claims. My cousin was quite convinced of it, however. It is claimed that the Wherlockes and their kin, the Vaughns, have unusual skills, can see the future, commune with the spirits, and other talents of that ilk. It is why they are a somewhat reclusive family. Needless to say, such, er, gifts gave them a great deal of trouble in the past. You will find ones who know of the family, but not many who know them personally and even fewer who know them well. Of course, my cousin told me of this in confidence." He glanced at each of the two younger men, who nodded their understanding. "Might I ask why you are interested in the family, m'lord?"

"I think I have met one, although I do not know which part of the family she springs from," replied Ashton.

"If you wish, m'lord, I can make note of what I know and as much of the lineage as I can and give it to you this afternoon."

"Yes, if you would be so kind, Marston, I would appreciate it."

"Allow me to offer you the household's felicitations upon your betrothal to Lady Hutton-Moore, m'lord."

"Thank you and thank them for me," Ashton answered and watched morosely as Marston left with the dirty dishes and a bowl full of scraps he would feed to his beloved cats. "I think I may be in some difficulty," he said to Brant as soon as Marston closed the door behind him.

"Do not fret over that now. You need to get that ring to your fiancée and make your displeasure known to Clarissa."

"The woman who may well have hidden her impoverished relative—stepsister, by damn—away like a dirty secret? I cannot help but fear what plans she may have for my poor aunts."

"She cannot act against them without your approval and acquiescence."

"But she can make them feel like dirt upon her pretty shoes."

"Perhaps, my friend, it behooves you to take some time to gain a better knowledge of just what sort of woman your fiancée is. Women are so well trained in the various artifices of society that one cannot always be certain what they are really like. Her dowry may save your family from debtor's prison, but at what cost?"

That was a question Ashton knew he would have to answer before he stood in front of an altar with Lady Clarissa. Perhaps it was time to survey some of the other heiresses.

By the time Ashton returned home late in the afternoon, his head ached. He was not particularly pleased to see all four of his friends waiting in his study, but he heartily welcomed the brandy Victor had brought along for them to share. It took several deep swallows of the smooth, mellow brew before he felt calm enough to indulge in the conversation his friends so obviously wished to have with him. Ashton decided to succinctly answer all their questions about Clarissa before they asked them.

"My fiancée was not pleased with the ring," he said. "She had obviously been anticipating the Radmoor emerald. Both she and her brother expressed surprise that I was at all annoyed by the announcement, claiming they had thought that everything had been settled. Even graciously offered to retract the announcement."

"An offer you politely refused, of course," said Brant.

"Of course. Mercenary bastard that I am, I need that money. I am barely hanging on as it is." He grimaced. "Unless some miracle befalls me, I will soon marry Lady Clarissa. I have no choice. Even less choice than I had thought for Lord Charles holds a rather large number of my father's markers."

"He threatened you?"

"Not precisely, but then such a thing is rarely done precisely, is it. The information was very delicately inserted into the discussion of the marriage contracts. However, the implication is very clear. Marry Clarissa or find myself facing a demand for immediate payment, something I could never honor, not without plunging my entire family into utter destitution. Part of Clarissa's dowry is already earmarked for the payment of those markers so I will get even less than I had hoped for." He shook his head when all four men started to speak. "No. No loans. The debts my father bequeathed me are almost more than I can bear. I will add no more."

"It would not be a matter of adding, but exchanging," said Brant, "but we will not argue that now. While we were waiting for you, Marston brought us the information on the Wherlockes as he promised."

Ashton studied the four very serious faces of his friends. "You are about to give me bad news."

"It can wait," Brant began.

"No. Spit it out."

"Well, even though Marston says he is not finished, the lineage he did give us is very impressive. The Wherlockes and the Vaughns are intertwined with many of the most important families in England. At the moment, what most concerns you, us, is one marquis of Salterwood, a Wherlocke, who married one Minerva Wherlocke, a very distant cousin. He bred one child on his wife, a girl, and died ten years almost to the day after his marriage. His widow then married the baron of Haverstile three years later and died within four years of her wedding, along with her husband, in a boating mishap. The baron adopted her child shortly after the marriage, making that child Penelope Wherlocke Hutton-Moore."

"Hell."

Chapter Five

"You should have heard her, Artemis," Penelope said as she kneaded the bread while her brother removed peas from their pods. "She was absolutely furious that Radmoor had given her—how did she put it?—some pathetic, tawdry little ring of sapphires and diamonds and not the Radmoor emerald." She looked across the kitchen table at her brother. "She truly cares nothing for the man."

"You suspected that all along," said Artemis, then opened a pod and rolled the peas inside into his mouth.

"I did, but feared it was my own jealousy making me think such things. After all, Radmoor is very handsome and a viscount, with a strong chance of gaining more titles. Even though his father leapt from scandal to scandal and bed to bed and apparently left little more than debt behind, Lord Ashton is still accepted in society. Except for the previous viscount, the Radmoors have a long and illustrious heritage. Marrying into that family would be quite a coup for the daughter of a baron who gained his title because he procured women for the prince."

"Really? You can get a title for that?"

"Oh, aye. Do not forget that some very high titles have been given to people simply because some king or prince begot them on the wrong side of the blanket. Compensation for the cuckolded husband, I suppose." She set the bread dough in a bowl and draped a cloth over it before moving to the sink to wash her hands. "So much anger," she murmured.

"At the Hutton-Moores'?" Penelope nodded and Artemis grinned. "So that is why you arrived here far earlier than you usually do."

"It is. Clarissa and Charles were so consumed by their anger, they did not notice me slip away." She frowned as she dried her hands. "I think they may have threatened Radmoor."

"With what?"

"There was something said about his father's debts. I think Charles may have gained hold of some of them, a lot of them, and now holds the markers over him like a sword of Damocles. Think, instead of a lot of men owed smaller sums, many of them willing to take payments or wait, Radmoor now faces one man who could bring him to his knees by simply demanding immediate payment of many debts."

"Clever," murmured Artemis and shrugged at his sister's scowl. "I did not say it was right, just clever. Evilly so."

She shook her head at his weak attempt to slither out of a scolding for his remark. "I also think they put the notice of the betrothal in the papers before there was any actual proposal made. Clarissa said something about the ring being an insult, one delivered because they had rushed the man." She gathered up a small basket of apples that had wintered over very well in storage, sat down at the table, and began to peel them. "It is the why of such machinations that I cannot understand."

"They want those titles in the family. Titles that actually carry a little power and respect."

"Perhaps. Charles would benefit through Clarissa. I fear Radmoor is quite firmly trapped. He is badly in need of money. He certainly does not have what would be needed if Charles called in those debts. It is sad when fathers decimate fortunes, leaving their families to suffer. From the way Radmoor's father behaved, I have to think that his parents did not have a happy marriage and the man then bequeathed his son the need to endure the same."

Artemis frowned as he snatched a slice of apple. "It would seem to me that some of the aristocrats do not want to give up anything. Not their fancy clothes, not their fancy carriages and fine horses, not the balls and the opera."

Penelope nodded. "That is some of it. They would rather plunge themselves into a miserable marriage that will last a lifetime just to be able to keep buying embroidered waistcoats from whatever tailor is *au courant*. I must say that, if Radmoor thinks Clarissa will give up even one small luxury while he repairs his fortunes and his lands, he has failed to see her clearly. Sadly, Clarissa is the sort of woman who will constantly remind him that *she* was the one who pulled him out of debt. Nay, I change my mind. The truly sad thing is that I think he would do his utmost to be a good and true husband, but Clarissa has no interest in that. She will turn what could be a good marriage into the same miserable, faithless union too many in society endure. The same sort of marriage his parents had." Penelope sighed and stared at the bowl full of apple slices in front of her. "I think that is what troubles me most of all. She will not make him happy."

"Do you care for him that much then?" Artemis asked quietly.

"I think I might. He has fascinated me from the first moment I saw him. But I do not have what he needs. Whatever inheritance was left to me is in Charles's hands and I doubt much of it, if any, will remain when I reach the age to take control of it. What little I get now, and that is given most reluctantly, is spent here. It would not help Radmoor anyway."

"But you would make him happy."

"Would I? He has three sisters, a mother, two aunts, and two brothers to support. If he loses even one of his properties, there goes a dower for a sister or a living for a brother. If he married a woman like me, one without a fortune, he would soon see the loss of one property after another and his sisters denied their seasons and thus a good and prosperous match. Two of his sisters are already past the age when they should have made their debut due to the family's lack of funds. I think all that loss would soon bring bitterness to the door."

"So it is not just clothes and carriages."

"Not with Radmoor. It is the futures of his siblings and the comfort of his mother and aunts."

"Pen! That fool what got hisself betrothed to the bitch is here! And he has brought four of his friends."

Penelope stared at Artemis in open-mouthed shock as that blunt announcement bellowed out in young Paul's choirboy voice echoed throughout the house. She recognized the words as her own but how had Paul heard them? Then she realized that Lord Ashton had undoubtedly heard them as well and groaned. After giving Artemis a fierce scowl for laughing, she buried her face in her hands.

"Pe—ne—lo—pe!"

"I will be there in a moment!" she yelled back. "Show them into the parlor!" She then looked at a cackling Artemis in horror. "I just bellowed like a costermonger."

"Stiffen your spine, sister. Clean the flour off yourself, set up a pretty tea tray. And go to greet your guests."

"But—"

"If you feel any embarrassment creep up on you, do try to remember where you last saw that rogue."

"Oh." She thought about that for a moment and then shook her head. "Not a good idea."

"Why not?"

"Because he was naked."

After glaring at her brother, who was laughing so hard he was in grave danger of falling off his chair, Penelope hurried to clean up and prepare a tea tray. Five gentlemen were waiting in her parlor. This, she thought, was probably going to be very embarrassing.

Ashton stared at the angelic-looking little boy who had opened the door. He could swear that the child's bellow was still echoing through the house. The badly muffled laughter of his friends told him he had not been mistaken in what he had just heard. When the child yelled out Penelope's name and the woman yelled back, Ashton was still too shocked to be surprised.

"Come in," said the boy. "I am Paul, cousin Orion's by-blow. The parlor is this way."

Following the boy, Ashton closely studied his surroundings. It was a spacious house and very clean. The furnishings in the parlor the boy led them into were of a good quality, but slightly worn. Ashton recognized two of the boys who had rescued Penelope playing chess at a table in the far corner of the large room. The looks they cast his way were not friendly ones even though their murmured greetings were very polite. Over his head he could hear what sounded like a small army moving around.

"You know them," the boy said and pointed at Stefan and Darius, "but I do not know you."

Ashton introduced his friends to the boy as they all found seats in the room on what proved to be surprisingly comfortable settees and chairs. They were the type of seats that were often banished to the attics and replaced by spindly, dainty chairs a man had to sit in with great care. He looked up from examining the once expensive but now worn rug beneath his feet to find the little cherub named Paul sitting on the table set between the facing settees, looking at him with an unsettling intensity.

"Did they really see you naked in a whorehouse?" Paul asked in his sweet voice, his dark blue eyes wide and filled with innocence.

The heat of an unaccustomed blush warmed Ashton's cheeks. He did not even bother to send a repressive frown toward the two other boys, knowing it would do nothing to stifle their laughter. He did, however, glare at his friends, who were doing a poor job of hiding their amusement. Facing the little boy again, Ashton wondered if the child was truly as sweet as he appeared to be. There was a glint in the child's beguiling eyes that made Ashton think Paul might not understand the full implications of what he was saying, but knew enough to know it was appallingly audacious.

"I was not expecting company at that time," he said.

"Are you really as big as a horse?"

"Paul!"

Penelope marched over to the table as all the men stood up. Paul hastily jumped off it and she set down a tray full of biscuits, fruit, and small cakes. She silently thanked the Fates for inspiring her to indulge in a frenzied bout of cooking. This visitation was going to be awkward enough without having been caught out with nothing to offer her guests. She then frowned at Paul, who was looking far too angelic, a sure sign that he was causing trouble. Considering what she had just overheard him say, however, she decided to reprimand him later. It was not a conversation she wished to have before five gentlemen of the ton.

"If you boys would be so kind as to leave us now, I would be grateful," she said. "And tell the others not to trouble themselves in sneaking down here. I intend to shut the door." She could tell by the way all three boys frowned that they knew any chance of eavesdropping was gone. The parlor doors were very thick.

"Did you give them *all* the cakes?" asked Paul.

"Nay. Now, please, away with you."

A quick glance toward the doorway showed Penelope that the other boys were already downstairs and peering around the edge of the door, obviously having slipped free of their tutor Septimus's guard. She was just about to tell them to leave when Artemis made them scatter. He brought in the pots of coffee and tea, bowed to the men, and then left, herding the other three slow-moving boys in front of him. The moment he closed the doors, she urged the men to sit down and busied herself serving each man some tea or coffee, hoping the mundane chore would calm her before there was any attempt at conversation.

Each man introduced himself, bowed, and kissed her hand before seating himself, and accepting his refreshments. Penelope became more and more alarmed with each introduction even as she attempted to note one thing about each man in order to remember him. Cornell

Fincham, tall, fair-haired, and handsome, whom she knew to be the third son of a royal duke. Brant Mallam, the earl of Fieldgate, a nearly beautiful man with dark hair and dark eyes. Whitney Parnell, the baron of Rye-croft, an apparently flirtatious and jovial fellow until one looked into his steel gray eyes. Victor Chesney, the baron of Fisherton, who looked almost bland with his brown hair and hazel eyes, until he smiled. And then, of course, Radmoor, the viscount who made her heart clench with want. Five handsome bachelors all seated in her parlor. The matchmaking mamas of London would hang her if they ever learned of this meeting.

By the time she took the only place left available near the table, Penelope's stomach was tied up in knots. The fact that this seat was next to Radmoor only made it worse. After all, he had seen her very nearly naked and she had seen him gloriously naked. The rules of polite society she had been taught did not cover such a situation. Nor had it instructed her in how to carry on polite conversation with five men who knew she had been tied to a bed in a brothel.

Ashton finished a delicious lemon cake and noticed a few smudges of flour in Penelope's hair and on one sleeve of her gown. For reasons he could not begin to understand, he thought such dishevelment only made her more adorable. "Did you make these?" he asked, waving a hand toward all the teacakes and biscuits and trying to break the weighted silence they were all locked into.

"Ah, aye. I mean yes, I did," she replied. "I like to cook. It helps me think. A cook I know well made the raspberry tarts, however. She is always sending food here, but the people she works for do not know that. They will not miss what she sends," she hastily added.

"The secret is safe with us," said Lord Mallam as he helped himself to another raspberry tart.

"Why have I never seen you at Hutton-Moore House?" Ashton asked, unable to play any more polite games, suddenly desperate for some answers to all the questions swirling in his mind.

Penelope silently repeated every curse she knew, knowing she would be ashamed later at how long that list was. It was apparent that Radmoor now knew exactly who she was, but she grasped at the very small chance that she could still persuade him that he was wrong. "Why should you have?"

"Your last name is Wherlocke."

"How do you know that?"

"It says so on the front of this house. There is a placard by the door that says WHERLOCKE WARREN."

"Oh. I had forgotten about that. My cousin Orion put it up." And she intended to kick him soundly for that the next time she saw him. "His idea of a little jest. It was either that or the BY-BLOW BUNGALOW."

Ashton did not know whether to be shocked or to laugh, and noticed his friends suffering the same torn sentiments. "This is where your family houses its . . ." He hesitated, struggling for the right word, one that would not cause insult, and then noticed that she had the glint of mischief in her eyes that he had seen in young Paul's.

"Naturals?" she said and grinned when Ashton's friends laughed. Even Ashton smiled. "Aye, it is, but it was not exactly planned that way. I fear my father was not faithful to my mother, hence Artemis and Stefan. When Mama married again, her new husband refused to house the boys, a refusal made only after the marriage was done, of course. My mother did not have the will or, mayhap, the true desire to fight the man on the matter and so Aunt Olympia gave me this house. It was sitting empty, you see, for it was no longer in an area that people considered completely respectable. I moved my brothers into this house. Then, one by one, the others began to arrive, starting with Darius, Uncle Argus's boy by a mistress who decided to get married and could not take the child with her. Argus bought this house from Olympia and signed it over to my brothers, and me, with himself as tentative head of the household until I come of age. There are ten boys here now and their fathers do their best to help with the money needed to raise them."

"Should they not be at school?"

"They attend when there is the money to send them but a tutor is usually all that can be afforded."

"And you live here? Is that why I have not seen you at Hutton-Moore House?"

"Nay, I do not live here. Charles and Clarissa do not know about this house as far as I know. I come here when I can. Fortunately, that is quite often. Until I am five and twenty I must stay with the Hutton-Moores."

Penelope decided the men did not need to know that she stayed because she feared it was the only way to be certain she could still claim that house when it legally became hers. Nor did they need to know that the will said when she was five and twenty *or* married. As far as she knew, the house her stepbrother and sister claimed for themselves was all that was left of the riches her mother had brought to her second marriage. There was still a chance she could lose that, too, and be left with nothing more than a tiny annuity, but she held out the stubborn hope that Charles could not actually steal that away as she suspected he had stolen everything else.

"You still have not answered the question as to why I have never seen you there," Ashton pressed.

"S'truth, none of us can recall seeing you anywhere," added Lord Mallam. "At not one society function."

"Have never even heard you mentioned of by the Hutton-Moores," said Baron Fisherton. "Yet you are a Hutton-Moore."

"Only in name," Penelope said, realizing that these men had obviously gone ahunting for information about her. "Only because the old baron felt it would make it easier for him to get his hands on all my father left behind if he adopted me. The pretense that I was one of them died a swift death when the old baron and my mother were buried. I was banished to the attics and nearly forgotten. That is why I can come here so often and no one knows. Or cares. As long as I keep out of sight, they do not trouble themselves with me. I rather prefer that arrangement now."

She smiled faintly when she saw how shocked the men looked. "I keep informed of all that is going on in my house through a few of the servants and, I blush to admit, eavesdropping. The house has a great many little nooks and passages the Hutton-Moores know nothing about. For reasons she never explained to me, my mother never told her husband about them and ordered me to keep them secret as well."

"And that is how you learned I was betrothed to Clarissa or from the paper?" asked Ashton.

"From Charles and Clarissa, but I did not really have to eavesdrop to learn that. Things got quite, er, loud after you left the house this morning, Lord Radmoor." And the anger of her stepsiblings had so filled the air she had felt choked by it, but that was not something she could tell these men.

Ashton grimaced and then stared at her in surprise. "You knew who I was that night."

"I did." She struggled to subdue a blush but a slight heat in her cheeks told her she was only partly successful.

"Nick me! Why did you not say something?"

"That potion did rather dull my wits, m'lord, and I did make a fumbling effort to explain." She frowned. "Are you here because you fear I will tell Clarissa about what happened that night?" Penelope was almost certain that Clarissa knew what had happened to her, all except for the fact that Radmoor would be the man sent to her. It was Charles's part in it all that she was not yet certain of.

"No, I . . ." Ashton rubbed a hand over his neatly queued hair. "I am not sure why I have come. To apologize?" He sighed when she shook her head and murmured, "no need." "No? I was somewhat condescending when you tried to tell me what had happened to you. In truth, I think it was the shock of finding out who you are and hoping you would prove my butler wrong that brought me hying over here. My butler was the one who gave us the information on the Wherlockes," he explained when she looked at him in confusion. "Do you know how, or rather, why you ended up there?"

"To begin with, I walked home from here at a later hour than usual, and alone. After years of doing so, I fear I had grown, well, overconfident. As for the why? Who can know? I certainly cannot guess." Penelope had a few very strong suspicions but no proof, so decided it was best to keep those suspicions to herself for now, especially since the man questioning her was now engaged to one of her suspects.

"What about the men who kidnapped you?" asked Lord Mallam. "Can you tell us anything about them?"

After looking at the very serious expressions on the faces of the men, Penelope shrugged and described her three assailants. She was not sure how these men could help her, or even why they should bother. Some odd sort of gentlemanly chivalry, or a matter of honor, she supposed. What she was sure of was that they would not believe her suspicions about Clarissa and Charles. The Hutton-Moores might not be accepted by all of society but they were still of the aristocracy. One had to be very careful about accusing such people of crimes, even when one was also of the aristocracy. Nor did she have the proof or the social standing she needed to make anyone even listen to her.

But I will get that proof, she decided, and turned her full attention back to the men. She could see they were outraged by what had happened to her and intrigued by the mystery of it. If that interest proved more than a passing fancy for them, they might well be of some help, but she would not allow herself to hope for much. In truth, she found herself hoping that their interest waned. If they persisted, she would find herself spending time with Radmoor, and when he married Clarissa, Penelope knew she would suffer all the more for having come to know him.

Instinct told her that getting to know Radmoor would not cure her of her infatuation. The night at the brothel had already made that light, dream-shrouded sensation into something more solid, deeper. Even worse, instead of her gentle, girlish dreams of sweet words and soft kisses, she now had dreams that left her trembling and aching with need, one far stronger than the mild want she had occasionally woken up with before. Lust had firmly clasped hands with infatuation. The only way to protect her heart was to stay as far away from Radmoor as possible, but as she blithely extended an invitation for the men to call again while she escorted them to the door, Penelope knew she did not have the strength to avoid him.

"What did they want?"

Penelope squeaked softly and jumped, startled by Artemis's silent arrival at her side. "They know exactly who I am," she replied as she went back into the parlor to collect the dishes.

"How did they find out?" Artemis moved to help her clean up after their guests. "We were careful."

"You were, but Radmoor saw the placard by the door. Then his butler rooted about and gave him a lot of information on our family. Now it seems Radmoor and his friends want to know *why* I was kidnapped."

"You know why."

"I do not really know why, but I think I know who. I could be wrong. I doubt it, but I could be letting my ill feelings toward Clarissa and Charles lead me into believing them capable of such a heinous crime."

"Who else could it be?"

Penelope shrugged. "I have no idea. I do not really know anyone else, do I? But I intend to look deep and hard for answers." She smiled. "So it seems do five titled gentlemen."

"And so do your brothers."

Artemis spoke in such a hard, cold voice that Penelope almost shivered beneath the chill of it. Her brother was becoming more man than boy. It made her heart pinch with grief over the loss of that sweet little boy she had taken care of for years. It was the memory of that little boy, however, that made her want to lock Artemis in the cellar so that he could not put himself in harm's way. She was certain that looking for answers as to why she had been kidnapped could prove to be very dangerous.

"Artemis," she began.

"I *will* find out who did that to you, Pen. Do not try to stop me."

She ached to do just that but knew it would be impossible. "Just promise me that you will be careful."

"I always am."

That was a lie and they both knew it. Wherlockes were rarely careful. As they headed toward the kitchen, Penelope resigned herself to worrying about her boys even more than she usually did. A little voice told her she would also be worrying about Radmoor but she gagged it. Radmoor was a grown man, betrothed to Clarissa. He could worry about himself.

"Are you serious in your intention to find out why Miss Wherlocke was kidnapped?" asked Cornell as he and the others followed Ashton into his study.

"Deadly serious," Ashton replied as he poured himself a brandy and waved the others over to help themselves. "If naught else, she is the daughter of a marquis, and despite what appears to be a very large family of virile males"—he ignored his friends' laughter—"she has no protector. I believe all those boys would do anything for her, but they are, after all, just boys." He sat down at his desk and put his feet up on it.

"So you have decided we must step into that role?"

Looking at his friends sprawled comfortably in their seats and watching him closely, he nodded. "Mayhap it is because I have sisters, but it chills me to think of what could have happened to her. Even I did not heed what she said and I consider myself a reasonable and fair man. Once my head cleared, I realized it was not just what she said that indicated her innocence and quality. There were many signs I just ignored. Someone ordered that kidnapping and I want to know who."

"I want to know why. She has nothing but ten little

boys, bastard get of her kinsmen, and a house in a neighborhood but one step away from unsavory," said Brant and then he frowned. "Thwarted lust?"

"Whose?" *Aside from mine,* Ashton thought with a sigh. "It appears she has been kept hidden away in the attics like some mad aunt. And, God rot it, *why* do the Hutton-Moores treat her so? Was it not *her* mother who helped pull them up to the precarious position they now hold in society?"

Cornell suddenly sat up straight. "It was. It was *her* money, *her* house, *her* good name." He nodded when the other men tensed and frowned. "Why is Miss Wherlocke not a much sought after heiress?"

"Her mother might not have had the sense to protect all her assets from the late baron's greed," Ashton said, but he did not believe strongly in his own words. "Mayhap her father's death was sudden and no will . . ." He stopped and shook his head. "Of course there was a will. The moment the man gained his title, what family he had near would have started clamoring for him to make one. I think the Hutton-Moores need a closer look."

"As does the late marquis of Salterwood. Mayhap he was as feckless with his money as he was with his seed."

"You need not help, any of you. *I* am the one who nearly dishonored her. None of you wronged her."

"The woman cares for ten by-blows simply because they are of her blood," drawled Brant. "How can I call myself a gentleman if I turn my back on such a woman when she is in need?"

They all toasted Penelope for her care of those whom many ignored or abandoned and began to discuss what information they needed to hunt down. Ashton could not shake out of his head the idea that his fiancée and her brother were involved. The thought kept whispering in his ear like a seductress. It was past time he looked into the affairs of the Hutton-Moores himself instead of leaving it to others.

Chapter Six

A high-pitched sound stabbed into Ashton's brain, bringing him to a full, reluctant consciousness. He groaned and put his pillow over his head. It did nothing to dim the sound of what had to be an army of excited women and the banging of luggage being brought into his home. He cursed. His family had arrived.

"M'lord?"

And so had his valet.

Ashton cautiously peeked out from beneath his pillow to find his valet Cotton looking down at him. In his hand was a tankard. The man had brought his cure for a night of drinking with friends. Although Ashton's stomach roiled at the thought of drinking it, he sat up and reached for the tankard. He gulped the potion down as quickly as he could and then sprawled on his back, eyes closed, until his stomach settled down again and the pounding in his head began to ease.

"M'lord, your family has arrived," said Cotton.

"I heard." Ashton eased his way out of bed, heartily regretting his night of drinking.

He should have considered the possibility that his family would rush to his side immediately after his letter reached them. His mother would be outraged by the trickery of the Hutton-Moores even as she hoped for the much-needed dowry Lady Clarissa would bring to the marriage. It was going to be difficult to answer her questions without adding to her concerns. Ashton prayed his head would clear enough to calm her worries with his answers instead of stirring up even more questions.

"I am ready now, Cotton. Let us attempt to make me presentable for"—Ashton glanced at the elegant clock on the mantel—"luncheon with my family."

It was time to sit down to the meal when Ashton finally joined his family and he still was not sure he was fit for the ordeal ahead. Everyone except his brother Alexander was there and he suspected Alex would appear before too long. He led his mother to the chair to the right of his. His young brother, Lucas, led the oldest of their aunts, Sarah, to the chair on Ashton's left. The rest of his family seated themselves. Ashton began to think he would need to inspect his coat for holes after the meal for everyone stared at him so steadily as the footmen served them.

"I brought the Radmoor emeralds, Ashton," his mother said once Ashton signaled the footmen to retreat.

"There was no rush to do so, Mother," he said.

Her sigh of distress struck him like a blow. Tradition required he give Clarissa the ring when she accepted his suit, followed by the bracelet when the wedding date was set. The earrings and necklace were to be given the day of the wedding. Ashton had a strong aversion to giving Lady Clarissa any of the jewels and not simply be-

cause she had tricked him into the betrothal. He had
planned to marry her. But now he did not trust the
woman. The moment he had discovered how Lady
Clarissa treated her stepsister, the unease he had felt
about marrying the woman had hardened into a deter-
mination to escape the trap the Hutton-Moores had set
in any way that he could. The only thing that kept him
from simply walking away from the woman right now
was the markers that Charles held.

"I do not wish to marry Lady Clarissa," he said. "To
put it quite simply, after the trick she and her brother
played, I no longer trust her. Or him. I have also discovered that she treats her stepsister, Lady Penelope Wherlocke, most unkindly."

"Does she make her sweep up the ashes like Cinder
Ella?" asked Pleasance.

Ashton smiled at his eight-year-old sister. "No, they
have a servant to do that. But they make her stay in the
attics." He kept a close eye on the reactions of the others as he spoke to Pleasance. "They never get her pretty
gowns or take her to a ball. I do not believe they even
give her the old gowns that Lady Clarissa has cast aside.
The house Lady Clarissa and her brother live in be-
longed to Lady Penelope's mother so you would think
they could at least offer her a decent bedchamber,
would you not?" Her soft gray eyes wide, Pleasance nodded, her fat blond curls bouncing with the movement.
"They keep her away from everyone and do not even let
her go visiting or meet with the guests who come to the
house." Aunt Honora looked almost ready to weep. "I
must consider what to do about Lady Clarissa's cruelty
to her stepsister."

"You certainly must," said Belinda who, at three and
twenty had the most to lose if he did not marry Lady
Clarissa. She had not yet had a season and was already

considered by many to be on the shelf. "How old was Lady Penelope when she was left in their care?"

"I am not sure," replied Ashton. "At a guess, I would say she was Lucas's age. Fifteen, mayhap younger."

And already caring for her brothers, even taking in more children. Ashton realized that, while no more than a child herself, Penelope Wherlocke had taken on the hard chore of caring for the abandoned by-blows of her own faithless father and her kinsmen. She had, without hesitation, found her half-brothers a home when her own mother had turned her back on the boys. And since she had obviously done that so well, her relatives had quickly decided she could care for their unwanted children as well. Ashton suddenly had to fight down a fierce anger over the way Penelope's relatives had treated her.

"I do not think I like your Lady Clarissa," said his sister Helen, a beautiful young woman of twenty who would undoubtedly be swamped with offers once he could afford to give her a season and a decent dowry. "Are we expected to live with you after you marry this woman?"

The reluctance to do so was clear in Helen's voice, but before Ashton could reply, the footmen returned with an array of sweets. He ordered them to clear the table of the last remnants of the meal, set the desserts out, and then leave them alone again. They were all capable of serving themselves and he did not want such important family business to be overheard and discussed by his servants.

He looked at his mother as the servants left the room. Lady Mary Radmoor was still a good-looking woman at nearly fifty years of age. There was no gray in her dark red hair and very few lines on her sweet oval face. Considering how poorly his father had treated her, Ashton was surprised that she did not look more careworn or bitter. There was a look of unease in her big blue eyes, however. Those eyes often made people believe Lady Radmoor was sweet but not very intelligent. That was a large mistake on their part. Ashton knew that, even as he watched her, his mother was carefully weighing the importance of every word he said.

"I have heard of the Wherlockes," announced Lady Sarah the moment the servants were gone again.

Leaning over to serve his mother some stewed apples, Ashton glanced at his aunt and nodded. "I gather they are a large family, especially if one includes the Vaughn branch on the family tree."

"They are indeed a large clan. They are also eccentric, a little wild, and very reclusive."

"So I have heard. Well, except for their being wild."

"Oh, they are wild. I believe it is because they are so gifted."

Ashton knew she was not referring to a gift in music or art. "Heard that, too, have you?"

Aunt Sarah nodded as she spooned clotted cream over her bread pudding. "When you have lived for three score and a dozen years, as I have, you hear a lot of things. You even hear enough tales about a certain reclusive clan to speak with some authority on them." She began to eat her pudding.

He wanted to politely wait for her to finish eating, but after only a few moments, he asked, "And?"

"*And* as I said, they are gifted. Nearly all of that blood are. Gifted or cursed, depending upon one's views of such matters. 'Tis said they can see the spirits of the departed, even speak with them. They also have visions, dreams that foretell things. I have even heard whispers that, occasionally, one is born who can read a person's thoughts. That tends to drive the poor soul mad, and who could be surprised by that? The current patriarch of the clan is rumored to be cursed in that way."

"Do you truly believe that anyone could read someone's thoughts? 'Tis impossible."

"I would like to think so," Aunt Sarah replied in all seriousness. "I have not claimed to believe all that is said about the Wherlockes and the Vaughns, about what gifts or curses they have. Yet it would explain some of the other things I have heard about them. Far too many of their wives or husbands walk away from their marriages and their children, excusing their inexcusable actions with tales of curses and sorcery. Far too many of their ancestors found themselves suffering the harsh, often fatal, punishments meted out for practicing witchcraft. They are intensely private, even reclusive, despite their ancient, honored title and their good looks. Many of the male children are schooled at home, and at both Harrow and Eton, tales linger of strange happenings whenever a Wherlocke or a Vaughn walked the halls there. There must be something there for such tales and rumors to persist for so long."

"Perhaps it is but envy," said Belinda, although her eyes sparkled with interest. "If they have more than their fair share of handsome looks, charms, or riches, there could be those who feel compelled to put a stain on such perfection."

"True, it could be that," said Lady Mary, but there was a note of doubt in her voice. "And they certainly sound like a family one could discuss for hours, but I must see to it that Pleasance gets some rest."

"I am not tired," protested Pleasance.

"No? Then it was simply because your head grew too heavy for your neck that caused you to nearly end up facedown in your pudding, was it?"

Ashton chuckled along with the rest of his family as

his mother led a heavy-eyed Pleasance out of the room. The rest of his family dispersed soon after, claiming a need to settle into their rooms. He suspected they all needed a rest. His letter could barely have crossed the threshold before his mother had been demanding they all pack and race to his side.

He retired to his study where, two hours later, his mother tracked him down. There was such a serious look on her face that Ashton poured her some wine. He was not sure if he was about to be interrogated or lectured, but sat back down behind his desk and tried to prepare himself for either one of those eventualities. The way his mother took several minutes to settle herself in the chair facing him and sip at her wine increased his sense of unease.

"How did you meet Lady Penelope Wherlocke?" she asked suddenly.

His mother had obviously spent her time thinking instead of resting, Ashton decided. He was not sure how to answer that question. After thinking it over for a moment, he decided to tell her most of the truth. It hurt to admit it, but after his father's behavior, his mother would not be shocked by talk of madams or brothels. He had no intention of letting her know how close he came to deflowering the daughter of a marquis, however. He took a deep breath and told her the whole tale with only a few important omissions and softening a few of the hard edges. In his tale, he was never naked and he had believed Penelope immediately. The chance that his mother would ever discuss the event with the boys who had rescued Penelope was slim, but he still sent up a silent prayer that it never happen.

"That poor girl," his mother said, and Ashton breathed a sigh of relief. She had believed him. His moment as a lust-crazed cad was still a secret, at least from his family.

"You do understand that honor requires you marry her and not Lady Clarissa."

"*I* did not kidnap the girl," Ashton said, smothering the spark of interest that rose in him at his mother's suggestion. "I only helped in the rescue." He sighed when his mother just continued to stare at him. "Mother, she has no money. All she has is a house in a barely respectable area of the city and ten boys to care for."

"Ten! She has ten brothers?"

"No. She has two. Two half-brothers. The rest are cousins. They are all bastards, Mother. As I thought on that most strange situation, I realized that, once she had settled her brothers and was seeing to their care so efficiently, all the men in her family saw her as the perfect caretaker for their own illegitimate children. 'Tis most admirable of her to care for ones most men ignore, but it makes it very unlikely that she will ever be accepted by the society she was legitimately born into.

"I loathe saying this, loathe the way it must guide my steps now, but we need money. We also need to remain a full part of society. Not only for Belinda, Helen, and Pleasance, but to find ways to keep our pockets full. Clarissa's dowry is lush, but it will quickly be diminished once our debts are paid, the dowry of each girl is set aside, and much needed work is done at Radmoor and our other properties. If I do not marry a hefty dowry, then we shall have to begin selling off the unentailed properties. Each one sold means less chance of a living for my brothers and less chance of a decent dower for my sisters. It will also mean less chance of regaining the fortune that was lost to us."

Lady Mary sighed. "I so wanted all my children to marry well, to marry for reasons of affection. For love. And do not scoff; it does exist. It is what makes a marriage a good one, keeps people together no matter what ill befalls them through the years. Instead, your father's foolishness has stolen that chance from you."

"I will be content," he said, knowing it was a lie.

"Not with that woman. She tricked you into this betrothal, could not or would not take the chance that you might change your mind or look to another woman. She hides her own stepsister away as if the girl is some guilty secret. Tell me, is this Lady Penelope a pretty girl?"

"Yes, but not in the conventional way."

"Ah, but those are the women who can bestir a man the most. That is undoubtedly one reason she is banished to the attics, well out of sight of the gentlemen who call upon the Lady Clarissa."

"Perhaps one of the reasons. Lady Penelope believes that house is hers but she will not come into full ownership of it until she turns five and twenty."

"And still they treat her like some poor, baseborn relation?" Lady Mary shook her head. "Worse and worse. Everything you say about Lady Clarissa makes me dread your marriage to her. Perhaps, well, there are other heiresses?"

"Do you think I did not look hard enough?" Ashton grimaced at the hint of anger in his voice and then sighed. "No, Mother. Despite my title and fine bloodlines, I am not the first choice of protective parents and guardians. My need for funds has become too well known, although I do not know how that happened as we certainly did our best to hide it. The Hutton-Moores seek a connection to a family with a heritage for they have little themselves. A heritage that may give them some power." Seeing the stubbornness in her expression, one that told him she could become troublesome about his marriage to Clarissa, he decided to tell her the whole truth about just how trapped he was. "Mother, Lord Charles holds Father's markers."

"God's bodikins! The swine! He threatened you when you called them on their base trickery, did he?"

A little stunned to hear his mother curse, Ashton just nodded.

"I know it is wrong to speak ill of the dead, but your father was a selfish man. Bone deep selfish. He never gave a thought to anything but his own pleasures and he beggared us in pursuing them. He ruined our lives with his follies. You must marry that conniving witch, I have a daughter who is three and twenty and another who is twenty and neither have had even one season, Lucas has had to leave school, and we stand at the doors of debtor's prison. I gave that man my youth, my loyalty, and six children and he betrayed me at every turn." She took a deep breath and visibly struggled to beat down her anger.

"I am sorry, Mother."

"You have nothing to be sorry for, Ashton. I should have done something, anything, to ensure that he did not rob my children of their futures. I failed you all. The only courageous step I ever made was when I slammed shut my bedroom door after I discovered I was carrying Pleasance. And in the end it saved my life. I did little to save all of you, though."

When he saw the glint of tears in her eyes, Ashton hurried to refill her wineglass. His mother had made only a few angry remarks about his father within Ashton's hearing, but it was clear that she had a lot of anger and hurt tumbling around inside her. He hated to hear her blame herself for any of the trouble they were in. A few sips of wine began to calm her and the tears in her eyes receded so Ashton retook his seat.

"You have nothing to be sorry for, either, Mother," he said quietly. "You had no power to stop him. The law makes certain of that, does it not?"

Before his mother could utter any response, there was a rap at the door. Ashton frowned when Marston stepped in at his call to enter, walked up to the desk, and handed him a letter. The strong scent of roses told him whom it was from. His sly betrothed wanted something. Ashton sincerely doubted it was a letter of apology or contrition he held in his hand. He found instead a barely disguised command that he accompany Clarissa to a dinner at the Burnages tonight.

The demand, the whole tone of the short missive, and the fact that Clarissa had given him barely two hours' notice of the event told Ashton that she knew about Charles's hold over him. Clarissa felt she had bought herself a husband. The woman obviously wanted a husband who would be hers to command and was not above using his financial troubles as the whip.

Ashton had every intention of refusing her command with a rudeness even less disguised than hers was, but then he recalled just who the Burnages were. Edward Burnage was a baron, his title only a generation older than the Hutton-Moores', but it was gained for something far more honorable than finding women to warm a king's bed. Burnage knew business, he knew trade, and he was a genius in both. It tainted the man in some ways but kept his pockets very full. There could be some benefit to be had in spending an evening with a man like that, and his friends. Even better, he thought and nearly smiled, it would sorely vex Clarissa if he talked trade all night.

"Is the messenger still here?" he asked Marston as he scribbled a curt reply on the bottom of the letter.

"Aye, he is, Radmoor," said a voice too young to be Marston's.

Ashton looked at the boy now standing next to a scowling Marston. "Hector?"

"You know this boy, m'lord?" asked Marston. "Ah, of course. You must have seen him at Lady Hutton-Moore's. I apologize for his intrusion. I told him to wait in the hall. He has been ill trained, I fear."

"Undoubtedly. Come here, Hector." Ashton bit back a grin at the scowl Hector gave Marston before marching up to Ashton's desk. "When did you become Lady Clarissa's page?"

"Yesterday. Pages are fashionable to have amongst the ladies. We could use the coin, too." He smiled sweetly.

"That is not why you are there." There was a glint of cunning in the young boy's amber eyes that told Ashton he was not going to get the truth from Hector no matter how many times he demanded it. Not yet.

"Nay? Why else would I be there, m'lord?" He tugged the letter from Ashton's hand. "I best get this back to the bi—, beauteous Lady Clarissa. She is the impatient sort and quick with her nails. And her fists," he muttered and then blushed. "Do not tell Pen that."

The boy was gone, Marston at his heels, before Ashton could say anything. Clarissa obviously abused her servants. The fact that he was not really surprised by that was yet another reason to escape her clutches. He had ignored far too much and was now paying the price for it.

"If that boy is new in service to Lady Clarissa, how is it that you know him?" asked his mother.

"He is one of the boys Lady Penelope cares for," answered Ashton. *And if she discovers Clarissa is hurting the boy, she will retaliate.* Of that, Ashton was certain. Just as he was certain it would not be wise for her to do so.

"Ah." Lady Mary smiled and nodded.

"What do you mean—ah?"

"He is a spy, Ashton. I suspect your friend Lady Penelope realized that, since she cannot always have her ear to the door, it might be wise to have another spying for her. That boy will be taken places she cannot go, either because she does not have the right attire or she fears the Hutton-Moores would find out."

"I wonder if she knows what they are about at all. I met some of the boys but briefly yet I would not be surprised to discover they have enacted some devious plan of their own. Lady Penelope obviously knows her stepsiblings far better than I do and I sincerely doubt she would want any of her boys near them."

"Probably not." Lady Mary glanced at the door. "So that was a Wherlocke. A fine-looking boy with unusual but beautiful eyes. Mayhap the rumor that claims the Wherlockes and the Vaughns are overblessed in looks is not just envy speaking." She looked back at Ashton. "He is definitely not with your fiancée for the coin, although his looks and guile will undoubtedly gain him a pocketful."

"I will get the truth out of him soon as I suspect Clarissa will be taking him everywhere with her. She probably thinks it enhances her status—that of a future viscountess."

"That letter was a little call for you to heel, was it?"

"Exactly. This time, however, I will answer it. She wants me to escort her to the Burnages."

"Ah, trade. Very successful trade, too. Every son, and even some of the daughters, from the time of the first baron seem to have the Midas touch. Undoubtedly had it before that but society paid little heed."

"Let us pray that a little of that rubs off on me. I have been betrothed for little more than a day and I already ache to cut the leash." He stood up. "If you will excuse me now, I must make myself ready. She expects me to collect her within two hours."

The evening was only half over and Ashton already felt as if his head could hold no more advice. Burnage, and many of his companions, knew of his financial troubles and just why he was mired in debt. His embarrassment over that faded quickly, soothed away when it became clear they knew exactly whom to blame for the dire straits he and his family were in. Ashton realized they admired him for trying to find a way out of the mess and not even blinking at the thought of entering into trade, something too many of his ilk believed was beneath them.

Lord Edward Burnage had the gruff honesty and good nature of a country squire but a keen mind to the making of a profit. Ashton did not know if it was because the man believed no son should suffer from his father's sins, or the man's evident dislike of the Hutton-Moores, but Burnage readily took Ashton under his wing. He also did Ashton the honor of believing the younger man understood what he was saying, respecting his intelligence.

Ashton's heart beat with the bright rhythm of hope for the first time in far too long. At first, his lack of money to invest in any of the schemes Burnage told him about only darkened his mood. Then Burnage gave him a suggestion that was like a ray of sunshine bursting through the dark clouds. A partnership with a friend or two. Ashton knew just whom to ask. He knew he could not raise the funds to make a decent investment on his own, but he could certainly raise a share of what was needed.

"Ah, I see that your lady is looking for you," Burnage

said. "Do you know where she bought those clothes for her page? I want to be sure I never take my business there," he added in a soft voice as Clarissa joined them, dragging Hector along with her.

Ashton knew he ought to take offense. It was, after all, a slur upon the taste of his future wife. Instead, he grinned. Hector was dressed in a violent blue coat, pale pink lace flowering at his wrists and throat, an elaborately embroidered waistcoat with what appeared to be every bird in England fighting for room on it, and shoes with garishly ornate silver buckles. His thick black hair had been lightly powdered, making it look a dull gray, and his queue was adorned with a fat pale pink bow.

He met the boy's gaze and found a dare to laugh glittering in those wide amber eyes. There was also a pinch of pain in the boy's expression and Ashton looked down at the thin arm Clarissa held. She squeezed Hector so tightly she had to be cutting off all flow of blood to the boy's fingers and her long sharp nails had to be digging into the boy despite his clothes. He reached out, snatched her hand off Hector's arm, and placed it on his.

"Have you come to tell me that you are ready to go home?" he asked.

"Yes, most assuredly." She looked around to make sure no one was close enough to overhear her, Burnage having moved away, and snapped, "I did not realize you had such a love of trade."

She was a beautiful woman with her big hazel eyes, fat blond curls, and lush figure, but Ashton could now see that her beauty was shallow. There was no kindness or heart beneath its gloss. Brant had seen that quicker than he had, but now Ashton's eyes were open. Open wide enough to know he could never spend the rest of his life with this woman. And Burnage, bless his merchant's heart, had just taught him ways with which he might yet escape that dire fate.

"Then let us take our leave," he said as he led her toward their hostess, the widowed Burnage's sister. He, too, wanted to get home. He had to make note of all he had learned tonight for it could be what gained him his freedom after years of servitude to his father's excesses.

Chapter Seven

"Careful, Paul."

Penelope grabbed the young boy before he stepped without thinking into the busy street. For someone already revealing a strong gift for foreseeing things, he could act as blindly as any small child at times. She did not usually take the active boy to the market with her, but today the younger boys were busy with their tutor and Paul had been so restless he had been making it difficult for the others to pay heed to the man. The older boys had simply and mysteriously disappeared. Even Hector had gone off somewhere when he should have been at his lessons. She was going to have to gather all the boys together and give them a stern lecture. They were all too young to run around the dangerous city on their own.

"What are you going to buy?" Paul asked as he hopped from foot to foot at her side.

"Something for a stew, I should think. Mrs. Stark's

daughter is still feeling poorly so she only had the time to bring us some bread, ham, and eggs. That will do fine for luncheon today and breakfast on the morrow but I must make you something to eat for your dinner tonight."

"Not mutton."

"Nay, not mutton. S'truth, I am not sure how to cook it correctly anyway." She was not sure Mrs. Stark did either for the last one Penelope had tasted had definitely warranted Paul's aversion to having any more.

She sighed when Paul raced to the window of a shop that displayed toy soldiers. They were well formed and painted beautifully. The perfect temptation for a little boy. Penelope wished she had the money right now to buy him a few. She could no longer be certain she would have it when she came of age and gained her inheritance. Although she had no proof yet, she was certain Charles and Clarissa were stealing from the legacy her parents had left her, supporting their rather lavish lives with her money. There was a strong chance she would find little or no money left when she finally gained control of her life. Not even enough to buy a little boy some toy soldiers and she found that too sad for words.

"Paul, we really must be going," she said as she took him by the hand. "You know it is not wise for me to be about too much in the light of day. What if Charles or Clarissa saw me? They might begin to watch me far more closely than they do now. It would be a very long time before I could slip away again."

"I forgot. Let us go and get some food then." He looked up at her as they waited for a wagon loaded with squealing pigs to roll by. "Do not be sad, Penelope. I will have those soldiers someday."

She hoped he was right and that he would have them before he was too old to enjoy them. "Now, off to the butcher's."

"Not over there!"

"We will be quick, Paul. Now, come along," she said as she tugged his resisting little body closer to the edge of the road.

Penelope finally saw an opening in the constant filing by of carts and wagons and started to hurry across the street. Paul cried out and started to pull her back again. She turned to look at him, not certain if he was having some premonition or was just being a naughty child, and saw the carriage racing toward her. Toward Paul. Instead of slowing down upon seeing someone in the road, it was gaining speed as it approached her. This was not the way she wished to die.

Ashton stepped out of the glover's shop muttering about the high cost of goods. His friends chuckled and Brant buffed him lightly on the shoulder. Ashton's mood was dark and he knew it, and it was wrong to inflict it upon his friends. He also needed to clear the haze of anger from his mind. They were headed to their club, where he hoped to talk over his plan for an investment with the men he wanted as his partners in it. That required a mind not taken up with thoughts of resentment or self-pity.

"They *were* priced too dear," said Brant, "but they are of the best quality and should last you a very long time."

"I hope you are right because, at such a steep price, they will be the last pair of gloves I purchase for a very long time," said Ashton.

"Is that not Lady Penelope?" asked Victor. "Just across

the road with that lad who is not as sweet as he looks. Paul, that is the name."

Ashton looked in the direction Victor pointed, across the road and down several yards to the right. His heart gave an odd little skip when he saw her. She was dressed in a simple blue gown; her hair was in an equally simple style, the sun bringing out the bright touches of blond and red in its depths. She looked like a tender country maid on her way to market, not the sort he would usually stare at, yet he found her beauty to be a balm to his soul. He realized that he had been blindly moving down his side of the road toward her and inwardly grimaced as he slowed to a halt. He was dangerously besotted but was not sure how to cure himself of the affliction. Worse, his grinning friends were right at his heels watching him act besotted.

A sound pulled his attention away from her as she began to cross the road. He did not need Paul's cry to see the danger bearing down on Penelope. He looked back at her to see her start to run in his direction but he knew she would never make it, especially not trying to drag a terrified little boy. The carriage was still gaining speed. Then she saw him. Ashton began to run toward her but she suddenly stopped, caught Paul up in her arms, and threw him toward Ashton. He had no choice but to halt and catch the boy. Paul was small and light but the force of his landing caused Ashton to stumble back several steps.

"Pe—ne—lo—pe!"

Ashton wanted to echo the boy's wail for he was certain he was about to see Penelope trampled by the horses heading straight for her. His friends started past him but he doubted they would be able to do anything. Even if Victor and Cornell reached the carriage they ran toward, they could never gain control of it before it had run right over Penelope. She had started running again but it was too late. Ashton pressed the crying boy's face against his shoulder, knowing that he had done what she had wanted by stopping his rescue of her to catch the boy, but cursing the fact that he could not save her, too.

"Jump!" he yelled but doubted he could be heard over all the others yelling and screaming.

She was fast, he thought a little hysterically, but he did not think she would be fast enough. Then, just as he braced himself to see tragedy unfold before his eyes, she cleared the path of the horses. Ashton had only begun to breathe again when he saw her clipped by the outside edge of the wheel. It hit her hard enough to toss her up off her feet. She would have hit the ground hard if Brant had not leapt out to catch her as she came down. The force of her landing in his arms threw Brant onto his back. Ashton rushed to their side, still clutching Paul in his arms.

"Is she hurt?" he asked Brant as his friend sat up, and fought the strange but violent urge to snatch Penelope out of his friend's arms. "Are you hurt?"

"I am bruised but hale," Brant answered, "but Lady Penelope may be hurt seriously. When I fell, I heard her head hit the ground." He looked down at the limp woman in his arms. "I fear this is not a swoon."

Ashton set Paul down and crouched by Brant's side. He felt the back of Penelope's head and softly cursed when his fingers encountered a gash. Just as he withdrew his bloodied fingers to pull out his handkerchief and press it against her wound, Victor and Cornell arrived.

"The carriage?" Ashton asked.

"Going too fast," replied Victor.

"Almost had it when he took a turn right after trying to run Lady Penelope down," Cornell said, "but got tripped up by a crowd of angry people joining in the chase. Victor had to grab a child who was nearly trampled by the fools."

"Did you recognize the driver, the carriage, or see anyone inside?" asked Ashton as he gently took Penelope from Brant's arms and then stood up.

"A hired hack, for certain. The driver had his face obscured with a scarf but he did not think to cover the scar of a wound that nearly took his left eye. There was someone inside, for when he took the turn, there was the sound of someone being tossed about, but the windows were covered." Cornell glanced at the crowd still lingering to watch the drama played out before them. "Victor and I could ask about. See if anyone knows or saw something useful."

"That might be wise. This was no accident. It was intentional."

Cornell nodded. "It was indeed. The carriage sped up. I believe we will find a consensus on that fact. How is she?"

"Nothing appears broken, but she hit her head hard. I will take her to her house and summon a doctor. Meet us there." He glanced at Brant, who had stood up but was favoring his right leg. "I think the doctor will need to look at Brant, too."

"Take the carriage. Victor and I will hire a hack if we need one."

Ashton nodded, and reassuring himself that Brant had hold of Paul and was steady enough to control the child, he strode ahead to where Cornell's carriage waited. He gently settled Penelope on the seat, climbed in, and sat down near her head. He then eased her partly onto his lap, supporting her head and neck with his arm. Paul and Brant sat on the seat across from him. The moment Brant shut the door, the carriage began to move and Ashton wondered when the driver had been told where to take them. He was a little alarmed by how fully his attention had been taken up by Penelope and her injuries. With all the other troubles he had on his plate, he did not need to be fascinated by the stepsister of his fiancée.

"Do you think she will die?" Paul asked, his voice unsteady and his eyes shining with barely restrained tears.

It was difficult not to shout at the boy. Just hearing the question was enough to make Ashton's heart pound with fear. He forced himself to be calm so that he could ease the child's fears.

"No. It is but a scrape upon her head." Ashton hoped the boy was too young to know how dangerous any head wound could be. "Her breathing is steady and the bleeding has begun to ease," he added, as much to calm himself as to take that haunted look from the child's eyes. "She is young and strong." The look Paul gave him told Ashton that the child, though young, was not innocent of the indiscriminate touch of death.

"If I had done a better job of catching her," began Brant.

"You did well, m'lord," said Paul. "It was a fine catch."

"Yes, it was," agreed Ashton. "It is not easy to catch a body hurtling through the air. I consider it a near miracle that I caught Paul. By catching her, you slowed her fall. Her wounds would have been far worse had you not been so quick."

"It is my fault," said Paul.

"How can you believe that?" asked Ashton.

"I did not tell her why we needed to get off the road. I did not see the why of it clear and it all happened so fast. I just knew we should not cross to the butcher's. She thought I was fretting that she would buy mutton."

It *had* happened with a numbing swiftness, Ashton realized. It had played out before him like some slow, macabre dance, but in truth, it had all happened in a moment or two. Everyone had been moving as fast as possible. Now that he watched it all again in his mind's eye, he realized how miraculous it was that Penelope and Paul had survived.

Ashton was just wondering how long it would take for Clarissa to hear about what had happened when the full import of what Paul had said hit him. "What do you mean you *knew*? Knew what?"

Paul blushed. "I know things, m'lord. Just that. Warnings and such but I have not gained the trick of it all yet. Pen says I have a strong gift for it to be showing itself when I am so young but that it will take me some growing before I can use it right."

He was opening his mouth to question the boy more, and perhaps try to dampen his pretensions, when the carriage halted before the house Penelope kept for the boys. Paul leapt from the carriage and raced into the house before he could be stopped. Brant was just steadying himself on his feet after alighting, and Ashton was lifting Penelope from the carriage, when half a dozen small boys burst from the house. Behind them strode a tall, thin young man who had the look of a Wherlocke about him. The young man waded through the boys, murmuring something that quickly calmed them. When he reached Ashton, he placed one elegant long-fingered hand on Penelope's forehead and then nodded.

"I am Septimus Vaughn, a cousin and tutor to this horde of little barbarians," he said in a voice that reached deep inside Ashton and calmed the fear he had been battling with since he had seen the carriage bearing down on Penelope. "She will be fine, but I suspect you would like to hear that from a physician."

Hastily introducing himself and Brant, Ashton said, "I would appreciate it if one of the boys could fetch one. Both Lady Penelope and Lord Mallam should be looked at."

"Olwen." The tutor turned toward a boy with wild raven curls who looked to be about Hector's age. "Fetch Doctor Pryne." The moment the boy raced off, Septimus looked at Ashton again. "Follow me. We will get her settled and ready for the doctor. Lord Mallam, perhaps you could wait in the parlor. Jerome, Ezra, please see to the comfort of the gentleman."

The two boys, who could not be much older than Paul, led Brant away while Ashton followed the tutor. Paul, Delmar, and one other boy hurried ahead of them to open the door of Penelope's bedchamber. A cradle tucked into a corner of the large, plain room told Ashton that Lady Penelope had been given the care of at least one of the boys while he was still an infant. He gently placed her on her surprisingly large bed and wondered what possessed her family to put such a heavy burden on her.

He stepped to the head of the bed as Septimus eased a cloth beneath Penelope's head. Ashton watched as the younger man delicately began to check her for any other injuries. He had to clench his hands into fists behind his back as he watched another man's hands move over her body. It was necessary. Ashton knew that. Yet a tight, hot ball of jealousy formed in his gut. When the man looked at him with eyes the color of a calm, sunlit sea, and just as fathomless, Ashton could not shake the feeling that Septimus Vaughn could see into his soul. It was embarrassing that he had so much difficulty fighting the strange possessiveness he had when it came to Penelope. He certainly did not want anyone else seeing the inner battle he was so obviously losing.

"Since you are lurking about, Delmar," Septimus said, "fetch me a cloth and some water. I want to clean this blood away so that I might better see the wound."

"Should we not wait for the doctor?" asked Ashton as Delmar hurried to do as he was told.

"I know Doctor Pryne quite well." Septimus began to gently pull the hair away from Penelope's wound. "He will appreciate the fact that all is readied for him. How did this happen?" he asked after Delmar set a bowl of water and a cloth on a small table by the bed and Septimus began to meticulously clean away the blood from her wound and her hair.

Ashton told the man all he could remember. Paul added his own views and opinions with a surprising clarity for one so young. Each time Ashton recalled what had happened, his conviction that it was intentional, that it was an attempted murder, grew stronger.

Septimus said nothing as he disposed of the bloodied water and rag, refilled the bowl from an ornate jug, and washed his hands. "What has Penelope gotten herself into now?" he finally asked as he returned to her bedside.

"So, you believe this was no accident as well," said Ashton.

"Most definitely this was no accident. Yet why should anyone wish to kill Penelope?"

"I think Mrs. Cratchitt is behind it," said a deep voice that was already familiar to Ashton.

Ashton turned to see Artemis, Stefan, and Darius standing in the doorway. He frowned as they moved closer to the bed to look at Penelope. All three boys looked like beggars, their clothes ragged and their faces dirty. They also wore the hard-eyed expressions of angry men, adding maturity to their young faces.

"Why should that woman wish to hurt Lady Penelope?" asked Ashton.

"Because of what she saw," replied Darius. "Bad things have happened at that place. Very bad things."

"We all now know that every woman there was not willing to join that hag's stable. My friends and I have every intention of seeing her closed down. We have already begun yet she has not acted against us."

"You are all lords, highborn and important," said Artemis. "If it was but one of you, she might try to silence you, but even she knows she cannot act against five noblemen. Penelope was the one who caused you to catch that woman at her foul games so it is Penelope she wants dead. Penelope she blames for the coming loss of what was a very profitable business. But I think it is more than that."

"What? Did Lady Penelope see or hear something else that Mrs. Cratchitt needs to keep a secret?"

"She saw the ghosts," said Delmar.

"Ghosts?" Ashton asked in disbelief. "You want me to believe Lady Penelope saw ghosts? That Cratchitt wants her dead because she saw some spirit floating about that hellhole?"

The look every other male in the room gave him was one of resigned disappointment. Ashton thought that unfair of them even as he recalled some of the things Penelope had said that night. She had called Cratchitt's a *sad place full of ill feelings and angry spirits*. She had also said that someone had died in that bed. He could still hear her say *poor Faith* in that soft voice weighted with sorrow. It was preposterous to think she could speak to the dead, he told himself, but that stern voice in his head did little to banish the belief that stirred to life in his mind and heart. He did not understand why even that flicker of belief existed, for he had never been a superstitious person.

"I am sorry you doubt us, m'lord," said Artemis, "but it is the truth. 'Tis Pen's gift. She said something to the men who kidnapped her and they must have said something to Mrs. Cratchitt. Whether the woman believes in Pen's gift or not, she may fear that Pen knows something. We have been trying to find out what secrets are hidden at that brothel, but have had no luck yet."

"Does Lady Penelope know you are spying on Cratchitt?"

"Nay, leastwise not in the way we are, and we do not mean to tell her until we find out something worth telling."

"And Hector? Does he follow that rule as well?"

"Ah, saw him, did you?"

"Of course I did. Clarissa drags him about with her day and night. She seems to think a ridiculously dressed little boy trotting at her heels adds to her prestige."

"Ridiculously dressed?"

Ashton ignored Artemis's amused question. "What do you think he will discover?"

"That the Steps are robbing Pen blind and were behind the kidnapping."

He waited for the shock over that blunt accusation to hit him, for a protest to form on his lips, but nothing happened. Ashton realized that he believed the Hutton-Moores were fully capable of such crimes. The moment he had learned how they treated Penelope, he had begun to see them more clearly and nothing he saw was good. The way they tricked him into a betrothal and held his father's debts over his head had only hardened that opinion. That was why he was not shocked, but had started to suspect such things himself.

Unfortunately, the suspicions of a group of boys were not enough to help him end the betrothal. Even if he could find another way to get the money he needed and pay off his father's debts, he could not end the betrothal on suspicions alone without causing his family to suffer through a scandal. His father had caused them enough suffering. Ashton refused to add to it.

"Why?"

"Money and lust, m'lord," replied Artemis.

"Charles lusts after Lady Penelope?"

Artemis nodded. "She does not see it but 'tis there. Did she not say she was brought to Cratchitt's for another man who would arrive on the morrow? I would wager what little we have that that man was Charles."

There was no time for Ashton to ask any more questions. A man who looked to be in his forties, built strong and wide with unkempt gray hair, stomped into the room. The bag he carried told Ashton this was Doctor Pryne. With a few curt words, the doctor expelled everyone but Septimus and Ashton from the room.

"I saw to Lord Mallam," the doctor said as he scrubbed his hands, immediately winning Ashton's approval. "Bruises, scrapes, and a badly wrenched knee. Got the boys putting cold cloths on it for now. I will wrap it before I leave." He studied the gash on Penelope's head and lightly prodded the area around the wound. "No crack in the skull. A good thing. A few stitches needed is all." He looked at Ashton and Septimus. "She needs to rest for at least a week. Now, get me more light here so I can stitch her head up," he ordered and Ashton found himself moving as quickly as Septimus did to obey that command.

Penelope moaned in pain at the first stitch. Ashton

started to reach out to her, thinking to hold her head steady for the doctor, but Septimus nudged him aside. The younger man placed one hand on her forehead and another over her heart. Penelope's face, pinched with pain, began to relax in sleep. She did not move or make another sound as the doctor tended her wound. Ashton wanted to deny that Septimus had calmed her with his touch, but he could not. He had seen it happen with his own eyes. The doctor showed no surprise or unease, either.

Doctor Pryne looked at Septimus when he was done bandaging Penelope's head. "Sure you will not join me in trying to keep some of the fools out there alive?"

Septimus shook his head as he moved away from the bed. "No. I cannot. Now and then, perhaps. Every day, patient after patient? Pain and more pain? It would break me."

"Fair enough. A shame, though. A demmed shame." Pryne moved to wash his hands. "She will be fine. As I said, keep her abed, at least for a few days, and make her go softly for the rest of the time until I can remove the stitches. She might be light-headed at first. Come for me if she shows any signs that she has bruised her brain. You know what to look for, lad."

"I do." Septimus began to escort the doctor out of the room. "What do we owe you?"

"Nothing. His lordship downstairs paid me handsomely. Best go and wrap his knee and let the fool put his breeches back on."

Ashton watched them leave and then looked at Penelope. They all believed she could see spirits. Paul believed he could foresee danger. The doctor believed Septimus had a gift that allowed him to ease the pain of injured or ill people. Rumors had persisted for generations, he mused, and then shook his head. He was a man of reason and control. He no longer thought Penelope and the boys were some family of charlatans, but he refused to believe in magical or mystical gifts. He needed proof to believe in such impossibilities and no one had shown him any.

Penelope groaned softly. Ashton took her hand in his and sat on the edge of the bed. He did not understand why he was so drawn to her but he acknowledged her hold on his interest. Her grip on his emotions, and his lust, were deep and firm. Even her strange belief that she could see and speak to spirits did not lessen it.

She slowly opened her eyes and Ashton was hit by the powerful force of lust and enchantment. He knew he ought to fight it, banish it, for he was, in a word, a fortune hunter. He was also betrothed to her stepsister, whether he had actually proposed to the woman or not, and he should not have to keep reminding himself of that very important fact. But he did. Every time he looked at Penelope, or even thought of Penelope. To touch Penelope as he ached to, he would have to be the worst of cads. What frightened him was how great a part of him was willing to don that shameful mantle. He feared he had more of his father in him than was comfortable.

"Paul?" she whispered, her voice little more than a hoarse croak.

"He is fine. He did not suffer even the smallest of bruises. Would you like something to drink?" he asked.

"Please."

Ashton stood up and looked around the room. Near the fireplace were a small table and two chairs. On the table were an ornate silver jug and two silver goblets. He hurried over to it, sniffed the liquid in the jug, and discovering it was cider, quickly poured her some. She looked asleep as he approached the bed, but the moment he sat down on the edge, facing her, she opened her eyes again.

Penelope started to reach for the goblet, her dry throat begging for reprieve, and saw how badly her hands shook. "I believe I may need your help."

The hint of petulance in her voice almost made him smile. Lady Penelope was not a good patient, he thought as he set down the goblet, and then settled himself on the bed right beside her. When he put his arm around her, doing his best to place it so that it would support her neck as well as her shoulders, she frowned at him.

"What are you doing?" she asked.

Penelope could not believe how good it felt to have him by her side. Her head was throbbing and her body did not have one tiny spot on it that did not ache. Yet the warmth of him seeped into her blood. She wanted to curl her body around his. She could not blame that wanton urge on Mrs. Cratchitt's potion this time.

"I was attempting to ensure that this cider goes into your gullet and not all over you or the bedclothes." He picked up the goblet and held it to her lips. "Drink it slowly. I have cracked my head before, and oddly, it tends to make one's stomach rebellious," he said as she sipped the drink.

"I suppose I must stay abed for days."

"Yes. Will that be a problem? Will the Hutton-Moores grow suspicious about your long absence?"

She drank the last of the cider, and once he had set the goblet aside, she leaned all her weight against him before he could move away. She wanted to enjoy his closeness for just a little while longer. "I will have Mrs. Potts help me to keep them away. She is good at making excuses for me and they are accustomed to the cook knowing what I am doing, though they rarely ask. I spend a lot of time in the kitchen." The soft warmth of his lips moved over her aching forehead and she shivered. "Thank you for catching Paul," she said quietly as she turned to look at him.

"You are most welcome." He gave in to temptation and brushed his mouth over hers, savoring the silken warmth of her lips beneath his.

"This may not be wise."

"Very unwise, but I *will* steal a kiss before I leave."

Penelope knew she should deny him, but she had no will to do so. At first he was gentle, almost tentative, his mouth moving over hers slowly and tenderly. When his tongue prodded at the seam of her lips, she cautiously parted them. He pressed his tongue into her mouth, exploring, stroking, claiming her with the depth of his kiss. Despite the pain it caused her, she reached out to hold him close. She could not fully smother a tiny groan, however. He cursed softly and leapt from the bed, leaving her with achingly empty arms and lips that still craved his kiss.

"I must go." Ashton wondered how he could even say those words when every part of him ached to crawl into that bed with her. "I will see you on the morrow. Rest," he ordered as he fled the room before he lost all control.

He almost ran out of her bedchamber and Penelope sighed. It was wrong to kiss him, to want him, as she did. Ashton was betrothed to Clarissa and he needed money to save his family. Penelope was not sure she had any. She also had ten children to care for and few men wanted that burden. If that was not enough to make any man run for the hills, there were her *gifts*. Few people outside of the family dealt well with those gifts, as shown by the many broken marriages that littered the family tree. If she let her heart, and her body, reach out for him, she could end up heartbroken and thoroughly disgraced.

It was a familiar litany and it had about the same meager effect on her good sense as it always had. Penelope closed her eyes and knew she ought to be concerned about how little that possible sad fate troubled her. Perhaps she would worry about it tomorrow.

Chapter Eight

"Are you listening to me, Ashton?"

Ashton blinked and looked at Brant. He frowned but it did little to banish his friend's amusement. It had taken two days to finally gather with his friends in their favorite club and start the discussion he had intended to have the day Penelope had been hurt. He should be discussing the possibility of an investment right now. Instead, he kept thinking about how sweet Penelope tasted, how her scent invaded all his senses, how perfectly she fit into his arms, and how badly he wanted her naked and in his bed. In her bed. In any bed. Pleasant as those thoughts were, they did not fill his pockets and that need was one he had to fix his full attention on.

"I was plotting how to speak of what I have gathered you all here to listen to," he said, glancing around their club to make certain no one was close enough to overhear them. "What did you say?"

"I but asked how the Lady Penelope fared."

"She is recovering. Young Paul has attached himself

to her like a leech but that will soon pass, I think. The other boys wait upon her as if she were the queen, but that, too, will undoubtedly wane. She says she will return to the Hutton-Moores' in a day or two if only to give Mrs. Potts some relief from lying for her."

And probably to escape him, he thought morosely. He could not stop himself from visiting her and kissing her every chance he got. Ashton knew she shared his passion, could taste the sweet temptation of it in her kiss, the way she shivered when he touched her, but they both knew what they did was wrong. He might not get free of Clarissa, and even if he did, he might still need to marry an heiress.

He shook those thoughts from his mind. Until he got some money, there was no solution to his many troubles. There was no more time to waste.

"We can discuss that strange but fascinating little family later," he said. "I have something else I must discuss with all of you."

Victor frowned. "You sound most serious. Another trouble?"

"No, praise God. A possible solution to the ones that plague me now. The answer to most of the problems I suffer through is money. I need some. Badly." He held up his hand to silence his friends when they all began to speak. "And I will not get it by adding more debt to that which weighs me down now or by shifting it about. I wish to discuss investments."

The look of interest in his friends' faces raised Ashton's hopes. He had feared that his friends would hesitate to dabble in trade, but he should have known they would not be prey to such prejudices. None of them was poor, by any means, but each would welcome some added weight in their purses. As precisely as he could, he told them everything Lord Burnage had told him and he could see their interest grow with every word he spoke.

Then the questions began. Ashton tried to answer them as precisely as he could. The only break in the barrage came when an unusually serious Cornell would call for another bottle of wine.

"I think it might behoove us to meet with Lord Burnage," said Cornell, his dark brown eyes holding an intent look Ashton had rarely seen in his cheerful friend. "It will help us decide which investment to make and, I think, he can be trusted to see us steered to the right people so that we are not fleeced."

"So you wish to partner with me in this?" asked Ashton, the burn of excitement sliding through his veins.

"Strike me blind! Of a certain I wish a hand in it. I would have tried it myself except that the outlay could have beggared me for a full year if I lost and I was never sure whom I could trust. I am a third son. Father has seen that I am not impoverished, but I will never see any lands or any more money than I have now. Someday I will marry and I shall need a house to put the wife in. I will also need something to be certain any children I have will be well cared for."

"And I could use some funds to improve my properties," said Whitney, his straight dark brows lowering as he frowned. "I keep hearing of new farming methods I should like to try at Ryecroft but they require money I cannot spare."

Victor nodded. "'Tis the same with me." He scowled at a stray lock of his brown hair when it tumbled over his brow. "Everything needed to make money seems to cost money, especially if it is some new machine or new breed of stock. I have no reluctance about dabbling in trade if it will get me what I need."

"Nor I," said Brant. "Victor is right. Near everything

needed to improve one's lands or fatten one's purse requires money. I have enough to maintain what I have
now but not enough to improve it." He grimaced and
then smiled crookedly at Ashton. "And of late, I have
developed an abhorrence of debt so borrowing what I
need is no option for me. And your face now tells me
where your thoughts are leading you. We do this for our
own benefit as much as we will do it for yours. And we
have all put aside monies to help you if you ever let go
your pride to let us."

"I thank you for that and for joining me in this despite that touch of selfish interest," Ashton said. "Part-
nering in this venture means less profit for each of
us—"

"And less loss if it all goes wrong. Alone, I cannot
bring to the table what is needed for an advantageous
investment. Together with the four of you, we can place
a handsome bet on the table."

"That was what I was hoping for." He signaled to one
of the footmen tending to the members of the club and
requested writing materials. "I shall send a note to Lord
Burnage requesting a meeting."

"Will you be able to attend one of his choosing?
From what you have said, the Lady Clarissa has you
tightly scheduled for the next fortnight."

"Business with Lord Burnage is of far greater importance than escorting Clarissa about town. I shall just
have to be cautious for I do not wish her or her brother
to discover what I am doing."

Victor rubbed a hand over his faintly dimpled chin.
"Afraid old Charles might try to tighten the chain he
has looped around your neck?"

"Exactly," replied Ashton. "I need time. With it and
luck, I may well be able to escape their clutches completely."

"So that you may more openly pursue the fair Lady Penelope?"

There was such laughter and knowledge in Victor's light green eyes that Ashton actually felt his cheeks heat with a blush. "Mayhap, although I should leave her be."

"Because of her large family?"

"Well, only a fool would not consider the fact that those boys come with her, but no, 'tis not that. She believes she can see and speak to the spirits of the dead." He sighed when they all just stared at him. "They all believe she can, too. Just as they all believe little Paul can foretell danger."

"Ah, that." Brant smiled faintly. "I heard most of that but thought it was just a child's fancy. You mentioned how Lady Penelope said she could speak to the dead once before but I paid that little heed as well. Just another fancy."

"They all share that fancy then. That tutor, Septimus, believes he can ease a person's pain or even heal. That gruff old doctor believes it, too."

"Yet you do not."

"There is no proof." He frowned and forced himself to be honest. "I will admit that Septimus appeared to calm Penelope when the doctor was stitching up her wound, and did so simply by putting his hands on her. I could see the look of pain on her face fade away the moment he touched her."

"And that is not proof? Mayhap all that is said about that clan is not just rumor," said Cornell. "Think on how long the rumors have persisted. Generations, Ashton. There have been the same whispers about those people for generations. Why should that not be because there is some truth sprinkled in all that talk."

"You cannot believe that someone can see or speak to ghosts," said Ashton.

"Why not? Not to say I do, but why should it not be so? And how is one to prove most of it? She claims she can see and speak to spirits but you cannot, thus she must be wrong in her belief? Seems most unfair a judgment to me. From all that is said concerning the secretive, reclusive nature of that family, I am surprised she mentioned it at all."

"It was at Mrs. Cratchitt's." He sighed when they all looked at him with keen interest and reluctantly told them all he had overheard, keeping only the name of the spirit a secret. "The older boys are busy trying to find out what the spirit meant. Their plan appears to be to lurk about the brothel dressed as beggar boys and spy on everyone."

"The young fools will get their throats cut."

"That is what I fear," agreed Ashton. "I had thought to go round to Cratchitt's just to see if they were being too bold, risking too much, but I must attend a soiree at Lady Stenton's this evening."

"Lady Stenton has a true skill for devising the most tedious entertainments," said Victor. "You can offer no excuse to save yourself from such pain?"

"None." Ashton idly drummed his fingers on the table. "Artemis believes Charles was behind Penelope's kidnapping, that he meant to enjoy himself with her for a while and then be rid of her. Greed and lust, Artemis said. I decided it might be best if I acted the dutiful fiancé for a while. Mayhap I will learn something that will either cause me to believe the boy's suspicions or try to make him look elsewhere for the villain behind the kidnapping. However, I am taking my mother with me and not only because it allows me to send Clarissa ahead with her brother. I intend to use Mother as a reason to leave early enough so that I might slip away and spy upon those foolish boys."

"Shall we watch over them whilst you dance attendance upon your fiancée?"

Ashton hesitated only a moment before accepting that offer. "I think they are canny lads, and if they do possess some strange skills, they may well learn what they seek to know without endangering themselves too much. But I am too much a man of reason, and all I see are boys risking getting their throats cut."

"Do not fear. We shall protect their tender young throats until you arrive."

Three long hours of bad food, bad music, and bad company and Ashton believed he had suffered enough to rightfully call himself a martyr to the cause. Clarissa looked breathtakingly beautiful in her green velvet gown, fashionably bundled up in the back and adorned with just the right amount of lace and trimmings. Her hair was done up in elaborate rolls of curls and tumbling softly down her back, the pearls and feathers decorating the curls highlighting the perfection of them. He was no longer impressed by that beauty, however, for he could now see the hardness in her eyes and hear the spite and cruelty behind her every word. Three hours in her company were two too many and Ashton began to look for his mother, who had kindly agreed to claim a sick headache the moment he required an excuse to flee.

"Had enough?" asked a young voice as Ashton stood in the doorway of the ladies' card room and searched the crowd of older women for his mother.

A glance to his left revealed that Hector had silently joined him, and Ashton smiled. "More than enough. Are you wearied of spying yet?"

"Near to." Hector stretched his neck so that he could

scratch an itch without ruining the falls of cream-colored lace at his throat. "Are you ever going to let her know that you know she has a stepsister she has been hiding?"

"Oh, most certainly. Tonight, with my mother joining me, was not the time. I do not wish any distractions when I confront her for I do not wish to miss her reaction."

"She looks to the left when she lies."

Ashton looked at the boy in surprise. "Clever lad."

Hector shrugged. "I know a lie when I hear it, m'lord. I can feel it. Do not really need to guess the twitch of it to know someone is lying to me but I still like to find out what the twitches are. She lies a lot. Lies, yells, curses, and slanders. But thought that, since you have to wed up with her, it would be a good thing for you to know."

"Yes, a very good thing."

Ashton caught his mother's eye and idly straightened the lace ruffles at his wrists. It was the signal they had agreed upon before leaving home. She gave him an absent smile and he hoped that was her way of agreeing. He looked back at Hector.

"Clarissa is not in the card room. Should you not be at her side?" he asked.

"Told her I had to go to the necessary as I was feeling ill." He grinned. "She always shoos me away when I say such things." He tugged at his red-and-gold-striped waistcoat. "I will be done with this soon, though. I cannot abide all this, this frippery. And she keeps me as busy as a body louse day and night. 'Tis clear that she thinks I need little sleep."

"Have you learned anything to justify enduring this torture?"

"Aye. You have matched yourself to a nasty piece of goods and her brother is one who would gut his own mother for a guinea. I wish Pen never had to go back to that house."

"Why does she?" Ashton idly wondered why he was having such a serious discussion with a boy of nine and decided it was because all of Penelope's boys held a maturity and wit far beyond their years.

"'Tis *her* house. She says she has to stay there to hold her claim to it, that it might be all that is left of her inheritance."

His mother's arrival halted Ashton's questions, even though a dozen more lingered on his tongue. He would have to find out later what the boy had discovered. Tucking his mother's hand in the crook of his arm, he properly introduced her to Hector this time. Ashton was astonished and somewhat amused by how thoroughly the boy charmed his mother. He then took full advantage of Hector's presence to save himself from a scene enacted by his angry fiancée. He sent the boy back to Clarissa with word that he had needed to take his mother home and would call on Clarissa soon.

"A lovely child despite those absurd clothes," said Lady Mary once they were seated in the carriage and headed home. "How could a mother give up such a clever, charming boy?"

"I am not sure why any of the boys were given up," Ashton said and then frowned. "Ah, that is not quite true. Lady Penelope's brothers were cast aside by her mother to please her new husband. I am uncertain of the fate of their own mothers, but odds are, they cast them aside as the others were cast aside."

"I recall that now. I can understand her, in some ways. Her husband was unfaithful. It must have been hard to see the proof of that."

"Possibly." Ashton wondered if his father had bred any children outside of his marriage but it was not something he could ask his mother. "I think she said the same was done with one of the other boys. It is not something I question for I suspect it is a painful subject."

"I think I should like to meet your Lady Penelope."

"She is not mine, Mother." He ignored the sharp pang of regret that struck him at admitting that.

"I meant only that she is your friend. Mayhap you could bring her to tea one day."

Ashton murmured an agreement, but doubted it would happen. It would be unkind in one way, offering Penelope a silent promise he could not keep. A man introduced a lady to his mother only if they met at some social occasion or if he had the intention of seriously courting her. He was already stepping far over the bounds of propriety and good sense by visiting Penelope so often and giving in to the need to kiss her, to hold her in his arms.

The moment he saw his mother safely home, Ashton traveled to Mrs. Cratchitt's. He was just descending from his coach and wondering what sort of reception he would face when he saw the boys. They rushed forward to tend to the horses, arguing with his coachman over who had the right to hold the team while their owner went into the brothel. Ashton stepped up to Artemis and loudly cleared his throat.

"Oh." Artemis stepped back from the coach, Stefan and Darius quickly moving to flank him. "'Tis you. Your friends have already had a word with us and gone inside. We do not need watching."

"I will confess that this guise of yours is quite clever and convincing." Ashton struggled to be diplomatic for he could see that he had stung the pride of Penelope's youthful protectors. They were too clever not to realize why he had come to this place. "But why do you think places such as this are always in need of boys to do this work or run errands? Throat cutting is naught but a sport in this part of the city. So is the snatching up of young, fair-faced boys. You would not like where you would be taken should that happen, nor what you would be forced to endure." All three boys grew a little pale, revealing that they had some idea, and he had to wonder where they were getting such worldly knowledge. "How much longer will you play this dangerous game?"

"It will end soon. We have heard enough already to know that it was Cratchitt who tried to run down Penelope. No hard proof of that, of course, but one should always know who one's enemies are."

"Quite true." Ashton wondered if he should have told the boys the description of the man his friends had gained but decided the boys were putting themselves in enough danger as it was. "And the other matter?"

"That has been more difficult to learn about."

"Artemis is close to getting an answer, m'lord," said Darius. "One of the ladies here has a liking for him."

Ashton grinned when Artemis blushed. "You mean to coax the truth from one of Mrs. Cratchitt's fillies, do you?"

"What say you?" Brant strode up to them and, grinning widely, looked Artemis up and down. "Ready to spread your wings, are you?"

"Nay, I but seek the truth." Artemis crossed his arms over his chest. "Pen said someone died in that bed and we mean to find out who, how, and why. Faith, that is the spirit's name, told Pen that she had been murdered."

Ignoring how Brant stiffened at the name "Faith," Ashton asked, "You are willing to risk your lives in this sty because Penelope claims a ghost spoke to her?"

"We are accustomed to people not believing us, but we know the truth. And what if Pen really can speak to the dead? The restless dead. What if this place has done more than ruined innocents? Is it not our responsibility to find out? You may close this place, but you know as well as I do that that witch will just open another brothel. If she has blood on her hands, she needs to be stopped, not just moved away."

Ashton rubbed his forehead, not sure how to deal with this belief in speaking to spirits. "Let us say, for the moment, that I believe Penelope sees and speaks to spirits. From what I overheard you speak of that night, the spirit said little that was helpful."

"We think the most important thing Faith said was that she is covered in sin," said Stefan.

"Aye," agreed Artemis. "And is this place not filled with sin? We are trying to find out if there is some room or cellar under this building and a way into it."

It made sense, Ashton thought, if one believed Penelope talked to ghosts. He was about to ask a few more questions when Victor, Cornell, and Whitney exited the brothel at a fast pace. Mrs. Cratchitt and two of her brutish footmen were close on their heels. The boys quickly retreated to the other side of the carriage team.

"What are you doing with those lads?" demanded Mrs. Cratchitt. "'Tis hard enough to keep boys about to do work without you lot cozening them."

"I was but discussing their fee for caring for my horses," said Ashton.

"Liar! Ye have been trying to ruin me! I know who is at the root of the slander being spread about me and my business. Well, begone! None of you are welcome here! Go and plague someone else, you bastards! If ye ever come back here, I will make ye sorry for it!"

Since his friends had already climbed into the coach,

Ashton sketched a bow to Mrs. Cratchitt and joined them. He hated to leave the boys but knew he would put them in even more danger if the woman suspected he knew them. Confronting Mrs. Cratchitt now would serve no purpose, could even lose him the chance to make her pay for her crimes. He was just not sure those crimes included murder.

"You never said the ghost's name was Faith," Brant said as the carriage began to move.

"Faith is a common name," Ashton said. "I did not wish to scratch at an old wound, especially not on the word of someone who claims a ghost spoke to her."

"The boys believe it."

"They also believe that Paul has the ability to see what *will* happen and that Hector can *feel* a lie."

"So you have no intention of helping the lads see if there is something under that hellhole? Not even just to prove them wrong so that they will cease this dangerous game?"

"What are you talking about?" asked Victor.

"Recall what I told you about all I overheard Artemis and Penelope say that night at the brothel." When Victor nodded, Ashton told him what the boys had said. "They are now lurking about that place trying to find out if there is something beneath the brothel and how to get down there if there is."

"Damn me. Think they might be right?"

"That a woman who drags unwilling young women into her brothel and forces them to prostitute themselves might have committed murder?" He sighed when his friends grimaced at his sharp words. "Sorry. It is just that every time I turn a corner, I stumble into a problem and it prods my temper. I need no more. I may not believe that a ghost told Penelope anything, but I do not find it hard to believe that Mrs. Cratchitt would kill someone or hide a body."

"And if she has murdered someone, or someone was murdered in the brothel, she could not safely toss the body in the river as so many others do," said Cornell. "Too great a risk of being seen toting a body around through the streets on the way to the river. Not many talk around here but I would suspect that woman is not one the local populace much trusts or admires. She would know it, too, and find another way to be rid of a body."

"So, bury it in the cellar," murmured Whitney. "Best place. She serves wine. Must have a place where she stores it. That usually means some room under the ground because it stays most even in temperature."

Ashton rolled his eyes. His friends were obviously keen on finding out if there really was a body in Mrs. Cratchitt's cellar, if she even had a cellar. He should have known they would be. They used the brothels but they expected to be serviced by women who knew the game, not ones dragged unwillingly into it by some hard-eyed madam. The thought of some innocent, no matter what her class, dragged from ones who cared for her and thrown into that sad life had outraged them all. It would be as impossible to stop them in whatever they planned to do as it had been the boys. Ashton's sojourn in London to find a rich wife grew more complicated every day.

The complications had begun the night he had seen Penelope tied to that bed, he thought as his friends discussed and discarded increasingly wild plans to get into the as yet undiscovered cellars of Mrs. Cratchitt's bordello. Even his growing dissatisfaction with his anticipated marriage had hardened into a cold hard truth.

From that moment on, he had lost control of his life. He had been tricked and threatened into a betrothal he did not want, now wondered if the money he needed was even Clarissa's to give, Penelope drove him mad with an aching need he had never felt before, and a pack of boys kept distracting him with concerns for their safety. All of them acting as if seeing ghosts, fore-seeing the future, and sensing lies were normal, and their firm belief in their supposed gifts was starting to weaken his firm resolve to be a man of reason. Toss in the facts that someone wanted to kill Penelope and his entire family hated his fiancée and he found himself lost in the midst of utter chaos.

It was time to take control of his life. His first step to-ward that goal was a good one. Investments. Ashton knew he needed to move on that as quickly as possible. He would also cease lurking about waiting for proof of the Hutton-Moores' dishonesty to fall into his hands. It shamed him that young boys were doing more to find out the truth than he was. It was time to thoroughly in-vestigate his fiancée and her sneering brother. It was also time to rid London of Mrs. Cratchitt. Even if she was not a murderer, she was a danger to all women.

"Find out whom she buys her wine from," he said, breaking into his friends' discussion.

"Ah, yes, follow the wine," said Brant. "Excellent. Then what? We are not going to be able to get within a league of that place without one of her thick-necked brutes espying us."

"No, but the boys can. Someone has to carry the wine into the place. If the boys know when it is coming, they can be there clamoring to help for a coin or two. We may even be able to turn the merchant to our side, allowing one of us to join his crew. In disguise, of course. The boys can certainly aid us in finding the merchant."

"Agreed," Cornell said.

One matter taken care of, Ashton thought with satisfaction. "I also want every scrap of information that can be gathered on the Hutton-Moores. My man obviously missed something and our methods thus far have not been serious enough, I believe. I will try to discover who was the solicitor Penelope's father and mother used. Penelope can help there. If he is corrupt, then all claims by the Hutton-Moores are in doubt."

"If they are, then the riches they claim may not be theirs. How could they think to continue such a fraud?"

"Having a viscount indebted to you certainly helps," murmured Vincent.

"Exactly." Ashton began to see how easily they could use him to hold tight to what was not theirs. "So will making sure that Penelope's wealth stays in their hands. If they make me complicit in their fraud, that will be even easier. They would think that, if I discovered the truth, I would be anxious to save my own skin, if only from disgrace, and protect them."

"But surely, if there is an inheritance, it will come to Penelope when she comes of age."

"*If* she comes of age."

"Strike me blind! This situation gets more knotted by the hour."

"So let us put our minds to unraveling it."

Chapter Nine

Penelope bit back a pithy curse as Doctor Pryne plucked the stitches out of her head. Some of her hair had been cut away from the wound, much to her dismay. She was not vain but she wanted to kill Mrs. Cratchitt for that alone.

Just thinking of that woman was enough to sour her mood. Nothing had gone right since that night. She was haunted by a ghost named Faith but had not yet been able to do anything to help the sad spirit find peace. The boys were running wild, and far too often, she did not even know where they were, although she had her suspicions. Charles and Clarissa were suddenly far too interested in where she was and what she was doing. A carriage had almost run her down. The worst of it all was that she was almost certain her infatuation with Radmoor had become something much deeper. Penelope had reluctantly faced the fact that she was in love with a man who would soon marry her stepsister, yet that had been but a shadow of what she felt for him now. She did not know whether to cry or to bang her head against the wall until her good sense returned.

For a fortnight Lord Ashton Pendellan Radmoor had invaded her home as often as he invaded her dreams. With each visit his embraces grew warmer, his kisses more demanding. Penelope knew what he wanted. She wanted it, too, much to her shame. Her weakness for the man troubled her so much she had begun to spend more time at her other house, recklessly putting herself under the watchful eyes of her stepsiblings. It was a madness she did not know how to cure. The way Ashton touched her, the way he kissed her, was pure sin and she ached to revel it.

He claimed he was temperate in all things, and she had often sensed his confusion, even his unease, with the passion that flared between them. Yet she could not see him thus. The way he kissed her, the way he could make her feel, and the way he had her aching to break every rule she had ever set for herself made him a sinful temptation in her eyes. And she was failing miserably in resisting that temptation.

"There, lass," said Doctor Pryne. "As good as new." He lightly slapped her hand away when she started to reach up to touch the healed wound. "Leave it be. 'Twill itch for a while and"—he patted her on the back—"your hair will grow back in soon enough."

She thanked the doctor and offered to walk him out, but he jovially refused, warning her to stay out of trouble as he left. The moment the door shut behind him, she raced to the mirror. It took several arrangements of her hair before she was certain no one would see where it had been cut. Suddenly, Penelope laughed. She was vain, at least about her hair. It was only hair, and plain brown hair at that, she sternly reminded herself as she left her room and started down the stairs.

The front door slammed open and Penelope's heart leapt into her throat. The ridiculously dressed small boy standing there was not immediately recognizable. "Hector?" Was that absurd costume what Clarissa thought a page should wear?

Hector sighed and stomped into the house, slamming the door behind him. He walked right past Penelope and into the parlor. A hundred questions pounded in Penelope's head. She quickly followed him and watched him fling himself onto a settee. She was just about to sit down across from him when she saw the bruises on his face. She leapt to his side, ignoring all his attempts to push her away.

"Clarissa did this to you, did she not?" Penelope rose to go and collect cool water and some cloths. "Wait right here."

Anger clawed at Penelope as she gathered what she needed to tend to Hector's poor battered face. When she had first caught wind of the fact that Hector was acting as a page for Clarissa, she had been tempted to yank him back to the safety of the Warren. Then she had thought on how that would bruise his youthful pride, and how he was doing it to try and help her. Instead, she had enlisted the aid of Mrs. Potts to keep an eye on the boy. Now she wished she had given in to her first impulse. She hurried back to his side, cursing her stepsister all the way.

"Why do you think Lady Clarissa did this?" asked Hector as he held a cold cloth against one cheek while Penelope gently cleaned the scrapes on the other side.

"I know what you have been up to, how you have been playing the page for her and spying for me. You have lived here long enough to know that very little can be kept a secret for long." She smoothed a salve over the scrape. "Any wounds aside from what you have on your face?"

He sighed. "She kicked me, too. In my ribs. I was careful, though. I protected my belly and my man parts just as Artemis taught me to."

Penelope felt torn between the urge to laugh and the urge to cry. His man parts, indeed. Her anger returned in a rush, hotter than ever, when she stripped the boy to his waist and saw the bruises forming along his ribs.

"She kicked you more than once by the look of it. What happened?" she asked as she inspected the wounds, relieved to find that bruises were all he had suffered.

"I spilled tea on her gown." He watched Penelope warily as he told her what happened. "She let out a screech loud enough to make your ears bleed and then she hit me. I fell and that was when I got the scrapes on the other side of my face. Then she stood up and kicked me, cursing at me like a sailor. Soon as she went stomping out of the room to go and change her gown, I left." He frowned. "She has hit me before. And pinched me and the like. But never like this. I think something has gone very wrong for her and I think I know what. Radmoor."

Although she was so furious she could hardly breathe, Penelope asked, "What has Radmoor done to put her into such a fury?"

"Nothing and that is the problem. He has not bowed to her or praised her eyes or brought her gifts."

"And because a man has not written odes to her toes, she beats a boy in her care?"

Hector's eyes widened at the fury in her voice. "She has a fierce temper and wants what she wants right when she wants it."

"You are *not* going back there."

"Nay. Decided that when I picked myself up off the floor."

That stark image was enough to snap the last tether on her anger. Penelope ordered Hector not to step one small foot out of the house and then left to confront Clarissa. During the ride in the hack, she struggled to bring the wild fury surging through her body under some control but it was difficult. The rage over what Clarissa had done to Hector was fed and strengthened by her own many grievances against the woman, not the least of which was that Clarissa had a claim on Ashton.

From the day her mother and the old baron had died, Clarissa and Charles had treated her like some embarrassing secret, as if she lived on their meager charity and owed them the courtesy of not shaming them by showing her face in public. They had banished her to the attics in her own home, never even shared a meal with her, introduced her to no one, and took her nowhere. Clarissa had even taken her mother's jewels, not one of which had been bought by the old baron.

Why have I endured it? she asked herself as she paid the driver and walked to the door of her house. For this house? To find out what Charles and Clarissa were doing with her inheritance? At the moment none of her reasons for lingering at the house made any sense. She was sure she could have found some other way to protect what was rightfully hers, to expose the criminal venality of her stepfather's spawn.

She found Clarissa in the parlor admiring herself in a small oval mirror. "Clarissa."

Clarissa turned to stare at Penelope, clearly horrified by Penelope's appearance. Penelope knew her gown was a drab, blue thing fit only for a maid to wear and that her hair was a tangled mess, but she did not think it was worthy of such shock. It also had to be a shock for

Clarissa to find her stepsister in the room she had chosen to meet her many admirers, a room Penelope had been banned from. Penelope knew when Clarissa saw the anger in her eyes. The way Clarissa eyed her so warily told Penelope the woman was wondering if Penelope had decided it was time to rebel. If so, Clarissa was going to think it was time to push Charles to stop dawdling and just get rid of her unwanted stepsister.

Ashton stepped out of his carriage just in time to see Penelope enter Hutton-Moore House. By the front door. She never went into the house through the front door. Alarm quickened his steps. He pushed past the startled butler and hurried toward the ornately decorated parlor where Clarissa liked to hold court.

"What are *you* doing here? I am expecting Radmoor and he does not wish to see such a slattern. Get out."

Clarissa's shrill command halted Ashton just before he reached the door. He looked behind him to see the butler approaching and curtly waved the man away. The butler hesitated for a moment and then obeyed the silent command. As stealthily as he could, Ashton moved to the doorway and saw Penelope. She looked adorably disheveled. Clarissa looked coldly furious.

"I have just come from tending the bruises you put on a boy of nine."

"Did the brat run crying to you then? Probably met you in the kitchens, eh? Ungrateful whelp."

"Did you even pause for but a moment to see if he *could* run after you had kicked him while he was huddled on the floor?"

"He ruined my gown! Do they not say *spare the rod, spoil the child*?"

Penelope stared at her stepsister. This journey to

confront Clarissa had been a waste of her time. She ached to beat the woman, hurt her as she had hurt Hector, but realized it would change nothing. Clarissa would never see that what she had done to poor Hector was wrong. In Clarissa's eyes, the only ones who ever did wrong were the ones who did not give her what she wanted or crossed her.

"You, *dear sister,* are a spoiled, vain, cold-hearted bitch."

Clarissa hissed out a curse and swung at Penelope. Penelope, accustomed to her stepsister's propensity to hit, was ready for it and caught Clarissa by the wrist. She then decided that such an attack deserved retaliation. And who better than one who had spent the last few years surrounded by boys? She idly punched Clarissa in the mouth. Clarissa stumbled over to the settee and sat down hard, her hand on her bleeding lip.

It had been an uncouth, even childish thing to do, but Penelope suffered no remorse. The woman deserved far worse for hitting and kicking a small boy. Penelope admitted to herself that the blow was also in retaliation for a thousand hurts and insults she had suffered at Clarissa's hands for far too long.

"Oh, you shall pay for this, Penelope, and pay dearly."

"How? By losing the small, cold bed in the attic you have so graciously allowed me? Denying me the right to go about freely in the society I was born into? Ah, but wait, you already do that. By making my life utterly intolerable? You have done that since the day my mother married your father, even before. But no more. Nay, not a minute more. I have stayed here because this is *my* house."

"Do not be a fool. It belongs to Charles."

Ashton noticed that Clarissa looked to the left as she spoke before glaring at Penelope again.

"Nay, Clarissa. 'Tis mine and well you know it. I can

do nothing about it now but one day I will see you and your brother thrown out of here. 'Til then, enjoy your stay."

"And just where do you think you can go? You have no money and you are Charles's ward."

"I do have a surfeit of relatives. I will go to one of them."

"Charles will not allow it. He will drag you back."

"Let him try." Penelope started toward the door. "And beware, sister. The spirits here are not very fond of you." Knowing how uneasy any talk of spirits made Clarissa, it was a petty dart to fling in parting, but it was also a satisfying one.

Ashton hurried down the stairs and out to his carriage. He had come to share tea with Clarissa, as ordered, but decided Penelope needed him. He was not sure he could hold firm to his temper if he faced his fiancée right now, either. The fury he had heard in Penelope's voice was enough to tell him that young Hector had not suffered a mere slap, but the details had sickened him. He knew many people believed harsh discipline was needed to raise a child right, but his mother had never condoned it. As far as he was concerned, he and his siblings had not suffered for the lack of it.

He was waiting by the door of his carriage when Penelope strode out of the house. She had taken so long to appear that he had nearly gone back in to look for her. The bag she carried told him what had delayed her. She had meant it when she had said she was leaving. Although he knew Penelope had a comfortable place to stay, the Hutton-Moores did not, yet Clarissa made no attempt to stop her stepsister from walking away. When Penelope caught sight of him, he bowed and waved her toward the open door of his carriage.

Penelope hesitated only a moment before walking

over to Ashton and allowing him to help her into his
carriage. She rested her head against the back of the
seat and closed her eyes while he climbed in beside her.
The carriage began to move and she opened one eye to
watch Ashton slide closer to her.

"Why were you waiting for me? How could you have
even known I was here?" she asked.

"I saw you enter," he replied and put his arm around
her shoulder.

"Did you eavesdrop on the conversation between
Clarissa and me?"

"Yes, and I had to move quickly to do so."

Penelope had to smile at his nonsense. Her fury had
eased while she had gathered what few belongings she
had. Even more so when she had stopped by Clarissa's
bedchamber and retrieved her mother's jewels. A part
of her was unsettled, certain she had given up too soon,
but mostly, she was relieved to be rid of the Steps. The
name the boys had given Clarissa and Charles suited them
well, even when prefaced with some unflattering word
the boys were so fond of using, she decided. They were
not of her blood and had never been family. They were
simply the Steps and she wished never to see or speak to
them again. At least, not until she ordered them out of
her house.

"Did you hear Clarissa say that I am Charles's ward?"
she asked Ashton, knowing that she ought to move out
of his light embrace even as she relaxed against him.

"I did and that could prove to be a problem for you,"
Ashton replied. "Perhaps you really should seek out one
of your relations and go to him." The words were hard
to say for he found that he did not want her to move out
of his reach. "The highest born, the one with the highest rank and the greatest power. By the time Charles
could get the courts to help pull you back into his grasp,

you would be of age and free of him. He could even lose the guardianship of you to one of your blood family."

"The highest would be Modred." She ignored him when he muttered the name in astonishment for most everyone had that reaction. "Modred Vaughn, the Duke of Elderwood. I will go to him if there is no other choice for me and I have no doubt that he would help. He might find the presence of the boys a severe trial, however. Do not misunderstand me. He is the kindest of men, but he has difficulty being near some people and I have never tested him with the boys."

"There are rumors that he can read a person's thoughts."

"I can see that you believe that as much as you believe I can see spirits," she teased and laughed when he blushed. "Aye, he can, but not as you think. Not as if every mind is an open book to him. He can grasp words and even whole sentences here and there, enough to know one's thoughts. Especially if they are born of strong emotion, and strong emotions are not always good ones, are they. If you place poor Modred in a room full of people, he will be beaten down by emotions, his mind battered by snatches of thoughts until he can hear nothing but the cacophony in his head. That is why he stays at the family seat with his aunt Dob, who works hard to teach him how to, well, to shield himself from such an onslaught. I know you do not believe any of this."

He kissed her cheek. "I am no longer sure what I believe. I saw Septimus ease your pain and Doctor Pryne obviously believes in that young man's ability to do so. I know Hector has a keen eye for a lie, too keen for a boy of only nine. I also know that everyone in the Warren believes in such things." He frowned as he struggled for the right words, ones that would explain but not of-fend. "The rumors of your family's gifts have been around for too long to discount them out of hand, but I pride myself on being a man of reason. I need proof."

"And for many of our gifts, that is hard to come by. Do not fear that I take offense."

The soft smile she gave him was more temptation than Ashton could resist. He pulled her fully into his arms and kissed her. The way her body fitted so perfectly in his arms caused his blood to throb with the need that filled him. It was madness to keep taunting his lust and wrong to keep tempting her to sate it, but he had no willpower when it came to Penelope, not when she was so soft and welcoming in his arms.

The carriage halted, bringing him to his senses. He ended the kiss and fought to tamp down the mindless urge to push her down onto the carriage seat and make love to her then and there. The desire turning her eyes a soft blue and the flush of passion's heat upon her cheeks did not make that easy.

Penelope inwardly shook herself in an attempt to regain her senses as Ashton helped her down from the carriage. She maintained a house for the illegitimate children of her relatives so she knew full well what she was so aching for. She also knew that Ashton had not closed his coat because he was cold. The hard proof of his desire for her had been very evident during their embrace. He was doing his best to be a gentleman. Penelope abruptly decided that she did not want him to succeed.

Everyone save for her brothers and Darius was waiting in the parlor when she and Ashton walked in. For one brief moment she feared something terrible had happened, but a quick yet careful check of their faces revealed no concern or fear in their expressions. She smiled a little warily at them even as she went to Hector's side to check his injuries, pleased to see that the bruising and swelling had grown no worse.

"I wish to take the boys to my cousin's home for an evening," said Septimus.

"Are you sure your cousin wants so much company?" she asked.

"Yes. Her nephew is there for a week and he is bored. He is accustomed to others of his age being close at hand to play with. Ones who understand," he added quietly.

"Ah." Penelope nodded. "Of course they may go. I just hope your cousin knows what she has unleashed upon her home," she added and grinned, ignoring the playful complaints of the boys.

It took but moments for the house to empty. It took only another moment for Penelope to realize that, for the first time since the night in the brothel, she was truly alone with Ashton. Suddenly nervous, she urged him to sit and hurried off to the kitchen to fetch some food and drink. By the time she returned with a tray, he was seated comfortably on the settee, smiling faintly at some drawings young Olwen had left on the wide, slightly scarred table placed between the settees, but he quickly stood and helped her set out the things on the tray.

"This is quite good," he said, sitting down again and tugging her down beside him. "Who is your artist?"

"Olwen," she replied. "Uncle Argus's boy. He is trying to perfect his art so that he might better draw some of the things he sees or dreams about."

"Olwen sees what will be as Paul does?" He poured them each some wine.

"Not exactly. It is so hard to explain, and because they are all still so young, it is hard to be certain exactly how their particular, er, skill will develop. Are you certain you want to hear this?" she asked and then sipped at her wine.

"How am I to come to a decision based on the reason I hold so dear if I do not have all the needed information?"

"None of us has all the information. It just is," she said and began to explain as best as she could the various gifts, or curses, her large family had.

Ashton listened to her tales, asking only a few questions. He was still unable to believe in all the things she claimed her family could do, but he did understand one thing clearly. The persecution of witches might be legally at an end, but the Vaughns and the Wherlockes still suffered. They watched wives and husbands turn from them, mothers and fathers turn from their own children, they had to remain secretive, and they had to suffer the fact that few people believed in their various gifts. He felt almost guilty for his doubt.

He held her close as they talked and drank wine. The quiet in the house wrapped around them, but it took Ashton a while to understand the significance of that quiet. All the boys were gone. Penelope had no servants living in the house except for the tutor and he was also gone. He was alone with Penelope. The last thin restraint he had on his desire for her snapped. The moment she finished a tale about her uncle Argus, Ashton pulled her into his arms and kissed her with all the hunger that had been knotting his insides for far too long.

Penelope was a little startled by the abruptness of Ashton's embrace. Then he thrust his tongue into her mouth and began to work his magic on her. In some dimly aware part of her mind she heard her wine goblet fall from her hand and she ignored it. She wrapped her arms around his neck and let herself be carried away by the fierce pleasure of his kiss.

Ashton soon had her on her back but Penelope made no protest. The press of his long, hard body against her made her blood flow hot and wild through her veins. She tilted her head back when he kissed the hollow at the base of her throat. The warmth of his mouth invaded her body as he kissed and nipped at the sensitive skin on her neck. His strong hands moved over her body, stroking her, and she trembled from the force of the need he was stirring inside her.

"This is madness," Ashton mumbled as he realized he had begun to undo her gown.

"'Tis a very sweet one." She kissed his throat, savoring the taste of him, and heard him groan softly.

"Penelope, I am close to taking you right here, on the settee in your parlor."

"Aye, it is, perhaps, not the best place for this."

He lifted himself up on his forearms to look at her. Her lips were kiss-swollen, her eyes a hot blue that he now knew was caused by desire. She wanted him. He wanted her. The greedy man inside him said that was enough. It shamed him to think he was becoming like his father. Although his father would never have paused to try and talk a woman out of allowing him to enjoy her favors, and that thought comforted him.

"You are an innocent," he began, thinking she might not truly understand how close she was to being deflowered in her parlor.

Penelope did not really want to discuss the matter, especially since such talk was rapidly cooling the heat he had stirred within her. "Innocent but not ignorant. Ashton . . ." She wriggled her hand beneath his fine linen shirt and echoed his soft gasp when she stroked the taut, warm flesh of his chest. "I manage a house filled with the bastards of my relatives. Artemis and Stefan prove that my father was as faithless as yours. I live a short walk from a part of London where every sin known to man can be purchased. I may be innocent in body, but I know more than I like to. I know where this will lead and I know I want to follow."

"I am not free—" Her fingers over his mouth stopped his words.

"I know that, too, and know that you may never be." She lifted her fingers and slowly traced the shape of his mouth with her tongue. "Fly free with me, Ashton. Let me soar with you for a while, at least until you speak vows to another that neither of us wish to break."

He stared at her, his body crying out to take her at her word while his mind lectured him on what was expected of a gentleman. The truth of her words shone in her eyes. She wanted him as much as he wanted her. The madness she stirred in him was a shared one. Ashton stood up and held out his hand.

"If we are about to tumble into sin, Penelope Wherlocke, let us at least retain enough dignity to do so in a bedchamber," he said.

She grasped his hand, nimbly hopped off the settee, and led him to her bedchamber. He knew where it was, but allowed her to take the lead. Ashton had hoped the walk to her bedchamber would cool his blood enough to restore his good sense, but his blood continued to pulse with need every step of the way. He shut the bedchamber door behind him the moment they stepped into the room and then he looked at her. Her undone gown was sliding off her shoulders, her full breasts almost completely exposed, and he decided good sense could go to the devil. For once he was taking what *he* wanted and he would deal with the consequences later.

Penelope saw Ashton's hesitation and feared that he

had regained control of his desire. She nearly laughed with joy when he caught her up in his arms and strode to her bed. She was already wrapped around him when they fell onto the bed. Drugged by his kisses, her passion running hot enough to blind her to everything around her, she only became aware of how rapidly he had divested them both of their clothes when his warm flesh pressed against hers.

"You are so beautiful," he whispered, crouching over her so that he could study her from head to toe and enjoying the way his body burned with hunger for every silken inch of her. "So soft." He ran his hand down her side from shoulder to thigh and then bent his head to slowly lick the hard tip of one plump breast. "As sweet to the taste as the finest nectar. I have ached for you since that night at Mrs. Cratchitt's."

"As I have ached for you," she said and lightly stroked his broad, smoothly muscular chest. "And I think we have talked enough."

"Yes." He ground out the word between tightly clenched teeth and then fell on her, almost able to hear the last thin thread of his control snap.

The moment his mouth closed around the aching tip of her breast, Penelope lost the ability to think clearly. She became deeply immersed in the desire racing through her veins, a desire stirred higher and higher with his every kiss, each stroke of his tongue against her skin, every touch of his hand. Her need was so great by the time he slid his hand between her legs that she barely even flinched over such an intimate touch. He kissed her as he stroked her there, his fingers dipping inside her. The ache he created there was not soothed by his touch; it grew worse. She needed more but did not know how to ask for it.

Ashton knew he could wait no longer to possess her.

He had dreamt of loving her slowly, of bringing her pleasure over and over, but he would have to fulfill that dream another day. If he did not get inside her soon, he would empty himself upon the sheets. He began to ease himself into her, groaning as her wet heat began to close around him. When he met the shield of her maidenhead, he kissed her and thrust hard, tearing through the barrier like some ancient marauder and capturing her gasp of pain in his mouth.

"It hurts only the once. I swear it," he said as he spread kisses over her full, soft breasts.

"I know." She wrapped her body around him again, holding him as close as she could as the pain eased and the pleasure returned. "What next?"

"Is the pain gone?"

"Oh, aye, I just feel so deliciously full."

Ashton groaned and began to move. He intended to go slowly, to be gentle, but the way she quickly caught and matched his rhythm, the soft sounds of pleasure she made, destroyed that gallant intention and need ruled him. When she gained her pleasure, her body rippling beneath and around his, he thrust deep inside her and let his own release take him beyond all rational thought.

Penelope was just shaking herself free of the bliss he had given her when Ashton climbed out of bed. She was so relieved when he did not immediately start to get dressed that she blushed only faintly when he fetched a wet rag and cleaned them both off. She pressed as close to him as she could when he climbed back into bed and pulled her into his arms.

"Penelope, I mean to get free of Clarissa and—" He sighed when she yet again pressed her hand over his mouth.

"No promises. No raising of hopes. What will be, will be. Let us just enjoy what we share," she said.

"I am working to escape their trap, you know."

"I know and I pray you succeed. For your own sake, if naught else. There are just too many complications for us to speak of a future now."

He grimaced. "I know, which is why I should never have even kissed you."

"Why not? I like your kisses."

Ashton knew she was not as blasé as she attempted to sound, but he laughed and kissed her. She was right. There were too many knots to untie to speak of any future for them now. But as he began to make love to her again, he promised himself that he would get free of debt and of Clarissa. Then Penelope would not be allowed to hush him when he tried to speak of their future. He knew now that the only future he wanted had Penelope Wherlocke in it.

Chapter Ten

"When will ye and Radmoor marry?"

Penelope forced herself to continue calmly with her sewing, but inwardly cursed Artemis for his blunt question. Finishing the neat row of stitches on the little shirt she mended gave her a moment to try and plan out the best way to answer his question. She finally raised her eyes to gaze at him with what she hoped was an expression of gentle confusion.

Ashton had done his best to creep away unseen just before dawn but she had known it was a wasted effort. There were no secrets in a house filled with Wherlockes and Vaughns, even one where many of the occupants were too young to have a full knowledge or control over their gifts. She had almost told him so, wanting him to come back to her bed and hold her, but she held silent as he kissed her and slipped away.

All the boys over seven were gathered in front of her and not one of them looked as if they believed in her guise of innocence. She would try to divert them from the matter but she would not lie. That, too, would be useless and could easily hurt their feelings.

"And why should his lordship marry me?" she asked. "S'truth, I believe he is already spoken for."

"And I think bedding the virginal daughter of a marquis ought to take precedence over all other promises made," snapped Artemis.

"Artemis, I may be innocent but I am also a woman full grown; a spinster in some eyes."

"That does not make his seducing you acceptable."

"Not even if I wished to be seduced?" she asked, and sighed when Artemis and the other boys looked even angrier. She was disappointing them and that hurt.

"Your reputation," Stefan began.

"I have none. No one save my family even knows me." That stung but she ignored the old pain. "And if the world did learn about me, once they learned about this place, I would have no good name to protect anyway."

"Because of us. Because we are all bastards."

"That seems unfair," muttered Olwen, his scowl causing him to look uncannily like his father, her uncle Argus.

"It is unfair but a lot of what society does is unfair," she said. "If all were fair and as it should be, I might have met Radmoor at some ball or soiree, we would have flirted a little, danced, and perhaps he would have courted me, learned to care about me, and asked to marry me. But here we are. I have naught and he needs money to keep his family out of debtor's prison. He may escape Clarissa's clutches, but he will still need to marry an heiress.

"I love him. I know he desires and cares for me. This is not just some careless lusting. Should we deny ourselves because some cruel twist of fate makes it impossible for us to be together as man and wife? I truly believe that, if not for the need to save his family, he would marry me. He said as much." *Or tried to,* she added honestly, but she would not tell the boys that she had silenced him each time. "I decided that was good enough."

"Do you think fate will be kind and fill his purse so that he can marry you?" asked Artemis.

"Nay, so you need not sound so derisive." She smiled a little, knowing it was a sad expression, when he blushed a little at her reprimand but still looked angry. "He makes me happy, and just for a little while, I want to be selfish and hold fast to that."

After a heavy silence and a lot of exchanged looks laden with silent messages she did not quite comprehend the meaning of, Stefan sighed. "Then it would make you unhappy if Artemis challenged him for a duel to defend your honor."

"Very unhappy." She cursed her own stupidity for not foreseeing such a consequence.

"I do not like this," said Artemis. "It is not right of him to take advantage of how you feel about him."

"He does not know," Penelope said, the hard note in her voice telling them that she did not want him told, either. "He calls it madness, and enchantment, and fears he is behaving as badly as his father, who was a faithless scoundrel and left his family in dire straits. I know my own heart and that is enough. S'truth, at this time I believe it would be cruel to try and make him fall in love with me.

"And who can say? Mayhap fate *will* be kind and give him what he needs so that he is free to choose me if he wishes to. Then I shall certainly do my best to make him see that what we share is far, far more than a passing madness."

"And what shall you do if he does marry another?"

"I will endure the pain and cure myself of this madness. I will *not* continue to be his lover. He would not ask it of me, either, as he is truly an honorable man. Right now he does not feel bound because he never asked Clarissa; she and Charles tricked him into that betrothal. If he says vows to a woman, however, he will keep them."

She could tell that they were still unhappy with the situation, but her word that she would not become some married man's mistress, no matter how much she loved that man, appeared to have taken the edge off their anger. Penelope could understand their worries and their anger. Every one of them was the result of some affair, shunned by many as if that were somehow their fault. They did not want her to entangle herself in the sort of thing that had tainted their lives. She loved them all, and appreciated their concern and their outrage on her behalf, but she could not let them dictate how she lived.

A movement in the shadows at the far corner of the room caught Penelope's attention. She squinted and soon made out the spectral shape of a too plump woman of middle years. When she saw that Conrad was also squinting into the shadows, she sighed. Conrad shared her gift. It was enough to confirm what she was seeing.

"Our neighbor Mrs. Pettibone has died," she said as she put aside her sewing basket and moved toward the ghost.

Alone. I am alone.

"Not for long, Mrs. Pettibone," Penelope said. "If you would just let go of this corporal world, you would move on to a better place and join the loved ones who passed before you."

Alone. I am all alone.

Penelope frowned. It was not unusual for one who had recently died to be terribly confused, but she had the distinct impression that the woman was speaking of far more than just discovering that her spirit was now separated from her body. "Artemis, I think Mrs. Pettibone has died unattended. I thought she had three daughters."

"Her daughters are in the country," he said. "They will not be back for a week, mayhap longer. I am not sure."

"Well, you are a clever fellow. Think of something to tell the watch so that he will feel compelled to go into the Pettibone House. The last thing her poor girls need is to come home to find their mother a week dead. If you know, or can discover, exactly where her girls have gone, I will send them word to come home now."

It took hours to sort out the problem of Mrs. Pettibone. The ghost did not leave, however. Penelope decided there had to be something the woman still needed, something concerning her daughters, and resigned herself to having Mrs. Pettibone's spirit around the house for a while. The Wherlocke Warren was, as her family liked to say, a clean house, void of unhappy spirits and what her aunt Olympia called unsettling energies. There had been the occasional spectral visitor, however, and she had accepted that. She would endure this one, too.

Her brothers, Darius, and Septimus disappeared during the turmoil of an interview by the watch and the carting out of poor Mrs. Pettibone's body, leaving her alone with the seven youngest boys. Their energy soon wearied her, and deciding it was a rare fine day and too good to waste, she rounded them all up for a walk to the park. The one she chose was across from Ashton's house but she told herself that was no more than a coincidence. It was a lie and she knew it, but she held to it.

She thought that if she repeated it to herself often enough, she might believe it and would be able to act appropriately surprised if Ashton found them.

Ashton stepped into the parlor of Hutton-Moore House and could tell by the look upon Clarissa's face that he was in for a show of her temper. After spending hours reveling in Penelope's warmth, he did not care. Clarissa had tricked him into this betrothal and her brother had blackmailed him into holding to it. Neither of them deserved his respect. He was also determined to escape their clutches as soon as possible. For the first time, he was even contemplating selling some of his lands to do so.

"I believe you had said you would be here yesterday, Ashton," Clarissa said as she sat down and waved one delicate hand to indicate that he should take the seat beside her.

Leaving the door to the parlor wide open, Ashton sat down in the seat across from her. There was no chaperone in the room, not even a maid. It smelled of a trap. Since they were already betrothed, he did not know why she felt compelled to play the entrapment game. If she was planning a seduction, it certainly was not because she had an uncontrollable passion for him. The only reason he could think of was that she wished to add one more link to the chain around his neck to be certain that he joined her at the altar. If fate was kind, he would break that chain and leave her standing there alone.

"There was a distraction I could not ignore," he replied and feared for a moment that he was about to get a lap full of hot tea.

"A distraction so great you could not even send round a note to say that you were not coming?"

"Once the hour set for our meeting had passed, I assumed you would know that I was not coming. In all honesty, I do not believe I ever promised to come to share tea with you. Since I had not agreed, or promised, to be here, I fear it never occurred to me to tell you that I was *not* coming."

Ashton sipped his tea and watched her struggle to keep her temper under control. Clarissa craved his title, the heritage of his family, and the chance to become a duchess. She did not want a man or a true husband, however. She wanted a lapdog. She and her brother might be able to force him to marry her, but he would be damned if he would bow to her every whim. His father's fecklessness meant he had to allow himself to be bought, but he would not be enslaved.

"Might I ask what this distraction was?" Clarissa asked, her attempt to put a light, sweet note in her voice ruined by the thrum of anger behind every word.

"The sight of a young woman fleeing your house with her baggage. Pitiful small amount of baggage it was, as well. Naturally, being a gentleman, I stepped forward to give her aid. Imagine my surprise when I discovered she was your sister."

"Stepsister," Clarissa mumbled, her cheeks losing some of their rosy glow.

Ashton continued as if he had not heard her. "A sister who had been living here all along. How is it that I have never met her?"

"She is a very shy girl and somewhat odd," Clarissa hastily replied, quickly glancing to her left as she spoke. "She has never cared for society and will not attend even the smallest dinner gathering. Now that I am to be wed and become your viscountess, she fears all the turmoil that will come as we entertain your many acquaintances as will be expected."

"Ah, well then, you must fetch her back and ease her mind." Ashton smiled at her and idly wondered if he looked as much like the indulgent but firm uncle he sounded like.

"What do you mean? How could I do that?"

"By telling her that we will be spending most of our time in the country. My lands have been sadly neglected, I fear, and it will take a lot of time to set them to rights. I shall want my wife beside me while that is being seen to. What with the houses, lands, and tenants that need seeing to, there will be little time left for frivolity and certainly no time for running to and from London." Ashton knew some would call him a cad and a liar for what he was doing, but he had to admit that he was enjoying it.

"But, surely, we will need to be here for the season. Your sisters need to find husbands," Clarissa said in a tone that implied she had just trumped him.

"Mother will take care of that chore. You do not need to worry about it. You will have more than enough to keep you busy, especially when the children begin to arrive."

"I do, of course, understand my duty to beget your heir, but—"

"And the spare. Do not forget the spare. I come from a large family, however, and that is what I desire to have for myself."

Clarissa narrowed her eyes and set her tea down with a snap. "I know what game you play. You nearly had me believing that nonsense, but I am on to you now. You seek to make me cry off, to run horrified from the very idea of marrying you."

"You imagine things, my dear. I but speak the truth." In a way, he did, but with a slight twist he knew would aggravate Clarissa.

She leapt to her feet and paced the room for a moment before whirling around to glare at him. "I have no intention of living in the country and being your brood mare."

Now the play would turn hard and mean, he thought, but said, "I am not sure you have much choice in the matter." Ashton picked a small lemon cake from the tray on the table and began to eat it as if he had not a care in the world.

"My money is not going to be wasted on cows and sheep and tenant cottages."

"*Your* money? Once we are wed, my dear, it is *my* money."

"Then I shall have my brother make sure you do not get full control of it."

He smiled at her and then dabbed at his lips with a prettily embroidered napkin. "Did you not read the betrothal agreement? The only thing that restricts my use of the money is that I may not touch a groat of it until we are married. After that, 'tis mine. You should have spoken out before the papers were drawn up and signed. Too anxious to be a duchess, I suppose." He could tell by the look on her face that she had not read a word of the agreement, had trusted in her brother to be sure all her interests were protected.

"The agreement can be changed and you will sign the new one."

Ashton sighed, acted as if he were actually thinking the matter over, and then shook his head. "No. I think not."

"You need me and that money more than I need you, you cocksure bastard," she hissed. "You cannot afford to break our betrothal because your precious family is but one step from debtor's prison. I am the one that will give you the money to save them. Best you remember that, sirrah. I care not what their fate is, but you do."

He studied her. Her eyes were narrowed and held a hard glitter. Her mouth was thinned in anger and her cheeks were flushed with it. He thought it odd that she could still look beautiful if one did not listen too closely to her words or look too deeply into her eyes. Ashton had to blame himself for missing so much about her character, for letting himself walk into the trap the Hutton-Moores had set for him. He had guessed that she had no warmth in her, but it was worse than that. Whatever man did marry her would find himself saddled with the worst of viragoes for a wife. Ashton was determined that that poor sod would not be him.

Ashton stood up and walked over to her. "My dear Clarissa, why ever do you think you are the one in control of this game? Your brother is. He will do nothing to risk this marriage he has worked so hard for. You may stomp your little feet all you like and curse him to the moon and back, but you will not get your way in this."

"Nonsense, my brother—"

"Wants to climb up society's rickety ladder and become someone of power and importance. He wants to dabble in politics. He is unable to do any of that without a notable family connection. Once we are married, that will be me. Trust me in this, the only conditions in that betrothal agreement are ones that give him some power over me and prevent me from simply turning my back on him once we are wed. You and your petty wants were never considered."

He caught her hand when she swung at him, having learned from how she treated Penelope and her page that she had a tendency to strike when angry. "I am trapped, no doubt about it, but it was not you who closed this trap around me. Sad to say, you were but the bait. Fool that I was, I never checked to see that the meat baiting that trap was rancid before I walked into it." He tossed her hand aside and started to walk out of the room. "I will meet up with you at the Hendersons' ball if I have the time."

It did not surprise him to hear something crash against the door a heartbeat after he had closed it. He had accomplished what he had set out to do, he thought, as he told his carriage driver to take him home, and climbed into the carriage. He had set brother and sister against each other. It might be only a temporary fissure in their relationship, but it was a start. Ashton just hoped it was enough to keep them tangled up with each other for a while so that there was less chance of Charles noticing that someone was asking a lot of questions about him.

He was actually humming a song when he walked into his house. As he handed Marston his coat, hat, and gloves, he asked about his family and discovered they were all out. His friends, however, were all awaiting him in his study. And drinking his brandy, no doubt, he thought with a faint smile as he went to join them.

"You are looking surprisingly cheerful," said Brant as Ashton entered the room and went to pour himself a brandy.

"I am hoping you are here to make me even more so." Ashton sat down on the plush settee next to a lounging Cornell. "I assume you have some news for me and are not here just to gaze upon my great beauty." He grinned when his friends all laughed and peppered him with insults.

"Well, some of our news will surely make you smile but I am not sure all of it will," said Cornell. "Lady

Penelope's solicitor, Mr. Horace Earnshaw, has definitely been corrupted."

"Or blackmailed," said Vincent. "We are not sure which."

"Mayhap both," muttered Whitney. "Corrupt the fool and then blackmail him."

"How? Or what?" asked Ashton.

"Not sure which came first," said Cornell. "Have been following the fool for two days and nights. He is not wise enough to hide his vices or he has suffered such vices for so long he has grown careless. He gambles and is not very good at it. Owes a lot. Not sure that is the real trouble, though. He goes to the Dobbin House every other night."

Ashton nearly choked on his brandy. The Dobbin House was a notorious brothel. It was rumored to sell children, especially pretty little boys, but had never been closed. The few times it was sacked by the authorities or some outraged morality group, there was no proof found that it was any more than an inn with maids that secretly earned a few extra coins on their backs. Not worth the time and trouble of prosecution. That did not stop people from believing the worst of it. If word spread that Earnshaw frequented such a place, he would soon find himself without clients and destitute. He could even find himself facing a hanging, as Ashton thought sodomy was still a hanging offense.

"From what little I have discovered about Penelope's father, he was a rake but not witless. It seems strange that he would have a solicitor with such vices, ones that leave him open to corruption and blackmail."

"May be that these things were not such a problem when the marquis first hired him and then the man simply paid no more attention to Earnshaw."

"Or he is the son of the man the marquis dealt with. If the man is already being blackmailed, then I am not sure what we can do to make him tell us what we need to know."

Brant frowned. "At least we can be sure that the man will not hesitate to abuse his client's trust to save his own skin. The only way to know if he will answer our questions is to confront him."

Ashton nodded. "Have any of you found a reason to believe it is worth it? Because of my father, I fear my mother did not have a great deal to do with society for many years. She knew a few things and what she did know seemed to imply that the marquis was a faithless swine but not given to financially profligate ways. His wife was also not without her own small fortune. The title and entailed lands went to his nephew but there should have been other properties and money."

"Exactly what we heard," said Whitney. "The man could not seem to stop himself from tossing up a skirt and many of the old men at the clubs had wild tales to tell of his lechery. But to a man, they said he was careful with his coin, almost tight-fisted. What was not entailed should have gone to his wife and, one would assume, to his daughter. For all we know, there may have even been something set aside for his sons. They were openly recognized as his from what I gather."

"It does seem as if that family does not hide its illegitimate children," agreed Ashton. "I might not approve of how they seem to toss them all in Penelope's lap but they do at least try to take care of them. Too few do. Well, was that the good news?"

"Some of it, although we cannot be sure of what use it is until we have a try at getting information out of the swine," said Brant. "The other news is that, although our investments are still young, there appears to be a good chance that they will pay off even sooner than we had hoped and pay off well. There are already high bids on the cargo the ship is to bring in."

"Then let us keep praying that the ship does not sink. At the moment, all I need is enough to pay off the markers Charles holds and then I can be free of Clarissa."

"Ah, Clarissa." Cornell sat up straight. "I fear your bride is not the sweet virginal darling she pretends to be. She may be cold, but she apparently has no aversion to using her fair flesh to gain what she wants."

"You were following her as well?" Ashton began to think Cornell enjoyed this work.

"I had my man Pilton trailing her around. I cannot be positive, since Pilton did not actually watch the pair performing the naughty deed, but she spent most of last night at Sir Gerald Taplow's. Since I have to doubt it is a matter of passion or love, there has to be a reason she is going to him. Shall I find out what it is?"

"If you can. One can never have enough weaponry when one faces down an enemy." Ashton frowned. "You are right to say it is doubtful she is madly in love with the man. I just do not see her succumbing to a great passion. She is, however, very ambitious. She craves all that society has to offer and needs to reign in its confines. There may be the answer to why she is spending nights with Taplow. Perhaps the easiest thing to do is figure out what he can give her."

"You really have no intention of going through with this marriage, do you," said Cornell, smiling faintly. "If you did, you would be at least a little annoyed that she is risking the bloodlines of your future heir."

"No, I will not marry that woman. I have even begun

to think that I will sell off some property if I must to dig myself out of this hole. I will make up the loss to my siblings in some other way."

"If you do decide to sell any of your properties, come to me first," said Cornell. "I know all that you have and would be pleased with any one of them."

"Then I shall tell you first. I am hoping that investment is the way out of the debt that now weighs me down, however. I want to be able to provide for all my siblings. It is what my father should have done."

"Do not fret over us, Ashton," said a voice from the doorway. "Better we all have to find our own way in the end than you tie yourself to a woman you do not want."

Ashton grinned at the sight of his brother Alexander. He stood up and went over to briefly embrace him for it had been months since he had seen the man. Only three years younger than he they had been close while growing up and remained so now. They even looked similar.

As Alexander settled in a seat and had some brandy, he caught up on the news. It surprised Ashton a little to see how eagerly his brother joined in with the spying Cornell was proving to be so good at. He had to wonder if his brother's travels in Europe were the simple matter of wanderlust Alex had claimed them to be. There were several shadowy groups within the government that dealt in collecting information on their allies as well as their enemies.

"You have gotten yourself into a tangle, brother," Alex said. "And at the heart of it all is the Lady Penelope if I am not mistaken. Pretty, is she?"

"I think so," said Ashton and ignored his brother's knowing grin. "I also think she has been royally cheated by the Hutton-Moores. Unfortunately, a young woman has little recourse in such matters."

"Hence this gathering of her knights. Well, count me as one of them. Even if there were not a fair damsel to be rescued, I would help, for I want you to be able to choose your bride, Ashton. You should not have to sell yourself because our father was a reckless fool."

"The final piece of news is that the next delivery of wine will be a fortnight from tonight," said Brant. "And the merchant, a gruff fellow by the name of Tucker, is more than willing to help us. Seems he has a young daughter and the tale of how Mrs. Cratchitt gains some of her fillies sickened and enraged him. He even wondered if one or both of the girls who had gone missing in the area may have been taken by her and wants to shut her down before any others go missing. Seems one of them was a girl his eldest son was courting."

"How could we have missed such a thing? How could we go there and not know that some of those girls were not willing?" asked Ashton.

"I fear once they are, er, broken in, the girls are apt to stay, afraid to go back home only to be shamed and shunned. Also, if Mrs. Cratchitt has murdered someone, there may be a threat of violence that holds them in the place." Brant shrugged. "And holds them silent." He stood up. "I should go now as I need to be at my grandmother's for supper and then escort her to the Hendersons' ball. Will I see you there?"

"If Mother is eager to go. She and Lady Henderson are old friends."

The others soon left as well, leaving Ashton alone with Alex. He asked a few questions about Alex's travels but his mind kept wandering to all that his friends had told him. He could almost feel the chains the Hutton-Moores had wrapped him in falling away but he told himself not to hope for too much, too soon.

"Investments. Tricked into a betrothal and threatened to hold fast to it. A murderous madam. A pretty young woman who is being cheated of her rightful inheritance. You have been busy while I have been aroaming," teased Alex. "And am I right to assume that the fair Penelope would be your choice of bride if you are freed to make your own choice?"

"Yes, she would be. But even if we clear all this away, there will still be problems with marrying her." He told Alex about the Wherlockes, about Penelope's belief that she saw ghosts, and the fact that unless his investments turned a healthy profit, he would still need money.

"Ghosts, eh? Intriguing. As for the money, sell whatever is not entailed. You do not need to sacrifice yourself for us. No one would wish it. Yes, it would be good to be out from under this debt without losing everything to pay it off, but we can live well off the lands that are entailed and find ways to rebuild our fortunes."

"The girls need dowries, Alex. They need to get out in society and find husbands. That costs money. Belinda is three and twenty. She really cannot wait around a few more years until I can gather up enough to give her a modest dowry. Then there is Helen. Is she to wait until we can marry off Belinda and then some as I try to gather a dowry for her, too?" He shrugged. "At the moment, I must concern myself simply with getting out from beneath the thumb of Charles Hutton-Moore."

"Then I think it is past time the whole family gathered round to discuss all the ways we can collect what is needed without costing you your future. We have seen the hell of a bad, unhappy marriage, Ashton. If our father had not been away so much, chasing after every pretty ankle he caught a glimpse of, we would have lived it. Do not ask us to watch you walk into one for our sake. And there is one thing you have not seemed to consider."

"What?"

"If your Lady Penelope is being cheated of her inheritance, when it is returned to her hands, she just might be the bride you have been looking for."

Ashton stared at Alex in open-mouthed shock for a moment. "Well, hell."

Chapter Eleven

The light dimmed and Penelope found herself squinting in order to read her book. She looked up and realized the boys were no longer in view. Her brief surge of panic eased when she heard their laughter off to her left. She just hoped they were not troubling anyone. They were good boys and mature for their age, but they were still just boys, after all. One thing she had learned in the years she had been caring for the boys was that, if there was trouble out there, they would find it or it would find them.

She looked up at the sky to see that a cloud had covered the sun. It did not look like a storm cloud, but she could see that the sun was a lot farther down on the horizon than she had realized. That could explain why the park was suddenly so empty. Everyone had been leaving as she had been reading, heading home for the evening meal or to prepare for some social occasion. The park was not a safe place to be at night, either. It was past time that she gathered up the boys for the walk home.

In a moment, she decided, and smiled to herself. She was reluctant to leave the peace she had found in the park. Her chances to enjoy such a lazy few hours were few and far between. One day, she thought, she would have a house with large private gardens she could sit in. Or a place in the country. A place where the boys could run about outside on a good day and do so in safety, under the watchful eye of the servants she would be able to afford.

It was a pleasant dream. She sighed. It would be even more pleasant if she could place a husband within the gardens or playing with the boys. Perhaps even a child or two of her own. Obviously even her dreams did not want to give her the false hope that Radmoor might be hers someday. He might well get free of Clarissa but he could not get free of debt unless he had money, money from a rich bride. She would never be rich enough for him, even if she gained possession of the house her mother had left to her.

The laughter of the boys drew closer, pulling her out of her thoughts. Penelope looked in the direction the noise was coming from and saw them all running her way. She frowned when she saw a small, furry creature running with them. Penelope had just decided that it might be a dog when all the boys stumbled to a halt in front of the bench where she sat. She looked down at the creature that sat near her feet, panting. It was small, dirty, and a mix of so many breeds she doubted anyone would be able to discern its parentage. She braced herself for the question she dreaded.

"Can we keep him?" asked Olwen.

"We found him hiding in the bushes," said Jerome.

"I always wanted a dog," said Paul.

She made the mistake of looking at the boys. Blue eyes, green eyes, brown eyes, gray eyes, and amber eyes. All were wide, innocent, and so full of pleading and hope only a person made of stone could refuse them. Penelope knew she was not, even when she tried her hardest to be so.

She looked back down at the animal. Even the dirty, shaggy fur hanging over its eyes could not dim the power of them. The huge, sad brown eyes were the last nail in the coffin of her resolve.

"Are you certain it is a he? Even more important, are you certain it is actually a dog?" she asked.

"Of course it is a dog," said Paul and he giggled. "We think someone threw him away because he is not perfect."

Those words hit her like a stab to the heart. *Why does he not just cut my heart out with a spoon?* she thought. Each one of the boys standing before her had been "thrown away."

"You can feel all his bones when you pat him," Paul continued.

"I would rather you did not pat it until it has been thoroughly bathed. At least twice."

She reached into the basket she had brought with her and took out the bread. To her astonishment, the dog sat up straighter, its ragged ears lifting up as if in attention. It never took its eyes from the bread as she tore off a piece, but neither did it rush at her to grab some or bark. She tossed the piece of bread at the dog and it caught it. Unfortunately, that so delighted the boys that she knew she had lost all chance, if she had had any at all, of denying them the dog.

"Oh, let me feed him," cried Paul. "Please?"

Penelope handed Paul a large chunk of bread. "Do not make the pieces too big or it could choke."

"So? Can we keep the dog?" asked Olwen.

"You will care for it. If it messes in the house, you will clean it up. And it does not put one paw into the house until it is thoroughly scrubbed clean."

The boys all cheered and then began to take turns tossing the dog pieces of bread. Penelope had to smile as she watched them even though feeding a dog every day would probably lighten her already light purse a lot more. She glanced toward the sun again and decided she could give the boys a few minutes more to play before starting the long walk home.

Penelope frowned as her gaze swept by the small pond while she was turning to watch the boys again and she saw something out of the corner of her eyes. She stared at the pond to see what had caught her attention and softly cursed, recognizing what the misty figure standing at the edge of the murky water was. London was full of ghosts, but she wished they would find someone else to bother. The multitude of spirits cluttering up the city was but one more reason she would love a house in the country, she decided as she started toward the spirit. People died there, too, of course, but not in such numbers and certainly not with such constant tragedy.

The misty figure grew more distinct as she drew near to it. Another young woman, she thought, and felt the pinch of sorrow. It was always hard when it was the spirit of someone who had been alive for far too few years, if only because it was always so sad when the young died. Most of the time death for one so young had been so unexpected that the spirit refused to believe it had happened. It made it very difficult to convince them to relinquish all earthly chains.

Beware.

"Nick me! *Why* do you all say that? Beware *what? Who? When?*" Penelope took a deep breath and let it out slowly, knowing there was no point in getting angry with a ghost. "Why do you linger here?"

For my love. Love put me here. Love must join me.

"Your lover drowned you?"

My love will return and I will hold him again.

"If you hold him, he will drown." Penelope frowned. "Is that the reason you linger here? To get revenge? I do not think it will work." She looked the ghost over carefully. "From what little I can see, you are wearing clothing from at least fifty years ago. I would wager that your lover is already dead. If he murdered you, he is roasting in hell right now. Is that not revenge enough? Let go of your need to have revenge. Seek your peace."

Beware.

Not for the first time, Penelope heartily wished she could slap a ghost.

"Pe—ne—lo—pe!"

Penelope turned quickly upon hearing Paul's scream of panic. She saw nothing wrong with the child. He was racing toward her with no sign of any injury. That did not mean everything was well, however. Something could have happened to one of the other boys. She took a step toward him, sternly telling herself that Paul was just a five-year-old boy, and although a very clever little fellow, he was still prone to childish fears. Whatever was scaring him did not have to be so very bad.

"Fall down!"

She frowned at what she thought was a very foolish command. The other boys appeared behind Paul, running toward her as fast as he was, and echoing his cry that she fall down. The fear she had been trying to calm abruptly turned to annoyance. She was about to ask them what silly game they were playing when the dog veered off from the boys and raced for the thick clump of beech trees farther down the banks of the pond.

Penelope was just thinking that she ought to help the boys go after the foolish animal when there was a flash of light from within the small grove. Something slammed into her shoulder so hard that Penelope stumbled and fell on her backside.

A man screamed in pain and she wondered what he had to scream about as she was the one who had been struck with something. She looked at her shoulder in disbelief. Blood was rapidly soaking the front of her gown. Someone had just shot her. *Who would shoot a woman strolling about the park with half a dozen boys and a creature that thinks it's a dog?* she asked herself, dazed by what had happened to her.

Pain tore through her body but she grabbed Paul as he ran up to her and pinned him to the ground beneath her. "Get down!" she screamed at the other boys. "Now! Down on the ground!"

Penelope saw them all fall to the ground and silently thanked God that they were obedient when it truly mattered. She looked toward the trees but could see nothing. Despite the way the pain was making her head spin, she caught the faint sound of a fleeing horse. A moment later the little dog burst from the cover of the trees and ran toward them with something in his mouth.

He is gone.

"Pen, you are bleeding on me," said Paul in a trembling voice.

She rolled off him and sprawled on her back, taking deep breaths in a vain attempt to ease the pain. Penelope knew she had to get the boys to safety but she was not sure how fast she could move. She looked at the ghost, who was slowly fading into the late-day fog forming on the pond.

"Would it really have been so hard for you to say, *Beware, there is a man in the trees with a pistol*"? she asked.

It is not over.

"Nick me, that was helpful," she muttered as the boys gathered around her. "Just give me a moment or two," she told them, "and we will go home." Not one of them looked as if they believed her. She did not believe herself, either.

Hector looked at the blood flowing from her wound. "You need care right now, Pen. Radmoor lives right over there." He pointed in the direction of Radmoor's home. "Paul, come with me. Radmoor can help us."

Before she could protest Hector's plan, he and Paul were running away. The dog sat down near her head and she frowned at what was hanging from his mouth. It looked to be part of the front flap of a man's breeches. That would certainly explain that scream of pain, she thought and almost smiled.

"Pen, what can we do?" asked Olwen as he knelt by her and took her hand in his.

"One of you find a clean bit of cloth and press it to the wound to help stop the blood from flowing," she answered, fighting hard to hold back the blackness creeping into her mind. "Once it stops," she continued, "we can leave here." She knew it was a lie but they all looked so frightened, she felt compelled to try and lift their spirits.

Jerome raced to the bench where she had been enjoying the peace of the park only a short time ago. He returned with her basket, took the scrap of linen she had draped over the top, and pressed it against her wound. Penelope nearly lost her battle against the encroaching darkness as pain seared through her. She clenched her teeth to stop a cry of pain but could not fully restrain a moan.

"I am hurting you," cried Jerome and he started to pull away.

"Nay, do not stop. It hurts no matter what you do, love," she said, "but the bleeding must stop. Hellfire, it hurts with me just lying here and trying to breathe. It is not your fault."

"Radmoor will soon come and help us," said Olwen as he patted her hand.

Penelope tried to smile at him but suspected it looked more like a grimace. The damp of the ground was soaking into her clothes but she knew that was not the only reason she was shivering. Shock was undoubtedly another cause, as was the loss of blood. She continued to take deep breaths but the pain was like a living thing writhing inside her. She knew she was too weak to get the boys away from here and began to pray that Ashton was home.

A disturbance in the hall cut short the discussion of investments Ashton was having with Alex. He started to rise, intending to go and see what the problem was, when the door to his study was slammed open. Hector and Paul raced in followed by a breathless Marston. The boys ran up to Ashton and grabbed his hands. That was when Ashton saw the blood on Paul's clothes.

"Hold, Marston," he ordered his butler and wrenched his hands free of the boys' hold to crouch down and grasp Paul by the shoulders. "Where are you hurt, child?"

"'Tis not my blood," Paul said, tears leaving pale streaks through the dirt on his face. "'Tis Pen's."

Ashton felt his heart actually falter in its steady beat. "Penelope is hurt?"

"In the park. Someone shot her. I was trying to warn her, to get her to lie down so she would be safe, but I must have done it wrong again. She has a big hole in her and was bleeding all over me when she pushed me down and the dog ran after the man who shot her but he got away and . . ." Paul stuttered to halt when Ashton placed one long finger over his lips.

"Is she alive?" he asked, fighting to keep his voice calm despite the panic gnawing at his insides.

Paul nodded.

"Where is she now?"

"In the park. Near the pond," answered Hector.

"Alex, ready a carriage," he ordered his brother as he stood up. "And a horse so that you can ride ahead of us with one of the boys and fetch Doctor Pryne." He started out of the room, the two boys close at his heels.

"Ride to where?" asked Alex as he hurried to follow them.

"The boy who goes with you can tell you where. Marston, tell the viscountess that there was an emergency I needed to tend to and that I do not know when I will return."

Once outside, Ashton began to run, not caring what his neighbors would think if they saw him. Only once did he pause in his race to Penelope's side, and that was to pick up a staggering Paul. The sight of Penelope on the ground, the other boys crowded around her, sent fear and rage careening through his body. When he found out who had done this, he would kill him. Slowly.

He gently nudged aside the white-faced boy holding a blood-soaked cloth against Penelope's left shoulder. "You did well, lad," he said as he tossed the cloth aside and replaced it with his handkerchief.

"Sorry to be such a bother," Penelope said, wondering if her voice sounded as weak and unsteady to them as it did to her.

"Idiot," he muttered.

Bracing himself against the pain he knew he would cause her, he lifted her enough to see if the bullet had exited her body or if it would need to be cut out of her. The relief he felt when he saw that the bullet had passed straight through was so strong he was glad he was already kneeling on the ground. It would have been humiliating to fall to his knees before the boys. It certainly would have done nothing to ease the fear he could see on all their faces.

He tore a strip off her petticoat, made a second pad to press against the wound on the back of her shoulder, and tied both pads in place with his stock. She made little sound aside from grinding her teeth, despite the pain he knew he was inflicting. By the time he was done, she was as pale as one of her ghosts and panting softly, the sheen of a light sweat upon her face.

"Ashton, get that piece of cloth from the dog," she rasped.

He looked at the filthy mongrel sitting near her head. "Are you sure that is a dog?" To his amazement, she laughed a little. "It went after the bastard, did it?" He gently tugged the scrap of material from the dog's mouth. "This is from the front placket of a man's breeches. And the buttons are silver." Ashton looked closely at the dog's mouth and saw a little blood on the dirty face. He winced. "That will be a wound it will be difficult to watch for."

"Oh, cruel man to make me want to laugh." Penelope frowned as a man stepped up behind Ashton. "I think I have lost too much blood, Ashton, for I am seeing two of you."

Ashton glanced back at Alex. "'Tis just my brother, Alexander. Did you bring the carriage?" he asked Alex.

"'Tis but a few feet behind me," drawled Alex.

"Ah, so it is. My apologies. I was obviously too enraptured by your handsome face to notice it." Ashton was pleased to hear the boys snicker, some of the fear on their faces fading. He then looked at Penelope. "I fear this will hurt."

"Everything hurts. What are you going to do?" she asked.

"Pick you up," he replied even as he did so.

Penelope knew he was being as gentle as he could be, but the pain shooting through her made her curse. She rested her head against Ashton's shoulder and struggled to wrestle the pain into submission. What she really wanted to do was give in to the darkness that promised her a respite from the pain, perhaps even scream, but she did not want to frighten the boys any more than they were now.

"Ashton," she whispered as he walked to the carriage, "if I should die—"

"You will *not* die."

"Just promise me that you will see that the boys are cared for."

He opened his mouth to argue with her and then decided against it. They were all frightened and an argument now could quickly become nonsensical. Nor did he want to hear her speak any further of dying.

"I promise."

"Thank you. They all know who their fathers are and that should be a help."

"Quiet. I promised. I do not wish to speak on that."

Penelope did not really wish to speak of dying, either, but she could not leave matters unsettled. His promise was enough to let her cease worrying about her boys. She knew Ashton was a man who would hold to his word. With her mind freed of that concern, the blackness she had been fighting swept over her and dragged her down into its depths.

Ashton felt Penelope go limp in his arms and looked down at her. The sight of her chest moving soothed away the panic that had rushed up to choke him. He was glad she had swooned. The ride in the carriage and getting her settled in a bed were going to add to her pain no matter how careful he was. Unconscious as she was now, there was a chance she would be unaware of it and he could only be grateful for that.

"It should not be fatal," said Doctor Pryne as he scrubbed his hands clean. "Just watch closely for a fever to set in. That could be. But she is a healthy young woman and that is strongly in her favor."

"What should I do if she does grow feverish?" asked Ashton.

"You? You mean to care for the girl, do you?"

"I do." Ashton did not care what the doctor thought; he was not going to leave Penelope until he was certain she was healed.

"First, send someone for me. I will tell you what is needed then. Having you care for her could ruin her, you know."

"Sir, she has a house where she cares for her family's bastards. As far as society is concerned, she is utterly ruined already."

"Hypocritical fools."

"You will get no argument from me on that. She only has the boys here to care for her. They may be clever lads, and far more mature for their age than many another, but they are still just boys. And except for her brothers, they see her as their mother."

Doctor Pryne shook his head. "You have the right of it. Well, get as much food and drink down her as you can. Broth or a very light meal of some bread and jam. Anything that is not too heavy. She will need that to keep her strength up." He idly touched the damp, muddy gown Ashton had flung over a chair when he had undressed her. "How did she get so damp?"

"The ground was damp and she was lying on it for a while ere I arrived. That is not good, is it?"

"No, but as I said, she is a young, healthy woman. Know who shot her? It was not an accident. Do not try to gull me. Who would want the lass dead? And that is what they wanted, for if that shot had gone a little to the right, it would have gone right through her heart."

That was something Ashton was all too aware of and it chilled him to the marrow of his bones. "I am not sure." He sighed when the man scowled at him. "I will not point a finger until I am, if only because that could send the bastard to ground. There are a number of us trying to find out, unceasingly searching for that proof. If he thinks we suspect him, the proof we need could easily disappear right along with him."

"Well, get it soon. A crack on the head and now a bullet wound. She has been lucky so far but that luck could soon run out."

The moment the door shut behind the doctor, Ashton sat down beside the bed and took Penelope's hand in his. He kissed her palm and held her small hand against his cheek. She gave no sign that she felt his caress. She had made little sound as the man had tended her wound and yet she had to have felt something. By the time Septimus had returned, his touch was not needed for Penelope had escaped the worst of her pain in her own way. It was as if she had pulled her spirit so deep inside herself that she was completely unaware of everything around her. Ashton was grateful that she might not have felt the pain but her utter stillness bothered him.

Her brothers entered the room and Ashton reluctantly gave up his place by the bedside. He decided to take the time to speak to Alex and get something to eat. From what little he knew about such things, caring for Penelope was going to take a lot of time and strength.

He found Alex sitting in the parlor with all the rest of the boys and Septimus. Ashton told them everything the doctor had said and soon found himself alone in the room with Alex. After a brief search of the room he found a bottle of wine and poured himself and Alex a drink. Just as he handed his brother the drink, Mrs. Stark bustled in with a tray loaded with bread, meats, and cheese. He thanked her profusely and gave her enough coin to stock the pantry with such items for he knew they would be needed over the next few days.

"You look too worried for a man who just heard that the wound is not a fatal one," said Alex when Mrs. Stark left them and he joined Ashton in helping himself to some of the food.

"She is too deeply asleep, or unconscious, for my liking." Ashton shrugged. "Yet that may be for the best. As far as I can tell, she was feeling very little of the pain the doctor had to inflict as he cleaned and stitched her wound. When Septimus returned and placed his hands on her, he said it was so." At Alex's curious look, he briefly explained what Septimus was rumored to be skilled at. "Not sure I believe he can take away pain, but I was not about to stop him from trying. She seems to have taken herself away from the pain. I but fear she may have gone too far, if that makes any sense."

"It does and 'tis a skill many probably wish they had. At the moment, the depth of her sleep is a small worry, however. Ashton, someone wanted her dead. Just as they did when they tried to run her down with the carriage."

"I know. I believe the carriage incident can be blamed on Mrs. Cratchitt, but this? This, I believe, is the work of the Hutton-Moores. Whether Charles himself tried to kill her or hired someone to do it does not matter. I cannot help but fear that he has already caught wind of the fact that someone is digging into his affairs. What better way to stop that and any possible troubles it might cause him than to be rid of the one who stands between him and what he wants."

"He would kill her for that house?"

Ashton shrugged. "Many have killed for far less. However, there may have been more left to her than that house and he has stolen it. He would not want that to be discovered."

"Lady Penelope is the one you want, is she not? Mayhap Charles has gotten wind of that."

"It is possible. Penelope thinks he does not know about this place, however."

"Penelope could be wrong."

It was possible, Ashton thought. Just because the man had not confronted her here or stopped her visits did not mean he did not know about the place. It would explain how Charles would have known where to find her so that she could be kidnapped and taken to Mrs. Cratchitt's. Ashton cursed as he immediately recognized the truth of that supposition. Charles knew; the man just had not yet bothered to do anything about it. At least not openly.

"He knows," he said to Alex. "The bastard has probably known exactly where she goes since the beginning. The danger to Penelope is that she does not know that."

"If Charles is guilty of all we think he is, then there should be some protection here. She does not even have a maid."

"No money for one. I would send a few of our servants here but I am not sure she would allow it. She has her pride."

"We can understand that well enough, can we not? She must be made to swallow it, however. It is not just her life at stake here."

"Very true and that will be the argument I will use."

Ashton was startled when Artemis burst into the room, but one look at the boy's pale face was enough to bring him to his feet. "What is wrong?"

"Fever."

Chapter Twelve

"So this is your emergency."

"Mother!"

Ashton stared in open-mouthed shock at the sight of his mother standing in the doorway, all the boys crowding behind her. Right behind the boys stood Alex. His brother shrugged. Ashton supposed he should not be so surprised that his mother would wonder where he and Alex had disappeared to after three days' absence. He had never considered the possibility that she would hunt him down, however.

"Is this where you have been for three days?" she asked.

"Yes." Ashton dipped the rag he held into the basin of cool water on the bedside table, wrung it out, and gently placed it back on Penelope's fevered forehead. "She was shot. The bullet went straight through but, either because she lost a great deal of blood or she caught a chill from the damp ground she was lying on, she has taken a fever. I thought of hiring someone to care for her, but decided the safest thing to do was to attend to her myself with the help of the boys. I do not know who shot her, you see."

Lady Mary moved to the side of the bed and looked down at the fevered young woman lying there as still as death. "Who would want to shoot her?"

"I told you, I do not know. I only have a few ideas and suspicions. No proof."

"There are a lot of us looking for that proof, however," said Alex as he stepped up beside his mother.

"How did you find us?" Ashton asked.

"The coachman." A movement by her feet caused Lady Mary to look down. Big brown eyes stared up at her through long speckled fur. "What is this?"

"A dog," replied Ashton, smiling faintly at his mother's look of doubt.

"We call him Killer because he charged after the man who shot Pen and bit the bastard right in his manly parts. I am Paul." Paul smiled up at her. "I am Orion's by-blow."

"Out. All of you out," said Alex and he began to clear the room of the boys who had slipped inside. "I will see if Mrs. Stark can make some tea for you," he told his mother and shepherded the boys out of the doorway.

Once the door shut behind Alex and the boys, Lady Mary looked at her eldest son. "That child looks and sounds as if he ought to be singing in the church choir. Until you hear what he says, that is. Manly parts? By-blow? Cursing?"

"I have begun to think that Paul says such things because he likes to shock people," Ashton said.

"Huh." Lady Mary removed her gloves, hat, and coat and set them down on a chair near the fireplace. "Is this

Lady Penelope? And she was truly shot?" When Ashton nodded, she shook her head. "Is she the only one who takes care of all those boys?"

"She has her two brothers, who are sixteen and fourteen years of age, plus Darius, who is thirteen, who help her." He silently prayed that his mother did not find out that those three boys spent a lot of time spying on a brothel. "Then there is the boys' tutor, Septimus Vaughn. Although I believe he is but newly out of Oxford."

"What about this Mrs. Stark?"

"She is the maid-of-all-work and only comes in for the day. The woman would help care for Penelope but she has an ailing daughter and six grandchildren to care for now. At times she cannot even come in for the day but she sends some food for them all."

"It is too much for this girl. Her relatives should be ashamed of themselves. When you spoke of it before, I had not realized that it was just her ruling over that pack."

"I agree that her family should be ashamed. The least they could do is hire some help for her."

"How long has she been feverish?"

"Since late the night of the shooting."

"Not so very long then. I have brought some clothing for you and Alex. And myself."

"Yourself?"

"I have come to help care for her."

"But—"

Lady Mary moved to his side and patted him on the shoulder. "She needs a woman's care, if only for her own sake. Think of how uncomfortable she will be when she awakes and realizes you were the only one at her side while she was too sick to see to her own needs."

Ashton sighed and nodded, knowing there was no argument he could make to that good sense. "I know *I* would feel so if the situation was reversed. You should not have to do it all either, however."

"I have every intention of letting you and the older boys do your share. Ah, here is our tea," she said, smiling at Alex as he entered and set the tray he carried down on the table near the fireplace.

At his mother's coaxing, Ashton left Penelope's side to share in the tea and a light repast with her and Alex. He was torn concerning his mother's presence. It would be good to have her tend to Penelope's more personal needs, but he found he also resented her interference a little. He wanted to be at Penelope's side round the clock as if he could personally fend off death himself. He decided he was badly in need of some rest if he could even think such a ridiculous thought.

By the time they finished their tea, his mother was in possession of every fact and rumor Ashton had. He was stunned that he had told her so much. It had even been difficult to hold back the truth of what was between him and Penelope. Her interrogation skills were astonishing. Ashton wished he could set her after the Hutton-Moores but he could never place his own mother in such danger, no matter how good the cause.

"Are you certain you should do this?" Ashton asked when she had him fetch her some writing materials so that she could make a list of what she needed to nurse Penelope.

"This is not the sort of fever one can catch," she said.

"I know, but taking care of someone this ill is an exhausting business." He waited to see how she would respond as she finished what appeared to be a very long list.

"Have the boys help you fetch these things for me," she said as she handed the list to Alex, who quickly left. She then looked at Ashton. "I have six children, dear.

Amongst the lot of you, you have contracted all manner of ills, broken bones, and gory wounds. However, I do believe I shall send for Aunt Honora."

"Would not Aunt Sarah be a better choice? She is stronger and, well, more sensible."

"Quite true, which is why she must stay to keep your siblings in line. Honora is very good at nursing the ill, Ashton. She nursed me through a childbed fever after I had Alexander." She stood up and walked to the bed. "Who is the doctor who tended the wound?" she asked as she uncovered Penelope's wound and studied it closely.

"Doctor Pryne."

"Roger Pryne?"

"I do not know the man's Christian name. Big man, graying brown hair, and a blunt way of speaking. Do you think you know him?"

"From that description, I feel sure I know him. An old school friend of mine married him." She sighed. "She is dead now. So sad it was, too. Not even five and thirty and she fell dead. A weak heart. What did he have to say about this wound and this fever?"

"The wound should not be mortal but the fever could be. He left the makings for a willow bark tea and told me to bathe her with cool water. Nothing more."

Lady Mary bandaged the wound again. "There is nothing more to do really. Do not look so worried, dear. I do not know this girl, but from all you have told me, she sounds as if she has the strength needed to fight this. No woman who could watch over ten boys and survive could ever be weak. Now, I need you to answer a few questions for me."

Ashton did his best as she proceeded to bombard him with questions. Some were of such a personal nature concerning Penelope that he felt himself blush like a schoolboy. It was one thing to take care of her personal needs when she was insensible, quite another to talk about them. However, when his mother ordered him to go and get some rest, he did so with as easy a mind as he could with Penelope still so ill. He did it because he knew his mother would fight as hard for Penelope's life as he did, and with a lot more skill. Together they would save her. He would not allow himself to think anything else.

Penelope winced. Her body ached all over. She struggled to remember what had happened before she had gone to bed. And why was she all alone? Why was Ashton not sleeping at her side? Had she slept through his leave taking?

Memories of the park returned in a rush and she nearly gasped. Someone had shot her. Keeping her eyes closed and her body still, she tried to concentrate on that wound. It ached, but no more than that, although she suspected it would hurt if she moved her arm. Her other aches had probably come from falling onto the ground after she was shot. She swallowed the panic that had stirred at the memory of that bullet tearing through her shoulder.

Her next thought was that she was thirsty. Very, very thirsty. Her mouth felt as if it had been stuffed full of wool, musty wool at that. She was suddenly desperate to rinse out her mouth and clean her teeth, certain she would feel so much better if she did so.

She cautiously opened her eyes and looked around. Even though her vision was a little blurry, she could see that she was in her own room in the Wherlocke Warren, much to her relief. As her eyes cleared of sleep's lingering haze, she gaped and could not fully restrain a gasp.

There was a woman sitting by her bed sewing what looked very much like one of the boys' shirts. A pretty, older woman dressed sedately but in clothes obviously made by one of society's best dressmakers. The woman suddenly looked at her and smiled. Penelope felt herself blush beneath the steady, sharp look in the woman's big, blue eyes.

"Ah, very good. You are awake," the woman said. "I am Lady Radmoor, Ashton's mother. You may call me Lady Mary. And I am not pressing you into any great intimacy with me by saying that. After my first year of marriage, I simply refused to answer to Lady Harold. But we can talk later. I suspect you need a drink and you would dearly like to clean that nasty taste out of your mouth." Lady Mary poured Penelope some cider and helped her to drink it down slowly. "Five days of fighting a fever and one of sleeping has probably left you feeling as if the army has tramped through your mouth in muddy boots."

Penelope was too stunned to say anything. She felt like a lifeless doll the woman played with as Lady Mary gave her what was needed to clean her mouth, brushed out her hair, and sponged her body clean. It was not until the woman had dressed her in a fresh night shift and tied a ribbon in her hair that Penelope finally shook free of her tongue-tying shock. Although the realization that a viscountess had just acted the maid for her threatened to shock her senseless all over again.

"It has been five, nay, six days since I was shot?" she finally asked in utter disbelief.

Lady Mary placed a tray of sliced apples and lightly buttered bread on Penelope's lap. "Eat some of this. Very slowly. I know Roger"—she blushed faintly—"er, Doctor Pryne prefers a patient to have broth, but he does not forbid a few foods that are gentle on the stomach. I strongly believe they are good for you, too." She sat down by the bed again. "You became fevered the very night you were shot. A few hours after you were brought home. The doctor believes that lying upon the ground as you did, and getting quite damp, together with your wound, is why the fever grabbed hold of you and would not let go. It is always damp by that pond. Then, of course, there is the fact that you had only recently recovered from another serious wound. You had not had enough time to regain your full strength, I suspect."

Penelope nodded slowly, recalling the chill damp that had slowly seeped through her clothes. She desperately wanted to ask where Ashton was. Her memories of the time since being shot consisted of brief, spotty visions of his face, of pain, and of heat. They could be memories of fevered dreams but she did not think so.

"Ro—Doctor Pryne said only that you were young and healthy and should be able to fight the fever. As the days wore on and your fever did not break, I fear Ashton grew a little short with the man. But the doctor proved correct. You had to fight the fever in your own way and in your own time. The wound never festered. In truth, it continued to heal very nicely, with quite astonishing speed. If not for the fever, one would think that you simply slept through the worst of it."

Ashton had been with her, she thought, and was dangerously pleased by that. The way Lady Radmoor kept stumbling over Doctor Pryne's name, nearly calling him by his Christian name every time she spoke of him, stirred Penelope's curiosity. She bit into a slice of apple and chewed slowly to stop herself from asking a few very impertinent questions.

"You are undoubtedly wondering why I am here," said Lady Mary.

Her mouth full of apple, Penelope just nodded.

"When Alexander and Ashton disappeared for almost three days, I decided I had to hunt them down. They are grown men, and like it or not, I know they are wont to, well, go off to indulge themselves, shall we say. However, they have never just abruptly disappeared. The only word I had from Ashton was that he had an emergency to tend to and that he did not know when he would return. Marston, our butler, told me that Alex went with Ashton. I finally got the whole tale of the two boys coming to the house and everyone racing to the park, and then confronted our coachman."

Penelope had to admire such persistence. "I am sorry they left you to worry so."

Lady Mary waved an elegant, beringed hand in the air. "'Tis the way of men. This time Ashton had a good reason so I did not box his ears." She grinned when Penelope laughed, but quickly grew serious again. "You were fevered, child, and he stayed to care for you. Alex stayed to help with the boys. What mother could fault them for that? However, I took over as is my wont. Ashton helped immensely, but I brought the much-needed woman's touch as did Honora, Ashton's aunt. With three of us working through the day and night, matters went much more smoothly. We even had the strength to help Alex and that lovely young man, Septimus, care for the boys."

"I hope they did not give you too much trouble." The idea of having so many people not familiar with her family's many *differences* lurking around the Warren made Penelope very nervous.

"No more than any other pack of boys. Quite a bit less, actually. I believe they were on their best behavior because of you. They do love you quite fiercely, my dear," she added softly and grinned when Penelope blushed. "Being boys, I suspect they do not say so, but trust me to know, they most certainly do. They were always slipping into the room to watch you breathe. Mostly the young ones, but your brothers and Darius did the same a time or two. For the younger boys, you are their mother for all that they call you Pen or cousin. Especially little Paul." She frowned. "Ashton told me the boy slept at the foot of the bed for the first three days or just outside the door. It was in the afternoon on the day I arrived that the fear you would die abruptly left him. He stated quite confidently that you would not join Mrs. Pettibone." She glanced around. "Is the woman still here?"

There were obviously few secrets left, thought Penelope. She supposed she ought to be grateful Lady Mary had not run from the house screaming about witches. Penelope looked toward where Mrs. Pettibone's misty form was seated by the fireplace. The woman's daughters must have returned by now so there had to be some other reason the woman's spirit lingered. She would have to solve that puzzle later, when she was stronger, and when some of her own troubles were cleared away.

"I fear so," Penelope said, almost smiling at the way Lady Mary was squinting toward the fireplace in an obvious attempt to try and see what she did. "Some spirits feel a need to linger here, to finish something. Soon I will solve the puzzle and then Mrs. Pettibone's spirit will find peace. She is quite harmless."

"You can truly see them then," Lady Mary said quietly. "Are there a lot of them?"

"In London there are quite a few."

"Well, that is no surprise, I suppose. I have always thought that, when we died, our spirit immediately went up or down."

"Most do. As I said, some linger because they feel a need to finish something. Some of their reasons for lingering are not always good ones, such as anger or revenge. Some are merely confused, unaware or uncertain of what has happened to them. Some are just not ready to give up earthly things even if they cannot touch or taste them." She shrugged and was somewhat surprised by how little the movement hurt her. "I have yet to meet a truly evil spirit. 'Tis my belief that hell does not let many escape its grasp, does not allow them to dawdle, if you will."

When Lady Mary nodded as if Penelope's words made perfect sense to her, Penelope sighed inwardly with relief. The last thing she wished to do was terrify Ashton's mother. "You are not afraid, are you."

"No. I am not absolutely certain I believe in such things but it all quite fascinates me. I can see why you try so hard to keep it all a secret from the rest of the world. Some would be afraid, and fear can be a dangerous thing." She grinned. "I will admit that I was a little unsettled when young Jerome got angry and things began to move about on their own."

"Oh." What a poor time for Jerome's gift to decide to bloom. "I was rather hoping that particular talent had eluded the boys."

Lady Mary stood up, took away the empty tray, and helped Penelope have some more to drink. "It is all most intriguing. I will say that I became more of a believer when I saw what Jerome did. Your brother Stefan moved quickly to put a stop to it." She set the empty tankard aside. "I can see how such things can have caused your family untold tragedy, yet it must be fascinating to live within a family blessed with so many miraculous gifts."

Penelope blinked slowly. She had never quite looked at it that way. Someday she might be able to, if she thought on the matter for a long time. Now she found it hard to forget the tragic side, especially in a house full of children cast aside by their own mothers. She was startled when Lady Mary patted her hand in a comforting gesture.

"Someday, child, when fear and superstition fade away," the woman said, "it will all be seen as the blessing it is."

The door to the room opened, ending Penelope's scramble for a polite response. Ashton and Paul entered, the dog trotting in right behind them. Penelope tried to keep her smile for Ashton one of simple greeting. She suspected Ashton's mother knew exactly what was, or had been, happening between her and Ashton, but Penelope saw no sense in openly admitting to it by word or deed. Lady Mary was a very kind woman, from what Penelope could tell, but the Radmoor family's future depended strongly on Ashton marrying an heiress. She could certainly not tell Ashton's mother that she accepted that hard truth but was bedding her son despite it. Penelope then noticed the small, ornate box Paul was carrying. It was her mother's jewelry chest.

"Paul, where did you get that?" she asked. She had thought it safely stored in her desk in their small library.

"I found it in the library," he replied as he set it down in the bed. "I thought you might want to wear something pretty. It might make you feel even better."

He opened the little chest of her mother's jewels and smiled at her. Lady Mary gasped softly. Penelope looked at Ashton, who merely cocked one brow in silent query.

Penelope sighed. "I did not steal them. They were my mother's and willed to me. I may not know much about the will and its reading but that much I do recall. The house and these jewels are mine. Every last piece in this box was bought by my father. Most to get back into her good graces when she heard about one of his affairs. Clarissa took them. I took them back. There are a few pieces missing but I will find them, too, when the opportunity arises." She poked through the box and pulled out a diamond and sapphire necklace. "Papa gave this to Mama on their wedding day. After his second affair, she put it in here and never wore it again."

Lady Mary leaned over the bed to touch the necklace. "It is lovely. I have always loved diamonds. Loved them too much to put them aside just because the man who gave them to me was a faithless cur. One particular necklace was always my favorite."

"But you never wear that anymore, Mother," Ashton said, desperately trying to turn his mind away from the mercenary wish that the box of jewels was bountiful enough to give Penelope the dowry he so desperately needed.

"You will wear them again," said Paul, smiling at Lady Mary. "You will get them back and a lot more, too."

Ashton saw how his mother stared at Paul in shock yet had the light flush of guilt in her cheeks. "Get them back?"

"Aye," said Paul when Lady Mary just stuttered out a few incomprehensible words. "Her ship has not sunk like everyone thinks. It was in a big storm but it just pushed the ship in the wrong direction."

"Mother? Did you sell your diamonds and invest in some shipping venture?"

Before his mother could reply, there was the sound of a contretemps in the downstairs hall. Afraid it might be some other threat to Penelope, Ashton ordered the women and Paul to stay there and hurried out of the room. He did not know whether to be angry with his mother for selling her diamonds without telling him or pleased that she had tried her best to help him. As he reached the bottom of the stairs, the man the boys were trying to keep out pushed the door wide open. The sight of Lord Charles Hutton-Moore at the door of the Wherlocke Warren was enough to banish all thoughts of his mother, precious family heirlooms being pawned, and secret investments right out of his head.

"So this is where you have been hiding," said Charles, lowering the cane he had obviously raised to swing at the boys. "Clarissa will not be pleased."

"I am not hiding, merely visiting these boys. Is there a reason for your visit, other than spying on me, m'lord?" Ashton asked.

Ashton studied Charles. The man was probably considered quite handsome by the ladies. Charles was big and strong with thick fair hair and clear blue eyes. He was also venal, sly, and, Ashton now knew, dangerous.

"Spying on you?" Charles smiled. "Not at all. I but seek word of my sister. Stepsister, if I must be truthful. Papa adopted the chit but it does make her m'sister. Lady Penelope Wherlocke? She spends a great deal of time here. I have allowed her to indulge in her little charity but she has never been gone for nearly a week. At first I thought she was staying away because she and Clarissa had an argument, but thought on how that has happened before, and again, Penelope has never stayed away for so long."

"Perhaps she but grew weary of sleeping in the attics." Ashton smiled faintly when Charles's eyes narrowed.

"Our family troubles are not yet your concern. As I said, Penelope has been missing for far too long. I grew increasingly concerned when I heard that there had been an attack upon a woman in the park near me. I merely wish to see for myself that she is unharmed."

A quick glance at Hector was all Ashton needed to confirm his opinion that Charles was lying through his teeth. The man was concerned that his attack on

Penelope had failed. Charles needed a body to prove his right to openly take everything that was rightfully Penelope's. Ashton wanted to throw the man out but resisted the urge. It was not just because the man held the late viscount's debts over his head, either. Charles was Penelope's guardian. Until she married, became of age, or was freed from his hold by her family and the courts, Charles had the law on his side. There would be some pleasure in showing the man that he had failed in his attempt to be rid of Penelope, but that would be severely dimmed by the knowledge that she would continue to be in danger.

"She has not been well," Ashton began, knowing it was a futile attempt to hold the man back.

"Ah, I see. Since you have also been conspicuously absent during this time, am I to understand that *you* have been caring for my ward?"

"Do not be foolish, m'lord," said Aunt Honora as she stepped out of the parlor, Alex at her back. "What man is capable of caring for someone who is ill? I and Lady Radmoor have had that honor." She looked at Ashton. "Perhaps you should take him to see his ward, dear. She cannot be moved yet, but he should be shown what good care she is getting. That should ease his mind."

A little stunned by how bravely his timid aunt Honora had just faced down Charles, Ashton nodded and started up the stairs. He signaled Charles to follow him with a negligent flick of his hand. The man walked through the silently glaring boys lined up on either side of the hall and Ashton was certain Charles had grown a little pale. It would be no surprise if he had. The fury in the gazes the boys sent Charles's way would make anyone uneasy. He also noticed that, subtle though it was, Charles had an odd gait, like a man who had suffered an injury to his more private parts. He was sorely tempted to see for himself it that injury was a bite from a dog.

Ashton just hoped that seeing Charles did not cause the barely recovered Penelope to regress. He was not sure of everything that had happened to her under Charles's roof but knew she had no fondness at all for her stepsiblings. The sound of rapidly retreating footsteps told him that she would be warned of the coming confrontation, however, and that had to be enough.

"'Tis Charles," said Paul as he tumbled into the room. "He has found us."

Penelope suspected the man had known about the Warren for a long time but she could not worry about that now. "Here, Paul, shove this under the bed," she ordered as she shut the box holding her mother's jewels and handed it to him.

She slumped back against the pillows Lady Mary had plumped up behind her, wearied by her moment of panic. Penelope was surprised when Lady Mary shifted her seat closer to the bed and took her hand. The woman intended to show Charles that there was a united front against him. She wanted to tell Lady Mary that was a dangerous stand to take, but before she could get the words out, Ashton walked in with Charles right behind him.

One look at her stepbrother was enough to make Penelope very glad for Lady Mary's support. She was fleetingly amused to see Mrs. Pettibone's spirit draw near the bed and face Charles. That flicker of good humor died a quick death when she met Charles's ice-cold gaze.

For a while Charles was all that was pleasant and gentlemanly. With a tone of deep concern he asked about her injuries and her health. His declaration that something needed to be done to catch the miscreant who had assaulted her was perfect in tone and in delivery. He even exchanged a little pleasant gossip with Lady Mary. Throughout it all, from beneath the bed, came a soft growl.

Penelope ignored the possible implications of the dog's hostility toward Charles and waited for the axe to fall. It was Charles's way to lull his victims into a state of calm with idle chatter and charm and then slap them hard with a piercing question or a bludgeoning statement. The moment he turned his well-practiced smile on her, she braced for it, determined to give nothing away in word or expression.

"You must thank the Radmoors most kindly for their help, my dear," he said, "as I have done. Then, once you are dressed, I shall take you home."

"No, Lord Hutton-Moore," said Lady Mary in a firm voice, "that will not do. Not at all. Penelope has but recently roused from a debilitating fever. To move her anywhere now could bring it back. As weak as she is from conquering the last bout, another would easily kill her. Since I am certain you do not wish her death on your hands, it would be best if you left her right here until her doctor says she may leave her bed."

Penelope saw the faint tick in Charles's cheek that indicated he was straining to control his temper. He was not accustomed to being thwarted. There was nothing he could do, however. Not only was Lady Mary right, but she was far higher born than he and arguing with her could easily prove to be social suicide. He could not even threaten Lady Mary with her late husband's markers for he had already used that tactic on Ashton. To try and wield that club on Ashton's mother, who had to already know about it yet still gave him orders, would be a complete waste of time. To try and dun a woman under such conditions, especially with the head of the household alive, would also be a grievous faux pas and he could not be sure that it would go unspoken of. Penelope nearly fainted from the strength of the relief that swept over her when, after a rather curt farewell, Charles left.

"That man did not come here out of any concern for you," said Lady Mary.

"Nay," agreed Penelope. "He came to see the body. He may not have pulled the trigger of the pistol used to shoot me, but he is definitely the one who put it in the hands of the one who did." She glanced at the way Killer eyed the door, the dog's whole small body still tensed to attack. "I believe, however, that he *was* the one who shot me."

"I do as well," said Ashton. "He now has an odd gait which could easily be from a rather, er, intimate dog bite."

Lady Mary looked at her son. "I think it is time you got some help from people who deal with criminals every day. A constable, or thief taker, or one of those fellows from that office on Bow Street. They help find criminals, do they not? If naught else, they could help to protect Penelope and the boys while you continue to seek out the truth."

Ashton nodded. "The moment I saw him at the door, I knew more needed to be done."

"Do you think he would try to hurt the boys?" Penelope asked.

"I think that man is not above using whatever is needed to get what he wants."

"Damn."

There was no more to say, for Ashton was absolutely right. Penelope had known from the day she had stood by her mother's grave that her stepsiblings did not want to share anything with her, even what was rightfully hers. As she had grown older, she had begun to fear that they would never let her reach the age of five and twenty or marry, but it had not been something she thought on for too long or too often. She had believed herself prepared for the hard truth that her stepsiblings wanted her dead, but it was still a bit of a shock. However, she could not wallow in self-pity. She had to get better, had to regain her strength as swiftly as possible, because now she truly was in a fight for her life.

Chapter Thirteen

Penelope heard a rap on the door and started to rise to answer it, only to have her way blocked by one of the burly footmen Ashton had placed in her home. She thought this one was named Ned, but she was still not sure which was which as they both looked remarkably alike. She sat down again as the other one answered the door. It was strange to have two big men wandering through her house during the day, and sometimes at night. Ashton always sent them home when he came for the night but that had not happened much lately and he did not stay in her bed, much to her disappointment. She could understand his reticence when his mother and aunt were there but they were gone now.

It had been two weeks since she had been shot, and although her shoulder could still give her a twinge on occasion, she knew she was completely healed. It had been three days since Ashton's family had left and she had begun to miss them the moment the door had closed behind them. She had never realized how much she missed the company of other adults, especially women, until she had enjoyed it for a fortnight. Or rather, part of a fortnight, she thought with a grimace as she recalled how she had been locked in a fevered state for most of that first week.

Ashton strode into the room and her thoughts scattered. She heartily returned his kiss, wondering if this would be the night he would cease treating her as if she were too fragile to endure any more than a kiss. The warmth in his eyes as he ended the kiss and sat down by her side gave her hope.

"'Tis very quiet in here," he said.

"The younger boys are at their lessons. Artemis, Stefan, and Darius are off spying. Now that you know when you will be able to get into the brothel, I had thought that would stop." She frowned. "It worries me that they spend so much time in that dangerous part of the city."

"They will be fine and it will be over soon." He put his arm around her and kissed her cheek.

There was a certain tone in his voice that made her suspicious. She leaned away from him and studied his expression. Penelope struggled to recall all she had been told as well as all she had overheard in the last few days and suddenly tensed.

"It is tonight," she said. "Or tomorrow night. You will be sneaking into Mrs. Cratchitt's tonight or tomorrow night."

"'Sneaking' is such a harsh word."

"Ashton." She was not surprised to hear herself nearly growl his name.

He sighed and rose to pour them each a drink of wine. She looked healthy, he thought as he served her the drink and sat back down beside her. It made it very difficult to act the gentleman. He wanted to push her down onto the settee and bury himself deep inside her heat. It was too soon, however, no matter how much certainty there had been in Doctor Pryne's voice when he had declared Penelope healed. By the look on her face, lovemaking would not make her forget that she expected an answer to her question, either.

"It is all planned for tomorrow," he replied. "And it will not be at night but in the afternoon. Tucker delivers the wine in the afternoon."

"Oh. Well, 'tis no matter. Spirits are not concerned about time. I should be able to see or at least sense what ones are there."

"What?! You are *not* going with us."

"Of course I am. How will you know if there are any murdered people in that place if I do not go?"

"We will know with the use of a shovel and our own eyes."

"Are you telling me that I cannot be a part of ending what I began?"

Ashton softly cursed. She had indeed begun this; there was no question of it. Whether one believed she had seen a ghost there or not, it was what was leading to an arrest and, undoubtedly, the hanging of an evil woman. The more information they had gathered on Mrs. Cratchitt, the more he and his friends were certain that people had died at that brothel, and Mrs. Cratchitt knew it. Or had done the killing herself. Ashton realized his greatest objection to Penelope joining them was that he did not want her anywhere near that ugliness.

"You are not healed enough," he said, making one last attempt to dissuade her.

"Oh, aye, I most certainly am. 'Tis not as if I ask to help wrestle the miscreants into their chains. I am healed enough to go along and see what happens, what is found there. To see that poor Faith finds peace." All the while she spoke, Penelope tugged at her gown. When her wounded shoulder was finally exposed, she pointed to it. "Does that not look healed to you?"

"Remarkably so," Ashton muttered and stared at the place where the bullet had torn through her soft flesh. The wound was still ugly and somewhat red, but it was otherwise completely healed. "How is it you have healed so quickly? I have seen many wounds, from a small cut to a sword cut or bullet wound gained in a duel, but none of them, even the smallest one, has healed as fast as this has. This is what so astonished Doctor Pryne, is it not?"

Penelope inwardly cursed herself for acting so rashly as she straightened her clothes. She had just wanted to prove to Ashton that she was healed enough to go with him when they brought down Mrs. Cratchitt. Instead, she now had to explain how it was she had healed with a speed that left even her a little stunned.

"You know that Septimus can ease a person's pain . . ."

"He can heal like that as well?"

"Nay. He can help make one recover from ills and wounds a little quicker, but no more than that. It was Delmar. I do not know whether it is just his touch or his touch plus Septimus's, but I could actually feel my wound heal at times. S'truth, I am not sure Delmar realizes what he has done for he was but holding my hand. I have not spoken to anyone about it yet." She placed her hand over his. "Please, keep it to yourself. Such healing gifts can prove as dangerous as they are wondrous. Everyone who has a disease or a wounded loved one seek out such people. The gift weakens the one who uses it, can even weary them unto death if it is not controlled and limited."

He grasped her hand and lifted it to his lips. "I will tell no one. Delmar should be made aware, however.

He could use his gift unthinkingly and give himself away."

Penelope wondered if Ashton knew that he spoke as if he believed. "Agreed. So, may I go with you?" She could tell by the look he gave her that he knew she would find a way to be there when they went into Cratchitt's cellars no matter what he said. It would just make life a lot easier for everyone if he would agree. "I will stay out of everyone's way."

"Only if you stay out of sight until I say you can join me."

"Oh, thank you, Ashton. I swear I will take not one tiny step without your permission."

His grumble of disbelief was silenced by her kiss. Ashton wrapped his arms around her and kissed her back. The wild, heedless passion she always stirred inside him began coming to life, clouding his mind and hardening his body. He had only just begun to taste the sweetness of her desire when her wound had abruptly deprived him of it. Ashton was starved for the taste of her, for the brush of her warm, soft skin against his. His whole body pounded with the need to be one with her. When Penelope pushed hard against his chest, he groaned a protest.

"Ashton, someone is at the door," Penelope said, struggling to sit upright. How had the man gotten her on her back so quickly?

It took a moment for Ashton to comprehend her words. When full understanding finally grasped his mind, he sat up and began to hastily straighten his clothing. Out of the corner of his eye he watched Penelope do the same. It embarrassed him to know that he had gotten her down on the settee and had been so close, so quickly, to feeding the need that still knotted his insides. He was a little astonished to realize that it also delighted him.

Then he heard an all too familiar sharp voice in the hall and his blood rapidly chilled. It was not for himself that he was concerned; it was Penelope. Clarissa's anger over his blatant disinterest in her had grown over the last fortnight. Every missed ball, soiree, or play only added to it. The fact that he had been proven right about how her brother would never let her end the betrothal had certainly not helped matters. Ashton was afraid that the rage bubbling inside Clarissa could explode all over Penelope. The feel of Penelope patting his hand as if to soothe him drew him out of his dark thoughts.

"Do not worry," she said quietly, bracing herself for what could be a very ugly confrontation. "Clarissa wants to be a viscountess, mayhap even a duchess, far too much to push you too hard. I doubt she would end your betrothal; even if she found you in bed with three naked women."

Ashton laughed softly even though the way Penelope seemed so unmoved by the thought that he could soon marry Clarissa stung. He did not want Penelope to be hurt by what he had to do to save his family, but he certainly did not want her to be indifferent to it. It was unkind of him but he wanted her to feel something more than passion for him.

"So here you are," said Clarissa as she marched into the room. "Cavorting with my own stepsister!"

"He is not cavorting, whatever that may mean," said Penelope.

"Of course not," said Septimus in a cheerful voice as he walked into the room, carrying several books and what looked like a ledger. "He has come to discuss numbers with me."

Clarissa scowled at Septimus. "Numbers?"

"Those little things you write in a column and add together so that you might see if you are still solvent?"

"What do you want, Clarissa?" Ashton asked when he was certain he could speak without laughing. "In fact, just how did you know to find me here?"

"I followed you. Do not dare to look so annoyed and insulted," she snapped. "I have every right to do so. *You* are *my* fiancé. You owe me your courtesy and your escort. I have been given little of either. Have you not heard the whispers? Every time I appear somewhere without my fiancé, I become an object of laughter and ridicule, and a greater one than I was the last time you deserted me."

"Then perhaps you ought to try discussing what events you wish to attend with me *before* you accept an invitation." Ashton watched her curl her manicured hands in a way that made him certain she wanted to claw his eyes out. "I have a great need to get my finances in order, to decide what debts to pay and what properties to improve without completely emptying the purse you will bring to the marriage."

"What do you mean? Charles holds most of your debts. When we marry, he will consider them paid."

"Is that what he told you?" It took no effort at all to make his laugh sound bitter. "Oh, no, my dear. Again, you failed to read what you signed. I get your dowry *and* I pay your brother for my father's markers out of that dowry. He found a very clever way to get you a husband yet not lose a great deal of money. Clever. Treacherous but clever."

Clarissa stared at Ashton in shock and then shook her head. She started to pace the room, muttering to herself about perfidious men. Penelope could almost feel sorry for her except that Clarissa should have known her brother well enough by now to be able to foresee such treachery. She easily shrugged away the tiny pinch of sympathy she did suffer. Clarissa had made her life miserable from the moment Penelope's mother had married Clarissa's father. Although Penelope did not believe in exacting any revenge for those slights and hurts, she had no trouble enjoying retribution handed out by the Fates. It would, of course, be far more enjoyable if there were still not the very real chance that Clarissa could end up married to Ashton.

"Be careful, Clarissa," Penelope said. "You nearly walked through Mrs. Pettibone."

Clarissa came to a halt so swiftly she stumbled and nearly fell. She looked all around her, backing up a little when she saw no one. Then she turned and glared at Penelope.

"Enough. I will hear no more of spirits. You best be very careful or you will soon join them." She pointed at Ashton. "And you had best cease making a fool of me or you, too, will be very sorry." She marched out of the room, slamming the parlor door behind her.

"She just threatened you," said Ashton, frowning after Clarissa.

"And you," said Penelope. "Perhaps it was because you did not stand when she entered the room."

"I had not invited her."

She grinned but quickly grew serious again. "I suppose we would be wise to heed her threats. In her way, she can be as dangerous as her brother." Penelope smiled at Septimus. "And thank you for coming in so quickly. How did you know she was here?"

"I happened to be looking out the window when her carriage pulled up outside." Septimus walked toward the door, but halted abruptly in his leave taking when another rap sounded at the front door. "Do you think she forgot a threat?"

One of the burly footmen appeared in the doorway and Septimus stepped back. "There is a woman with a child at the door, m'lady. She demands to speak to the one who, er, takes care of the brats." He blushed. "Her words, m'lady."

Penelope sighed and nodded, dreading what was about to happen but not for her sake—for the child's. "Send them in here."

A moment later a tall, voluptuous woman strode in dragging a little raven-haired girl by the arm. She tossed a bag at Penelope's feet. Penelope looked into the wide, dark blue eyes of the little girl, saw the hurt there, and had to fight the strong urge to leap up and slap the beautiful woman holding her.

"This one belongs to Quintin Vaughn. I am Leona Mugglesby and I was his mistress near seven years ago." She pushed the little girl toward Penelope. "I went looking for him first."

"I believe he is in India," Penelope said.

"Oh, is he now? Not that his people saw fit to tell me that. But I know Maggie O'Hurley who used to be Orion's mistress and she told me about this place. So, here she is. You take her. Maggie says you do not hesitate to take one of these devil's spawn. That be what she is. Devil's spawn."

The low rumble of thunder sounded and the woman turned white. "See? See what she does?"

Penelope looked out the window. There was an ominous black cloud that did not appear to cover much more than her house and the one next to hers. She looked at the little girl and saw the turmoil in her wide eyes. She reached out, took the child by the hand, and pulled her close enough to put an arm around her. Out of the corner of her eye, she watched Ashton sit down, all thought of respect for the woman obviously gone.

"You think this girl is doing that?" Penelope asked with what she hoped was an appropriate touch of scorn.

"She is! Do you think I believed it at first? Of course not. Then I started thinking on all that's been said of you lot and I knew. Well, you can have her. I will not be having that spawn of Satan near me no more. Ow!" She spun around to find seven scowling boys behind her. "Are these more of them?"

Before Penelope could think of an answer, the boys all shoved their way past the woman. Delmar led them and he had obviously been the one to kick the woman. They placed themselves between her and the little girl. Penelope was so proud of them but feared what painful memories this confrontation might be stirring up in each of them. She did notice, however, that with the presence of the boys, the threat of a storm had eased.

"What is your child's name?" Penelope asked the ashen-faced Leona, wanting the woman to leave before she added to her cruelty with even more unkind words.

"Juno. That is what Quintin said to name the child if it was a girl. He patted me belly and talked to her all the time. Cursed her, he did; I am that sure of it. Well, now he can have her. He can keep her cursed as she is or re-move it, I care not."

"You may leave now," said Delmar as he moved to place his hand on Juno's shoulder. "She is ours now. Go away."

To Penelope's surprise, the woman obeyed Delmar with great speed. "Juno," she said as she looked into the child's eyes, "do you know your papa?"

"Yes," she replied. "He used to come visit me and Mama a lot but then he came one day when Mama had another friend with her. He left but he told me he would always love me and would be back someday. Will he come here? Will he know where I am?"

"He will." Feckless though her kinsmen were, they did love their children in their own way. Penelope just wished it were not the way of a bachelor who had found some woman to care for his child while he played about. "These boys live here, too." She introduced the child to everyone. "There are three older boys, too, but you will meet them later. I will let them all tell you about themselves. Now we must find you a place to sleep."

"I am sorry about the storm," Juno whispered.

"Do not fret, love. We are used to such things here." She looked at the boys. "There will need to be some shifting about so that she can have her own room."

Septimus stepped closer and picked up Juno's bag. "We will see to it, Pen."

The moment they were all gone, Penelope slumped in her seat and closed her eyes. When Ashton wrapped his arms around her, she huddled against his warmth and fought the urge to cry. It had been three years since the last child had been left with her. She had forgotten how ugly it all was.

"Is it always like that?" Ashton asked.

"Almost always," replied Penelope.

"Do you really think that little girl had something to do with that storm cloud?"

"Quite possibly. It *is* gone now, is it not? Disappeared when the boys came and stood by her."

Ashton sighed. "Ah, Penelope, I know not what to believe."

"You do not have to believe, Ashton. Just to know that they are but children, good children, not *devil's spawn*."

He kissed the top of her head. "I know that, have no doubt of it. Someone needs to teach your kinsmen not to be so careless, however." He smiled when she giggled, relieved to hear the sadness that had shrouded her was fading.

"'Tis said that we are like rabbits. Very fertile. It may not be their fault entirely."

Ashton's mind suddenly filled with the image of Penelope well rounded with his child. The joy that rushed through his veins startled him. He scrambled for something to distract him from such dangerous thoughts.

"I believe this calls for a celebration," he said as he leapt to his feet.

"I do not think we should celebrate a little girl's mother casting her aside like that."

"No, but we can tell her that we are celebrating her arrival at the Wherlocke Warren, welcoming the first girl to the family." He bent down and kissed her frowning mouth. "Set out your finest dishes and linens and have all of you wear your finest clothes. I will be back with a feast."

Penelope watched him leave and shook her head. It was a wonderful idea but one could never be sure if a child saw things in the same way as an adult. She decided she would risk it. If nothing else, it should help to let the poor little girl feel accepted for what she was.

"That went far better than I had thought it would," said Penelope as she sat down next to the chair Ashton was sprawled in before the fireplace in her bedchamber. "She looked so happy."

"Good. At least we will not have rain." He grinned when she laughed. "I still find that hard to believe, you know."

"So do I, but I have heard of an ancestor who was said to be able to do it. Unfortunately, he was burned."

"Ouch." He got up, grabbed the pillows from her bed, and placed them on the floor. "Come sit with me here." He sat down and held his hand out to her.

Penelope sat down beside him, settled herself comfortably in his arms, and sighed with contentment. "I am fully healed, you know."

He kissed the back of her neck. "I know. 'Tis just difficult to rid my mind of the image of you racked with fever."

She turned in his arms and kissed his chin. "I could help to banish that image."

Ashton slowly fell back against the pillows. "Are you certain? 'Tis well entrenched."

He stroked his hands up and down her slim back when she lowered her body on top of his. The way she smiled at him made his blood run hot. It was a mix of amusement and beguilement. And there was no doubt that he was thoroughly beguiled. She kissed him, and as he savored the sweet heat of her mouth, he undid her gown.

There would be no sweet kiss good night this time. After seeing her wound, seeing how firmly it was closed and healing, he knew he did not have to wait any longer to taste her passion again. It was not until he had tugged her gown off and tossed it aside that he realized he might have to savor her later. It had been too long and his body was too hungry.

Penelope tugged and pulled at Ashton's clothes until he was gloriously bare-chested. She sat astride him and ran her hands over the smooth, hard breadth of his chest. Her whole body ached for him. Her dreams had been filled with the memory of the time they had made love and now she was nearly desperate to make those dreams come true. She reached for the placket on the front of his trousers, the hardness she felt there only adding to her need for him.

Ashton groaned as the feel of her fingers brushing against him while she undid his breeches drove him mad. "In a rush, love?" he asked and ran his hands up and down her slender legs.

"It has been a long time." She freed him from his breeches and clasped his erection in her hand, savoring the hard, hot length of him. "You wish to go slowly?"

"No." He pushed her onto her back. "It has been a long time." He shoved up her shift until she was bared from the waist down and then rubbed himself against her. They both groaned. "I will go slowly next time."

Penelope gasped as he thrust himself deep inside her. She clung to him, rising to meet his fierce movements. He muttered things against her neck as they both grabbed greedily for the pleasure they could give each other. Penelope wished she understood what he said, but her mind was too clouded with rising desire. And then the bliss she had so ached for swept over with a force that had her crying out his name. She clung to him as her body shuddered with the force of it and he plunged deep inside her to find his own.

Ashton came to his senses with his face still pressed against Penelope's full breasts. *And such fine breasts they are*, he thought with a grin, and kissed each nipple. She wriggled with pleasure beneath him and he grew hard.

Just as he was about to begin the dance all over again, he heard a noise and tensed. He wanted to tell himself it was his imagination but he was certain the sound he had heard was that of a heavy foot vainly trying to creep up the stairs. Since the footmen had left for the night, as had Septimus, he was the only one in the house with a heavy foot. When Penelope opened her mouth, he pressed a finger against it and cocked his head in a listening poise. He was pleased to see her eyes open wide with understanding a heartbeat later.

Ashton had just finished securing his breeches when Penelope handed him the iron from the fireplace. He glanced over at her standing next to him dressed only in her shift with the ash shovel in her hand and could not help but grin. Just as the latch to their door started to move, he heard a crash from downstairs. Not thieves, he decided and swung hard at the man who stepped into the room.

To his astonishment the big man only swayed, then straightened and glared at him. Ashton winced when Penelope swung her little iron shovel and hit the man in the back of the head. The man fell to his knees and Penelope nimbly leapt over him, pausing in the doorway to look back at Ashton.

"The children," she explained even as more crashes sounded from downstairs.

"Go."

When the big man started to stagger to his feet, Ashton hit him again, and then ran past him to try and see what was happening downstairs. It sounded as if someone was doing his best to destroy Penelope's home. That enraged Ashton and he started down the stairs. As he touched his foot on the bottom step, all the boys came racing down, armed with whatever they could grab. The last clear thought Ashton had was that he was glad the older boys had returned from their spying and then he headed straight into what quickly became a melee.

Penelope held Paul and Juno by the hand and cautiously made her way down the stairs. It had been quiet for a little while and she was certain she had heard some men run out of the house. She knew for a fact the one who had tried to sneak into her bedchamber had fled. When she reached the door of her parlor, she did not know whether to weep or laugh.

Ashton was sprawled on the floor with his back against one of her overturned settees, her brothers flanking him. The other boys sat on the floor facing him and it was obvious that they were discussing the battle that had wrecked her parlor. A wide assortment of sticks, bats, and fireplace utensils were scattered around the floor.

"I assume you won," she said as she stepped into the room.

Ashton looked around the room and grimaced. "We will clean it up."

"No need to do so tonight. Any injuries?" They all shook their heads even though she could see bruises and scrapes on every one of them. She looked at Ashton. "Do you know who they were? Not thieves."

"No, not thieves. Just another warning from Mrs. Cratchitt." He stood up and put his arm around her shoulders, ignoring Paul's muttering about being squished. "There will be no more after tomorrow."

Penelope turned her attention to getting everyone back to bed, all the while praying he was right. Next time the enemy could well arrive to give a warning with pistols and knives.

Chapter Fourteen

Little of the afternoon sun penetrated the narrow, filthy alleys around Mrs. Cratchitt's brothel. Penelope shivered. It was as if a dark cloud of evil blanketed the place. The memories of her short sojourn in the place did not help her to look at it with anything but dread. There were eight armed men lurking in the shadows of the alley with her but that did nothing to still her lingering fear of the brothel and its owner.

"Do you see anything?" whispered Whitney as he moved to stand beside her.

Penelope smiled faintly. She knew he meant ghosts. It was amusing how Ashton and his friends always wanted to talk about the many gifts the Wherlockes and the Vaughns had yet still claimed that they did not really believe in them. She wondered if they had yet realized how often they acted like believers. Nevertheless, she supposed curiosity was much better than fear.

"Aye," she said as she watched Faith try to touch Brant and the man shivered, glancing around in puzzlement for the source of the sudden chill he felt. "Six by my counting."

"Stap me. There are six bodies in there?"

"Could be more. Not every spirit lingers, not even ones who have been murdered. After all, if life has been naught but a misery, why stay?"

"The one you saw first, the one called Faith. Is she—"

"Aye, she is, but it is too late to pull Brant away from here."

Whitney cursed, muttered an apology, and then stared at his friend. "This will kill him. He thought her a faithless jade."

"I know. She came to me because she wanted him to know the truth. And truly, who would not believe what a vicar told him?" She patted Whitney on the arm. "You will all need to stand by him until the worst is past."

"It *is* an ugly business."

"Oh, I very much fear, as concerns Faith, it is going to get very ugly indeed." The more she had thought about Faith, the more Penelope had decided a sweet, innocent vicar's daughter did not run off with a soldier. Someone had taken, or sent, Faith away from home and lied to Brant. "There they go," she said, effectively diverting Whitney from asking any more questions about Faith.

Penelope could sense the tension in the men standing behind her. Victor and Cornell stood tensed and ready alongside five big, rough men from the Bow Street Office. The cooperation of such men had not been all that hard to get for they had already been keeping a very close eye on Mrs. Cratchitt. There were also rewards offered for finding people who had gone missing and she suspected the men from Bow Street hoped to find a few of those people inside the brothel. She knew the girl Tucker's son had courted was there

and had heard that the merchants had gathered a reward together for finding her. The Bow Street men
would not go home empty-handed.

A part of her wished to flee back to her house, to
crawl into her bed and pull the covers over her head.
There was going to be so much sadness and anger soon.
Penelope stiffened her backbone. This was why she had
been given such a gift. It was her duty to see that the lost
souls haunting Mrs. Cratchitt's found some peace.

It was only a few moments after the men took the
kegs of wine inside when Artemis and Stefan ran out
and signaled them to join them. Penelope halted the
men and handed them heavily scented cloths they
could tie around their noses and mouths if needed. Instinct told her that they would indeed be needing them.

They all trotted off toward the brothel and Penelope
followed at a much slower pace. She silently ordered
Artemis and Stefan to the wagons with one sharp jab of
her finger. She was not surprised when they obeyed
with no argument. Their white faces had told her that
what she was about to walk into was far more than they
could bear and she thanked God that she had insisted
that Darius never even set foot in the place today. She
tied the scented cloth around her face and followed
Whitney, who had kindly slowed his pace so that she
could catch up.

Ashton kept his cap pulled low as he followed Tucker
and his son into the brothel. Penelope's two brothers did
their best to keep Mrs. Cratchitt and her two thick-necked
men from reaching them too soon. Tucker also kept up
a constant stream of chatter in an attempt to drown out
Mrs. Cratchitt's demands that they stop as they wove their
way through the kitchens and into a large pantry. They

had just reached the door Tucker said led to where the wine was usually stored when Mrs. Cratchitt's men finally shoved the boys out of their way. Before she could put herself between them and the door to the cellars, Tucker's son darted forward and opened it.

The smell was all that was needed to confirm everyone's suspicions. The man from Bow Street who had posed as Tucker's worker moved quickly, grabbing Mrs. Cratchitt and holding a pistol to her head. Ashton set down the keg he had been carrying and pulled out the small sack Penelope had stuffed with heavily scented cloths. He did not want to know how she had known that they might need such things. Thoughts of her facing the stench of rotting bodies, seeing such things, were too horrible to contemplate for long. He ordered the white-faced boys to go and call the others in as he handed the scented rags to the other men. He then tied one around the nose and mouth of the man holding Mrs. Cratchitt.

"What are you doing?" she screeched. "I told you to leave the kegs in the kitchens. The cellars have something rotting in them. The stench would spoil the wine."

"Aye, and we know what be rotting down there," growled the man holding her. "Got yourself a new one buried down there, eh? Shoulda buried it deeper, ye foul besom. Then the stench would not be giving away your crimes."

"I have done nothing! If there is something down there, it is not my doing, not my business at all. I thought it was the cess in the streets acreeping in there, is all. Can you not give me one of those cloths?" she asked piteously.

"Nay. Take yourself a deep breath. Smell a hempen necklace, do ye?" He looked at Ashton and the others. "You lot go on down there if you can stomach it. Soon's my men get here, I will be tying this bitch up and joining you."

One glance at Mrs. Cratchitt's men told Ashton they would do nothing. Tucker, his son, and Brant started down the narrow wooden steps. Ashton was about to follow them when the other men arrived. They quickly helped the first Bow Street man tie up Mrs. Cratchitt and her men, all loudly protesting their innocence until they were roughly gagged. Then he saw Penelope enter behind Whitney. He shook his head at her as two of the Bow Street men pushed past him to hurry down the steps, leaving two others to watch the prisoners and two more to go and guard the two doors so no others could flee the place. Cornell and Victor hesitated a moment and then went down the stairs. Ashton tried to stop Penelope as she made to follow them.

"Nay, Ashton, I have to go," she said.

"It will not be pretty," he said even though he could tell by the determined look in her eyes that she would not heed him. "It is already worse than I ever imagined it would be."

"I know and I fear it is going to be hardest on your friend Brant. 'Tis his Faith."

"Ah, Christ, no."

Whitney slipped by him and nodded. "Damned if I know what is true or false now, but if she says it is so, that I do believe." He hurried down the stairs.

"Penelope, you do not have to go down there," Ashton said, not surprised by the hint of desperation in his voice.

"I do. This is what my gift asks of me. There are restless souls down there, Ashton. They need me to help them find the peace they deserve." She took him by the hand and led him down the stairs, pausing only to get out of the way of Cornell, who raced back up the stairs muttering something about more shovels and blankets. "Go help him, Ashton."

"Penelope—"

"Nay. I will not be swayed in this."

He pressed his cloth-covered mouth to her forehead and then hurried after Cornell. Penelope slowly walked down into what she could only call hell on earth. The smell came from a young woman hanging in chains on a far wall. She could not have been dead for many days but the vermin so common in the dark alleys and the places lining them had done their gruesome work. What horrified Penelope the most was that the keys to the girl's chains hung near but just out of reach. The cruelty of such a thing was beyond her understanding. Next to the body the Bow Street men were taking down was the woman's spirit but what caused tears to sting Penelope's eyes was the spirit of a small boy who stood beside her.

Help him. He has found me.

Recognizing Faith's voice, Penelope spun around to see an ashen-faced Brant staring into the grave he had dug open. The shovel slipped from his hands as he fell to his knees. Penelope quickly moved to his side and placed her hand on his hair. Even as she wondered how he could tell it was his Faith, he removed a small ring from the finger of the corpse. When he looked up at Penelope, tears running freely down his cheeks, her heart broke at the depth of the grief she could read in his eyes.

"How?" he asked. "Did her lover desert her?"

Penelope saw Faith shake her head. "There was no lover, Brant."

My father lied. My father threw me into hell for a pouch of gold.

"Ah, nay." It just kept getting worse, Penelope thought

and wondered how much more any of them could endure. "Truly, there was never anyone else."

"Is she here?" he whispered and looked around. "Can she tell you what happened to her?"

"She says her father lied to you, that he gave her away for a pouch of gold."

"Her own father sold her to a brothel? A vicar?"

Lady Mallam paid. Warn them.

"Warn who?"

My brothers and sisters. Warn them.

"I will see to it. So will Brant."

"What does she want?" Brant asked. "Anything. I will do anything to make up for what I did. I believed her father. I failed her. I should have believed in her and no one else. I should have searched for her."

"Brant, the man is a vicar with a sterling reputation. Of course you believed what he said. Faith wants us to tell her brothers and sisters what was done to her. I think she fears they are in danger. They must be warned in case their father has an idea to make some more coin on any of his other children." She watched as Ashton and Cornell moved to Faith's graveside and began the grim task of putting her body in a large blanket and wrapping it up tightly.

No blame lies with him.

"If I had but looked for her," Brant said.

"Nay, she does not blame you." Penelope rubbed Brant's back as Faith whispered the whole ugly tale of her fate into her mind.

A harsh cry distracted Penelope from watching Faith watch Brant. She looked around and found Tucker's son clutching something and knew he had found the girl he had been courting. "I must help the others," she told Brant as she stood up. "They need to find peace."

Brant grabbed her by the hand. "Despite all I thought,

I never stopped loving her, never stopped hoping she would return to me and explain it all."

"She knows. But you must let go of her now, Brant. She needs peace."

Penelope began to make her way from spirit to spirit, getting what little information she could from them, and helping them to finally let go. She ignored the looks of the men who continued the grim work of uncovering the bodies. Finally, only Faith was left. Her spirit lingered near Brant, who no longer wept but clutched the little ring and stared blindly at the blanket-shrouded remains of his lover.

"Brant," she said, pulling his gaze to hers. "Let her go. This is not the place for her but she cannot leave it unless you let her go. She needs to move on."

Tell him to find love again. He must not let grief and betrayal bind his heart.

"I will," she whispered. She watched Brant stand up. Finger by finger he loosed his tight grip on the ring.

"Farewell, love," he whispered, kissed the little ring, pocketed it, and moved to help the other men.

Just as a smiling Faith disappeared, one of the Bow Street men joined Penelope and said, "Got the sight, eh?"

Penelope nodded toward Brant. "It was his fiancée who started this search." She looked around and counted ten holes. "So many." She frowned for she suddenly realized she had seen more than ten ghosts.

"'Spect there be more." He nodded when Penelope paled. "That woman has had a brothel here for nigh to ten years. I sent Tom off to get more men. There be a lot more ground to search. Cellar runs to a large room on either side of this one. Funny them leaving things like rings and bracelets with the dead."

"Burying all proof that these poor souls were ever here."

He nodded. "Got the right of it." He sighed heavily. "The little lad was the hardest."

"His name was Tim."

"Aye," said Tucker as he stepped up to them. "Butcher's son. Recognized his wee cap. His mam made it for him and he was that proud of it. Disappeared three years ago."

"You got more names?" the Bow Street man asked Penelope and quickly pulled out a bit of paper and lead to write down the ones she gave him, all seventeen of them.

"It might be difficult to explain how you got those names," Penelope said when she was done.

"I will think of a fine lie, no worry there. No more ghosts?"

"Nay."

"Was hoping you could help us see if there were others buried here. This list implies there are at least seven more. Save some time and sweat if we could know where they all are."

"I can do that. 'Tis not only the spirit I see. I can sense where the dead are buried. Get me something to mark the places and I will walk through the rest of this hell."

"We will be taking Meggie and Tim home to their folk," said Tucker. "They will send the rewards round to Bow Street. The butcher had gathered one, too." Tucker looked at Ashton and his friends. "Good men. Not many of their sort would do this."

Penelope managed a small smile. "They are very good men. Not one of them was certain I had seen a ghost but they still worked hard to find the truth. I am sorry for your son's loss."

Tucker nodded. "He be grieving, but knowing is always better than not knowing." He walked away.

The Bow Street man brought her a small sack of kindling he must have snatched from the kitchens and Penelope began the sad task of finding other graves. By the time she was done, the total number of dead had reached two and thirty and she was exhausted in mind and soul. She climbed up the steps to find the brothel utterly silent. Penelope idly wondered how many had been dragged away to face prison, a trial, and undoubtedly, a hanging. After what she had seen, she found that she simply did not care what happened to any of them.

She stepped outside and found herself immediately wrapped in Ashton's strong arms. Penelope tossed aside the cloth she had worn over her face and pressed close to him. She tried to find some strength and comfort in his arms. "Brant wants to take Faith home now," he said. "I have already sent the boys home."

"Thank you."

"Let me take you home as well."

"Nay, we will go with Brant."

"Penelope, you look utterly exhausted."

"Is it a long journey?"

"No, her father is the vicar in a small village just to the south of the city."

"Then I will come with you."

"Why?"

"Because I have seen Faith. I have talked with her. Brant may have questions." She sighed. "It may also be something needed to get Faith's brothers and sisters to see the truth about their father and that was what Faith asked of us."

Ashton frowned. "Brant might have questions but surely those can wait? S'truth, mayhap this is something he should do alone. You can always warn her brothers and sisters later."

"Nay. You see, there is something Faith told me that I did not tell Brant. I need to tell him. I am just not sure how. If the confrontation with the vicar does not bring the whole ugly truth out, I shall have to speak up."

"What could be uglier than a man selling his own daughter to a brothel?"

"Oh, the vicar did not do that. He did sell Faith in a way, taking coin and letting someone else drag her away. I think he also suspected what fate awaited her but did not care. It was that someone else who saw that the poor girl was sold into that hell."

Ashton had a very bad feeling about what she would say, but he still asked, "Who?"

"Lady Mallam."

Ashton pressed his face against her neck and cursed for a long time before he lifted his head. "Let us get this over with."

Brant refused to allow Faith's body to be put anywhere but on a carriage seat. Penelope could understand his aversion to her remains being treated like luggage, but it meant that he rode alone with the dead. Perhaps it was for the best, she decided as she joined the others in the second carriage. The man needed time to grieve privately. It might give him the strength to endure the next blow.

She leaned against Ashton as she struggled to forget what she had seen in those cellars. All four men were silent and Penelope suspected they were also trying to fight back the ugly memories of that place. It was hard to conceive how anyone could have such a complete disregard for life. Mrs. Cratchitt was a monster.

"He is eaten up with guilt for not looking for her," said Whitney, abruptly breaking the heavy silence.

Ashton nodded. "It will take him a long while to understand that he did nothing wrong in believing the word of a vicar all thought was such a pious man."

"How would a vicar in a little village south of London know where to sell his daughter?"

After a quick glance at Penelope, who nodded, Ashton told them about Lady Mallam's part in it all. "We all know she was not happy with his choice but I never would have thought her capable of such a crime against an innocent woman."

Once their shock had passed, Ashton's friends began to discuss how they could help Brant and what should be done about Lady Mallam. Penelope closed her eyes and allowed herself to dose lightly against Ashton. She was not looking forward to the confrontation with the vicar but she needed to make certain that her promises to Faith were fulfilled.

When the carriage stopped, she sat up and blinked her eyes. It took her a moment to shake off her weariness. Just as she was about to ask what they should do next, Cornell cursed and leapt from the carriage. Whitney and Victor quickly followed. As Ashton helped her out, she saw that Brant had already grabbed the vicar and was dragging him toward the carriage where Faith's body rested.

"This is not good," muttered Ashton.

"I do not see what is wrong with him being angry at the man who sent his own daughter to her death," said Penelope as she hurried to keep up with his long strides.

"I cannot be sure how far Brant's anger and grief will make him go, and I do not think it is a sight for them to see." He nodded toward the house.

At first Penelope saw only the house. It was a pretty thatched-roofed cottage surrounded by flower beds. She wondered how anything so pretty and innocent looking could house such a man. Then she saw the children.

There were eight of them. Four boys and four girls. They all stood just outside the door of the house watching Brant's rough treatment of their father with wide eyes. She suspected seeing five gentlemen who were so obviously of the aristocracy only added to their fear.

Just as she took a step toward them, the largest of the four boys began to move toward the carriage where Brant had opened the door and was shoving the vicar inside, his siblings hesitantly following him. "Ashton, do not let the children see the body," she said as she caught up with him. "Try to keep them back. They should not see their sister like that."

"Look upon what you have done to your own child," Brant said as he reached in and yanked the blanket back to reveal Faith's body. "You lied. She never went off with a soldier. You sold her to a brothel and she died there."

"No! No!" The vicar tried to scramble back, to put some distance between himself and the body of his child. "I never sent her to such a place of sin."

"But you sold her to someone, did you not? Got yourself a fat bag of gold for her, too."

Penelope glanced at the children and could tell by their expressions that they had knowledge of the money. She was pleased to see that Ashton had Victor's help in holding them back from the carriage but nothing could save them from hearing the whole ugly truth of what had been done to Faith. They would be warned about their father as Faith had wanted, but Penelope could not help worrying over how deeply it would hurt them.

"I needed money!" the man shouted and cried out when Brant tossed him to the ground. "I have so many children and being the vicar here does not pay well. What was I to do? I could barely keep food on the table."

"You could have let me marry her as I intended to do. I spoke to you of it, gave Faith a ring. We would have been wed as soon as the banns were read. That would have helped."

The vicar shook his head. "No, she would not allow that. She threatened my position. I had to do it."

"She?"

It was only one word but Penelope knew she was not the only one who heard a lot in that one small word that was alarming. Fury. Grief. Dread. Cornell and Whitney quickly moved closer to Brant. She began to doubt her opinion that it would be best if Brant heard the truth about his mother from the vicar's own lips. What the man had just said was as good as pointing the finger right at Lady Mallam. Only that woman could be *she* and Brant had the wit to know it. He looked dangerous.

The vicar obviously sensed the danger he was in for he began to scramble backward, like some strange crab. Brant kept pace with the man's awkward attempt to escape. It was an eerie dance made all the more so by the way Cornell and Whitney moved to keep pace with Brant. Penelope felt her insides tighten painfully as she waited for something, anything, to happen.

"You said *she*." Brant's voice sounded more like a predator's growl than any other voice she had ever heard. "*She* threatened to take away your position here. There is only one who could do that. Aside from me, that is. Are you telling me it was my own mother who paid you and then took Faith away?"

The vicar opened his mouth but nothing came out. To Penelope's astonishment, the oldest boy abruptly pushed past Ashton and Victor and confronted Brant. She saw a flicker of hope lighten the vicar's face but the hard, furious look of disgust his son gave him vanquished it.

"I am Peter Beeman, his eldest son," the boy said. "It was Lady Mallam who came to have a private talk with Father just before our Faith disappeared. I cannot tell you what was said but suddenly there was money again." Peter sighed, his eyes gleaming with tears that he struggled to keep from falling. "I would rather we had Faith." He glanced toward the carriage. "We will bury her. I will not have my father lead the service—"

"Peter!" Beeman shouted but quailed when Brant glared at him.

"It would be a blasphemy considering he is the one who sent her to her death."

"I did not!"

Peter stared down at his father, his siblings slipping up to stand beside him all wearing the same look of utter disdain and fury. "Yes, you did. You knew there was no chance she would ever return to us. That is why you told the lie about her running off to Spain with a soldier. I have no doubt you have already composed the letter telling us she has died. You but waited for the right time. And just where did you think a woman who was so adamantly against our Faith marrying her son would send the girl? I think she told you. Mayhap not directly, but she said enough that you knew what our sister's fate would be and you did not care."

"No, son, I would never."

"I mean to bury her in the plot near my home," said Brant, both he and Peter ignoring the sputtering vicar. "I will send word when it is time for the ceremony. You and your siblings are welcome. Your father is not. Believe me in this"—he looked down at Beeman—"I would throw you out of this cottage, this village, if not for these children." Brant looked back at Peter. "You will tell me the moment you think he is trying to be rid of any of you or to hurt you in any way. I may not be able to do so legally, but I now name myself your guardian. Treat me as such."

Brant started to get into the carriage but his friends quickly moved to his side. And Victor asked, "Do you need us to come with you to confront your mother?"

For one long moment, Brant stared at the blanket-wrapped form of the young woman he had wanted to marry and then looked at Victor. "I have no mother."

Chapter Fifteen

Ashton stared down at a sleeping Penelope, her face still streaked with tears. It had been a horrific day. He worried about Brant, but knew his friend had meant it when he had insisted Ashton take Penelope home and stay with her. Cornell, Victor, and Whitney would watch over Brant, he assured himself. The man had not really requested any assistance, but he had it. Ashton suspected his other friends were in for a very uncomfortable time. The way Brant had said he had no mother had held a deep note of finality to it.

He could not believe what the woman had done. Since the day he had met Brant when they were still boys, Lady Mallam had ruled her son with an iron hand. As Brant had changed from boy to man, he had rebelled against his mother's control but he had remained a dutiful son. She had gone too far this time. She had murdered the woman Brant loved simply because she had not approved of the match of her son and a lowly vicar's daughter. They could not prove that

Lady Mallam's intention was to cause Faith's death but placing a sweet country innocent, the daughter of a vicar, in a brothel could only lead to the worst of consequences.

And how had the woman known about Mrs. Cratchitt's? How had she known who to get to do her filthy work for her? It might not hurt to see if one could find out the answers to those questions. Lady Mallam was not going to take well to being disowned by her son. Considering what she had done the last time Brant had stood firm for what he wanted, Ashton believed she would bear careful watching.

What Penelope had done at the brothel had stunned him, too, but in a good way. It had been astonishing, almost miraculous. No one could watch her speaking to the dead, helping them find peace and seeking the truth from them, without believing. It was either believe or think her utterly mad. And Penelope was not mad.

He had ceased a long time ago to think her some charlatan who made money off the gullible people of the world, but he had never fully believed that she had some special gift that allowed her to speak to the dead. He had seen her insistence that she could speak to the dead as an adorable eccentricity, curious about her family and their claims but very doubtful that anyone could do the things she claimed they could do. That doubt was fully vanquished now. He was feeling just a bit like an ass.

Since he now believed that Penelope could see the dead, could even find where the bodies were buried, it meant there was a good chance that the whispers about the Wherlockes and the Vaughns were all true. There was an alarming thought. It was even more alarming when he realized that the house he was taking her back to was packed full of Wherlockes and Vaughns. Twelve

of them. How many more of them had gifts? Had Penelope been telling him the truth when she had spoken of
all the children having such unusual skills?

He had not seen that yet, but had noticed odd things
about a few of them. There was no denying Hector
could tell when someone lied but was it a keen eye for
such tics and twitches that gave a person away or a true
gift? Septimus most definitely had a touch that eased a
person's pain, even a highly respected doctor believing
in that gift. Paul claimed he could see things but complained that he had not learned how to give his warnings in a way that helped anyone. The boy had certainly
known when there was danger approaching several
times.

That sort of thing was not so hard to accept, he
thought and nodded to himself as he gently stroked
Penelope's hair. However, a boy who could help heal
with just a touch? A little girl who caused a storm when
she was unhappy? Another boy who could toss things
around without lifting a finger?

Ashton frowned. He had seen that; he just had not
wanted to let the memory of it stick in his mind. Now
that he was trying to be accepting of the miraculous, he
could let himself think of the time when the men had
ransacked the house. Jerome had definitely been hurl-
ing things at the intruders yet he had never lifted a finger.

He leaned his head against the back of the seat. It
was something he could turn round in his mind again
and again but it would make no difference. He was
caught up in a world he did not fully understand and he
had to accept that.

The carriage pulled to a halt in front of the Wherlocke Warren an hour later. Ashton nudged Penelope
awake, smiling at the childish way she rubbed her eyes.

Promising her he would return later, he gave her a kiss at the door and handed her into the care of her brothers. In desperate need of a bath and a change of clothes, he leapt back in the carriage and ordered his driver to take him home.

Penelope stood in the doorway for a moment and watched Ashton's carriage disappear before shutting the door. It was going to be a lot of work but what she really needed was a long soak in a hot bath. She could still smell the dead on herself and she wanted that dark scent gone so that she could begin to dim the power of the memories of all she had seen today.

To her relief, one of the footmen, or NedTed as she had begun to call the two men in her mind, immediately offered to bring hot water up to her bedchamber. It was nice to have servants, she mused as she went up the stairs. Half the way up the stairs she suddenly realized that there had been something different about the house. She paused and stared back down into the hall. Her brothers stood at the bottom of the stairs, grinning up at her. That was suspicious in itself. Then she gasped as her mind finally grasped what was different.

Where was the destruction caused by the men who had broken into her home last night? They had not had time to clean up much before going to the brothel yet the hall looked cleaner than it had before the attack. She ran down the stairs and into the parlor, stopping in the doorway to gape at the room, which had been an utter mess only hours before. The few broken pieces of furniture were gone, replaced by pieces far better than she could afford.

"Who did this?" she asked, sensing her brothers and NedTed behind her.

"His lordship sent over some men to give me and Ned a hand in cleaning up the mess," said the one who was obviously Ted. "They brought a few things with them from the attics of Radmoor House 'cause his lordship said he could see that some of your furniture was badly broken. Sent some maids, too, and they cleaned everything to a real shine for you."

Penelope went through the rest of the downstairs although the damage had not been as severe in any of the other rooms. Everything was scrubbed clean and she found several more pieces of furniture she had not owned or bought. She did not know whether to let her pride rule and complain about Radmoor taking charge without her knowledge, or simply accept a kindness. Penelope saw Ted walk by with two buckets of steaming water and decided she would consider the matter while she bathed.

Ashton sank down into the hot tub with a sigh of pleasure. That pleasure vanished rapidly when his mother strode into the room. He grabbed a washing rag and placed it over his privates. She might be his mother but he was far past the age where he could comfortably allow her to view him utterly naked.

"So modest," Lady Mary said and giggled as she sat down on the bed and looked at him. "Was it very bad? I noticed your man walking by muttering about burning your clothes."

"Was what so very bad?" The look she gave him told Ashton she was not going to let him play that game, that somehow she had found out where they had gone today. He sighed. "Yes, it was very bad. How did you know?"

"Gossip is already starting to wend its way through London." She nodded when he cursed softly. "It appears there were a few gentlemen there rather early in the day. One even got dragged off to the Bow Street

Office before he was identified and released." She smiled. "'Tis difficult to recognize an earl when he has none of his trappings on."

Ashton laughed. "I am surprised they would admit to where they had been."

"From what I have heard, there are many obviously false explanations for why they happened to be in the area to see what happened. It was a gruesome business with everyone in the place being dragged off and questioned. It is a tale that is too good to be silent on even if one has to lie, badly, about why one was near a brothel. The tale has also spread like fire through the tradesmen, who then tell their customers, who then tell their employers, and so on. There were not a hundred bodies, were there?" she asked softly.

"No. There were thirty-two including the woman Brant had wanted to marry." He told his mother all about Faith and what they had discovered at the vicar's. "Is there talk of Penelope?"

"A little," said Lady Mary as she stood up. "No one recognized her or even got a good look at her. There are a few who say she must have been there because some woman in her family or a friend was taken and killed. Well, enjoy your bath before the water chills." She paused in the doorway and frowned. "I have always considered women who run brothels naught much more than vermin for making their living over selling other women, but this Mrs. Cratchitt—well, she is a monster, is she not?"

"She is. I but wish there was some way to punish her aside from a hanging, some long, painful punishment."

"There is hell, m'dear, and that is where that monster is surely going," she said quietly before shutting the door behind her.

Ashton hoped his mother was right. That woman had taken the lives of two and thirty people and he knew three were utterly innocent. There was no doubt in his mind that others were, too. He wondered how many men were feeling appalled that they had ever gone to that woman's brothel or were wondering if they had been given some stolen girl who then ended up buried in the cellar. Since the dead cannot speak, except to ones like Penelope, Ashton doubted that many of society's men would trouble themselves over the matter for very long.

It was nearly time for the evening meal before Ashton was done bathing, resting, and dressing. He had even had a brief talk with Alex, who had been sorely disappointed that he had not been able to join them today. Alex was still too busy trailing after Penelope's solicitor.

Just as he reached the bottom of the stairs, Clarissa arrived. Ashton scoured his mind for some memory of an event or a meeting they had agreed to but found none. It was obviously time for another lecture on his neglect. He cordially invited her into the small blue parlor, leaving the door wide open. He also whispered to the footmen to go and find his mother immediately. He still suspected that Clarissa would try to be caught in a severely compromising position with him so that he would be honor-bound to join her at the altar. The woman obviously felt she could seduce him if she could just get him alone for a while. Ashton wanted to tell her that she could dance naked through his bedchamber and he still would not touch her, but bit back the insult.

After they were served some wine and a few light cakes, he sat down opposite her. "To what do I owe the honor of this visit?"

"Ashton, we are betrothed yet rarely see each other," she said. "I but thought we might take some time to talk."

"About what?"

"How about we discuss what invitations you would accept?"

"I assume you have something in mind."

"There is a rout at the Dunweldons' on Thursday and a lovely supper promised at the Burnages' on Friday. I am sure that one of those should suit you."

Since it had been a while since he had checked on his investments, he said, "The supper at the Burnages'." He could tell by the fleeting look of annoyance that crossed her face that that was not the one she wanted him to choose.

"As you wish. There was one thing, just a bit of gossip, but I thought you might be able to make it clearer to me. Some of the tales I have heard have been quite wild."

"Tales about me?"

"About you and your friends going into a brothel today with some of those rough men from Bow Street. 'Tis said you went in to find bodies and brought out over a hundred."

"Two and thirty. They were murdered women, and a boy, and had been buried in the cellar. Mrs. Cratchitt will surely hang as will many of her associates."

"Why should you do such a thing? What matter if she has killed a few of *those* women?"

"Not all of them were of that life, Clarissa. The woman kidnapped young women and forced them into it. Do they not deserve justice? Are you attempting to defend a woman who killed so many people?"

Clarissa sipped her wine in an obvious attempt to

wash away a sharp remark. "Of course not. It is just a little embarrassing for me to have to hear the talk."

"Talk of how my son did his best to bring justice to so many people and put a monster on the gallows?" asked Lady Mary as she strode in, helped herself to some wine, and sat down next to Ashton.

"No, not that. I am sure he was very brave," Clarissa said. "And he is an honorable man. 'Tis just that such a thing is best left to those people who deal with criminals."

Ashton wondered why Clarissa was so concerned. The tale did not tarnish him. It may make some people wonder why he should even bother, but there was no embarrassment in being talked about because he brought a vicious killer to justice. Then he frowned, wondering if she feared that Mrs. Cratchitt would talk a little too much now that she faced a noose. The men who had kidnapped Penelope had talked about how a pretty lady had wanted her taken out of the way. Since he was certain the man who was supposed to come and enjoy himself with Penelope the next day was Charles, it could be possible that Clarissa had been fully complicit in the plan.

They really had to track down that solicitor, he thought. All they had at the moment were rumors and suspicions. They needed to see the will, a list of the late marquis's assets, and other information. Ashton actually, briefly, considered slipping into Hutton-Moore House and searching for the will. Charles had to have a copy of it somewhere. He suddenly realized that Clarissa was looking at him as if she expected an answer to a question, one he had not heard.

"I am sure there was no lady there leading the men around by talking to ghosts, dear," Lady Mary said, and

Ashton silently thanked her for her gentle nudge in the right direction.

"Why would you think such a thing?" asked Ashton. "Do not say that is one of the rumors skipping through the ton." He shook his head. "One has to wonder who makes up such tales and why so many people believe them."

"Just how big a fool do you think I am?" Clarissa said, her temper finally flaring beyond her control. "I have seen you with Penelope, seen you at her house. I know you are fully aware that she claims she can see and speak to the spirits of the dead. You did not even blink an eye when she told me to be careful because I walked through Mrs. Pettibone. And there was no one there! What I truly want to know is why are you associating with my stepsister?"

"I believe I told you that I was there to discuss my finances with young Septimus. The man is a genius when it comes to finances."

"You are in debt! What is there to discuss?"

"How to get out of it."

"By marrying an heiress just as you are doing. It is the traditional way a lord replenishes his fortunes. Yet you talk of investments? That is so common.

"I think there is something going on between you and Penelope. She was there at the brothel. A friend of mine heard it from her aunt, who heard it from her cousin, who heard it from her butcher."

"Ah, well then, who am I to doubt the truth of what your friend said."

Clarissa glared at him but doggedly continued. "Penelope was there and I know it. Her name is already stained beyond saving because she insists on caring for all those, those field colts. Now she will sink even lower when the world hears of how she was marching through the cellars of a brothel finding the dead for those Bow Street men, men who are not such a very big step from being criminals themselves. Even being the daughter of a marquis will not save her when it is known that she was there while all you oh-so-noble gents were digging up the bodies of whores."

When Ashton opened his mouth to say something, his mother silenced him by placing her hand on his arm and squeezing lightly. He was not sure what angered him most, the way Clarissa talked of Penelope's boys or the way she so obviously intended to spread the word of Penelope's gift and destroy her in any way she could. What he feared most was that it would have people flocking to Penelope's door trying to get her to find their loved ones or speak to them. She would have to go into hiding.

"My dear young lady," said Lady Mary, "may I first say that your language is atrocious. A lady does not say such things as 'field colts' or 'whores.' It shows a distinct lack of breeding and could even make one doubt your morals. And you should think very carefully about what you say concerning your stepsister. She is part of your family and whatever mud you fling at her can all too easily splash you as well."

After such a sound scolding spoken in a soft, proper voice, Clarissa was speechless. She stood up, curtseyed to Lady Mary, and turned to Ashton, who had come to his feet when she had. Reluctantly he escorted her to the door to collect her things and see her to her carriage. It was not until he was helping her into her carriage that she finally spoke again. Ashton was sure it was not shame that had held her silent but fury.

"You should not press me too hard, Ashton," she

hissed. "My brother may want this marriage for his own reasons and he may be cheating me out of my dowry, but I promise you, he will never let you have Penelope."

She slammed the carriage door in his face and Ashton frowned after it as she was driven away. It seemed that Artemis had been right—Charles wanted Penelope. Ashton had to talk himself out of grabbing a mount, riding to Hutton-Moore House, and pounding Charles's face into the floor. The man had definitely been behind her kidnapping and had meant to take his pleasure of her before ridding himself of her. If, as they suspected, he was behind the shooting, then he may well have decided he could no longer wait to satisfy his lust.

Shaking his head, he walked back into the house. He badly wished to go straight to Penelope but it had been too long since he had shared a dinner with his family. As he rejoined his mother, he did wonder, however, if there was a gift among the Wherlockes and Vaughns that would help him get the truth, maybe even find the will. It was something to think about.

Ashton greeted the footman who opened the door at the Wherlocke Warren. "Everything quiet?" he asked as he handed the man his hat and coat.

"Aye. Ned walks the gardens every now and then. Sees naught."

Ah, Ashton thought and had to smile. This one was Ted. He had to wonder what had possessed his mother to hire identical twins as footmen. Just a whim, he supposed, or a very strange sense of humor.

"He is careful not to do so with too much regularity, is he not?" he asked Ted.

"Aye, m'lord. I do the same out the front. No one will be setting any clocks by us."

"Good. Very good."

"Her ladyship and all them others have already retired, m'lord."

Ashton almost nodded, expressed his regret, retrieved his things, and left as any gentleman should. Then he thought of all he had been through today and decided he was in no mood to play the gentleman. He needed to be with Penelope. His footmen would never indulge in gossip nor would any of Penelope's family so it should be safe to break some rules.

"Quite all right, Ted," he said as he started up the stairs. "Her ladyship is expecting me."

That was not entirely true. He had said he would return but that had been hours ago. Penelope could easily have decided he was not coming and gone to sleep. She, too, had had a very wearying day. So, when he stepped into her bedchamber to find her curled up beneath the bedcovers, he grinned. Curled up around her was just where he wanted to be, needed to be, and he began to shed his clothes.

It was the tug of her night shift being removed that woke Penelope out of a sound sleep and she feared she had slipped into a nightmare. A strong male body, fully aroused, pressed against her, and her brief moment of panic fled. She recognized the scent and feel of the man now holding her close and nuzzling her neck. Still, it would not hurt to tease him for his presumption.

"Oh, nay, Ted," she whispered huskily. "You must go. Ashton could be here at any moment." She choked on her laughter when Ashton started to tickle her unmercifully in retribution.

"Wretch," he said when he got her pinned beneath him.

"That was for your arrogance in slipping into my bed uninvited."

"Ah, so I need to be invited, do I?" Ashton leapt nimbly from the bed and stood at attention beside it. "My dear Lady Penelope, would you be so kind, so gracious and generous, as to accept my humble self into your bed?"

Penelope looked at his groin, where his staff stood at attention as well, thick and bold as it stuck out from his lean, strong body. He really was a beautiful man, she thought, and wondered how long she could get him to stand there so that she could savor the sight of him. It was a cold, damp night, however, and they had both suffered through a grueling day.

"Humble is the very last thing you appear to be, but get in the bed." She lifted the bedcovers. "Best hurry. 'Tis cold in this room and very soon you will not be looking so manly."

Ashton laughed and got back into the bed. "How do you know what cold can do to a man?"

"Do recall that I spend most of my time with ten boys. Whether I wish to or not, I learn about all manner of bodily quirks and functions."

"Yes, boys do find such things endlessly fascinating." He wrapped her in his arms and began to nuzzle her neck again. "I meant to arrive sooner so that I could sup with you and the boys but my family was all at home and wished my company."

"Much more important. And did you think to sit upon one of our new chairs?"

"Ah, that."

"Aye, that. More arrogance, but I swallowed my first surge of pride and did not choke on it, so I thank you."

"You are most welcome."

"But, well, should you not be trying to sell what you are not using?"

"I doubt the pieces brought here would raise enough coin to make it worth the time and effort."

She nodded as she ran her hands up and down his strong back. "Those with money want only the new and the fashionable. Those without the money probably do not have the room for it anyway."

Penelope murmured her pleasure when he began to feast upon her breasts. His touch, his every caress, set a fire burning inside her that only he could quench. She did not think she could ever get enough of his touch and tried very hard not to think of how he might soon be touching someone else this way, a wife he chose for the money to save his family. Placing her hands on his cheeks, she lifted his face to hers and kissed him, using her hunger for him to banish such sad thoughts.

The wild need he stirred within her soon pushed aside all thought of the future. Penelope offered herself up to his every touch freely and wantonly. The way he made her blood run so hot it burned away all good sense was more than welcome after the dark day she had spent.

The strong desire only she had ever made him feel burst to life inside Ashton as she turned to sweet fire beneath his hands. He kissed his way down her soft, taut belly as he slid his hand between her silken thighs. The heat he found there only added to his great need for her. He knelt between her legs, draped them over his shoulders, and kissed her there. Her whole body jerked in shock, and she tried to retreat, but he held her firm as he licked and kissed her, making love to her with his mouth. When her body arched in his hold and she started to cry out, he pressed his mouth closer and savored every tremor of her release.

Setting her trembling legs back down, he kissed and

licked his way back up her body. He smiled into her
wide, passion-dazed eyes and then kissed her even as he
joined their bodies with one fierce thrust. She cried out
and he hesitated, thinking he had hurt her, but the way
she wrapped her body around his eased his fear that he
had been too rough. He did not hold back then, letting
the ferocity of his need rule him. Astonishment briefly
cut through the blinding force of his release when her
body clung to his, her wet heat rippling around him as
she found her pleasure for a second time.

Penelope did not return to her full senses until Ashton had finished cleaning them both off and pulled her
back into his arms. Then the heat of a blush spread
from her cheeks all the way down to her toes. He chuckled and kissed her hot cheek, annoying her. He had no
respect for her modesty, she thought. What he had
done had driven her mad with pleasure, but now that
the pleasure had faded, she could hardly look at him.
One glance at his smiling mouth had her recalling
where that mouth had just been, causing an embarrassing ache there as if her shameless body was crying out
do it again.

Turning so that she could press her cheek to his
chest and listen to his heartbeat, she idly wondered
what he would do if she so boldly ignored any sense of
modesty he might have. Then she recalled the sight of
him standing naked by the bed and nearly cursed. Men
did not have much modesty at all. But he might just go
as mad as she had if she kissed him so intimately. It was
an intriguing idea that soon had her kissing her way
down his chest to his hard stomach. When she kissed the
lightly haired spot just below his belly hole, his erection
bumped against her chin and he groaned. She smiled
against his hot skin. If he groaned at that light inadver-

tent touch, he just might yell as loud as she had with what she intended to do next.

"Ashton? That, er, kiss you gave me? Is that some strange foreign trick?" she asked.

"Not that I know of," he replied, not surprised that his voice was so hoarse and unsteady he nearly squeaked, for her mouth was so very close to where he ached for her kisses he thought he might go mad if she did not give him at least one little kiss. Mayhap even a lick or two, he mused, and nearly groaned again.

"Then it would not break any rules or traditions if a woman returned such an intimate kiss?"

"Ah, no." The way she lightly ran her nails up and down his thighs had him shaking like an untried boy. "In truth, a man would be most heartily grateful, I should think."

"Oh, good." She slowly ran her tongue along the length of him and felt him shudder.

"Oh God."

It was the last coherent thing Ashton said for a very long time.

Chapter Sixteen

"Now here is a sight I never thought I would see."

Ashton's first clear thought was one of astonishment that Penelope, whom he had thought was fast asleep, could go tense so quickly. It seemed as if every inch of her delectable little body had gone as stiff as an overly starched cravat. He was tempted to see if her hair was standing on end. He smiled as he kissed the back of her neck.

Then it penetrated his sleep-dulled mind that some-one had spoken, that someone was seeing him and Penelope in bed together. Naked. Wrapped in each other's arms. The room heavily scented with the love-making they had indulged in for long hours during the night. That someone had the voice of a mature female and an accent that bespoke education and good breed-ing. His heart sank as he realized that all the troubles and complications he had been wrestling with had just increased—tenfold.

"Best hold firm to that sheet, Ashton," Penelope

murmured. "Could you give us a moment of privacy, Auntie?"

"No."

"Have it your way."

"I usually do."

It was not easy, but Penelope managed to sit up with the sheet held firmly against her. It helped that Ashton also sat up, holding firm to that part of the sheet covering the bottom half of his body. For a moment she was distracted by the sight of his smooth, hard chest, but her aunt's loud *ahem* pulled her free of the thought of kissing him there. Penelope sighed for she did not really want to talk to anyone; she wanted to make Ashton writhe and yell like she had last night. She frowned at her aunt, who stood in the doorway with her arms crossed beneath her much-admired bosom.

Lady Olympia Wherlocke was a very impressive woman. A little taller than most women, and some men, with raven black hair and sky blue eyes, she drew many admiring glances. She was strong, confident, and only three years older than Penelope. Penelope was always amazed by how imposing her young aunt could be. Olympia was even more imposing than usual at the moment, backed as she was by all the boys and their tutor, who had his hand placed firmly over young Juno's eyes.

"'Tis a little early to come calling, Auntie," Penelope said, grimacing inwardly when Olympia simply quirked one perfectly arched brow. "I was unaware that you had planned a trip to the city."

"I had not planned one but I was suddenly compelled to come. Drawn here, you might say. Called to your side."

"Not another one," muttered Ashton.

After giving Ashton a brief, cold stare, Olympia returned her attention to Penelope. "It was as I was racing to your side that a new element was added to the mix of feelings and portents pulling me onward. I now believe I know what that new element was." She gave Ashton another hard glare. "I hope you can explain everything to my satisfaction."

"More or less," replied Penelope, "but do you think we could do all this explaining in the parlor in a little while? A few moments of privacy would be greatly appreciated. Ah, nay, actually, let us gather in the breakfast room. I am feeling a bit peckish."

"I cannot imagine why."

Ignoring her aunt's sarcasm, Penelope said, "Please, Auntie. I will tell all over breakfast. There is simply too much to explain to do it here and now." *And I would much rather explain it all with my clothes on,* she thought crossly.

"Fair enough, but I suggest you be quick about joining me there."

There was a certain tone to Olympia's voice that made Penelope uneasy. "Am I to prepare for more surprises?"

"Possibly. I have the very distinct feeling that I am not the only member of the family feeling compelled to rush to your aid."

"Damn."

"In truth, I believe your uncle Argus will be arriving within the hour." Olympia shooed everyone out of the room as she turned to leave and, as soon as the doorway was clear, shut it firmly behind her.

For a moment Penelope stared at the door and then groaned. She quickly got out of bed and yanked on her shift before turning to face Ashton. He still sat in the bed holding the sheet over his groin and looking an endearing mix of confused, embarrassed, and alarmed. If her uncle Argus really was on his way to the Wherlocke

Warren, there might be a good reason for that last one. Uncle Argus was a rogue, but he expected the women of his family to be sweet, innocent, and impervious to seduction. He had been known to get very angry with any man who tried to seduce one of the Wherlocke or Vaughn women. While some of those men had deserved all they got, she did think her uncle was very hypocritical in his attitudes.

"We best hurry," she said. "Auntie is not a patient woman. If she thinks we are taking too long to join her, she could come back here."

"But if we were taking a long time to appear, it could easily mean that we decided to—"

"Exactly." Penelope cursed the heat in her cheeks for she hated to blush. "That thought would not deter Auntie."

"So she really is your aunt?" Ashton asked as he got out of bed and started to dress. "She cannot be much older than you."

"She is only three years older than I. She was the youngest of eight children. My mother was the eldest. Between them are six brothers. Uncle Argus is the third-born son."

"Are you intending to tell her everything?" He moved to help her do up her gown.

"One must be completely truthful when dealing with Aunt Olympia."

"And this Uncle Argus if he arrives?"

"Aye, him, too." She decided it was not a good time to tell him that her uncle could simply make Ashton tell him everything he wanted to know with the power of his eyes and his voice. "And if Olympia feels he will arrive, then he will. I am sorry," she said as she hastily tied her hair back with a blue ribbon to match her gown. "I have complicated your life beyond measure."

Ashton took her into his arms and held her close. "You have, but so have I. More so than you have, actually. So has fate. So has my family." He leaned back a little and briefly kissed her. "Who knows? Mayhap your aunt and uncle can help us to untangle this mess, most of which really is of my own making. The moment I met you, I should have turned away from Clarissa and taken a good hard look at things. The answers were there. I have seen that since I was trapped into this engagement. I had just decided to take the quickest route out of my difficulties by marrying money."

She smiled sadly and stroked his cheek. "And if you had taken a good look, all you would have seen was what was already there—all those responsibilities a man like you cannot ignore. There is also the small matter of all those markers Charles holds." Penelope took him by the hand. "Come. Olympia is neither a prude nor a complete tartar. She will frown and scold but she will not condemn."

"Not *you* leastwise," he muttered as he followed her out of the room.

Ashton's concern proved to be warranted, Penelope mused as she swallowed the last bite of a hearty breakfast. The moment the children left, even the older ones ordered out by Olympia, her aunt fixed a severely condemning scowl on Ashton. This was not going to be a comfortable confrontation, Penelope decided. She was a little astonished that Ashton showed no real lack of appetite beneath her aunt's gimlet stares.

"I assume the wedding will be soon," said Olympia.

"Nay," Penelope replied, firmly burying the hurt that knowledge always caused her. "There is to be no wedding."

"You are the daughter of a marquis, the niece of an earl, the—"

"No need to list all of my impressive connections, Auntie. Ashton is fully aware of them. He and his friends have been doing a lot of poking about. I will explain the why of that in a little while," she hastily added when she saw her aunt's eyes narrow at the mere thought of someone investigating the family.

"Then there will be a wedding."

"Nay. Ashton is already spoken for." She grimaced when her aunt looked at Ashton in a decidedly murderous way. "I knew that from the very beginning."

"I see." Olympia took a sip of her tea before saying, "No, I do *not* see. Not you. You are not like so many of our other relations. You are not heedless, not reckless, and certainly not given to tossing away all good sense for the sake of passion. You better than all of us know the price paid for such things. You care for a houseful of the consequences."

"The fault is mine," said Ashton. "I erred in two ways. The first was that I should have left Penelope alone. The second was that when that proved impossible, I should have backed away from Clarissa, avoided that fatal meeting with her brother that ended up with me engaged to the woman."

"Ashton." Penelope patted his hand. "Charles has tied you neatly in a knot and you know it. Auntie, before we wade into that tangle, allow me to tell you how Ashton and I met," said Penelope, and after taking a deep breath to steady herself, she told Olympia the tale of her kidnapping and all the other troubles that had plagued her since that night.

"You should have written to us, called upon us for help. That is what a family is for."

"I intended to do just that as soon as I could figure

out what was happening. And if it was anything more than coincidence. I know how uncomfortable this city can be for many of you. I did not wish to pull all of you to London simply because I was having a run of bad luck."

"Bad luck? You call what has happened to you simply bad luck?" Olympia shook her head. "Someone wants you dead, Pen, and I think you know who that is as well as I do."

"Aye, I do, but is it Clarissa, is it Charles, or is it both of them? I am certain Charles was behind my kidnapping but the madam's hired scum mentioned a woman, too. No one actually said the names of the people who had paid to have me put there, however. Clarissa did hint at it the other day but that is only my word against hers. We also think Mrs. Cratchitt was responsible for some of the things that happened to me because she felt I knew things that could get her hanged."

"Other than the fact that she kidnaps young women and forces them to become whores?"

"I said something to the men who carried me there, something about someone dying in that bed. If they told her what I said, and we now know she did kill a lot of people, she would not have wanted me telling anyone about it, would she? You see our problem, do you not? What was done by her? What was done by Charles or Clarissa? I think each has tried to kill me but we have no proof of that. If we are going to accuse a baron of trying to kill me, we need proof. Charles may be a somewhat new baron, the honor scoffed at by much of society, but he is still of the gentry. It is very hard to just point a finger and accuse one of the gentry. One needs indisputable fact. Ashton, his friends, my brothers, and Darius are all working hard to find out the truth."

"The truth is that Charles does not wish you to reach

your majority or marry. He will lose everything if that happens. But we can argue over that later. Aside from this fool getting himself caught in Clarissa's web, why can you not get married?"

Penelope sighed, realizing that her aunt would not be diverted for long with talk of murder and mystery. She looked at Ashton and cocked one brow, silently asking him if he wanted to tell her aunt Olympia everything. He was doing what he had to do to save his family from utter ruin and he might not wish to share those troubles with her scowling aunt, a woman he did not know. Penelope breathed a sigh of relief when he patted her hand and looked straight at Olympia.

"My family is destitute," he said bluntly. "My father was faithless, extravagant, and irresponsible. He left us all so deep in debt that my only choices are to wed an heiress or walk away from everything the Radmoors have built since the time of Elizabeth."

"That still does not explain why you cannot marry my niece and do not try to tell me you were not the one who took her innocence," said Olympia.

"I know what I have done is wrong but I never lied to Penelope about what my plans were or how they could not be changed no matter what I wanted. I have two brothers, three sisters, two aunts, and a mother I must support. I loathe the fact that I am naught but a fortune hunter, but needs must when the devil drives, and all that. And Charles holds all my father's markers. He can easily ruin my family with them."

"Do you have some strange aversion to Penelope's money?"

"I do not have any money, Auntie," Penelope said. "A small pension or whatever one might wish to call it, some money from the fathers of the boys, and that house that Charles claims is his. It is not enough to save

Radmoor and his family from debtor's prison. Charles will never allow him to pay those markers off slowly for he is determined that Clarissa marry a man of high title and a long heritage. Ashton needs a lot of money."

Suddenly Aunt Olympia tensed and looked toward the door. A moment later Penelope knew why. Every hair on her body stood on end. She glanced at Ashton and saw him pull up his sleeves and stare at the upright hair on his arms in astonishment. Uncle Argus was here.

A tall, broad-shouldered man strode into the breakfast room, detached a grinning Darius and an equally happy Paul from his body, and shooed them out of the room. Paul was not Argus's son but the boy adored the man and the man adored him. That man shook back his long black hair and fixed a dark, fierce gaze on Ashton. Penelope quickly put her hands over Ashton's already glazing eyes and scowled at her uncle.

"You will not do that to Ashton," she snapped. "There is no need. We are keeping no secrets, and will answer all questions."

Argus rolled his eyes and sat down next to Olympia. "You allow a man no fun." He began to help himself to what was left of the food.

Ashton pulled her hands away and stared at her in confusion. "What did he do? One moment I was ready to stand up and greet him, or accept a fist to the mouth, and the next? Well, I am not sure."

Penelope sighed. "Uncle Argus, I would like to introduce Ashton Pendellen Radmoor, the viscount of Radmoor. Ashton, this is my uncle, Argus Wherlocke, Sir Wherlocke, and he has a gift for making people want to tell him anything and not recall that they did."

"Truly?" Ashton stared at Sir Argus with interest.

"Ashton, the man just tried to force you to tell him all your secrets! Why are you looking at him as if he is the solution to all your problems?"

"Do we not have a few people we need some answers from?"

"Oh." She looked at her uncle, who gave her a beguiling smile. She did not believe it for a moment. Uncle Argus was at his most dangerous when he looked so sweet.

"Tell me all while I fill the hole in my belly," Argus said and began to eat.

Yet again Penelope told her whole story, her troubles, Ashton's troubles, and all of their suspicions. She hoped no more of her relatives showed up because she was getting weary of telling it all. She especially hated to keep saying, aloud, that she and Ashton could not marry for it hurt each time she did so.

"So toss aside that scheming bitch Clarissa and marry our Penelope," said Argus.

"I do not have the money he needs," protested Penelope, trying not to lose her patience over having to repeat herself. "I just have a house and a small fund. Charles holds all the markers left by Ashton's father, and if he calls them in, that will utterly ruin Ashton's family. They could easily all end up in debtor's prison." *Please let this be the last time I have to say this,* she added silently.

"Of course you have money. Damn, girl, your father was so tight with a coin it screamed. He had a lot of properties that were not entailed and a small fortune in the funds. God knows what else he had. If the Hutton-Moores have told you that you are poor, they are lying. Your father would have made sure that everything that was his became your mother's and yours with few ways open for a second husband to get his hands on any of it. He would have left something for his sons as well. Did you not read the damn will?"

"It was read to me by the solicitor, Mr. Horace Earnshaw," Penelope said quietly. "I fear I was grieving so when it was read that I did not pay close attention. There was so much my mother and I had not agreed on and I knew that I would never be able to take back any angry words or come to an understanding. She was gone and the distance that had grown between us would never be crossed. It broke my heart. I did ask for the will once, but Charles told me the solicitor had it. I wrote the man a letter but he never responded and"— she shrugged—"I fear I forgot about it after a while. Things can get a little busy here. But—"

"It would help if you had a servant or two," Ashton muttered.

"What are you grumbling about?" said Argus. "Of course she has servants. Who was that burly fellow at the door?"

"One of my mother's footmen. I had him and his brother come here after Mrs. Cratchitt's men broke into the house and started to destroy it."

"Why did you not hire some, girl?" Argus stared at her in confusion, an expression that made his harsh face look almost boyish.

"Because I do not have any money. I have enough for us all to live here, clothe, and feed ourselves, but little more. What extra coin I had I have used to pay Septimus to tutor the boys. And to be quite blunt, it is a pittance, and if he was not family and so fond of the boys, he would soon find a new position."

Argus sat back in his seat and dragged a hand through his hair. "But I have sent you money every week. I know the others send money near every month. I cannot remember the exact sum, but it would certainly be enough to hire a maid or two."

Penelope stared at her uncle and then, as a cold knot formed in her belly, she looked at Ashton, who was frowning. "They have known about this house since the beginning. They have found some way to take most of the money sent to me." She looked at her uncle. "Did you send it here?"

"I believe most of us did. Are you saying they managed to get their greedy hands on the money we sent to our children?"

The hair on Penelope's arms was standing up again and she knew that, although his voice was almost pleasant, her uncle was furious. "I believe they have. I just do not know . . ." She stopped speaking as she saw the ghost of Mrs. Pettibone standing near the fireplace with her head hanging in shame. "Oh, Mrs. Pettibone, did you steal it?"

Nay. He did. He said he was your brother. Said you were trying to steal from him and all. He gave me a little each time I took a packet.

Penelope blinked. That had to be one of the most understandable conversations she had ever had with a ghost. It was obvious that what she had done had weighed on Mrs. Pettibone for a very long time.

"It is fine, Mrs. Pettibone, I forgive you."

The children?

Clearly Mrs. Pettibone's skill with words had already faded. "They will forgive you, too. It is not your fault that you believed Charles. He is very persuasive and you have been taught that a man rules."

Aye. They do.

Penelope was not about to get in an argument with a ghost about that although a part of her wanted to. "Find your peace, Mrs. Pettibone."

Hell. I am a thief.

"Nay, you were lied to. It is Charles who will pay. Let go, my dear. Let go."

When Mrs. Pettibone suddenly smiled beatifically and slowly faded, Penelope looked at her aunt and uncle. "Charles told Mrs. Pettibone some tale about me stealing from him. I suspect the *and all* includes many a slander upon my reputation and good reasons why he could not just take me to a magistrate. So, she took any packet she could get ahold of and gave it to him. He always gave her a little money to show his immense gratitude. Why the woman did not stop and ask why, if I was stealing from him, I was posting the money to myself instead of just carrying it to the house, I do not know." Penelope knew her voice was tart and short with bitterness but she could not help it. Charles had stolen from her boys, and for that, she wanted to see him pay.

She frowned. "It was odd. The first thing she said was clear and precise. No rhymes, no short words that give a clue but not enough. She spoke to me as if she were right here, alive. Yet when she first appeared, she was just like the others, and after she made her little confession, she went back to short sentences or one word. Has not said a word in between then and now, either."

"Perhaps she was just saving her strength, practicing what she needed to say so that she could confess it all quickly and clearly," said Ashton, and then he shrugged. "It was just a thought."

"A very good one. I may see ghosts and speak with them but I fear the only thing I am sure of about them is that they almost all seek peace."

"The man who stole from our children will pay us back," said Argus. "And I will see that Septimus is given a nice sum to make up for wages lost to the bastard."

"Thank you, Uncle. Sad to say, I am not sure there

will be any of the money to retrieve. It was undoubtedly spent on fine clothes, fine wines, carriages, and horses. The trappings that Charles so loves."

"Then we will take our money back in trade."

"We can plan that out later, Argus," said Olympia. "I want to see this solicitor."

"Once my curiosity about the will was roused again, I began trying to arrange a meeting with him," said Penelope. "I started by writing a letter every other day, then every day, then two a day." She shrugged. "Yesterday I sent him four."

"Perhaps he has not replied because he is buried beneath the letters," drawled Olympia.

"I have things to do today," said Argus, "but we will all hunt the man down on the morrow. Has anyone tried to find the will at Salterwood House?"

"It is called Hutton-Moore House now," said Penelope and almost smiled when her uncle fell into a low muttering of curses. Perhaps she had erred in not sending word to her relatives about her troubles.

"And I need to visit with the boys and little Juno," said Olympia.

"Juno?" Argus frowned. "A girl?"

Penelope explained who Juno was. "She is still a little uncertain but the boys are already very protective of her."

"Damn. A girl. Best write to Quintin. He may still be sending money to that bitch to pay for the girl and it had best come to you now."

"Of course." She smiled faintly. "I wonder if her dear mother considered her loss of income when she so callously rid herself of her daughter."

"She will be made aware of it very soon and I would not wish to be her when Quintin finds out what she did."

Penelope winced. Her cousin was well known for his temper. However, if the woman had a change of heart simply because her purse was now lighter, she would find that she had lost all chance of retrieving her little girl. Penelope would never let that woman near Juno again.

"We will be staying with you," said Olympia but she was staring at Ashton.

Ashton nearly grimaced. He had finally been able to get Penelope back into his arms and now she would be taken away from him again. Argus was grinning at him and Ashton had a strong urge to kick the man.

"Bit like shutting the stable door after the mare has fled, Olympia," Argus drawled as he stood up and started toward the door. "Never thought you a prude."

"Someone should be in this family," she called after him but he just laughed as the door swung shut behind him. "You may leave now," she said to Ashton.

Penelope grasped him by the arm when he began to stand up and held him in his seat. "Nay. This is my house, Auntie. I am one and twenty and not a child. As my uncle so indelicately put it, the mare has fled. I know what I am doing would be frowned on by everyone in society if it was discovered, but so would taking care of the illegitimate children of my relatives. I want my time with Ashton," she said quietly and he grasped her hand in his. "I need it and for once in my life I intend to do what I want."

"Fine." Olympia stood up. She walked around the table and looked into Ashton's eyes. "Stay. But if you break my niece's heart, I will make you very sorry you were ever born." She patted Penelope on the head and then strode out of the room.

"Your aunt is a very beautiful woman," Ashton said quietly.

Penelope suffered a sharp pinch of jealousy. "Aye, she is."

He nodded. "She is also very scary."

"True, she is."

"My mother would love her."

They looked at each other and laughed.

Chapter Seventeen

"This seems a poor place for a solicitor," muttered Olympia. "I cannot believe your father would entrust his money and important papers to a man who lived in such squalor."

Penelope slid her hand into Ashton's and stared at the building. It *was* a squalid place in a squalid area. Then she frowned. There was also someone dead in there.

"Best we go on up and see the fool," said Argus, starting toward the door, Darius at his heels.

"Nay," Penelope said. "At least not with Darius. Someone is dead in there." She was not surprised to hear Ashton and Argus curse; they seemed to come up against a wall everywhere they turned.

"The solicitor?" Ashton asked.

"I am not certain."

She stepped back and stared up at the filthy windows. Some were broken and the holes had been stuffed with anything at hand. It was not until her gaze reached the fourth floor that she saw something. At first she thought it was just that one window up there was amazingly clean but then she saw something move. From what little she could recall from the reading of the will, it was the solicitor in the window, or rather, his spirit. Her stomach churned a little. He had not died easily.

"Mr. Horace Earnshaw is dead," she said.

"Feared that was it," muttered Argus while Olympia just kept staring at the window, a look of deep concentration on her face.

Help me.

"Too late," she murmured and then looked at Darius. "Do you recall the Bow Street man who led the others at Mrs. Cratchitt's?"

Darius nodded. "Mr. Dobson."

"Can you go and get him? Tell him that I have found another body and bring him here."

"I will go with him," said Ashton. "If you do not mind, I believe we will take the carriage."

Argus nodded. "Good idea. This is a dangerous area."

"We will go as fast as we can," said Darius as he jumped into the carriage with Ashton.

"Should we not go up there?" Argus asked as the carriage rolled away. "We could find some of the papers we need to look at."

Olympia slowly shook her head. "Only the will and Penelope shall have to try to get the man's spirit to tell her where it is. Everything else was taken. Poor fool took a long time to die but he did do one last good thing. He did not tell them where that will was."

Help me.

"I cannot, sir," Penelope said, staring up at the forlorn and gruesome ghost. "You must accept what has happened to you."

"How long do you think it will take Darius and Ashton

to fetch that Dobson man back here?" asked Olympia, glancing around with a frown and slowly extracting a pistol from her reticule.

"Not very long, I should think. With all that happened at the brothel, I made him and his men a tidy sum. The merchants had gathered rewards for two of their own who had gone missing. Dobson thought there might be more to come if they can match the bodies, at least some of them, to a list of missing people they have."

"I had not realized they did that sort of thing."

"They do a great many things. Dobson, and I am ashamed that I never asked his name, told me a great deal about them as I marked where more bodies were buried. I had not realized just how much but will certainly keep them in mind if I ever have trouble in the future. I but wish he could have gained some rewards for finding someone alive," she added quietly.

"Have you been to question Mrs. Cratchitt about who paid her to have you kidnapped?" asked Argus.

"Ashton says he will try to do that," Penelope replied, "but he has been warned that she is not being cooperative. At least she was not when they took her away. 'Tis not as if helping anyone will save her from a hanging."

"I will go with Ashton when he goes to see the bitch," said Argus. "She will tell me what we need to know."

"Penelope, my dear," Olympia said, "you do realize what the murder of the solicitor means, do you not?"

"That someone fears we are getting too close to the truth."

"Yes, and that puts you in a great deal of danger."

Penelope sighed and nodded. "I know, but considering all that has happened to me thus far, I think I have been in a great deal of danger for a while. I was wondering on it and think that Charles can no longer wait to get his hands on everything. He has debt, perhaps, or is just greedy. The latter I think. We have been most careful since I was shot."

"You have and the fact that Lord Radmoor has saved your life three times and Paul's once and done his best to protect you is why I did not pummel him the moment I realized he had seduced you," Argus said.

"I think the seduction was mutual." Penelope blushed when her uncle grinned.

"You love him."

"A great deal."

"Well, let us hope we find that you still have enough left to solve his problems."

"I do not know what of my inheritance will be left, but I do know if we prove Charles has attempted to kill me, has killed Mr. Earnshaw, and has stolen from me, that he will be completely discredited. Enough proof and he will hang or be transported. Then I may help Ashton in a very big way."

"How?"

"I will hold those cursed markers then, will I not, and I can burn them."

Ashton hopped down from the carriage after Dobson and his two men did, then swung Darius down. The boy raced to his father's side. Argus put his arm around the boy as Penelope talked to Dobson. From what little he had seen since Argus had arrived, the man truly did love his child, and appeared to be very fond of the other children, too. Now that he knew Argus and the others had been sending money, a goodly sum by the sound of it, his anger over the way the children had been left in Penelope's care faded. They had sent her more than enough to have hired plenty of servants. However, he still thought the Wherlocke and Vaughn men could be more cautious. Ashton was not certain he believed Penelope's assurances that they were, but that they were just too damn fertile.

He scowled when yet again the image of Penelope rounding with his child slipped through his mind. It was not good for him to have such dreams but he could not shake free of them. Ashton looked at Penelope and hurried to her side for she looked pale. Whatever had happened to Earnshaw had obviously not been pleasant. He took her hand in his just as Dobson and his men started to go into the building. The Wherlockes began to follow but Dobson turned to face them.

"I think you lot ought to stay here," Dobson said.

"No," said Argus. "I believe you need us to go with you."

Ashton shivered. Argus's eyes were like fathomless dark pools and his voice stroked one's mind. The man was dangerous. He could turn any person's mind so cloudy he spilled every secret he had. To Ashton's astonishment, Dobson just scowled at the man.

"I ain't sure what you be doing but you can just stop it," Dobson growled and then eyed Argus warily when the man grinned. "Fine. You can come in as I might be needing Lady Penelope's help, but I think the boy best stay here."

Darius started to protest but his father sent him to the carriage with a few quiet words. As the boy scrambled up on the box next to the driver, he did not appear to be disappointed.

"Do you know who your family is, Dobson?" Argus asked as they climbed the dark, narrow stairs.

"Nay. First clear memory I got is some small orphanage run by a harsh besom named Mrs. Creed. Why?"

"Because very few people can tell what I am doing to them and resist it. Mostly ones in our family."

Dobson snorted as he opened the door to the solicitor's rooms. He stopped abruptly and then cursed. "Poor sod." He looked back at Olympia and Penelope. "'Tain't pretty."

"We know," said Olympia, and Dobson shrugged before leading them all inside.

Ashton took one look at the remains of Horace Earnshaw and nearly followed Dobson's two retching men back out of the room. He put his arm around Penelope when she swayed a little. Olympia paled, hesitated a moment, but then slowly began to walk around the room. Argus stood, hands on his hips, and stared down at the mess that used to be a man.

"That ghostie here, m'lady?" asked Dobson.

"Aye," Penelope replied as she stepped closer to the desk, holding Ashton's hand tightly. "He does not understand. He cries and asks me to help him."

"No help could fix this mess. See if you can get him to tell you what happened and who did this. Weren't no common thieves." He crouched by the body. "Common thieves just stick a knife in you, take what you got, and leave. They don't be lurking about taking little pieces off a man."

Argus crouched on the other side of the body. "Did the face first."

"Mr. Earnshaw," Penelope began, wanting to shut out the rather gruesome conversation her uncle and Dobson were having concerning the solicitor's body.

Help me.

"I cannot. Look at your earthly remains, Mr. Earnshaw. There is no help I can give you save to help you find peace."

Bastard.

"Who? Who did this to you?"

He had them hurt me.

"Mr. Earnshaw, do you not wish the man to pay for causing you so much pain?"

He watched. Enjoyed it.

Penelope shivered at the thought that anyone could enjoy seeing what had been done to Mr. Earnshaw. She rubbed her forehead as she struggled to think of some way to pry the information she needed out of a ghost. They were not known for being cooperative or even very coherent.

"Mr. Earnshaw, do you know who I am?"

Salterwood's brat.

"And you have been cheating me for years, have you not?"

Needed money.

"But you did not do it alone, did you. Who helped? Who shared in the theft?"

Charles.

Penelope pushed down a surge of excitement. Charles was a very common name. She needed more.

"Charles who?"

Bastard. Wanted it all.

"All of what?"

Salterwood's fortune.

"Charles did?"

Bastard. Hid some.

"Hid some what?"

Papers. In the floor.

"Where in the floor?"

Under board. Third from left.

"And Charles wanted those papers?"

The ghost nodded. *Bastard.*

"Mr. Earnshaw, you will find peace if you unburden yourself."

Did. Under floor.

Penelope saw the ghost suddenly cringe in terror and she cursed softly as he disappeared. Sometimes, she thought darkly, all her gift gave her was a headache. It was also obvious from the look on the spirit's face that Earnshaw had committed more sins than stealing from his clients for it had not been the look of a soul about to find peace.

She looked at Ashton and frowned. He was looking a little pale. Then she heard the conversation Dobson and Argus were having as they crouched by the body. The two men were still calmly discussing which parts of poor Mr. Earnshaw had been cut first. Her stomach roiled and she fixed her attention on her aunt.

"It was Charles but Mr. Earnshaw did not give me his surname so it does us no good," she told Olympia.

"No. Too many named Charles." Olympia sighed. "There were three of them. One leaned against the desk while the other two cut the poor fool at his direction. They gagged him so that his screams would go unheard. Not that that would have caused them very much trouble in this place."

Dobson stood up and looked at Olympia with interest. "You got the sight, too?"

"Not like Penelope. What I see is the shadows of what happened especially if it was violent. Unfortunately, the shadows are not always clear enough to see faces. Mr. Earnshaw endured for a long time but then his heart failed when they threatened to castrate him." She smiled faintly when all three men winced. "The will is here."

"Ah, aye, he did tell me that." Penelope pointed to the floor. "Third board from the left wall. Under it."

"You think this Charles wanted that?" asked Dobson.

"He is my stepbrother, and with Mr. Earnshaw's assistance, I believe he has been stealing from me for years. That is why we came to see Mr. Earnshaw today. To confront him."

"Then why'd he take everything else?"

"Because he thought the papers he wanted were there? Or mayhap he wanted to confuse whoever found Mr. Earnshaw's body." She frowned. "Or Charles might have thought he could find something of interest in Earnshaw's papers. Knowing my stepbrother, he would not hesitate to blackmail someone."

Dobson scratched his cheek and nodded. "Blackmail can fill your coffers fast. Too bad you did not get that surname. Could end this all right now." He frowned at Argus and Ashton, who were trying to pry up the floorboard with dented fireplace tools. "Hey, you two weak-bellied women," he yelled to his men, "get in here and help these fellows."

Penelope left the room with Olympia as the men set to work. Once outside, she took a deep breath. The air in London was not sweet but she needed to clear the stench of death from her nose.

"At least now we are sure it is Charles," said Olympia.

"True. I just wish Earnshaw had given me the cursed surname, or at least mentioned the word 'baron.'" Penelope sighed. "Not that it would have done me much good in trying to charge Charles with a crime. I certainly could not tell a judge that a ghost told me."

"No. Just as I could not tell a judge that I saw it all in the shadows. Penelope, about Radmoor—"

"I love him, Auntie. Even when he is being a little pompous, I love him. He has stood by me and helped me in every way he could. He and his friends."

"I know. What I was going to say was, if you do end up

with money, enough money to help him and his family, are you going to wonder if that is why he marries you?"

"I had not considered that until now," grumbled Penelope and gave her aunt a cross look.

"Mayhap you should."

Penelope thought about it for a moment and then shook her head. " *If* I have some fortune left, *if* I can destroy those markers, and *if* Ashton asks me to marry him, I will. That is, *if* he will accept the boys. I cannot leave them. Too many have done that to them already and I love them. I could never hurt them like that. A lot of *ifs*.

"But I am certain that Ashton cares for me. He might not love me as I do him, but I think he could, especially if the chains Charles has wrapped around him are cut. I also know he would be a good husband and father. Faithful. I just do not try to think on it too much because there are still so many problems left to solve. And if he does not wish to marry me even if we solve all the problems, I will accept that, too. Better to lose him than to have him as an unwilling husband."

"Fair enough, but I do think you will soon find yourself very rich. We just need to keep you alive until that happens."

The men arrived before Penelope could say anything. Dobson's two men carried the blanket-shrouded form of Mr. Earnshaw. She winced when they dropped the body so that they could signal a hack. Penelope supposed they saw so many bodies they had grown callous about the dead. Not callous enough to keep from retching, however, she thought.

Ashton stepped up beside her and handed her a packet. "Dobson took a quick look and decided it was ours so we could take it."

"But you have to let me see it if it's needed," added Dobson.

"Of course," replied Penelope.

Dobson patted his coat. "I took the list that was with the packet. It names the ones he worked for. Their papers are all gone and I be thinking they will want to know that."

"Most assuredly." She smiled at him. "Why, I would not be at all surprised if they wished to reward anyone who gets those papers back for them."

He winked. "Just what I was thinking." He frowned toward where his men were loading Mr. Earnshaw's body into the carriage and arguing with the driver, who was loudly objecting to having a dead body in his hack. "This was a bad one. Just like that poor woman chained up at Cratchitt's. It be the cruelty of it that makes it worse than another killing. You find out anything about who did this, you let me know. I might not be able to clamp the irons on a man because of what you learned, but it could lead me in the right direction so's I can find what I need."

"Agreed."

"Ah, and we found the man with the scar that nearly took out his left eye."

"One of Mrs. Cratchitt's?" asked Ashton.

Dobson nodded his head. "Pulled out of the river a few nights back. Throat cut. Fools wrapped him tight in an oilcloth and that left a lot of him to be recognized. One of her other men did so. So, no need to talk to the old besom about who tried to run m'lady over with a carriage. She will be hanged soon so, if you do have anything else you think she can tell you, best not wait too much longer." He tipped his hat to Penelope and Ashton. "Call for me if ye have a need. You know where to find me."

"I truly hope we do not have to find him again,"

Penelope said quietly as Ashton helped her into the carriage. "But I fear we will. This is not over yet."

"No. No, not yet," Ashton said. "Are you going to look?" he asked, lightly touching the packet she held.

"Soon."

It took all of Penelope's willpower not to tear the packet open immediately. She held it tight all the way home. Once settled in the parlor with something to drink and eat, she sat down next to Ashton and opened the packet. She took out several deeds to property she had not even known her father had, sheets of paper with an accounting on them, and the original wills of her mother and father, not the copies that Charles had hidden away somewhere.

"Nick me," she said as she read her father's will. "I was to get two thousand pounds per annum. I never saw that. A few hundred but never two thousand. Ah, of course. My guardian was to give it to me. At first it was the new marquis, then the old baron after he adopted me, and then Charles. I have obviously been robbed for years. And it says here that Stefan and Artemis were to get one thousand per annum and a small piece of property. Each."

"Both to be distributed by the guardian," said Ashton. "It does appear that every guardian you have had decided you had no need of such largess but it is Charles who concerns us now."

"Aye, Charles. He has been pocketing most of four thousand pounds a year." She read on, shaking her head in disgust. "There are gifts listed for all the old servants and I know those were never paid out." She put her father's will down. "I do not think Mother obeyed it, either. I do not understand that."

"Perhaps Earnshaw was stealing from her, too," said Argus.

"That could be. It is not as if Father left her destitute, however. The properties he held that were not entailed go to her, except for the two small ones for Stefan and Artemis, so we did not even have to stay in the dower house as we did. I can, in a way, understand her hesitancy to give the boys anything. She was devastated by Papa's unfaithfulness. Yet, to not give Jones, the old butler at Salterwood House, his pension plus the generous gift Papa left him? That seems so unlike Mama. She liked Jones but he only got a pittance from the new marquis and had to go live with his sister when he was pensioned off. Did she not even notice that? We were in the dower house at that time."

"Your mother would never have questioned a man to see if he was doing as he should," said Olympia. "She probably felt the marquis would do as he should and never gave it another thought."

Penelope thought of how her mother behaved with men and had to agree. Despite the way her father had been, her mother had never stopped acting as if men knew everything. As she had grown older, it had begun to annoy her. The way her mother had turned aside the boys just because the baron said he would not have them in his house had crushed her last hope that her mother might someday grow a backbone.

"What does your mother's will say?" asked Argus. "It may answer some of your questions."

"In other words, I should have listened when it was read."

"You were grieving. I doubt that anyone who truly cares for the person who just died hears much at the reading of the will."

Penelope just smiled a little, not completely ready to forgive herself, and then read her mother's will. She had to take several deep breaths to keep from weeping.

Just holding the will made her painfully aware of how much had been left unresolved between her mother and her. Ashton began to lightly rub her back and she sent him a brief smile of gratitude for his concern.

"Mother wanted every provision of Papa's will to continue to be honored. 'Tis an odd thing to say so mayhap she did have some suspicions. She also left Mrs. Potts a very nice pension plus a sizable gift. I know that was never given out. Mrs. Potts is sixty. I think she would like to rest now after a life of service but has complained now and then about having little money to do so and no promise of a pension from Charles. Ah, and here, just as I did remember, I was to have all of her jewels and that house."

Ashton sorted through all the deeds on the table. "The deed to that house is not here."

"I suspect Charles managed to gain hold of that. It is difficult to prove ownership without it. My word against his is not enough."

"Quite possibly although I suspect there are others who could verify your claim." He frowned as he studied the deeds. "There are some very fine properties here. Who cares for them?"

"I have no idea. I did not even know about them although Mama's will gives them to me. Two are actually part of her original dower and the rest are properties Father obtained. She even left a nice gift of money to Charles and Clarissa despite how poorly they treated her."

"We need to have a nice long chat with Charles," said Argus. "And after that, I want to go and talk to the new marquis. To deprive Jones of his earned pension cannot be allowed to stand. They have stood by our family for generations. Them and the Pughs. That will have to be fixed."

"Aye," agreed Penelope. "George is a pompous little

man but he cannot be allowed to break Wherlocke tradition. We count too much on the loyalty of those people for him to cause even the tiniest rift."

"And he needs to understand that one must never cheat the women or the children in the family who are dependent upon your care. That, too, is unacceptable. I believe I know something about him and what I recall leaves me unsurprised that he would do his best to cheat you and your mother, even your servants. He has a skill at sensing a person's weakness and has always used it to line his pockets. His mother taught him that. She saw the usefulness of such a talent almost immediately. She is one of the ones I wish *had* deserted her child. He may have become a better man. But we will sort him out."

Penelope briefly felt sorry for George, but only briefly. Her family had few rules they followed but helping the women and children in their family and taking good care of their loyal servants were ones that were never broken or bent. George would soon learn the error of his ways, and always be watched closely. She noticed Ashton looking a bit bemused.

"What is it?" she asked.

"Aside from the fact that one of you is named such a common name as George?" he asked and grinned when they all laughed. "It is your outrage over how the servants were cheated. I feel the same but know I am one of a few who would, sad to say."

"Remember what we are, Ashton. At times our very lives have depended on the loyalty of our servants. We have found a few families whose loyalty is taught from the cradle. They have stood by us for generations and have always been treated well and rewarded well. They know it and teach their children that they can only benefit from being utterly loyal to us. George threatens

what has been established and we cannot afford that."
She smiled at her uncle. "But you will put him on the
right path, will you not, Uncle?"

"Most assuredly."

"And will have a great deal of help in doing so," said
Olympia, briefly allowing her anger at George to show,
but she quickly shook it aside. "Now we have to decide
what to do about Charles."

"We could start legal proceedings against him, I suppose," murmured Penelope. "Cousin Andras Vaughn is
a solicitor. We could always ask him to at least look at all
of this and see if there is anything that can be done. I
think the biggest problem here is that Charles is my
guardian. That gives him a great deal more power than
I have."

"Then we see to changing who your guardian is,
using the fact that he has cheated you of your inheritance for years to push for that change."

"Do you think that can be done?"

"I am not sure, but I do not see why not. We have
more in our family with the power to turn the courts to
their side than he does. Shall we begin?"

"And let him know it?"

"Most assuredly, my dear. That is part of the game."

Ashton inwardly shivered at the cold smiles exchanged
by Olympia and Argus. He prayed he never got on the
bad side of this family. He also prayed that the game they
planned did not put Penelope in even more danger.

Chapter Eighteen

Penelope smiled down at a sleeping Ashton. She lightly trailed her fingernails up and down his strong thighs. He made a soft noise of pleasure and shifted slightly. She kissed the hollow at the base of his throat.

"Ah, 'tis morning," he said and lifted one hand to stroke her back.

"What a clever man you are." It was barely dawn but she saw no need to be precise.

He grinned and then groaned softly when she lightly nipped his stomach. It astonished him that she could still stir such a wild aching lust inside him. It was possible that he had made love to Penelope more than he had made love to all the other women he had known combined. He had also been far more creative, aroused, and satisfied. If it was merely a brief, mad lust, it should have begun to wane but it had not.

Ashton wondered if it was because Penelope was so passionate and so comfortable with that. The few women he had known in his life had liked to be made love to but rarely liked to make love to him, and then only did so halfheartedly. Penelope gave as freely as she took. Then she ran her hot little tongue down the length of him and he no longer cared to puzzle out the why of it all.

She teased and tormented him with her too clever tongue and her nimble fingers until Ashton thought he would go mad. When she finally gave him what he craved and slowly took him into her mouth, he knew he would not be able to enjoy the delight for very long. The moment he felt the last threads of his control begin to fray, he sat up enough to grab her by the arms and start to pull her up his body. He fell back against the pillows as he kissed her.

"Ride me, Penelope," he whispered against her throat.

A little uncertain, Penelope did her best to join their bodies. As he slid home inside her, she trembled from the pleasure of it. Ashton grasped her firmly by the hips to urge her to move and she quickly grasped the rhythm he sought from her. But desire was swift to grab hold of her and rule her completely, leading her into finding her own rhythm. When Ashton placed his hands over her breasts, she held them there, stroking him from his fingers to his elbows. And then the bliss began to sweep over her, tumbling her into that place where only pleasure ruled. In a small part of her desire-clouded mind she was aware of Ashton joining her there a heartbeat later.

It was not until they had cleansed themselves and were regaining their strength in each other's arms that Penelope began to feel a little uneasy about her behavior. She loved Ashton and believed what they shared was but one way to express that love. Yet she had heard that many men did not believe ladies were capable of such passion. Did she demean herself in Ashton's eyes by reveling in their physical joining as much as he did?

"Ashton?" She stroked his hair.

"Yes?" Ashton idly fondled her breasts as he licked her throat, his sated body already stirring with renewed interest.

She swallowed nervously as she struggled to decide the best way to ask her questions. "I have heard it said that a true lady does not, well, she does not—"

"Enjoy making love?"

"Aye."

"That, my sweet, passionate Penelope, is the sort of nonsense that has ruined many a promising young marriage."

The relief she felt was almost overwhelming. "Truly?"

"My word on it. 'Tis foolishness such as that which causes even good men to set up mistresses."

"Ah." Penelope was pretty sure that was not the only reason. Some men just felt it was their right to have as many women as they wanted no matter how warm their bed at home.

Ashton moved so that she was neatly pinned beneath him. "I like my passionate Penelope." He slowly moved against her, mimicking the act he fully intended to indulge in once more before he had to leave. "My sweet lover." He almost grinned at the way her breathing grew a little uneven and she blindly parted her legs a little more so that he could continue his play with more ease.

"I am not sweet."

"Oh, but you are." He kissed her. "Purely sweet." He circled each of her nipples with his tongue. "And here? Raspberry tarts." He continued to torment her breasts with playful kisses and gentle nips. "At first I feared this was wrong, that I was allowing lust to rule me as it had ruled my father."

"Nay, Ashton—"

"No need to try to soothe my fears again, love." He drew the hard tip of her breast into his mouth and suckled her. "I have never felt like this or acted like this and I am almost thirty. I was temperate in all things and did not find it any great trial. My father was behaving like a rutting goat by the time he was eighteen." He kissed his way over to her other breast and gave it the same treatment.

"Eighteen?" Penelope struggled to keep her mind clear for he had never fully explained about his father and she believed it was something she needed to hear. *He better hurry up, though,* she thought.

"Yes, and he never stopped, not even after he married my mother." He began to inch down her body, one slow kiss at a time. "I thank God that she finally locked her bedchamber door against him nine years ago." He moved past the place he intended to feast upon in a moment to kiss his way down her leg and was certain he heard a murmur of disappointment. "At best guess, it was a year later that he caught the pox."

"Oh, Ashton. Thank God your mother was spared that." Penelope knew it was only the brief cold slap of his words that gave her the ability to utter such a complete, coherent sentence. As he kissed his way up her other leg, the wild need only he could awaken in her was already returning.

"He did not stop his rutting until shortly before he died so God alone knows just how far and wide he spread it." He traced the shape of each of her hipbones with his tongue. "He finally brought his ravaged body home so that the family he had so shamed and ignored now had to suffer through his increasing insanity. Then, one night, he ran naked from the house, screaming that there were mermaids in the pond and he would have one. We could not catch him in time. He flung himself into the water. By the time Marston and I caught up to him, he had drowned."

"Oh, I am so sorry for you."

He propped himself up on his forearms and looked at her. "Do not be. He was no father to any of us. Ever. There was a touch of sadness at lost chances, something I believe we all suffered, but no more. What I am trying to say is that, at some point, it finally sank into my poor, stunted male brain"—he grinned when she laughed—"that I was letting that fear control me so I cut myself free of it. And this is not wrong. What we share is beyond words."

"Aye, it is."

"And I mean to revel in it, including gorging myself on the sweetness of you." He bent his head and slowly licked her.

Twice he took her to a shattering release. To Penelope's astonishment, she still ached to have him deep inside her and she murmured a complaint when he urged her up onto her hands and knees. She did not think she had the strength or the patience for any more games.

"Grasp the head board," Ashton said, not surprised by how rough and thick his voice was for he was shaking with his need for her.

Penelope did as he said and gasped when he joined their bodies from behind. Shock over the unusual position faded quickly, burnt away by desire. Her last clear thought was to wonder just how many ways one could do this.

They were both dressed and ready to go downstairs before Penelope found the courage to ask, "Ashton, you have told me that you have no imagination and that you were temperate, so how is it that you know so much about, well, *this*." She blushed and waved her hand toward the bed.

He grinned and then kissed her. "Books." He kissed her again. "And beautiful inspiration."

"Books? There are books written on such things?"

"Yes, and they are the fabled pirate treasure of every boy who reaches the age to start thinking on women." He saw the shocked look on her face and laughed.

"Boys will never change," she muttered and followed him downstairs.

"Shopping?" Penelope looked at her aunt then her uncle and then back again.

Argus nodded and tugged Darius close to his side. "I decided to take the older boys out to a tailor I know. He does fine work and is not a thief, never pricing his clothes far beyond reason. So we are off to get these brothers of yours and Darius here measured for some new clothes. Septimus is coming along to help."

Penelope looked at each of the boys and Septimus, who was not much more than a boy himself. She could see their eagerness. Argus had undoubtedly insisted Septimus go so that he could also get a few new clothes. It would certainly make up for the young man's meager wages. She did not have the heart to deny any of them just because her pride pinched over the fact that she had never been able to give them such a treat. That, she knew, was not her fault. She looked at her aunt Olympia, who stood holding the hands of Juno and Paul.

"I intend to take Juno and Paul out for a wander." Olympia softly instructed the children to stay where they were and, grabbing Penelope by the arm, dragged her to the far end of the room. "If that little darling's mother spent any of Quintin's money on that child's clothing, I will eat my shoes. I saw Juno's things and they are little better than rags. I suspect the woman bought that one pretty dress just to drag her here."

"I know," Penelope muttered, "yet the mother was dressed quite exquisitely and warmly. But, Aunt—"

"No. Do not argue. You have been consistently and monstrously robbed. Argus and I agreed that we all should have kept a closer watch on this place and you. 'Tis bad enough that the rogues in our family feel free to leave you with the burden of raising their children, especially when you began this when you were little more than a child yourself. Consider this an apology for that unforgivable neglect. And they are our family, too. Now, we have already told the other boys that we shall take them out on the morrow," she said as she led Penelope back to where the others waited near the door.

Before Penelope could even think of a reasonable protest, they were all gone. That left her alone with six little boys. Not even Mrs. Stark was around, having left the house an hour ago. The woman's daughter was still too sick to be left alone all day. Penelope had also hoped to have a woman-to-woman talk with her aunt, but that would now have to be arranged for later.

She sighed and collected her sewing. When she stepped back into the parlor, she found the younger boys already gathered there playing a game or reading a book or drawing. They were being amazingly well behaved and she had to wonder what promises her aunt and uncle had made to them to get such a result. For a moment, she wanted to complain, her pride ruffled by the apparent usurping of her place, but good sense intervened. She ruled in the matter of the boys and she knew it. She had made a family for them. If, now and then, aunts, uncles, cousins, or wayward fathers wandered by spreading their largesse, she would not let it trouble her, but share in the boys' joy over whatever gifts they got. She would, however, make certain that the boys understood that not every visiting relative would be so open-handed, if only because they could not afford to be, and that not every father would include every child in his attention and generosity. Her family was mostly kind, loved the children they bred no matter which side of the blanket they were born on, and were generous, but they could also be unintentionally thoughtless. She would not let her boys be hurt.

It was not until it was time to begin cooking for the evening meal that Penelope ceased her work. She stretched as she stood up, a little astonished by how much work she had accomplished in a few hours. Her mending basket had only two items left in it. Penelope then grimaced, knowing it would quickly fill up again. She turned to the boys and was about to ask Conrad and Delmar to come help her in the kitchen when the dog growled.

"How bloody cozy," sneered a familiar voice, which rapidly built a hard ball of fear in her belly.

Penelope slowly turned around to face Charles and had to struggle to hide her shock. He looked terrible. His clothes were a mess and she suddenly feared for TedNed, whichever of the twins had stayed with her while his brother went with Olympia. The footman would never have let Charles into the house without a fight. The fact that Charles had obviously won that fight was astonishing. Charles also looked ill, his face flushed and his eyes gleaming with a too bright light. Penelope prayed that was from the excitement of a hard-won fight.

"What are you doing here?" she asked. "Where is my footman?"

"Bleeding on your steps."

"Bastard. What do you want?"

"Everything you have, you useless little bitch. My mistake was in thinking I would enjoy a bit more than your lands and money, have a little taste of what you have been giving Radmoor so freely. That little game failed and I suddenly figured out why. That bitch Cratchitt brought Radmoor to you, planning to cheat me on being the first. Everything has gone wrong since then. I should have just killed you the first chance I had years ago."

He lunged and grabbed her by the arm. All the boys and the dog moved forward to protect her, and Penelope felt the muzzle of Charles's pistol push hard against her temple. Pressed against him as she was, she could feel the hard shape of another pistol inside his waistcoat. He had obviously come well armed.

"You brats stay right where you are or I will shoot this bitch." Charles glared at the snarling dog. "That mongrel, too. God, how I ache to shoot that little cur. Now, back away. Faster, faster. You do not wish to make me feel threatened, do you?"

Penelope suddenly noticed something else about the man holding a gun to her head. He smelled bad. Charles never smelled bad. Perhaps the only good thing she could ever had said about Charles if someone had asked was that he was always clean. It had almost been an obsession with the man. But now, there was a nose-wrinkling odor about him. Even his breath was foul. A heartbeat later she knew what it was. Charles was indeed ill. Very, very ill.

"Charles," she said in as calm a voice as she could muster, "you are not well."

"I know I am not bloody well," he yelled. "I am sick. Hell's teeth, I think I am dying. And 'tis all your fault!" He aimed his pistol at Killer. "And that thrice-cursed cur!"

Her cry of alarm was drowned in that of the boys. The shot fired so close to her head left her ears ringing. Penelope realized she had closed her eyes and slowly opened them. There was no bleeding corpse of a dog to be seen, and if the fury in the expressions of the boys was any indication, none of them had been hurt, either. The boys took one unified step toward Charles, and Penelope silently cursed when her captor pressed the muzzle of yet another pistol against her head.

A movement near the fireplace revealed the homely face of the dog peering out from beneath a chair. Penelope suspected that was where the beast had ended up when Jerome had flung it out of danger. He had obviously been honing his skill. She was just wondering if the child had enough skill to remove Charles's gun from his hand when Charles cursed. The muzzle of the pistol began to tremble against her temple. Penelope's heart leapt into her throat so quickly she almost choked.

"I do not know which one of you little bastards is doing this, but you had better stop it right now," Charles said, his voice a hard, cold snarl. "Ere you finish playing that trick, I will have shot her or you could make me shoot her by accident as I struggle to hold firm to my pistol." The pistol grew still. "Now back up again, you little abominations of nature. Cod's body, someone should have been sent out to drown your kind at birth ere you could became a plague on the rest of us."

"We may be abominations, sir," said Delmar, never taking his eyes from Charles as he took a step back, "but we would never attack women and children and never live fine and high off what is not ours."

Delmar was a lot cleverer than she had ever guessed, Penelope realized as she listened to his very adult words. Unfortunately, that cleverness could easily get him killed right now. It was dangerous to poke at a rabid dog, and Charles was as close to one at the moment as a man could get.

"Delmar," she whispered in warning.

"That brat begs for killing, Penelope," said Charles as he started to drag her to the door. "You need to teach him how to treat his betters. Respect for his elders and all that, eh? I might have had a bit more for mine if the pig had not been such a fool. Showed him, though, eh? Who is the fool now, Papa?" he muttered.

She shivered at the implications of what Charles had just said. Arguments had peppered the relationship between the old baron and his heir, but she never would have thought Charles capable of killing his own father. The fact that her mother had been with the old baron at the time of his death had either been a matter of a callous disregard for innocent life or Charles had intended it to be that way.

"He drowned," she said. "The boat sank. You cannot plan for a boat to sink. It is impossible to plan for a storm."

"You can pay good coin to get a boat scuttled in a way that the damage is seen too late. That storm that blew up was just good luck. Meant no one looked too closely."

Charles had killed her mother, as well as the three others who had worked on the boat, along with his father. Penelope was dazed by the confession, one that was tossed out as casually as if he had been speaking of the weather. Charles had planned for that boat to go down, not caring at all that innocents drowned along with his brutish, greedy father. The sickness she could smell on him now had not made him mad; it had only sharpened a madness that had obviously been lurking in his veins all along.

"Patricide," she whispered.

"Hah! As if that has not been done many times. Sometimes a man gets bloody tired of waiting around for what is rightfully his." He kicked shut the door to the parlor and locked it.

Penelope silently cursed her habit of leaving the keys in the locks of all the inner doors. She winced as she heard the boys started kicking and pounding on the door. Charles abruptly shot the door, and even through the ringing in her ears, she heard a high-pitched curse.

"Jerome!" she cried as she tried to pull free of Charles. "We are unhurt!"

Tightening his grip on her, Charles began dragging her up the stairs. He kept his arm around her and yet another gun pointed at her head, glancing behind him every step of the way. He was either afraid that the footman would rouse and come after him, or he did not believe that a thick door was enough to keep him safe from six little boys. She began to think that all the weaponry he carried was not to fend off large footmen.

Penelope tried to drag her feet, but he simply hefted her up a little higher as he walked. "You will not get away with this."

Charles snorted. "Could you think of nothing more clever to say, witch?"

"I am not a witch."

"Of course you are. The whole lot of you are. Everyone knows that. It did not take me long to dig up the truth on you and that family of yours. They made a mistake when they did not burn the lot of you years ago."

He shoved her into her bedroom so forcefully, she stumbled along for several steps and fell against the side of the bed. By the time she regained her balance and was steady on her feet again, he had slammed shut her bedroom door, locked it, and pocketed the key. No matter how desperately she wanted that key, she had no intention of getting within reach of the madman. When he staggered over to the small table where she kept the drinks to help himself to Ashton's brandy, Penelope eyed the distance to the window. It would be a long fall but she had a better chance of surviving that than she did if she stayed in reach of Charles.

"You can cease plotting, witch."

"I told you, I am not a witch," she said and wondered why she was even bothering to argue with the man. About all it did was keep him from shooting her right now.

"And I say you are. The Wherlockes and the Vaughns. All witches. Told you. I searched out the truth on you. My father wanted your mother's money, no question of that, but he also hoped she might have some useful witch's tricks. Well, failed there, too, the old sot." He took a deep drink of the brandy. "She was useless. Just filled the demmed garden with noisy birds."

Penelope felt her eyes sting with tears but fought them back. She could not let her lingering grief for her mother deter her thoughts now. Yet her mother's affinity for birds did not deserve such scorn. A woman with such a gentle gift had also deserved a happier life than she had been given. Penelope decided it was a bad time to begin to forgive her mother for her weaknesses.

"And you? Ghosts? What the bloody hell use is seeing ghosts?"

"They can tell you who killed them."

He glared at her. "Well, that knowledge does you no good, does it. Who will listen to you? Your lover? The man who is supposed to marry my sister? She is none too happy with you for that, I can tell you." He chuckled and took another drink. "She had her heart set on being a viscountess and I would have made sure she did not have to wait too long to be a duchess."

"What can killing me possibly gain you, Charles? There will be plenty of witnesses to this and none of them ghosts."

"And why should I care? I am dying, I told you, and it is all your fault."

"Why? Because our dog bit you when you tried to kill me in the park?"

"He nearly bit my balls off! I am rotting! I could not go to a doctor, could I? Not a good one. I could not trust one of those self-righteous twats not to tell someone!" He started to tear at the buttons on his breeches. "Want to see what that cur has done to me?"

That was the very last thing she wanted to see and started to inch toward the window. Then a thumping at the door drew his attention. Somehow the boys had gotten out of the room. She was just opening her mouth to tell them to run, when a softly cursing Charles shot at her door. There was a screech and a sudden scrambling from the other side of the door.

"Boys? Are any of you hurt?" she called out, her eyes widening as Charles produced a very large knife.

"Just a scratch," Jerome called back.

"Get out of here!"

They were brave little boys and she did feel proud of them. She was also terrified. Charles was insane. Her boys were risking far too much in their attempts to help her.

"Yes, get out of here, you little bastards," said Charles. "I can take care of you later."

"There is nothing to be gained from hurting any of them." She was pleased to hear the boys hurrying down the stairs. "They have nothing that you want."

"No? I wager they will get all your money if you die. Well, I am tired of stealing little pieces of it. I want it all and you are going to make out a will giving it all to me."

"And you expect me to give you everything I have so that you will be rich when you kill me? You are mad."

"I have worked too hard for this to give up now. Who knows? Once you are dead and I can freely go to a doctor, I may yet be miraculously saved." He shrugged and started to advance on her. "I do not really care. I just do not want to see everything I tried so hard to get and might well be dying for to go to a bunch of little bastards."

He lunged and she barely dodged him in time. Penelope leapt toward the window and was just getting it open when he grabbed her. She began to fight him. Recalling what he had said about his injury, she tried to hit him in the groin, but Charles revealed a true skill at avoiding such attacks. He had obviously done a lot of brawling.

The ease with which he had subdued her both terrified and infuriated Penelope as he dragged her toward her writing table. It did not give her much hope for escape. For a man who said he was rotting and dying, Charles had an enormous strength that she had no defense against. She could only hope that the boys got away and someone would keep them safe until Charles was made to pay for his many crimes.

"Write that will," he demanded, pressing the knife against her throat. "Everything comes to me."

"What about Clarissa?" she asked as she picked up her quill.

"She will be taken care of. Hellfire, with you gone, she will be marrying that fool Radmoor, eh? You can think of that while you roast in hell with the rest of your ilk."

Writing a will might buy her some time, Penelope thought as she began to write. She was not sure what miracle might happen to get her out of this trouble, but she refused to give up hope. She was in danger and at least one of the boys had been wounded by Charles's shot through her door. That could well alert her relatives in the city. Penelope just prayed that there were ones who could easily decipher whatever dreams, visions, or warnings they got. The very things that so often got her family condemned might be all that could save her now.

Chapter Nineteen

Ashton strolled into the conservatory to find his mother and came to such an abrupt halt he swayed. Sitting with his mother was Lady Olympia Wherlocke, Paul, and Juno. He had meant to ask his mother what all the packages were that he had seen in the hall. It pained him to refuse to let her go shopping anytime she pleased but they could not afford such things at the moment. That was not a subject he could go into right now, however.

"Ashton, dear, look who I met whilst shopping," his mother called to him, waving him over to the seat next to her.

There was something different about his mother, Ashton thought as he moved to join her. She shone. He did not think he had seen her look so happy in years. It was going to be difficult to take that joy away but he would have to tell her that she needed to return some, if not most, of what she had just bought. For now he would let her revel in her pleasure.

He bowed to Lady Olympia, winked at Paul, and smiled at Juno. Helping himself to some tea, he took his seat next to his mother. Seeing Olympia made Ashton all too aware of how many hours he had been apart from Penelope. He was far beyond besotted, he thought with an inner smile as he sipped his tea.

"Ashton, dear." Lady Mary grabbed him by the hand, nearly causing him to spill his tea. "I have such grand news. Paul was right. My ship was not lost. Well, not lost as in sunk, just lost. It came in yesterday!"

His mother was practically bouncing in her seat. "Your investment brought you returns?" He wished she had not already spent them, but could not bring himself to criticize.

Lady Mary grabbed up a piece of paper that had been precariously tucked beneath the tea tray. With a wide smile, she handed it to him. Ashton's eyes widened as he read the amount of her returns. It was not enough to save them, but it was a good start.

"This is wonderful," he said and kissed her on the cheek.

"I even got my necklace back."

He eyed the necklace around her neck and found himself wondering how big a bite retrieving it had put in the sum he was looking at. Then he cursed himself for an ungrateful son. His mother deserved her pleasure in what she had done and definitely deserved a few pretty things. The returns her investment had brought were still a windfall for them. They did not solve his trouble with the Hutton-Moores but the money would solve most of the others.

"It is fine, sir," said Paul, his words a little garbled as he tried to speak around a mouthful of cake.

"Paul, dear, finish what you are eating before you try to speak," said Olympia.

Even from where he sat, Ashton could hear the sound of Paul gulping down what was in his mouth. His mother and Olympia hid smiles behind their cups of tea but their sparkling eyes gave away their silent laughter. Paul, he decided, was going to take a lot of work before he could be unleashed upon the world.

It was then that Ashton realized he wanted to help with that. It was not only Penelope who had wormed her way into his heart but also her boys. And girl, he mused with a glance at a sweet-faced Juno. Somehow, he had to get what was needed to shake free of the Hutton-Moores so that he could take on that job. Whether he did it by getting the money to pay his debt or by proving they were murderers, thieves, and kidnappers did not matter at the moment. It was going to be a big job as eight of her children were still very young but he felt no trepidation about it at all.

"It will be fine, sir," Paul said again. "It will all be settled soon."

Ashton was about to ask just how it would all be settled when both Olympia and Paul went dead white. "What is it? What is wrong?"

"Penelope," they said at the same time.

"Is she hurt?"

"We have to get to her," said Olympia as she stood up. "M'lady, may I leave the children here for a while?"

"Of course," said Lady Mary, revealing no astonishment at this odd behavior of her guests.

"But . . ." Paul began to protest. "She is hurt! I need to see her!"

Olympia bent to kiss the top of the boy's head. "You will but, brave and clever though you are, you are but a boy of five. Stay here. I will fetch you when she is safe again."

Ashton was on his feet, his heart pounding with fear

for Penelope. He realized that, at some point during his time with her, he had become a believer. Not just in Penelope, but in the others. He suspected there would be other things he ran across in her large and somewhat eccentric family that he would struggle with, but most of the doubts he had were gone. There was no doubt in his mind at the moment that both Paul and Olympia had sensed that Penelope was in danger and he ran to fetch his pistol from his study.

He met Olympia hurrying into her coat in the front hall. "Do you know what the trouble is?" he asked her as he donned his coat.

"No," she answered as they ran out to her waiting carriage. "I just feel her fear. And"—she took a deep breath—"at least one of the boys has been hurt."

It was not until they were seated and the carriage racing toward the Wherlocke Warren that Ashton asked, "You cannot tell how badly or where the danger is coming from?"

Olympia closed her eyes for a moment. "Charles. It is Charles. And I think two of the boys have been hurt but neither very badly." She looked at Ashton. "It ends today."

He pushed aside a shiver of primal superstition at the look in the woman's sky blue eyes. Ashton took her at her word. He just wished he knew where it was coming from. Then he could apply his beloved reason to it all.

"There!" Olympia cried as she leaned out of the window. "'Tis cousin Leo riding to the Warren. And I think that is cousin Andras with him."

As Ashton yanked the woman, he glanced out and saw two men on horses weaving their way precariously and swiftly through the throngs that always crowded the streets of London. "Do they have visions, too?"

"No. One of ours has been hurt. We all, well, feel it. I

suspect young Chloe told Leo what he needed to know as she does have visions. It is the same as what brought Argus and I to London. A connection, if you will. I am of the belief that it was formed many years ago, when what we are was a very, very dangerous thing to be."

That made a strange sort of sense. They were threatened as a whole, every one of their blood in constant danger of being denounced as a witch. A death sentence until recently. With their skills, developing some sort of warning that danger was near one of their own was merely a way to guarantee that at least some of their blood survived those dark times.

His thoughts swerved to Penelope. She was in danger and he was not reaching her side fast enough. He knew now that she had been protected by only one footman as he had seen Ned by the carriage. That would have allowed Charles a very good chance of getting to her.

Nothing could happen to her, he told himself. Fate could not be so unkind as to let him see what he could have and then snatch it away. He was so close to being free of the Hutton-Moores, either through gaining the money to pay them off or proving them guilty of serious crimes. Ashton wanted the chance to stand before Penelope, a man free of debt and with coin in his pockets. That dream was within his reach and he would not allow Charles or fate to deprive him of it.

The two men who had passed them on horses were already there when the carriage pulled to a halt before the Warren. Ashton nodded to both men, who were tending to the boys as Olympia introduced them. He noted that they both carried the mark of the family, that almost annoying handsomeness and that air of confident power. Ashton supposed one would have confidence if one came from a family that had survived centuries of persecution.

He wanted to race into the house to find Penelope but beat down that blind, primitive instinct. Seeing Ned tending to his brother, he moved to speak with them. He was astonished by how battered the big man was. Ashton had chosen the twins to protect Penelope and the boys because they were big and strong and excellent fighters. Yet it was apparent that someone had badly beaten Ted. It was hard to believe the elegant Charles capable of such a feat.

"He ain't right in the head, m'lord," said Ted. "You could see it in his eyes."

"Just the one man then? Lord Charles Hutton-Moore?"

Ted nodded and winced. "Just the one. He may look a fine gent but he has done a lot of hard fighting, brawling, m'lord. I thought I was facing a gent and got me instead a groin-kicking, ear-biting, eye-gouging street tough. Confused me and all just enough for him to win." He shook his head again and winced at the movement. "There truly be something wrong with the man. Something very wrong."

"He is ill," said Olympia as she moved to stand next to Ashton. "The boys say he spoke of how he is dying, of how he is rotting away. They also believe Charles was the one bitten by Killer. He has locked himself and Penelope inside her bedchamber." She nodded when a carriage careened to a halt before the house. "Ah, here is Argus." She hurried over to halt the new arrivals from storming the house, the other two men quickly joining her in the effort.

"You did well, Ted," Ashton said. "I begin to think Charles had the added strength insanity can often bring."

"M'lord, if the man truly believes he is dying, he has the strength of that, too. Man sure he is dying, well, he ain't going to care what happens to him like most folk would. Ain't got any fear left, does he."

"No, he does not and that makes him very dangerous indeed." Ashton strode over to where the Wherlockes were arguing about what to do. "We need a plan quickly," he said. "As my footman just said, we have a man in there who believes he is dying so he has no more to fear, thinks he has no more to lose."

"Bad. Very bad indeed," said Argus. "I could try to convince him to let us in."

"Do you not need your eyes for that?"

"I do but not always and even then it might do more harm than good. Delmar is a healer. He says Charles is right to believe he is dying, that he is rotting away with an infection. The boy says the poison has gotten into the man's mind. It is, well, unpredictable to try to make a madman do as you will him to."

"I can get you in," said Jerome as he nudged his way into the circle of adults and older boys.

Ashton looked at the boy and then at the bandage on his thin arm. "You have been injured."

"'Tis but a scratch and Septimus has already taken most of the pain away. Charles shot at us through the doors. Once into the parlor, and when we got out and went after Penelope, he shot at us again through her door. The first bullet skinned Delmar on the arm, the second skinned me. It will make no difference to what I can do."

"And just what is that?"

"I can unlock that door. Been practicing. I got us out of the parlor and we were locked in there. If we do it that way, he will not even guess we are coming."

"Andras and I will see if there is a way in through her window just in case you need help," said Leo.

Watching the two men run off, Ashton had to wonder how they thought they could get in through the window without alerting Charles, but shrugged aside that concern. "Are you certain you can unlock the door without a key, Jerome?"

"I am, sir," replied Jerome, "though I cannot say how quick I will be."

"What do you need?"

"I have all I need right here." Jerome tapped his head.

"Go," said Argus. "I sent Septimus to fetch Dobson and I will wait here for now. If you fail and Leo and Andras fail, I will try to use my skill on the man."

A cry of pain from inside the house convinced Ashton. He could wait no longer. With Jerome at his side, he entered the house and began to creep up the stairs. It occurred to him that, despite their gifts, the Wherlockes could be as helpless as anyone else in certain situations. Strangely enough, that comforted him even as it annoyed him that none of them had a skill that would be very useful at the moment. Unless, he mused, glancing at Jerome, the boy could do what he said he could.

Once outside the door to Penelope's bedchamber, Ashton had to fight his urge to try to kick his way in. He could hear a struggle going on inside and soft cries of pain. There was a low voice to be heard as well and he suspected that was Charles. What the man was doing revealed his madness. There was no way he could kill Penelope now and get away with it. There were seven witnesses to his attack.

Jerome edged up beside him and stared at the keyhole. Ashton wished there was something he could see to tell him if the boy was successful or not. The only thing he had to judge that the boy was doing anything at all was the look of intense concentration on Jerome's face and the unblinking stare the boy fixed upon the lock. Hearing what abuse his Penelope was suffering inside made it difficult to just crouch there beside the still, silent boy and wait.

He tensed as he heard a soft click. Jerome sagged a little and nodded. Ashton was almost afraid to touch the door latch. Afraid that the boy had failed and equally afraid that he had succeeded. To think of a child having such a skill was a little alarming. Cautiously he eased the latch down and his heart started to pound with hope and the promise of an upcoming battle. It was unlocked.

Penelope signed the will she had written and then swung around to stab Charles with the sharp end of the quill. He hissed a foul curse and swung his fist at her. She managed to elude a straight punch to the face but the hard fist connected painfully with the side of her head, causing her to fall from her chair. She scrambled out of his way when he lunged for her. The glint of the knife was all the impetus she needed to forget the throbbing in her head and fight for her life.

She ran for the window again. Just as she started to hurl herself out, Charles grabbed her by the skirts and reeled her back in. But as she had been hanging out of the window for that one brief moment, she had seen something that gave her hope. The faces of two of her cousins looking up at her. Her family was gathering, and if she could just stay alive long enough, she would be saved.

Her life with the boys had taught her how to fight and fight dirty simply through the number of squabbles she had broken up. Her brothers had even taught her a few things so that she could defend herself if she needed to. They were not enough to save her life from a madman if she were on her own, but she no longer was. All she needed was a little time.

Penelope began to use everything she could get her hands on to beat at Charles. She scratched, bit, kicked, and punched when he grabbed hold of her and threw things when she was free. Despite her efforts, he finally pinned her to the floor.

"What? No witch's tricks to save yourself with?" Charles sneered, his mouth so smeared with blood from her fist that it made for a chillingly gruesome expression.

"I am not a witch," she said. "You, however, are a thieving, murdering bastard."

"Watch what you say, bitch." He lightly caressed her throat with the flat side of the blade. "I am the man with the knife and now it is only to my benefit that you die."

"What was it before? Anger?" *Keep him talking,* she thought, glancing toward the door and certain that she could see it opening.

"Fun." He laughed. "I was annoyed that you had gotten away from me at Cratchitt's but I also needed to put an end to all the prying your white knights were doing."

"You cannot be so insane that you think you will not hang for this. There are witnesses this time, Charles. A lot of witnesses."

"It does not matter. I am a baron. A bunch of little bastards and a servant cannot put the noose around my neck. As far as the authorities will be concerned, I will have been in Spain."

"Paid liars will not free you of this murder charge."

"Let us just put that to the test, shall we?" He raised the knife.

Penelope braced herself for the blow, praying she would see it coming in time to at least move out of its way enough to make the wound painful but not mortal. He leaned back enough to add strength to his blow and she found her hands free. She reached out to catch him by the wrist and struggled to stop the downward plunge of the knife.

Just as she feared she was not going to be rescued this time, two gunshots rang out. Charles's body was flung back from hers. Penelope quickly scrambled out of the way even though every instinct she had told her the man was dead before he hit the ground. Then, suddenly, she found herself in Ashton's arms and she clung to him.

"The boys," she said. "He shot at the boys."

"Jerome and Delmar got a little flesh wound on an arm," Ashton said as he stroked her hair and watched Penelope's cousins look over Charles. "Dead?"

"Quite thoroughly," replied Leo Vaughn.

A moment later Dobson and some men showed up. He quickly took down all the notes he needed to report the crime and close the case. Ashton halted him as he began to leave, however.

"I think we need to go to Hutton-Moore House now," he said.

It was the last place Penelope wanted to go, but she nodded. "Charles claimed the authorities would believe he was in Spain. There is a chance that he and Clarissa intended to slip out of the country as soon as he had rid himself of me."

"And there may be more proof there of their crimes," said Dobson, who was already striding out the door.

Penelope said a quick thank-you to her relatives as she and Ashton hurried after Dobson. She was not surprised to look out of the carriage window and see the adults in her family who had come to rescue her, along with her brothers, following them. The moment they pulled up in front of what would soon be the Wherlocke House again, she was glad of their company.

It was quiet in the house and there were trunks lining the hall ready to be packed into a carriage. Penelope suspected those trunks held a great deal more than clothes. It would be just like Clarissa and Charles to try and take all they could in case they were not able to return and claim her wealth. A wealth she was not sure of yet, she reminded herself as she followed Ashton up the stairs, both of them matching Dobson's quiet steps.

Even before Dobson flung open the door to Clarissa's bedchamber, Penelope had guessed what they would find. He had given her no time to speak, however, and the wide grin on his face told her that had been intentional. Clarissa was sitting astride a man, both of them naked and, for a moment, completely oblivious to the fact that they were no longer alone.

"Now, I had heard she was cold," murmured Leo as he peered over their shoulders. "That looks mighty warm to me." He placed a hand over her eyes just as Clarissa noticed the people standing in the doorway and screamed.

Things began to happen very rapidly. Clarissa and her lover, Sir Gerald Taplow, were forced to get dressed beneath the watchful eye of Dobson. Her cousins, uncle, and aunt were in the study searching through the papers. Ashton helped them even as he kept a close watch on Penelope who, with her brothers' help, was going through the trunks to make certain they held only clothes. She had made it clear that she was letting Clarissa go but that the woman would leave with nothing that was not hers.

"You sure you want to let her go?" Dobson asked as he watched Clarissa order her trunks packed, her lover no longer in sight.

"We really do not have anything we can charge her with, do we?" Penelope noticed that Clarissa revealed no grief over the fact that her brother was dead. She had been more upset over the things Penelope had liberated from her luggage.

"Nay, not a thing. From what the lot in the study say, she never even signed anything save for the betrothal papers." He winked at her. "Lord Radmoor has already burned them."

Talk of burning papers made Penelope recall what she had wanted to do the moment she had regained control of her life, her house, and whatever money might be left. When Olympia came out of the study to hand Dobson some of the papers Charles had stolen from Earnshaw, Penelope slipped away to join the others in the study. Even as she stepped up to Ashton, she knew he held the markers Charles had been holding over his head.

"These are mine, I believe," she said as she snatched them from his hands.

"Yes, they are." He was not sure what she was going to do and his thoughts were not clear enough to guess. Penelope Wherlocke was a very rich woman and they had only begun to look through the papers they had found.

"Good." She gave them a quick glance to be sure they were the markers she sought and then threw them all into the fireplace.

"Penelope!" Ashton hurried over to the fireplace but there would be no salvaging the markers. "That does not clear the debt."

"Does it not?"

"No. This is all yours now and that means the debt I owed is also now owed to you. I am sure Charles bought them with your money as are you."

This was not sounding good. "You cannot expect I

would dun you for your father's debts? Not after all you have done for me?"

"I did what any man must do. As I will continue to do." He kissed her and started toward the door. "You are certain you are not hurt."

"Nay, I am not hurt." *But I think I am about to be,* she thought.

"Good, then, since everything is in order and you have a great deal of help, I must be on my way." He started out the door.

"When will you be back?"

Penelope inwardly cursed herself for asking the question. It sounded weak, as if she was begging him to return. She would if she had to, but with so many standing around hearing every word they said, she could not, would not, humble herself.

"As soon as I have put some things in order."

"Well, hell," she muttered as she watched him leave.

"A man has his pride, m'lady," said Dobson as he moved to stand beside her.

"Bugger his pride," she grumbled and Dobson laughed.

"I thought it a very fine gesture," said Argus. "In time he will as well."

"Uncle, for months the man searched for an heiress or at least a woman with a healthy dowry for a bride. It is what got him entangled with the Steps. What am I right now?"

"A very wealthy woman. Daresay when we are done, you will be an heiress."

"And where is the man who was looking for just that?"

"Now, Pen, he just said he had a few things he needed to straighten out."

"What things?"

"His debts, I suppose."

"Which brings us back to that wealthy bride. Which brings us back to me. I am now wealthy and he could marry me, thus clearing up the last of his debts."

Olympia stepped up and put her arm around Penelope's shoulders. "A man can be a foolish beast," she said, ignoring the grumbled complaints of the men in the room. "An heiress for a bride, a whopping big dowry, was what he had been looking for. He did not expect anything more than a mildly satisfactory marriage, was willing to sacrifice himself for his family. Then, he met you, and suddenly that just was not good enough. From what Lady Mary told me, Radmoor has been very busy trying to get out of debt before he marries, has long expected to get out of his betrothal with Clarissa. Now, Penelope, he is determined that money not stand between him and his wife. I would say that he wants to come to you as an equal or at least as a man with no debts and some money in his purse."

Penelope thought about that for a moment. It did make sense and her aunt was well known for her ability to read people. It did not ease the sting of his abrupt departure by much, though. It still held the stink of pride about it, as well. And if Ashton nurtured hopes of coming to her as an equal in wealth, by the looks of what her family was discovering, that could well take years.

"It is still just his pride," she muttered. "Or it is me." She hoped she did not sound as pathetic to the others as she did to herself.

"It is not you," Olympia said firmly. "It is pride and men can be very odd when it comes to pride. A man's pride is easily stung."

"Mustn't make fun of a man's pride," said Dobson, pausing in his collection of more of the papers Charles had stolen from Earnshaw. "Sometimes it is all a man has left."

"It might have helped if he had told me what the *things* are that he needs to straighten out and how long he thought it might take him," said Penelope.

"He will be back when he is ready," said Olympia.

"Will he? Well, that is just fine. We shall see if I am willing to take him back when he is ready, shall we?" And she would be and they all knew it, but she silently thanked them all for not saying so. A woman had some pride as well.

Chapter Twenty

Two weeks was long enough, Penelope decided as she absently devoured her substantial breakfast, barely tasting the food she was shoveling into her mouth. She ignored the way the boys watched her warily as she ate. Penelope knew her moods had been unpredictable of late, but she felt she had good reason for that. The man she loved had seen to the moving of her and the boys into the larger, well-staffed Wherlocke House and then left her there so he could continue to *straighten out a few things*. Whatever that meant. Two weeks seemed enough time to *straighten* things. Where was he?

Her confidence in his feelings for her had faltered badly after the first week with no word or sight of the man. It would have collapsed completely during the second week if not for the visits of his family, his mother and his sisters assuring her that he was working hard. *Working hard for what?* she had ached to ask, but good manners had always stilled her tongue.

She had hired her cousin Andras as her solicitor and they spent many hours going over the tangled records kept by the old and new barons as well as all the papers her parents had left behind. Clarissa was destitute but Penelope found herself a little richer every day. Clarissa was also far away in Yorkshire now, having married an aging earl with embarrassing haste. The woman should have hesitated a little, Penelope thought and almost smiled.

Clarissa had undoubtedly thought she was marrying an old man she could easily manipulate. Instead she was now tightly secured on a distant, remote estate where it was rumored the old earl worked diligently to produce the heir he so desperately needed. Dobson had assured Penelope that Clarissa was well secured by the wily old earl, who was as strong as an ox and would probably live another twenty years. He had told her that he and the earl had had a nice long talk and the man had no intention of allowing his young wife to go where she pleased, when she pleased, or to have any control over any money, especially the money that would be left to the children he wanted. The woman would be spending her breeding years in Yorkshire giving the earl as many children as he could breed off her.

Wherlocke Warren was no longer her concern, either. The boys were with her, and Uncle Argus was busily restoring the place to its former glory and then some. The family had purchased the Pettibone House and were already in negotiations for two others in the area. Penelope was fairly sure they planned to bring the area back to its former respectability and make it a family enclave. It would allow more of their family to come to London and live unconcerned about curious neighbors seeing things that could refresh old rumors about them.

Everything was working out so well except for her relationship with Ashton. At the moment, she had none, was not even enjoying an affair with the man. She spent far too many nights lying in a too cold bed missing him. Her fears, her grief, over that state of affairs were rapidly turning into anger. He at least owed her an explanation for his desertion.

"It will be fine, Pen."

Penelope looked up from her congealing eggs to find Paul standing by her chair. "Will it? Did you see that or but hope it is so?"

"I know it." He patted her shoulder. "I know it. So does Olwen."

She found that boy standing at her other side holding one of his drawings. "You have had a vision?" She struggled not to let her hopes rise.

"Aye." He thrust the drawing at her. "See?"

Her first thought was that Olwen's drawing skills had vastly improved. The house in the picture was a huge English manor house, stately and massive with wings on each side of the main building. *The window tax alone must be crippling,* she thought and idly wondered if that still stood. On the vast lawn in front of the manor were her boys and little Juno. Horses could be seen in the distance. Then she looked at the couple standing behind a pair of windows that reached from the ceiling to the floor, staring out at the children on the lawn. The man was definitely Ashton. He stood behind her, his graceful hands curved around her belly. Her very large belly.

"This is truly what you saw?" she asked Olwen, hope leaping to life in her heart with such speed and strength it was almost dizzying. It was the first real taste of hope she had had since Ashton had walked away two weeks ago.

"It is. There were other things I think I will add later as it is a good drawing. Belinda was there with a man in a very fine uniform. Almost all of the Radmoors were there. And do you see this man over here?"

A tall man stood in the shadows at the edge of a stand of trees. "Brant. Oh, dear. He is alone, very alone. I can almost feel it."

Olwen nodded. "He will be for a while. He is wounded and needs to heal. So, you see? It will be fine."

"I hope so." She gave a little start when a small hand slid over her stomach. "Delmar?" She looked at the boy who had nudged Paul aside and he gave her a brilliant smile.

"You can wait for Ashton for he will come, but you might want to hunt him down and give him a kick," Delmar said as he removed his hand. "Babies need their fathers."

"B–b–" She cleared her throat. "Babies? Not baby?"

"Nay. Babies. Two. A girl and a boy. Ashton *will* come for you but, I think, it might be best if you hurry him along."

Penelope sat there for several minutes with her hands pressed to her belly. She had suspected she was with child, for all the signs were there, but she had pushed the concern aside with hard work. There was no ignoring it now. Her confidence in Paul and Olwen's predictions faltered for only a moment. If they said she and Ashton would be together, then they would be. And if she had to nudge that prediction into coming true, she would do so.

She looked at her brothers, who both simply quirked one brow in her direction, revealing that they, too, believed in what Paul and Olwen said, but were leaving the decision in her hands. She stood up and grabbed the last of the cinnamon rolls. As she hurried off to her bedchamber to dress appropriately for pushing a man onto the path fate had chosen for him, she ignored the laughing cheers of her family.

Ashton was shaking but he was not sure if it was with delight or shock or a little bit of both. He was rich. Filthy rich, at least as compared to what he had been. Unbeknownst to him, his friends had gathered up enough money to almost double their investment and asked only that he repay his share of the original investment. Pride had nearly made him refuse, but he had swallowed it. They had given him a gift, helped him in the only way they knew how, and he would not hurt or insult them by refusing it. He had thanked them profusely, paid the rest of his share out of his much improved funds, and was still struggling to accept his vast change in fortune.

"I can pay Penelope for those markers now," he mumbled and winced when Cornell smacked him on the back of his head.

"She burned them as a gift to you," Cornell said. "Consider it a thank-you for all you did although I believe it was inspired by a great deal more than gratitude."

"Yes." He suddenly grinned, his future looking so bright it nearly blinded him. "Yes, it was."

"And she certainly does not need the money. The lady is an heiress. Word is already leaking out about that."

Ashton quickly set down the papers he held when he realized he had started to crush them in his hands. Penelope would soon be besieged by men eager to share in those riches. Men would be doing their best to woo *his* Penelope into their arms. That could not be al-

lowed. He blinked away his growing fury at all those unknown men when a brandy was shoved into his hand.

"Drink," said Victor. "A toast to our success!"

All five men cheered and drank the brandy. Ashton
felt calmer when he was done, his mind cleared of
shock over his good fortune and jealousy over suitors
Penelope did not even have yet. Then he grimaced. He
had not even sent her a note in a fortnight. Wooing her
back into his arms might not be so easy.

"So, when will you marry the girl?" asked Brant.

"As soon as I can," replied Ashton without hesitation.
"Once she will speak to me again. I just realized I have
not even sent her a note in the fortnight since she and
the boys were moved into Wherlocke House. Kept
thinking I would see her soon and could talk to her in
person. Much better than a note."

"Except when it has been a fortnight since you last
spoke to her."

"There is that."

"You shall just have to woo her," said Cornell. "Flow-
ers, mayhap some bonbons, although I suspect the children will eat all of them. Ah, and what about the
children? You will not have her without them."

"I know. I do not mind. The west wing at Radmoor is
already being readied for them."

"Confident bastard."

"I was until about a moment ago. I shall just have to
explain everything and beg for her forgiveness. Penelope cares for me. She is not a woman to take a lover
unless she did care for the man."

"Fool, she loves you. Any idiot can see that."

"Some idiots like to hear the words before they get
all cocky and sure of themselves."

"Yet you are having a wing of your house prepared
for her children."

"That was as much out of hope than anything else." He frowned when he heard someone approaching the door, Marston's low somewhat urgent voice and measured footsteps following. "Now what."

The door to his study opened and Ashton's eyes widened. There stood his Penelope, an apologetic Marston peering over her shoulder. She was dressed as fine as he had ever seen her, having obviously bought herself some new clothes. The green of the gown brought out the green in her eyes and complemented the soft, creamy rose of her skin. The gown was cut a little low in his opinion, far too much of her lovely soft bosom exposed to the eyes of others. A kick to his chair brought him to his senses and he stood up.

"Penelope, can I help you?" he asked and was not surprised to see Cornell roll his eyes.

"I need to speak to you," she said, some of her bravado seeping away as she looked at his friends.

Before she could succumb to utter cowardice, turn around, and run for home, his friends began to excuse themselves. Each man stopped to bow to her, wish her well, and kiss her hand. She held on to Brant's hand and stared up into his shadowed eyes. Olwen was right. The man had been wounded and needed to heal.

"Olwen says it will be fine," she whispered and then blushed at the weak attempt to give comfort when it had not been asked for.

"Does he?"

"Aye, I just thought it might help if you knew that."

"Oddly enough, even though I am not sure I believe in all these things, it does." He bent down to kiss her cheek. "Do not bludgeon him too much, m'dear."

Penelope knew she was blushing when Ashton walked past her to shut the door behind his friends. She heard him murmur something to Marston before shutting the door and then frowned. Was that the sound of a key being turned in a lock?

She turned to face him and all her well-practiced words dried up in her throat. He was so handsome and he was smiling at her as if she was the best thing he had seen in years. Then she frowned. If he had wanted to see her, he could have come to Wherlocke House. She was not the one who had been in hiding.

Ashton saw the soft welcoming look upon her face suddenly firm into a frown. Anger turned her eyes more green than blue. He should have kissed her while she was still looking soft and welcoming, he thought, and then inwardly shook his head. They needed to talk. He grinned to himself. Then they could kiss. He pocketed the key he had just locked the door with, for he intended to keep her in his study until she forgave him his idiocy and then he intended to do a lot more than kiss her.

"It has been too long," he said.

"You knew where I was," she replied, fighting to keep hold of her anger with him and not fling herself into his arms as she so ached to do.

"Penelope, a man has his pride," he began and then looked at her in surprise. "Did you just growl at me?"

She had but she would have all her hair pulled out before she would ever admit it. "Do not be ridiculous. Ladies do not growl. You were going to tell me about a man's pride?"

"Pride can make a man act like an idiot. I suddenly realized how rich you were, in land and coin. I wanted to at least be clear of debt when I came to you."

"You did not care about such things when you courted an heiress, when you courted Clarissa. How is my money different than theirs?"

"It is not, except that it is yours and I cared about

what you thought of me." He rubbed a hand over his head. "No, I cared about how I felt in your eyes. I did not want to be that fortune hunter any longer. I never did, to tell the truth. It always made me uncomfortable. But with you, it made me more than uncomfortable. When you burned those markers, I felt as if a huge weight had been lifted off my shoulders and then it was back. I was already in debt to you and we had not even discussed marriage. That was when I knew I had to do something."

"Straighten out a few things?"

"Yes, straighten out the remaining debts and find enough money to pay you for those markers."

"I do not want you to pay me for those markers. That was a gift. They had been the reason you had become ensnared in Clarissa and Charles's trap and I wished to free you completely from it. I certainly did not wish you to remain chained down by debts your father made."

He stepped closer and placed his hands on her shoulders. "I know that now. Up until a few moments ago, I was still planning to pay you back but my friends made me see sense. Sometimes one just has to accept a gift." He brushed a kiss over her lips, forcing himself not to take more just yet. "I thank you."

"You are welcome. And that was it? The markers?"

"No, not all of it. I made an investment, you see, and was waiting for it to pay some results. It has." He grinned. "I am now a wealthy man."

"So, you do not need a wealthy bride."

"No, but I do need you. I want you as my bride. I know you cannot fully understand, but I needed to free myself of debt and put some money in my purse before I asked you to join your life to mine."

"That is what Aunt Olympia said. All that puzzles me is why you should feel so with me and not the others."

"Because I cared nothing for them. To me they were more dowry than women. I knew I would be a good husband, faithful and kind, but I really felt little for any I courted and less than nothing for Clarissa. If not for those markers, I would have walked away from her at the start. But you, I could not bring myself to act the fortune hunter with you. I wanted to go to the woman I love with a full purse and no need of her money. I wanted the world to know that I chose her not for the weight of her purse, but because she was the only woman I wanted." He leaned back a little, uneasy as he saw tears glistening in her eyes. "This makes you cry?"

"You love me." She finally gave in to the urge that had been gnawing at her from the start and threw herself into his arms.

"Yes, I love you." He savored the feel of her in his arms again, wondering how he had lasted even a fortnight without feeling her there. "I was about to come to you, beg your forgiveness and woo you."

"Oh, there is no need. I forgive you. I might not fully understand it all, it being a man's way of thinking, but I forgive you. I also love you. More than I can say."

"Then show me, Penelope Wherlocke," he whispered against her neck.

"The door," she began as his fingers nimbly began to undo her gown.

"Locked."

"Cocky."

"Hopeful. Very, very hopeful."

Penelope let herself drown in the heat and passion of his kiss. They stumbled toward a settee, leaving their clothing in their wake. She was shaking with her need for him and the tremors that rippled through his body told her he suffered from the same hunger. By the time they fell together onto the settee, she had nothing left on but her stockings.

Ashton looked down at the well-kissed, delightfully tossled woman in his arms and his whole body hardened with his need for her. He was panting as if he had run for miles and was pleased to see that she was doing the same. The wildness was still there and he rejoiced in it.

She moaned her welcome as he joined their bodies with a slowness that had her gritting her teeth in need. He moved in and out of her with an equal slowness and she thought she would go mad. Every nerve and muscle in her body tautened with hunger and her desire roared through her veins. She did not want slow and easy. She wanted to be possessed with fire, ferocity, and blind need.

"Ashton, cease playing with me," she said as she rubbed her feet over the backs of his legs.

"I like playing with you." He was not sure how much longer he could do so, however, as his mind was clouding with passion's heat and his body was screaming for release.

"Do you now?"

Penelope trailed her hands down his strong back and slowly ran her nails over his taut buttocks. The way he trembled at her touch, sweat beading on his brow, told her she was on the right track. Smiling faintly, she slipped her hand between their bodies and did the same just above where their bodies joined. He groaned. She tightened herself around the hard length of him and almost undid herself with the way it made her desire soar. He gasped and shuddered. She did it again. He finally gave her the ferocity she craved, pounding into her until they both cried out with joy.

"Penelope," Ashton said when he could finally speak

again, "have you been reading some of those books?"
He smiled when she giggled.

"Actually, there were quite a few in the library at
Wherlocke House. Naturally I had to hide them away so
the boys could not find that, er, pirate treasure."

"Really? There are naughty books at Wherlocke
House?" He grinned at her. "And you read them? Sinful
child."

"I peeked at a few." She blushed. "I think whoever
wrote them and drew the pictures had some very grand
ideas of the size of men and just what a person is capable of doing. I am sorry, Ashton, but some of the things
I glimpsed in those books are impossible, if not posi-
tively painful looking."

"I agree, all except on the size of men." He laughed
when she slapped him on the shoulder. "Ah, my Penelope, I do love you."

She brushed her lips over his. "I love you, too. Ashton?"

He touched a finger to her mouth. "And I love the
boys. I have already begun making changes to the west
wing of Radmoor Manor so that they may have rooms."
He frowned at the glisten of tears in her eyes. "Are you
going to cry again?"

"I did not cry before. 'Tis just a little dust. You need
to get the maid in here."

"I also may still have doubts about what you and your
family can do, will confess that some of the things can
make me uneasy, like what your uncle Argus can do, but
I do not care. It neither frightens nor repulses me.
Those were the things you were most concerned about,
correct?"

"Very correct." She stroked his cheek. "Thank you,
Ashton, and do not worry about your doubts hurting

any of us. We understand that those who have not lived with such things as we have cannot always accept them as we do. It has always been the fear, the whispers of witches and such, that we cannot abide."

"I am not surprised." He idly began to caress her breasts. "I hate for this moment to end as my mother will be eager to keep you busy and at her side as she makes wedding preparations."

"How long does that sort of thing take?"

"I am hoping I can keep her to the three weeks needed to read the banns."

"It could take longer than that?"

"Easily." He studied her face and smiled. "In a hurry?"

This was not the way she wished to tell him, Penelope thought. Yet if she hesitated, she would find herself in a precarious position. Three weeks was not so bad as she was carrying twins and everyone expected them to come early. Any more than that and they would be raising eyebrows everywhere at the birth of the children.

"Three weeks. No more."

He blinked. "You are sounding very firm. I will speak to Mother, though, if you really feel that way."

"Ashton, I would love to have a big wedding, love to make your mother happy as she plans and shops and all of that. However, any more than three weeks and I shall not fit into any wedding dress made now."

Ashton sat back on his heels and stared at her for a moment. Then he stared at her pretty, flat stomach. Then he stared at her again.

"Am I guessing right in thinking that you are already carrying my child?"

"Aye, I am." She squeaked when he lunged at her and hugged her almost too tight. "So, I need not say I am sorry for ruining your mother's wish for a big wedding?"

"No need to say you are sorry at all." He kissed her with all the love and joy he was filled with. "I do believe I had a hand in this." He stroked her stomach. "How are you feeling?"

"Hungry all the time. I fought with Artemis over the last piece of apple pie last night. He lost." She grinned when he laughed for she could hear the joy in his voice.

"But not ill?"

"Nay. Oh, a tiny little bit in the evening, but if I have a biscuit or piece of toasted bread and lie down, it passes. I was only sure this evening. I had guessed at it but pushed it aside with all the work that needed doing."

"Because you were not sure of me. That is why you came here tonight. You needed to make me take a stand."

"That was some of it. Everyone assured me that you would be back. It was Delmar who told me I might want to come and give you a kick so that you would find your way back to us a little faster. He confirmed what I had been trying to ignore, that I carry your children."

He was kissing her belly when she said that, so Penelope decided it might take him a moment or two to fully grasp the meaning of her words. She stroked his hair as she waited and knew the exact moment the words struck home. His mouth stilled on her belly and his long, strong body that caused her so much pleasure grew tense, but not in the way that would give her any delight. Slowly he lifted his head and stared at her.

"Did you say children? Not child, but children?"

She leaned up and kissed his cheek. "Aye, fear so.

You are at least speaking more coherently than I when Delmar first told me."

"Twins?"

"Aye, Papa, twins. One boy and one girl."

He took her into his arms and held her until the worst of the shock passed. "Are you certain you are fine?"

"Very certain. We are good breeders, Ashton. We have our children easily and rarely, very rarely, lose a woman to childbirth. I will be fine."

Ashton wriggled around until he was on his back and held her on top of him. "I cannot think of any time my family has produced twins," he said as he ran his hands up and down her slim, soft back. "Yours?"

"Not that I know of but they are not all that unusual in the Wherlocke and Vaughn family. I *will* be fine, Ashton. I will. Trust us to know such things if naught else. There was not a glimmer of worry in any of the boys. Not one. All they were interested in was that the children not be bastards."

"I am glad they pushed you to come here."

"And if we are about to be pulled into all the business of a hasty wedding, I think I do not wish to talk anymore." She smiled as she stroked his body with hers and he grew hard beneath her.

"Neither do I. I do love you, Penelope, my fruitful little nymph."

"Shall I call you my handsome satyr?"

"Only if there is such a thing as a faithful until death type of satyr."

"I think there might be now."

He laughed and kissed her, eager to make love again. Ashton believed he would also be eager to make love to Penelope no matter how many years and children they had together. He had started out a fortune hunter but ended up with riches no man can find in his purse. Love, he thought, as he gave himself over to the wildness he and Penelope shared so well, that was true wealth.

An enchanting new novel from New York Times *bestselling author Hannah Howell that will make you believe in the power of destiny—and desire—all over again . . .*

SHE SEES HIS FACE EVERYWHERE . . .
Lady Alethea Vaughn Channing is haunted by a vision of a man in danger—the same man who she has seen in dreams time and time again. She doesn't even know his name, and yet she feels the connection between them, knows she is the only one standing between him and disaster . . .

. . . YET THEY HAVE NEVER MET
But rakish Lord Hartley Greville is capable of protecting himself, as he has proven more than once in his perilous work as a spy for the crown. If he's to carry out his duty, he'll need to put aside the achingly beautiful woman with the strange gift. And yet, when Alethea's visions reveal a plot that could endanger children, Hartley will not be able to ignore the destiny that binds them together—or resist the passion burning between them . . .

Please turn the page for an exciting sneak peek of
IF HE'S WILD,
coming in June 2010!

Alethea Vaughn Channing looked up from the book she was trying to read to stare into the colorful flames in the massive fireplace and immediately tensed. That man was there again, taking shape within the dancing flames and curling smoke. She tried to tear her gaze away, to ignore him and return her attention to her book, but the vision drew her, ignoring her wants and stealing her choices.

He was almost family for there was no denying that they had grown up together. She had been seeing glimpses of the man since she was but five years old, although he had been still a boy then. Fifteen long years of catching the occasional peek into his life had made her somewhat proprietary about the man, even though she had no idea who he was. She had seen him as a gangly, somewhat clumsy youth, and as a man. She had seen him in dreams, in visions, and had even sensed him at her side. An unwilling witness, she had seen him in pain, watched him weep, known his grief and his joy and so much more. She had even seen him on her wedding night, which had been oddly comforting since her late husband had been noticeably absent. At times, the strange connection was painfully intense; at others it was only the whisper of emotion. She did not like invading his privacy yet nothing she had ever done had been able to banish him.

This was a strong vision, she thought, as the images before her grew so clear it was as if the people were right in the room with her. Alethea set her book down and moved to kneel before the fire, as a tickle of unease grew stronger within her. Suddenly she knew this was not just another fleeting intrusion into the man's life, but a warning. Perhaps, she mused as she concentrated, this was what it had all been leading to. She knew, without even a hint of doubt, that what she was seeing now was not what *was* or what *had been*, but what was to come.

He was standing on the steps of a very fine house idly adjusting his clothes. She could smell roses and then grimaced with disgust. The rogue had obviously just come from the arms of some woman. If she judged his expression right, he wore that smirk her maid Kate claimed men wore after they had just fed their manly hungers. Alethea had the suspicion her vision man fed those hungers a lot.

A large black carriage pulled up. She almost stuck her hand in the fire as a sudden fierce urge to pull him back when he stepped into it swept over her. Then, abruptly and without warning, her vision became a dizzying array of brief, terrifying images, one after another slamming into her mind. She cried out as she suffered his pain along with him, horrible continuous pain. They wanted his secrets but he would not release them. A scream tore from her throat and she collapsed, clutching her throat as a sharp, excruciating pain ripped across it. Her vision man died from that pain. It did not matter that she had not actually seen his death, that the fireplace held only flame and wispy smoke again. She had suffered it, suffered the cold inside his body as his blood flowed out of him. For one terrifying moment, she had suffered a deep, utter desolation over that loss.

The sound of her servants hurrying into the room broke through Alethea's shock as she crawled toward the table where she kept her sketchbooks and drawing materials. "Help me to my seat, Kate," she ordered her buxom young maid as the woman reached for her.

"Oh, m'lady, you have had yourself a powerful seeing this time, I be thinking," said Kate as she steadied Alethea in her seat. "You should have a cup of hot, sweet tea, you should, and some rest. Alfred, get some tea," she ordered the tall, too thin butler who no longer even attempted to explain the hierarchy of servants to Kate.

"Not yet. I must get this all down ere I forget."

Alethea was still very weak by the time she had sketched out all she had seen and written down all she could recall. She sipped at the tea a worried Alfred served her and studied what she had done. Although she dreaded what she had to do now, she knew she had no choice.

"We leave for London in three days," she announced, and almost smiled at the look of shock on her servants' faces.

"But, why?" asked Kate.

"I must."

"Where will we stay? Your uncle is at the town house."

"It is quite big enough to house us while I do what this vision is compelling me to do."

"And what does it compel you to do, m'lady?" asked Alfred.

"To stop a murder."

"You *cannot* meet with Lord Hartley Greville."

Alethea frowned at her uncle who was only seven years older than she was. She had been too weary to speak much with him when she had arrived in London yesterday after three days on the road. Then she had slept too late to breakfast with him. It had pleased her to share a noon meal with him and she had quickly told him about her vision. He had been intrigued and eager to help until she had shown him the sketch she had made of the man she sought. Her uncle's handsome face had immediately darkened with a scowl.

"Why not?" she asked as she cut a piece of ham and popped it in her mouth.

"He is a rake. If he was not so wealthy, titled, and of such an impressive lineage, I doubt he would be included on many lists of invitations. If the man notches his bedpost for each of his conquests, he is probably on his third bed by now."

"Oh my. Is he married?"

"Ah, no. Considered to be a prime marriage candidate, however. All that money and good blood, you see. Daughters would not complain as he is also young and handsome."

"Then he cannot be quite so bad, can he? I mean, if mothers view him as a possible match for their daughters—"

Iago Vaughn shook his head, his thick black hair tumbling onto his forehead. "He is still a seasoned rake. Hard, cold, dangerous, and the subject of a cartload of dark rumor. He has just not crossed that fine line which would make him completely unacceptable." He frowned. "Although, I sometimes wonder if that line is a little, well, fluid as concerns men like him. I would certainly hesitate to nudge my daughter in his direction if I had one. And, I certainly do not wish to bring his attention your way. Introduce a pretty young widow to Greville? People would think I was utterly mad."

"Uncle, if you will not introduce me, I *will* find someone else who will."

"Allie—"

"Do you think he has done anything that warrants his murder?"

"I suspect there are many husbands who think so," muttered Iago as he turned his attention back to his meal, frowning even more when he realized he had already finished it.

Alethea smiled her thanks to the footman who took her plate away and set several bowls of fruit between her and Iago. The moment Iago silently waved the footman out of the room, she relaxed, resting her arms on the table and picking out some blackberries to put into her small bowl. As she covered the fruit with clotted cream, she thought carefully over what she should say next. She had to do whatever she could to stop her vision from becoming a true prophecy, but she did not wish to anger her uncle in doing so.

"If wives are breaking their marriage vows, I believe it is for more reason than a pretty face," she said. "A man should not trespass so yet I doubt he is solely to blame for the sin." She glanced at her uncle and smiled faintly. "Can you say that you have not committed such a trespass?"

Iago scowled at her as he pushed aside his plate, grabbed an apple and began to neatly slice and core it. "That is not the point here and well you know it. The point here is whether or not I will introduce my niece to a known seducer, especially when she is a widow and thus considered fair game. A rogue like him would chew you up and spit you out before you even knew what had happened to you. They say he can seduce a rock."

"That would be an intriguing coupling," she murmured and savored a spoonful of her dessert.

"Brat." He grinned briefly, and then quickly grew serious again. "You have never dealt with a man like him."

"I have never dealt with any man really, save for Edward, and considering how little he had to do with me, I suppose dealing with my late husband for a year does not really count for much."

"Ah, no, not truly. Poor sod."

"Me or him?" She smiled when he chuckled. "I understand your concerns, Uncle, but they do not matter. No," she hastily said when he started to protest. "None of them matter. We are speaking of a matter of life and death. As you say, I am a young widow. If he seduces me, then so be it. That is my business and my problem. Once this difficulty is swept aside, I can return to Coulthurst. In truth, if the man has anywhere near the number of conquests rumor claims, I will just disappear into the horde with barely any notice taken of my passing."

"Why are you being so persistent? You may have misinterpreted this vision."

Alethea shook her head. "No. 'Tis difficult to describe, but I *felt* his pain, felt his struggle not to weaken and tell them what they wanted to know, and felt his death. There is something you need to know. This is not the first time I have had visions of this man. The first was when I was just five years old. This man has been visiting me for fifteen years."

"Good God. Constantly?"

"No, but at least once a year in some form, occasionally more than that. Little peeks at his life, fleeting visions mostly, some clearer than others. There were several rather unsettling ones, when he was in danger, but I was seeing what was or what had been. Occasional dreams, too. Even, well, feelings, as if we had suddenly touched in some way."

"How can you be so sure that this vision was not also what happened or had already happened?"

"Because amongst the nauseating barrage of images was one of a newspaper dated a month from that day. And, of course, the fact that the man is still alive." Alethea could tell by the look upon her uncle's face that he would help her, but that he dearly wished he could think of another way than by introducing her to the man. "I even saw him on my wedding night," she added softly.

Iago's eyes widened. "Dare I ask what he was doing?"

"Staring into a fireplace, just as I was, although at least he had a drink in his hand. For a brief moment, I felt as if we were sharing a moment of contemplation, of loneliness, of disappointment, even a sadness. Not an inspiring vision, yet, odd as it was, I did feel somewhat comforted by it." She shrugged away the thought. "I truly believe all that has gone before was leading up to this moment."

"Fifteen years of preparation seems a bit excessive," Iago drawled.

Alethea laughed but her humor was fleeting and she soon sighed. "It was all I could think of to explain why I have had such a long connection to this man, to a man I have never met. I just wish I knew why someone would wish to hold him captive and torture him before killing him. Why do these people want his secrets?"

"We-ell, there have been a few rumors that he might

be working for the home office, or the military, against the French."

"Of course! That makes much more sense than it being some fit of revenge by some cuckolded husband or jealous lover."

"That also means that a great deal more than your virtue could be in danger."

"True, but it also makes it far more important to rescue him."

"Damn. I suppose it does."

"So, will you help me?"

Iago nodded. "You do realize it will be difficult to explain things to him. People do not understand ones like us, do not believe in our gifts or are frightened by them. Imagine the reaction if, next time I was playing cards with some of my friends, I told one of them that his aunt, who had been dead for ten years, was peering over his shoulder?" He smiled when Alethea giggled.

Although his example was amusing, the hard, cold fact it illustrated was not. People did fear the gifts so many of her family had. She knew her dreams and visions would cause some people to think she had gone mad. It was one reason she shunned society. Sometimes, merely touching something could bring on a vision. Iago saw all too clearly those who had died and not yet traveled to their final destination. He could often tell when, or why, a person had died simply by touching something or being in the place where it had happened. The only thing she found unsettling about Iago's gift was that, on occasion, he could tell when someone was soon to die. She suspected that, in many ways, he was as alone, as lonely, as she was.

"It does make life more difficult," she murmured. "I occasionally comfort myself with the thought that it could be worse."

"How?"

"We could have cousin Modred's gift." She nodded when Iago winced. "He has become a hermit, afraid to touch anyone, to even draw close to people for fear of what he will feel, hear, or see. To see so clearly into everyone's mind and heart? I think that would soon drive me mad."

"I often wonder if poor Modred is, at least just a little."

"Have you seen him recently?"

"About a month ago. He has found a few more servants, ones he cannot read, with Aunt Dob's help." Iago frowned. "He thinks he might be gaining those shields he needs, but needs to gather the courage to test himself. But, then, how are we any better off than he? You hide at Coulthurst and I hide here."

"True." Alethea looked around the elegant dining room as she sipped her wine. "I am still surprised Aunt Leona left this place to me and not to you. She had to know you would be comfortable here."

"She was angry that I would not marry her husband's niece."

"Oh dear."

"Quite. I fear she changed her will when she was still angry and then died before the breach between us could be mended."

"You should let me give it to you."

"No. It suits me to rent it from you. I keep a watch out for another place and, if this arrangement ever becomes inconvenient, we can discuss the matter then. Now, let us plan how we can meet up with Lord Greville and make him understand the danger he is in without getting the both of us carted off to Bedlam."

*   *   *

Two nights later, as she and Iago entered a crowded ballroom, Alethea still lacked a sound plan and her uncle had none to offer, either. Alethea clung to his arm as they strolled around the edges of the large room. Glancing around at all the elegant people, she felt a little like a small blackbird stuck in the midst of a flock of peacocks. There was such a vast array of beautiful, elegant women; she had to wonder why her uncle would ever think she had to worry about her virtue. A hardened rake like Lord Hartley Greville would never even consider her worth his time and effort when there was such a bounty to choose from.

"Are you nervous?" asked Iago.

"Terrified," she replied. "Is it always like this?"

"Most of the time. Lady Barnelby's affairs are always well attended."

"And you think Lord Greville will be one of the crowd?"

Iago nodded. "She is his cousin, one of the few family members left to him. We must keep a sharp watch for him, however. He will come, but he will not stay long. Too many of the young women here are hunting a husband."

"I am surprised that you would venture forth if it is that dangerous."

"Ah, but I am only a lowly baron. Greville is a marquis."

Alethea shook her head. "You make it all sound like some sordid marketplace."

"In many ways, it is. Oh, good, I see Aldus and Gifford."

"Friends of yours?" Iago started to lead her toward the far corner of the ballroom, but she was unable to see the men he spoke of around the crowd they weaved through.

"No, friends of the marquis. He will be sure to join them when he arrives."

"Misery loves company?"

"Something like that. Oh damn."

Before Alethea could ask what had caused her uncle to grow so tense, a lovely, fulsome redhead appeared at his side. If she judged her uncle's expression correctly, he was not pleased to see this woman and that piqued Alethea's interest. Looking more closely at the woman's classically beautiful face, Alethea saw the hint of lines about the eyes and mouth and suspected the woman was older than Iago. The look the woman gave her was a hard and assessing one. A moment later something about the woman's demeanor told Alethea that she had not measured up well in the woman's eyes, that she had just been judged as inconsequential.

"Where have you been, Iago, darling?" the woman asked. "I have not seen you for a fortnight."

"I have been very busy, Margarite," Iago replied in a cool, distant tone.

"You work too hard, my dear. And who is your little companion?"

"This is my niece, Lady Alethea Channing," Iago said, his reluctance to make the introduction a little too clear in his tone. "Alethea, this is Mrs. Margarite Dellingforth."

Alethea curtsied slightly. The one Mrs. Dellingforth gave her in return was so faint she doubted the woman even bent her knees at all. She was glad Iago had glanced away at that precise moment so that he did not see the insult to his kinswoman. The tension roused by this increasingly awkward confrontation began to wear upon Alethea's already taut nerves. Any other time she knew she would have been fascinated by the subtle, and not so subtle, nuances of the conversation between her uncle and Mrs. Dellingforth, but now she just wanted the cold-eyed woman to leave. She leaned against Iago and began to fan her face.

"Uncle, I am feeling uncomfortably warm," she said in what she hoped was an appropriately weak, sickly tone of voice.

"Would you like to sit down, m'dear?" he asked.

"You should not have brought her here if she is ill," said Mrs. Dellingforth.

"Oh, I am not ill," said Alethea. "Simply a little overwhelmed."

"If you will excuse us, Margarite, I must tend to my niece," said Iago even as he began to lead Alethea toward some chairs set against the wall.

"Not a very subtle retreat, Uncle," murmured Alethea, quickening her step to keep pace with his long strides.

"I do not particularly care."

"The romance has died, has it?"

"Thoroughly, but she refuses to leave it decently buried."

"She is quite beautiful." Alethea sat down in the chair he led her to and smoothed down her skirts.

"I know, that is how I became ensnared to begin with." He collected two glasses of wine from the tray a footman paused to offer them, and handed Alethea one. "It was an extremely short affair. To be blunt, my lust was quickly satisfied and, once it eased, I found something almost repellent about the woman."

Seeing how troubled thoughts had darkened his hazel green eyes, Alethea lightly patted his hand. "If it is any consolation, I, too, felt uneasy around her. I think there is a coldness inside her."

"Exactly what I felt." He frowned and sipped his drink. "I felt some of the same things I do when I am near someone who will soon die, yet I know that is not true of her."

"What sort of feelings?"

He grimaced. "It is hard to explain, but it is as if some piece of them is missing, has clearly left or been taken."

"The soul?"

"A bit fanciful, but, perhaps, as good an explanation as any other. Once my blind lust faded, I could not abide to even touch her for I could sense that chilling emptiness. I muttered some pathetic excuse and fled her side. She appears unable to believe that I want no more to do with her. I think she is accustomed to being adored."

"How nice for her." Alethea sipped her drink as she watched Mrs. Dellingforth talk to a beautiful fair-haired woman. "Who is that with her now?"

"Her sister Madame Claudette desRouches."

"They are French?"

"Émigrés. Claudette's husband was killed for being on the wrong side in yet another struggle for power and Margarite married an Englishman shortly after arriving."

"For shame, you rogue. A married lady? Tsk, tsk."

"A widow, you brat. Her husband died six months after the wedding."

"How convenient. Ah, well, at least Margarite did not stink of roses. If she had, I might have been forced to deal with her again."

Iago scratched his cheek as he frowned in thought. "No, Margarite does not use a rose scent. Claudette does."

Alethea stared at the two women and briefly wished she had a little of her cousin Modred's gift. It would make solving this trouble she had been plunged into so much easier if she could just pluck the truth from the minds of the enemy. She suspected she would quickly be anxious to be rid of such a gift, however. If she and Iago both got unsettling feelings from the two women, she hated to think what poor Modred would suffer with his acute sensitivity. Although she would prefer to avoid both women, she knew she would have to at least approach the sister who favored roses at some point. There was a chance she could gain some insight, perhaps even have a vision. Since a man's life was at stake, she could not allow fear over what unsavory truths she might uncover hold her back.

"I believe we should investigate them a little," she said.

"Because they are French and Claudette smells of roses?"

"As good a reason as any. It is also one way to help solve this problem without revealing ourselves too much."

Iago nodded. "Very true. Simple investigation. I even know a few people who can help me do it." His eyes widened slightly. "Considering some of the lovers those two women have had, I am surprised they have not already been investigated. Now that I think on it, they seem overly fond of men who would know things useful to the enemy."

"And no one has seen them as a threat because they are beautiful women."

"It galls me to say so, but you may be right about that. Of course, this is still all mere speculation. Nevertheless, they should be investigated and kept a watch on simply because they are French and have known, intimately, a number of important men."

Alethea suddenly tensed, but, for a moment, she was not sure why she was so abruptly and fiercely alert. Sipping her champagne, she forced herself to be calm and concentrate on exactly what she was feeling. To her astonishment, she realized she was feeling *him*. He was irritated, yet there was a small flicker of pleasure. She suspected that hint of pleasure came from seeing his cousin.

"Allie!"

She blinked slowly, fixing her gaze on her uncle. "Sorry. You were saying?"

"I was just wondering if you had a vision," he replied in a soft voice. "You were miles away."

"Ah, no. No vision. Just a feeling."

"A feeling?"

"Yes. He is here."

ABOUT THE AUTHOR

Hannah Howell is an award-winning author who lives with her family in Massachusetts. She is the author of thirty-two Zebra historical romances and is currently working on a new historical romance, IF HE'S WILD, coming in June 2010! Hannah loves hearing from readers and you may visit her website: www.hannahhowell.com.

More by Bestselling Author
Hannah Howell

More by Bestselling Author
Fern Michaels

__About Face	0-8217-7020-9	$7.99US/$10.99CAN
__Wish List	0-8217-7363-1	$7.50US/$10.50CAN
__Picture Perfect	0-8217-7588-X	$7.99US/$10.99CAN
__Vegas Heat	0-8217-7668-1	$7.99US/$10.99CAN
__Finders Keepers	0-8217-7669-X	$7.99US/$10.99CAN
__Dear Emily	0-8217-7670-3	$7.99US/$10.99CAN
__Sara's Song	0-8217-7671-1	$7.99US/$10.99CAN
__Vegas Sunrise	0-8217-7672-X	$7.99US/$10.99CAN
__Yesterday	0-8217-7678-9	$7.99US/$10.99CAN
__Celebration	0-8217-7679-7	$7.99US/$10.99CAN
__Payback	0-8217-7876-5	$6.99US/$9.99CAN
__Vendetta	0-8217-7877-3	$6.99US/$9.99CAN
__The Jury	0-8217-7878-1	$6.99US/$9.99CAN
__Sweet Revenge	0-8217-7879-X	$6.99US/$9.99CAN
__Lethal Justice	0-8217-7880-3	$6.99US/$9.99CAN
__Free Fall	0-8217-7881-1	$6.99US/$9.99CAN
__Fool Me Once	0-8217-8071-9	$7.99US/$10.99CAN
__Vegas Rich	0-8217-8112-X	$7.99US/$10.99CAN
__Hide and Seek	1-4201-0184-6	$6.99US/$9.99CAN
__Hokus Pokus	1-4201-0185-4	$6.99US/$9.99CAN
__Fast Track	1-4201-0186-2	$6.99US/$9.99CAN
__Collateral Damage	1-4201-0187-0	$6.99US/$9.99CAN
__Final Justice	1-4201-0188-9	$6.99US/$9.99CAN

Available Wherever Books Are Sold!

Check out our website at **www.kensingtonbooks.com**

Romantic Suspense from
Lisa Jackson

See How She Dies	0-8217-7605-3	$6.99US/$9.99CAN
Final Scream	0-8217-7712-2	$7.99US/$10.99CAN
Wishes	0-8217-6309-1	$5.99US/$7.99CAN
Whispers	0-8217-7603-7	$6.99US/$9.99CAN
Twice Kissed	0-8217-6038-6	$5.99US/$7.99CAN
Unspoken	0-8217-6402-0	$6.50US/$8.50CAN
If She Only Knew	0-8217-6708-9	$6.50US/$8.50CAN
Hot Blooded	0-8217-6841-7	$6.99US/$9.99CAN
Cold Blooded	0-8217-6934-0	$6.99US/$9.99CAN
The Night Before	0-8217-6936-7	$6.99US/$9.99CAN
The Morning After	0-8217-7295-3	$6.99US/$9.99CAN
Deep Freeze	0-8217-7296-1	$7.99US/$10.99CAN
Fatal Burn	0-8217-7577-4	$7.99US/$10.99CAN
Shiver	0-8217-7578-2	$7.99US/$10.99CAN
Most Likely to Die	0-8217-7576-6	$7.99US/$10.99CAN
Absolute Fear	0-8217-7936-2	$7.99US/$9.49CAN
Almost Dead	0-8217-7579-0	$7.99US/$10.99CAN
Lost Souls	0-8217-7938-9	$7.99US/$10.99CAN
Left to Die	1-4201-0276-1	$7.99US/$10.99CAN
Wicked Game	1-4201-0338-5	$7.99US/$9.99CAN
Malice	0-8217-7940-0	$7.99US/$9.49CAN

Thrilling Suspense from
Beverly Barton